WITHDRAWN

Gilligan's Wake

Gilligan's Wake

Tom Carson

Picador   *New York*

GILLIGAN'S WAKE. Copyright © 2003 by Tom Carson. All rights reserved. Printed in the United States of America. No part of this book may be used or reproduced in any manner whatsoever without written permission except in the case of brief quotations embodied in critical articles or reviews. For information, address Picador, 175 Fifth Avenue, New York, N.Y. 10010.

Picador® is a U.S. registered trademark and is used by St. Martin's Press under license from Pan Books Limited.

www.picadorusa.com

Library of Congress Cataloging-in-Publication Data

Carson, Tom.
    Gilligan's wake : a novel / Tom Carson.—1st ed.
      p. cm.
    ISBN 0-312-29123-X
    1. United States—Social life and customs—Fiction. I. Title.

  PS3603.A775 G45 2002
  813'.54—dc21

2002029256

First Edition: January 2003

10 9 8 7 6 5 4 3 2 1

For my mother and Arion

I

This Tiny Ship

SKIPPERTOO AND GET ME HOME, I MEAN IF YOU REALLY WANT TO hear about it. They took away my facial hair and gave me a small hat. Please to ignore dead bird around neck, hokay? We were seven, like the Mercury astronauts. But all that came after I'd done my time in the booby hatch.

Eisenhower on the rebop, waving yo-ho to a U-2 and a boo-hoo to Batista. So hipped am I on clinching my Houdini exit from the old burg, where the specimen before you wore a sweatshirt laundered only by my tears, that I don't even feed the mailbox a snack for my best high-school buddy after Dobie skywrites me an epistle exhaling how gassed he is the New Frontier is here. When the thousand days start clicking off, I'm hanging on by my goatee in North Beach. The coffeehouses are losing steam, the topless bars aren't so much as a gleam in Carol Doda's plastic surgeon's scalpel. On the sidewalk outside City Lights, with avid periwinkle peepers but a poor Christmas salting his ever waggable chin, even Ferlinghetti's looking like he doesn't know where his next trochee's coming from. Hello, hi, "Can you believe this *fog*?" he says, clutching my arm, which what with Fisherman's Wharf north by northwest and the Rice-A-Roni streetcar going dingding practically in our ears makes me think, wow, he's never had a dull moment.

Then he put on some lip about the big "Ask not" recital that got beamed our way this San Fran A.M. out of snowy—doubly snowy, in the transmission-flaked ghost dance our coast's early risers blinked at—Washington, DeeCee. "And so the Harvard sonovabitch asks Robert *Frost* to write him an inaugural poem, for Christ and Buddha's sake," Larry sniffed, huffing himself up to his full height just as some middle-aged square doing a walk-by in a mackintosh gave us a look like he hadn't known our kind was still roosting in the nabe. "Pass *that* torch, Jack! They'll never learn. That monosyllabic, meter-crazy Vermont retard—he ever stops by *my* woods with miles to go before he croaks, I'll take two forks and stab him in the ass with them! Why wasn't it Bill Car-los Bills? Hell, what about *me*? I'd have been there like a shot off a shovel." We know you would, Ferl, I said, and made to split. Larry always reminded me of a St. Bernard who'd gotten bombed on his own brandy cask. A dog on a long MacLeish, Corso used to say.

But me, I'm toking on a modest hope that things are looking up. Even if Rexroth did call it *déjà lu*, in a slam that accused me of counterfeiting bongos and beret to pull a fast one on easy readers—"If I'm any judge," which he was in all but robe and gavel, "this kid knows North Beach like the back of Allen Ginsberg's hand"—my little book *Wake Me When It's Over Daddy-O: Proems 1957–1960* has sold a couple of copies, and my girl, who got hers for free, looks good in a leotard. And even better out of one, even if I can't quit missing Thalia Menninger, who never knew what she meant to me. For our bread, Suze is girl-ing the java urn at a place called the Vertigo-Go. Then, just three months into Camelot, JFK banana-peels us with the Bay of Pigs.

Bam, ogle me on the move with a few other scraggly cats and chicks down Columbus Avenue to Montgomery Street and Union Square, lipping "Hands off Castro!" and shoving our "Fair Play for Cuba" leaflets at a sluice of snap-brims all doing the lunch-hour hurry-hurry. Ferlinghetti's rounded up whoever isn't on a reading tour or in Tangiers with Burroughs to show some angry beard. Soon a red light holds us up and we accordion, which is when the tagalonging crewcut we were hoping was plainclothes says he's with the *Chronicle*. That's all Ferl needs:

"When governments write bad poetry, poets have to govern. And *this*," he says, puffing himself up to his full heat, "is a *bad poem*, in my professional opinion. You remember what Shelley said," and if you're fast you see the crewcut's brain go "*Winters?*," but Larry is tearing along: "I mean I don't know where Allen and Gregory are on this, we each go our own way, but to me the 'free' in free verse has always been a *verb*, you see. The way Fidel did Havana, I want to free verse. Free *verse!*" he hollers, jerking his head up at the rest of us. "*Free* verse!" And my Suze, who's in black from her Feiffer-feet to the witch hat on her middle-parted hair and looks like she's just guessed where all the flowers went, is nudging in and saying, "Larry, it's turned green, like really green, green like my eyes, we gotta go."

Across from a scary-looking mausoleum just short of Union Square, some burlies are hoisting a sign that makes me wonder if I'm on peyote.

It's a clock with twelve hands all holding coffee cups, and underneath it says, "There's Always Time For Some More Maxwell House!" I mean, sometimes I think the straights know things we don't, out in the crazy heart of America. The whole bit's gone a little haywire, we aren't moving, now I see that Ferlinghetti's in a face-off with a couple of wharf rats up from the Embarcadero who think our gang is what's wrong with this picture, and that's why they've just knocked FaFaFaFair Playayayay ffor CubaCubaCuba in a long scoop down the gutter. The fat one with the hair like shaving cream is tearing off his cap and lipping away at Larry like a one-man what's-up-doc cartoon, and the shrimp in the sneaks and red sweater next to him has hard and frightened eyes for me, why me? I know I don't know him from Adam.

Then someone hollers "Watch yourself, Maynard!," in the same brain-blink that my inner radar pings a toppling world of uh-oh up above. When I look the coffee clock's come loose, did it jump or was it pushed?, and is avalanching toward me from the sky. I try to protect myself with my "Leave Fidel Alone!" sign, but it's too late, because *time has grown a thousand feathers that I have to try to name. The clouds keel like old sails in a washing machine*, hey pops which way to Alcatraz?, and Suze's face is skidding at me from all directions under her witch's hat, her mouth making the big O, as Larry jumps back like a circus lion in a movie running backwards and I think Corso never liked me. Off in a corner of this scene, which I couldn't sort out with a colander, a lanky detective was hauling a drenched blonde out of the big blue drink next to the Golden Gate.

While a ship with nowhere to get to sailed calmly on.

■

I came to in a Jasper Johns, not representational like you would know of what but undeniably sturdy. Big on white, a use of pigment so tactile it made your eyeballs feel like workingmen's thumbs, and shapes of sheriff's badges in rows and uninhabited aisles in an as yet unrecognizable pattern. This is either prison or a dream, I thought; not noticing the false dichotomy. After a minute or a week, part of the painting opened up, and a nice Negro lady Jasper had hidden back of it said, "With us again at last! It's about time. You must be starving. I'll just go fetch Dr. Troop."

Dr. Troop? I knew no Dr. Troop. Nor can I peg the cat who soon comes nimbly ambling in as if the air behind his heels is still begging for more autographs, a square but clearly some sort of glamor boy in his particular square world. Grown-up baby blues and teeth I groove on, better tended than the Taj Mahal I wonder if I'll ever get to see unless I build my own, out in the yard where the doghouse used to be.

Troop sits down on a bit of here that Jasper's just decided is a chair, and as he hikes a pack of Larks from his breast pocket I dig the monogram—"KFT"—on the blue shirt underneath his lab coat. Just like the ad, he holds out the pack to me: "Sure you don't smoke?" he asks, when I shake my head. "I suck 'em down like popcorn on fire myself, couldn't have made it through med school otherwise. Hopkins was rough stuff, believe me," just like he'd flown a Douglas SBD Dauntless torpedo bomber over Midway or something. "So's everything since been. My patients had just better pray the Surgeon General's boys don't turn up anything too scary, because I'm not about to give these babies up."

He Zippos one and blows some smoke that kills the painting, now it's just a room I'm in. Then he gives me another gander at the Taj. "Anyway, hello," he says, and calls me by a name I've never heard before.

"Whoever that is, it's not me," I told him. "I'm Krebs—Maynard G. Krebs."

Troop looked a little disappointed, but not surprised. Making his cigarette act as glad to be near him as if it was a bird and he was St. Francis of Sinatra, he gave a glance at the window he'd brought in with him, which gazed back admiringly. The next bit seemed to be up to your correspondent.

"Well," I said, my own earlier check of points south of my goatee not having turned up anything out of whack, "I guess the first question is, what kind of doctor are you?"

"The best." Troop flashed me a quick Taj. "I'm your psychiatrist. You're in the Mayo Clinic."

"Yeah, well—hold the Mayo for me, will you, Doc?" I joked weekly, I mean weakly. Troop's face told me he was slightly tired of having to pretend that he found that one wry, that he thought it cut the mustard, that he greeted it with relish. He thought it was a bunch of baloney. Then again, someone must have had some lettuce to install me in this pad, and Thalia Menninger was a tomato.

"Man, am I hungry," I said. "I sure could use a crab sandwich on sourdough bread from Fisherman's Wharf right now. But what am I doing here?"

"Returning appetite is a good sign," Troop said. "You've had a breakdown, damn near as bad as they come, and I wrote the book on those. It's on sale in the gift shop, if you feel like chipping in for my retirement fund. The big words aren't too hard. Your mother practically had to Scotch-tape you together to pack you in the car over here."

Mother? I thought. I, Maynard Krebs, had no mother. And certainly no father, as even Troop didn't dispute. As he took a drag, his cigarette's glow briefly reddened his retinas, like two tiny stop signs. But I was feeling woozy, and Troop was stubbing out a bird:

"Well!" he said, smacking his knees and calling me by the wrong name again, he must be a busy man. "Just wanted to say howdy-doo, give you a peek at who's been taking care of you since Old Man Sky fell down and conked you on the head, and welcome you back to our program. I'll have Julia bring you up some lunch. No can do on the crustacean, I'm afraid, but I'm sure she's got something in the kitchen almost as good."

"Hey, Doc?" I said.

He was about to step out of the painting. But he turned all the way around—with his whole body, not just his head. Some trick, I thought; the feet must go like so, then so.

"Just how far are we from North Beach?" I said. "I'd like to ask some cats I know to come dig this white flag."

Troop hesitated, which was nice of him, considering. "I'm honestly sorry," he said, "because they say it's a helluva town. But you might as well know that you've never been in San Francisco. Oh, maybe with your folks, on home leave when you were a kid; your mom didn't mention anything like that, but we didn't have time to go over everything.

Much less under it! But we're in Rochester, Minnesota, and that's where you've always lived."

He split. A second after that, he left. My noggin felt as heavy as Coit Tower, my goatee weighed a ton. But I had to get it and the rest of me up. I came off the bed and went straight to my knees, which turned out to be bare; I was wearing some sort of gown. Figuring out I couldn't stand if it was life or death and that I must be drugged, I dragged Maynard, G., and Krebs across cold floor and then more floor to the window like I was ready for Andrew Wyeth, who'd started painting *Maynard's World* at an easel just behind me.

I didn't know what I was on, but I must have been higher than the snows of Kilimanjaro. For a few seconds, I hallucinated that I saw a metropolis of ivory and paste, dominated by a stubby pencil stabbing upward like the giveaway spiking in a lie-detector test. On the far side of the river it faced, I could see a mansion with pillars like fat cigarettes, topping a hill planted with endless rows of upright Scrabble tiles. Beyond it were bunched miles of pastel homes, mingled with older liver-spottings of slowly browning brick and leaking greenery the hue of my Suze's tender, mocking eyes.

Down near the water's edge, a gaunt group of outsized men was struggling to raise a mast or antenna. Blind cars shot past them toward gang-a-gley. Gang-a-gley?

Langley. The way my brain said it turned that humdrum name into a sound that both harbored the ogres and augured the harbors of tales heard from diaper days on. But I must have stepped into a puddle-piece of someone else's addled, jigsaw-puzzled life, and no one in sight could explain it to me: not the history teacher plucking at his rubber-banded wrist, not the Scrabble-loving woman with the patriotic rain hat in her lap. Not the bourbon-sipping gargoyle moodily watching a helicopter settle on his lawn, not the empty space still shaped like a girl turning toward me, crossing her arms like a magician's assistant to cover up twin winks I'd never seen in sunlight, but the magician had.

Then I heard a splatter-pop that I mistook for musketry, but they must only have been shooting a movie. As soon as "The End" showed up, I blinked it all away.

Saw fields, a power plant. A peeling sign that read EGAN'S GARA. Dead sky. And winter that stretched to the ends of the earth.

■

When the drugs wore off and I could walk again, a week or another blink later—it was hard to tell here in the Mayo, when half an hour felt like all day—they moved me out onto the ward. There were maybe a dozen of us in all, though it was hard to tell that too; everyone had several faces, the dingy gowns all looked alike, and we were all indifferent to everything. I think Troop put something in the water.

Holden Caulfield, who had the bunk left of mine—unless I lay with my feet on the pillow, in which case he was on the right—was just a nasty piece of work no matter how you sliced him. Kooky, but I hit it off better with Cpl. Ira Hayes, a full-blooded Pima Indian who'd helped hoist the flag on Iwo Jima. Once people quit taking pictures of him, he'd gone back to the reservation and hoisted a few more. Now he was in pretty bad shape. He looked a little like Tony Curtis, which was cool; I dug Tony in *The Great Impostor* and *Some Like It Hot* the most. Farther down our row, Edsel Ford spent most of the day just staring out the window, pressing his fingers to the glass and saying "Me?" in a soft voice whenever a car zipped by.

Nixon, who was pregnant, had my old room off the ward. Troop said he'd been back six times so far. Not a mingler, but you could peek in by pretending you were on your way to the can while they fed him his daily cottage cheese and ketchup. You might lose your own breakfast, though, because he wasn't easy to look at, with an adult head and torso and the arms and legs of a malformed child, the whole thing in a blue suit on the bed. We'd hear him screaming in the night like there was murder in his thighs, trying to bring out a new Nixon. One day, pop-pop, his hands would poke out of his sleeves, and black wingtips slither out his pants-cuffs. Sometimes it took him years, Troop said.

Years, wow. I guess people can get used to anything if it's them. But I was me, and that was Maynard Krebs and not the other G., and I never stopped thinking about North Beach, or wondering how could I get word to Ferlinghetti. He'd come out for Castro, he'd come out for me. He owed me that much, I thought. I knew he had a thing for Suze in some bald-pated, white-hairs-curling-out-the-workshirt, bright-eyed older-fellow way but that was all right, after all he was a much more established poet in our scene than I was, he'd taught us all a lot and anyhow I could hardly picture Suze's face or her green eyes. She was going away and all I could see was the flow of her light brown hair as she glided past Columbus and a row of lookers on her way to history, I guessed that must be long ago but it was hard to tell in here, so long, so long, so long. There was something in the water but Troop would never admit it.

In my dreams, Larry was often there. Sometimes he had Moe and Curly with him. Tiny planes dangled in the night, bombing us out of our gourds. We fired our Kerou ack-ack gun and fled to join Fidel; in the Sierra Mastre, there we felt free. I saw the best mimes of my generation destroyed, running through Ghirardelli Square at noon in flight from angry pedestrians.

Then the lanky detective I had watched raising a blonde little friend of all the world out of the sea near the Golden Gate would push away my blue bedspread and come sit beside me a while. Only it turned out that he didn't want to solve mysteries anymore: "I'll tell you, son, once Hitchcock showed me what life outside of Bedford Falls would *really* be like, it made me dizzy," he said affably. "I hustled back to Capra like a rabbit." Saying which, he looked up past his shoulder. "Wouldn't *you*?" he asked.

That's the way it was. Alack and shite gave way to living dolor. Brett Sommers surprised us, in her slack klugmans there I felt free. Bewitched, I dreamed of Suze's eyes, blinking at me from inside a bottle. She was wearing acres of green petticoats, and I called her the hyacinth girl; sometimes we even talked alike. With a wiggle of her nose, she married Sergeant York. But she was mother-naked now, and those were the wrong eyes in the bottle, and I knew that wasn't allowed. She swallowed the eyes and then I fled, I flew like a nun.

The elevator at the end of the hall was the size of a phone booth, but must have been capacious for all that: "Max. 99" read the sign on its wall. Stepping out, I interrogated a couple of loafers: *Who is the third son who walks always beside you?* I was still hoping to find Suze, but Vic Morrow and vic morrow and vicmorrow kept me in this petty place from day to day. Rats were patrolling Room 222, gunsmoke made the sea be yesterday, oh Dr. Kildare F. Troop I'm on to you: *I know what the Mayo Clinic is.* And Nixon never let up screaming screaming Why does Nixon scream why does Nixon scream why does Nixon scream *Why does Nixon scream so loudly in my one and only brain*

Believe me, most mornings it comes as a relief to learn I'm awake. When dawn wells up in the sky, she knots me together. Then we'd sit around the Cleaver Ward in our robes and gowns, waiting our turn to be led down to breakfast and wondering why our ward had the name it did. The one across from us was called the Burt Ward, and every schizo in it wore a mask and hopped around like batty robins.

"There'd just better be some *cee*-real left when I get down there," Ira Hayes used to grunt—"that's all *I'm* gonna say." We all tried not to drink the water, but Troop knew that we'd have to if he kept us long enough. Since Nixon wouldn't have been fed yet either, we'd hear his grunts and howls from his room, and Holden, who had a way of turning into Gore Vidal before your very eyes, would start in on his favorite joke. "Doctor Troop!" he'd yelp, although Troop wasn't there. "Can Nixon come out to campaign?"

"Why, *Holden*," one of us always played along. "You know that Nixon has no arms and no legs."

"Oh, we don't want him as a *candidate*," Holden would snicker in his malicious prep-school whine. "We just need to use him as a *power base!*"

"Ragh. Urgh," we'd hear from Nixon's room. "Gagh. Cough."

Then Julia would unlock the door, and we'd shuffle out to the stairs that took us to the cafeteria. "Man, I'm draggin'," Ira Hayes would groan. "My feet feel like they're made a' bronze this mornin'." That was *his* favorite joke.

"Which one were you, anyhow?" I asked him one afternoon, when we were all sitting around the Cleaver Ward.

"In the picture? I still am. Second from the left, I think." He stood up to demonstrate for us, his arms straining toward an invisible flag as it went up and away from him; of course, it just looked goofy, with him in his flapping Mayo gown. Then his fingers started shaking, the way they always did, and he dropped his hands fast, wiping them on his gown. "Shit, but I could use a drink," he said, trying to sound at home with it. "Yeah, some fuckin' firewater over here for fuckin' Tonto, whatcha say, Doctor Troop—Sergeant Stryker, Major Treaty, Colonel Custer, General Hospital. Man, if I ever get out of this place . . ."

"You know what I'd like to do?" Holden said dreamily. He was lying on his bunk face upwards, watching a blue treasure map waft from his Chesterfield to the ceiling. "I think I'd like to shoot a really, really famous musician. That's what *I'm* going to do, if they ever let me out of here. Maybe I'll even get his autograph first!" he giggled. "God, it'll be beautiful. I hope you can all be there."

"Sure, Holden," Ira said, grateful for the change of topic. "But not Gene Krupa, okay?"

"No, not Gene Krupa," Holden said, with a strange, far-seeing smile. "Bigger."

"Nobody bigger'n Krupa in my book," Ira shrugged. His hands had finally stopped trembling. "Blast away at whoever you want."

"If they ever let *me* out," I said, surprising myself, "I'd like to go sailing."

"Me," Edsel Ford said at the window. For all we knew, the car going by outside just then really was an Edsel—the one his father named for him. From the sound of it, the traffic was heavy just now: "Me-me-me-me-me-me-me," he said.

Then he said, "Mom?"

■

"Gil—"

"Krebs," I said firmly, before Troop could finish. "Call me Maynard G. Krebs."

"Whatever. Well, that tears it," he said, tearing up a fat little booklet on his desk. "The truth is, we're not making progress. You're not responding as well as you should."

"The truth is, there just isn't a whole lot on the ward to respond *to*, Doc," I said. "Unless you're finally coming clean about the water, daddy-o."

"There is nothing in the water except water. But do you know what's in the basement?"

"No. But I don't want to go down there."

"The basement," Troop said, "is where we perform electroshock therapy on the patients we can't help the normal way. It's a last resort, but then," he grinned, "that's what some people call us."

"Do it to Julia, not to me," I said. "Being the only black person in the whole Mayo Clinic has been driving your nurse absolutely goofy, Doc, or hadn't you noticed?"

"You think she's black? That's damned interesting. You must not know any real Negroes." Troop jotted down something on a pad. "Oh, by the way," he said, "I hate to be the one to tell you this. But hell"— with a sudden, Lark-packed chuckle—"that's how it goes when you're-in-*charge*! Or so my predecessor, the great Dr. Benway Casey, used to say. Tony is no longer with us."

"Tony?"

"I meant Ira. Ira Hayes is dead."

"Oh."

"He has been for some time," Dr. Troop said gently. "Maybe *you* just hadn't noticed."

"Oh again," I said.

His voice went back to its usual chipper briskness. "At any rate, I've scheduled you for your first session."

"Will it help?"

"Who knows? We're really just guessing about whatever it is a jolt of kickapoo joy juice does to whatever's happening in there. But I can guarantee that it'll take your mind off Ira, that's for *damn* sure. Boy, did *he* hate it."

"When are we doing this?" I asked.

"You, not we. But—well, right now," Troop said. "I mean, it's not as if you've got that much else besides that little bit of broccoli on your plate, is it?"

"I guess not," I said. "Let's go."

I followed Burleigh, Troop's nicotine-stained assistant, down the stairs. The room at the bottom had that unshaded but creviced, crime-scene basement light. I stepped over a cardboard box marked "Xmas ornaments," and hesitated like the joint was booby-trapped. Its familiar gray-green-white cover now a witch's hat, an old Scribner paperback lay open and face down on the floor. As I heard Burleigh call "Who's next?," the basement's combined glare and dankness were like the moon, the almost silent whistles, the dull trees and the smell of peat at town's end.

Out of habit, I started to move toward the sofa. But then I saw I couldn't sit there, since there was a doghouse on it. Plunking myself down instead in a lawn chair with frayed webbings, I felt Burleigh's hands attach the electrodes to my ears.

I wondered if this was Maynard G.'s last stand. On my ward alone, Edsel Ford had turned into a car, and thought his mother was one too. Holden Caulfield was just itching to turn into an assassin. Nixon was slouching toward himself as always, hoping someone would ask him to carve the rough beast. Ira Hayes was all over the map, since he'd turned into a Marine, a photograph, a statue, a memorial, a pauper, a drunk, a corpse, and Tony Curtis. At the start, all he'd been was an Injun; and that was just the Cleaver Ward. Who knew what other metamorphoses were going on in all the Mayo Clinic's other wards, besides Dr. Kildare F. Troop? Maybe it made me the odd man out here in the Sally fields, but I didn't want to turn into someone new, voyaging out past full fathom five to parts unknown. I only wanted the electroshock to prove that I could still be what I was, which was Maynard G. Krebs.

ZZZZT!

vast wasteland teenage wasteland sons of he woe gee ma john wayne newton minow who minow *Minnow* Me now No no Krebs *ZZT* Krebs *ZZT* Maynard Krebs who's next *ZZZT ZZZT*

Ocean waves.

Here it came now. "Boom!" went doom.

Her nipples in sunshine. What I had run there to tell her: he was gone. Then doom went boom. Here came everybody but me.

■

Too late to save me, Ferlinghetti, or maybe Dobie, finally got a message through. It said "Maynard! I'm with you in Rochester" and I said *Look here is a postcard that calls me Maynard I am Krebs I tell you I am Krebs ZZT ZZT.* And I said "I bet you wouldn't do this to Papa" and Burleigh said *We did he thought he was Hemingway there was no cure for it but me ZZZT* oh man what I'd give for some reefer now *ZZT ZZT.*

Why couldn't I remember anything? I used to be able to remember things practically while they were still happening. Somewhere in a part of what was gone now, Thalia or maybe it was Suze and I used to know whole chunks of our favorite novel backwards and forwards. We'd play a game that she named Memory Substitutions, changing names and garbling lines on purpose to turn the passages we knew by heart—each other's heart—into jokes that only we understood.

"In my younger and more vulnerable years," I'd start, "my father gave me a dead animal that I've been turning over with a stick ever since." Hugging her knees at her end of the sofa, she'd giggle, with the light brown hair that flowed in two waves from a central part on her high forehead unveiling her mouth as she tossed her chin, and say in an incredulous voice: "Can't reread the *Washington Post*, old sprout? Why, of course you can!" Or else we'd reverse the game, and rearrange everything *else* we knew—old songs, TV shows, other books, news of the day—to make it refer to our shared text, and so to us:

"Daisy, Daisy—give him your answer, do," I'd sing. *"He's Jay Gatsby—all for the love of you."* And then I'd wait for her to decide what came next.

". . . Don't swerve to hit that floozy! That drive must be a doozy," she'd croon within seconds, giggling, her eyes' twin pools of dilute green light bright, eager, tender, mocking and observant all at once.

"But don't you beg, back in East Egg—" and then I hesitated, even

though it wasn't her turn. But she thought it was, and our two voices tangled: *"For another man to love yooo!"* I tried out, just as Suze sang, *"Why don't you escape the zoo?"*

Then we'd stop. But soon she'd wiggle free, because she was virgo intacta and she had to go, back up the stairs quick-quick and out the kitchen door. So I'd beat off, a boat against the current, borne ceaselessly back to her ass; and if you find that unromantic, I think you know nothing about youth. But skip her.

Skip her.

In the basement, when I wasn't getting electroshocked, they'd put me on laundry detail. I didn't like it, because laundry was the cruelest chore—breeding clean clothes out of the dead wash, mixing Tide and Joy, and so on. There was so much of it, so much more than I thought there would be from our now reduced numbers, a million airy pieces to fluff and fold, and yet all of it kept billowing, teetering, swarming up damply to swamp me, *fear death by laundry,* and I said "Doc be a lovey tonight and take me off the laundry detail" but he wouldn't, and gingerly I handled laddered hooks and many buttons, tender buttons, I had not thought Suze had undone so many, was she merry as she did it, was she merry and I cried, and still I cried "Krebs Krebs" to dirty socks.

But "Your goatee's gone," Holden, who had a way of turning into Paul Lynde before your very eyes, told me snidely when they brought me back up to the ward one day. Since there was no mirror other than his snicker, I touched my chin, and found it bare except for glue. Airplane glue, so clear and pearly when you squeeze it out to fit the bridge to the deck of a PT boat or join the wing and fuselage of a Curtiss P-40 with the sabre-toothy Flying Tigers snarl pasted on the snout, but soon glaucomic as it makes maps of nonexistent countries on your fingers. Even though I hadn't done it in years, I sniffed mine—and boom, hey daddy-o, I was back in front of Troop, and I said *Just tell me Doc please What was in the water* and Troop said *Kim Novak you damn fool Kim Novak was in the water The water by the Golden Gate* and afterwards naked in lockup with the lights out I whimpered *krebs i was krebs* and the food stinks here.

If I could only say
alia Mennin
If I could only say
Suze

Now I didn't have a name anymore, but there didn't seem to be much call for one. Here on the Cleaver Ward, Ira's old bunk was still empty, and one day I saw its mattress was gone, letting the bare framework underneath show. Wearing a red sweater Edsel Ford had given me before he too went away, I had taken to standing at the window in his place, since he'd made good his escape and it seemed like someone ought to watch the traffic. I never started saying "Me," though. I still knew the difference, and I wasn't that far gone.

The cars went past and by and on out of the frame, but then one stopped to drop off a new prisoner. When the pirate who had captured her let her out and caught her arms to show her to us up here in the Cleaver Ward, I saw she had no top on, and that struck me as hard, since it was still and always winter and now there was dirty snow on the ground. Even Captain Teach must have thought so, because he'd just let her put on a dirty prison shift with stains down the front. Then the wind did a wild dance and kicked the light brown hair back off her face, and two green eyes looked up as if the wind had come from me.

"Her," I said, and pressed my fingers to the hard, hard glass.

Next to me, Holden's face was just as hard. "That cooze was sleeping with a *professor*, man, can you believe it?" he said. "I know which one, too—I thought he was after *me*! I wouldn't have gone along, but I did think better of his *taste* back then. By the way, I'm sorry about your dad. But if you ask me, *she* deserves whatever she gets."

But maybe now that could include me, I thought. The door was open, since there wasn't one anymore, and I flew out, ran down the stairs and past all the other doctors and machines everywhere in that awful, horrible hospital, until I was outside. The attendant was leading her away somewhere, and dirty snow had started swirling all around us, it was dirty when it came out of the sky, *and I remembered what the G in my old name had stood for they were right* and I caught her, and I was trying to say, I was trying to say *Thalia Thalia* and then *Suze Suze* and I said "Susan" and she said "No I'm Tuesday" and the attendant said "I'm a whole weekend, baby, let's get going" and they did.

Live long and prosper merimee quaquaqua nicknick *oh Isadora ZZT* dirty snow *remember remember* april one one nine seven four *WOn't get fOOLed ag gag gag* ill again *ZZT* nick nick and me now would be lost *ZZT* nick and me now would be lost quaqua nicknick *ZZT* cast off outcast and the cast aweigh can you sail sail away oh I can sir can sir Can Sir *ZZZZZZT* middleaged father 46 year old artificer please go gently nicknicknick *ZZT ZZT* And I think we had better bag it quit just give up on this land business and reversible thumbs too the works and go back to the beach crawl into the water and be fish with no eyelids our old *ZZT* huckfins and a gill again the

II

The Skipper's Tale

ONE DAY BACK IN THE WAR, I WAS SITTING IN THE OFFICERS' CLUB on Tallulabonka or someplace with a couple of the other skippers— Kennedy, McHale. We were all in the PTs, which believe me was no fooling, buddy, when it came to going in harm's way. The truth is, we probably weren't helping the fucking war effort any more than if our tubs were named for Barnum, but it looked good in the newsreels. MacArthur quit the Philippines, we got to play taxicab. I don't think my boat ever fired a single torpedo that hit anything.

McHale and I went back a ways. My charter-fishing business in the Florida Keys went bust after I made the mistake of taking a boatload of crazy Cubans someplace they wanted to go and I didn't, so I joined the peacetime Navy in early '40. McHale was already in, running a cutter by day and a poker game by night down in the Panama Canal Twilight Zone. That's where he and I hooked up, chasing the same sassy-hipped piece of local poon and downing brew like there was no tomorrow, which it turned out there wasn't. So the both of us were right on the spot to volunteer for the PTs when they started training the first squadrons down there, right after Pearl Harbor.

He and I were the old salts in our squadron. That tickled the bejesus out of us both, since we weren't all that old and had both been failures up to then. Most of the skippers were more like Jack, a lot of fancy-pants rich kids in khakis hot-rodding it on the bounding main. They'd whip their boats around these islands like flivvers on a back road near, I don't know, Dartmouth or someplace, like they figured Dad could always buy them another if they cracked this one up.

The way things turned out, I guess you could say Jack's Dad sure did.

He was a pretty cool customer then. Always friendly with McHale and me, but still like he thought that was funny. You knew that half his brain was someplace else, and you could bet your last pair of shined shoes that wherever it was was more interesting, and for damn sure had better food, than Tallulabonka. A skinny guy who liked to wear shades and didn't keep a Lucky Strike going awake or asleep like the rest of us, even though he'd smoke a cigar once in a while just to show us we shouldn't take it personal. I never knew where he got the cigars.

We called this joint the officers' club, but it was really just another shack made out of panfried-looking palm fronds, with flies buzzing around like they knew something we didn't and one of those damn "Paris, France 10000 Miles" directional arrows stuck on it. Anyway, the three of us were talking hump, the way you do wartime or peacetime and Tallulabonka or home whenever there's beer and you can't get a ballgame on the radio. McHale and I were doing most of the jawing.

"Remember ol' Screw-Me Susie, back in the Zone?" he asked, nudging me with that gap-toothed, dirty grin of his. Which was about the most obscene sight that you could ever hope to see, this side of Minnie Mouse's snatch. I was, I think, the more sensitive of the two of us, I guess. Well, who gives a blueberry shit.

I swigged some down. "Oh, what a gal," I said.

"Hell, yeah. I think there was one time she took you on for lunch—and about three *more* of us on for dinner. Talk about a night that'll live in Infamy, N.J." He always told his crew that's where he was from. "Ony thing I can't remember," McHale had started to bust a gut, "is which one of us lost the coin toss, and had to buy her her fuckin' ginger ale afterward." As I blinked and swigged some more, Minnie got another workout, with McHale's eyebrows wig-wagging her in. "You ever do anything like that, Jack?" he asked.

"Well, I never had to pay for the ginger ale, if that's what you mean," Jack said, with a nice smile. "Back in college," and he knew we knew which one, so Harvard was just another fly buzzing around, "my housemates would complain because I never had any cash on me. But I never got used to carrying it, or keys either. Never had that clear a notion of just what pockets were *for*, men. But you know, Mac, the funny thing is," he grinned, "they always let me into the Stork Club anyway. And even though I'd be happy to bring you two fellows along with me, I'm not completely sure you'd make the grade."

It's hard to explain, but it wasn't snotty. It was more like Jack *had* just taken us into the Stork Club with him, and we'd had a great time there. Later in the war, when I switched over to the submarine service, my boat picked up a shot-down carrier pilot who was a senator's son or something, and this bird was frantic to pretend we were all the same kind of

Americans. The guy just didn't get how we wanted him to act as different as we knew he was, so we could make up our own minds on what we thought of that. But that wasn't how Jack worked his rap sheet. He knew his life probably sounded pretty damn swell to you if you were most people, so he'd let you be part of it for a second, quick joke about Baaastin here, fast flashbulbs-at-your-best-table smile there. At the same time, even so, as soon as he let you be part of it, it was like *he* wasn't anymore. He'd gone someplace else again, and not Boston either. Like I said, hard to explain.

"Say, Jack," McHale wanted to know. "You ever bang a movie star? I know your dad knows a couple or a few, so tell us. Well? Didja ever nail one of those broads?"

"Not yet," Jack said, looking out past Dickinson Inlet at the U.S.S. *Monroe*. Then it was like he'd decided he had to give us a little more of himself on this one, taking himself away first as usual. "Even though, believe me, Mac, a couple of times I was *this* close," he said, holding up a thumb and finger of the same hand that was holding his cigar. "And not in my father's house, either," he added, which made me think there might be more to this whole being-rich business than McHale or me was ever going to know. "But what the hell, piss on that noise—I guess the war got in the way."

"War got in the way of lots of things for everybody," I said, not sure where that one had surfaced from. I guess I hadn't been able to help but think how maybe I hadn't known old Screw-Me Susie like McHale had known old Screw-Me Susie. But even so, I was probably missing life back in the Zone, where the beer wasn't 3.2, she had shacked up with just me for a whole weekend once when Mac got detailed over to the Cristobal district on SP duty, and nobody was dying. If you like gals whose morals are as loose as what they use to prove it with is tight, there's nothing like being on American soil but out of sight of the padres and schoolmarms, with Old Glory flying when you step outside afterwards like a roof between you and God.

"Not me," McHale said. "Hell no I wouldn't mind some available pussy, even if it had Ethel Merman's face riding shotgun. But I'm in my fuckin' *prime* out there, and don't nobody forget it. Me and Bilko have a bet going about which one of us is going to come out of this son of a bitch with more loot."

"So do we and the Russians, I think," Jack said. "At least, that's what my father's friends are saying, now that they've spent some serious time in Washington at a dollar a year." He smiled, but not at us. " 'While England slept,' " he muttered, like it was an old song title or something.

It was late in the day. Off in the sky, a Douglas SBD Dauntless torpedo bomber was heading out above the sun, far off and so close to immobile that it looked like some lonely kid's model. "Wonder what's going on?" McHale, who had seen it, said. "Those birds don't usually go out alone."

A minute later, it was still hanging there. "Man, those Dauntlesses are slow," McHale said. "No wonder the Japs knocked so many of them out of the sky, when they were coming in at Midway."

"So we build some more," Jack shrugged.

"What for?" McHale was getting exasperated. "So the Japs can knock *them* out of the sky?"

"Look, Mac," Jack said, his face pivoting on the stub of his cigar. "Whatever you are, you're not dumb. Even Binghamton knows that. But you still don't know what this war is about. It isn't about us out here in the South Pacific, trying to look like heroes and not get killed at the same time. It isn't even about Midway. It's about whether they run out of planes before we run out of planes, and—well, I don't know if either of you fellows has ever seen Detroit, and I know I've never seen Tokyo. But Mac, all fooling aside? You'd *love* these odds at Aqueduct."

"Oh, fine. Fine," McHale said. "That's great, Jack, and I'll be sure to have the chaplain write both my wives it's a done deal. But so then tell me, why ain't I in Washington? Or Detroit? What the fuck are *we* doing here?"

"Trying to look like heroes and not get killed at the same time," Jack recited, kidding him along. "Anyway, what happened to being in your prime—your *fuckin'* prime, Mac? You want to let Bilko win walking away?"

"I'd like to stay in it, that's all," McHale grumbled. "My fucking prime."

"Wouldn't we all," Jack said. He stood up, with a grin like autumn leaves with a pack of Chiclets in the middle. "Well, gentlemen. Pleasant dreams," he said. "I've got a night patrol, and just how did you two sons of bitches get out of it, anyway?"

■

Well, little buddy, you've probably figured out it was the next morning when all of us on Tallulabonka heard that the 109 hadn't come back. No sign of Jack or any of the crew. Mostly because he thought he should, Binghamton sent a couple of boats out to cruise around the Telmi Strait for traces, and they didn't even turn up any debris.

That's how it went in the war, but McHale was down in the dumps about it. "God damn goddam everything to bastard shit anyway," he bitched. "Jack didn't know it, but one of my boys from the 73 had six Imperial quarts of booze and two Nip flags with fake bloodstains hidden in one of the 109's depth-charge canisters. And now it's all just getting sharks drunk and nervous at the fucking bottom of the Telmi Strait."

Four or five days later, Binghamton ordered McHale and me to hightail our boats down to Ireidahonda for a couple of fast supply runs. Whenever we weren't in action, they'd use the PTs to ferry ammo, rations, 3.2 beer, movies and replacements around to all the different cogs of the war effort on all the little islands. It wasn't bad duty so long as you remembered to keep an eye peeled for half-submerged sea mines in the channels.

From the half-dozen or so times we'd done it by now, both me and McHale already knew old Nick. He was the supply officer on Ireidahonda and its kid sister island Alwok, and a good one. Had a tent up called "Nick's Snack Shack" to feed hamburgers to the pilots and bomber crews that used the airstrip there, played poker like it was chess or something and his opponent wasn't you, got along with officers and EM both. But there was something anxious about the way he did every-damn-thing, all the way from Hi Nick to See ya 'round—like he was watching you with his lips and ears, not just eyes, to make sure you were up to speed on what a relaxed and ordinary Joe he was, and thought well of him for it.

This time, his clipboard had my boat hauling C rations, smokes, a dozen cases of 3.2, a shovel, and *Mrs. Miniver* to a crew of Seabees building a new airstrip over on Fondawonda. McHale was taking ammo and *Blondie's Blessed Event* to an Army recon platoon on Liltiti, which was the smaller of the Big Gazongas. But then Nick started tapping a pencil against the clipboard, and I swear you could see sweat whiter than his skin start on his hairline and make his five o'clock shadow slick.

"Wait—wait," he muttered, like Halsey would have his hide if he got this one wrong, or maybe just for the hell of it. "No, now I'm, uh, 'god damn' sure!," flashing a weak smile. "They've already had *Mrs. Miniver* on Fondawonda." I'll tell you, that put a Minnie on McHale's mug. "I'm switching the movies."

"Sure they don't need any 3.2 on Liltiti?" McHale asked him, with a wink that told me not a lot of it would get there if they did.

"Hell, no, they don't, Mac, and you know it," Nick said. "The Big Gazongas are a combat zone."

If you don't know, little buddy, 3.2 was the low-alcohol-content brew that Uncle Sam shipped all over the Pacific. The idea was we wouldn't get too drunk, and brother, they knew what they were doing. You practically had to glug the cubic equivalent of Lake Superior to get as deep in the bag as every sailor, GI, and gyrene was determined to get anyway at the drop of a hat, come hell or high 3.2. Put it this way, in the Florida Keys I'd been damn near as skinny as Bogart. Now, well, last Christmas McHale and I had had to arm-wrestle every day for a whole week to see who got stuck being the base Santa Claus that morning, putting on a wool union suit and some cotton batting in that heat to go around and Ho-ho-fuck-the-Navy-ho-ingly hand out Lucky Strikes and gum, which they got most days anyway, to the EM. I usually lost.

While they were loading up our boats, Nick took the two of us over to the Snack Shack for some burgers. Maybe we should have been down to the dock supervising, but Nick seemed like he was desperate to make a good impression on somebody, and just now we two were the only citizens around. He flipped the burgers himself, pretty awkwardly but with concentration to make up for that, you could tell he was sick with fear at the thought that you might try to start an interesting conversation with him during it. It was really too damn hot for burgers, but McHale and me always were a pair of firehouse dogs when it came to any kind of meat on a griddle.

"Either of you want coffee with these?" Nick asked, putting down two burgers for each of us. "I've got some brewed."

"Always got time for good Joe," McHale said. "And if I'm reading that can's label right, you're talking about real Maxwell House—not that powdered crap we drink on patrol."

"I guess I'll have some too," I said. So he brought us each a cup. Had none for himself.

"These are fuckin' good, Nick," McHale said through his first burger. "What were you in civilian life—short-order cook?"

"Lawyer." The way it dropped out of his mouth and hit his shoe like a dead mouse, I could see that it was a thing he'd spent his whole life expecting to take pride in once he finally got to be one, and now he was someplace where he couldn't. It was all a little strange, what with the way he had an apron on and wasn't eating with us, as if he'd made a last-minute snap decision that we'd like him better if he didn't. His face was all about sweating out tough choices about things that didn't make a damn bit of difference.

"Ever pull any sea duty, Nick?" McHale asked him.

"'Fraid not! I'm a shore rat. I guess the Navy knows best—anyway, I try to do mine," he said with a queasy smile. If McHale wanted to piss on him for that, the smile said, he'd hold McHale's johnson while he did it. Hating him with his teeth and dark eyes the whole time.

"Oh. Well, you're not missin' much." McHale took another bite. "'Cept the war, of course," he said thoughtfully, chewing.

I really didn't want to bust out laughing along with him, but it *was* funny. After a second, Nick reached around and took the apron off, and started to brush the table clean of the bits of bun and beef McHale had just spewed out.

"I've seen a little of the war," he said, once we quit laughing. "You know, it's kind of hard to miss wherever you are, so long as we're all out here. Anyway, not everyone can skipper a PT boat—somebody's got to pump gas. And sometimes planes come over here too at night and drop the occasional bomb on my tent, even if I've never been in combat up in the Big Gazongas."

"Aw, shit. He didn't mean nothing by it," I said. Which was true, since I knew McHale didn't mean anything by *anything*. "Sorry, Nick. That was lousy thanks for good chow."

"Well, I wasn't expecting any thanks," Nick said, flashing a smile that was a little too eager to show up and then to get itself over with. "You hadn't finished eating yet."

"We have now, though," I said.

"Whuffafugoomean?" McHale said, bits of bun showing through his lips. "Ffgotanowononmplate."

"Take it with you, for Christ sake, Mac," I said. "They've gotta be done loading now, and we both need as much sun's we can get. Or do you want to run your boat smack up against Liltiti in the dark?"

"Maybe that's what Jack did," McHale said. "Hell, maybe I'll be the one who finds him—and then tears him a new one for losing all *my* supplies, too."

"You mean Joe Kennedy's kid?" Nick said. "Is he still missing?"

"And presumed dead," I said. "But I didn't think he'd ever done a supply run for you, since he's Binghamton's pet and always gets the glamor jobs. Do you know him?"

"Of him," Nick said. "He doesn't—or didn't—know of me, obviously. My family didn't exactly move in the same circles his did, Stateside. Or here either, I suppose," he added, glancing at McHale and twitching that my-movie's-stuck-in-the-projector smile of his like he wasn't sure if he was making up, sucking up, or just giving up.

"Well, we better shove off," I said. "Come on, Mac."

"Oh, fine—so let him take me to *court,* the weaselly shithead," McHale was saying, as we got down to the dock. "He just got my goat. Tapping his pencil and flipping his burgers and fiddling around with his apron, and doesn't the dumb son of a bitch know that every GI in the Pacific theater has seen *Mrs. Miniver* six fucking times? I swear, I'm going to toss the fucking thing over the side before we make Liltiti, and when I tell 'em what I've done those poor bastards in the foxholes are gonna start crying and lining up to suck my dick from pure gratitude. We're dodging Nip bullets in malaria up to our hips, and they give us Greer fucking Garson to pound pud to? I don't know about yours and I don't want to, big buddy, but my little piggy just says uncle and goes 'wee, wee, wee' all the way home. You know, sometimes I wonder what in hell we're fighting for."

"You do? Well, I'll be damned," I said. "I never knew you thought about it. Well, see you back on Tallulabonka tomorrow, Mac, God willing."

"Or whoever," McHale said. "I don't give a shit, do you?"

■

Stern to bow, his boat and then mine worked our way out of the narrow channel between Ireidahonda and Alwok. Then I set a course due south by northwest for Fondawonda, straight on out past the big blue in between Donovan's reef and Bomarzo. McHale and the 73 peeled off west by north-south toward the Big Gazongas, and pretty soon we lost sight of them in all the gilded fish scales that the sun was putting on the sea.

I was pretty sure that we could make Fondawonda by sunset even though, because of all the cases of C rations and 3.2 loading down the bow, my boat was making even choppier headway than usual. But there hadn't been anywhere else to stow them. Remembering what McHale had said he was going to do to *Mrs. Miniver,* once we were out of sight of Ireidahonda I told a couple of the boys to man the .50 calibers for some target practice. Then I started heaving reels of *Blondie's Blessed Event* up in the sky like some damn discus thrower. The sun would catch them just before the bullets did, at least the ones we hit.

"Bye-bye, Dagwood!" we'd holler out every time another reel hit the water, whether we'd plugged it on the way or not. "Screw you up the ass, Mr. Dithers. So long, Daisy—yeah, 'give us your friggin' answer do' ta *this*! Woof!" We felt kind of let down that Hollywood didn't make longer movies, once we were back to riding in the quiet that settles in at double intensity after any kind of shooting. Because it's unnerving, you try to keep the voices going anyhow, but they always come out puny and you have to wait until you've got some good practical excuse to talk before it sounds normal again.

Which we had. My senior torpedoman was a little fellow from Chicago name of Laprezski, we just called him Ski. "Hey, Skipper," he called up to me. "You really think those Seabees are gonna need *all* this beer?"

"Don't think I wasn't searching my heart and asking for guidance about that self-same question, boys," I said. "But we're gonna look awfully damn stupid turning up off Fondawonda with nothing but a shovel." Even so, a dark mass had already started showing on the horizon to starboard beyond the cases stacked in the bow, so I knew it was now or never. "Well, a couple dozen cans more or less aren't gonna make much of a nevermind," I called down. "Pass one on up here to me, willya? Do. Not. Throw. The beer can at me. Not at eighteen knots, Algligni, you idiot. Pass."

Well, it was the usual foam and minnow piss. But it tasted better with the salt air gluing new skins on our warm faces, the .50 cals sticking up port and starboard like praying-mantis architecture on some insect cathedral, the gray torpedo tubes turning into big thumbs pointing the way every time we slewed, and the orange and pink purple of the lowering sun making toy-sailor silhouettes out of my crew as they did less and less of whatever they did and Fondawonda started hiking herself up on her elbows in front of us, the way Susie used to in the good old days in the Zone, and our boat scooted toward her like a spoon on a gigantic blue bedspread. I knew my buddy McHale didn't have a whole hell of a lot of use for God, or for any of His works except McHale, and sometimes I was tempted to agree with him about everything but the last part. But the Lord was sure a breathtaking stage manager for some mighty rotten vaudeville revues, and I guessed I wasn't the first or last to think so. Even dogs probably did, whenever they took a break from sniffing and relieving themselves in a corner of the floorboards.

When it's your place of work, you sometimes forget that the sea is the sea. But I had seen somebody else realize it once, when he was small. That was when I still had my own boat in the Keys, and rented it out for excursions. The little boy I remembered best from that time couldn't have been over five, and maybe I ought to've said the hell with the money and told him and his folks to come aboard anyhow, but I didn't.

You know how kids that age behave like they haven't figured out yet how to manage being all of themselves at the same time? When this one raced out onto the pier, he was nothing but a pair of legs. With knees that weren't used to being bare in winter, and looked like they'd blink if they could. But seeing the whole Atlantic there, with nothing between him and it, turned him into just a face.

It was like he'd forgotten which job his eyes had, which one his mouth did. Just kept widening them all, for insurance. If he'd been older, he'd have goggled like that at the first dame he saw naked. So I had a picture of how it felt for a little kid to take in all that blue for the first time, and understand that grown-up men went out on it until they got too tiny to be spotted by everyone they'd left behind on land.

The memory of it used to knock on different doors around my skull like it was looking for a room. I never could put a name to the mood he sometimes popped up from, except that it was where I stashed the stuff I knew better than to ever try bringing up around McHale. He'd probably have gotten a bang out of being the guy who wiped the glow off that kid's mug.

I hadn't. But I knew his father couldn't afford to charter my boat even for the minimum three hours, and had already tried to spare Dad the embarrassment of having to hear that from me head-on by doing my best to act disgruntled and damned busy swabbing out bait buckets as soon as I saw him coming. He'd just gotten out of a sad-looking black tow truck with "Egan's Garage, Rochester Minn." painted in white script on the cab door, a mighty mystifying sight in Florida until I spotted his missus sitting inside it. One look was enough to tell me that the reason he'd brought her all the way down here from up there in the middle of the Depression, despite being so short on ghelt that he had no other transport but his work vehicle, was to give her a chance to do the last of her coughing in sunshine.

So we had the conversation that neither of us wanted to, because Egan knew what I'd been trying to tell him by carrying on with my chores. But he had to ask me anyway, because of that mute profile in the passenger seat. She wanted to keep their boy beside her, but he probably didn't know she was dying or even how to spell "tuberculosis," and he scrambled out of the truck to run down to the pier after his dad. That's when he stopped short, looking like he'd just found his next mother— not even knowing yet that he was going to need one, but staring at the ocean with everything he had in him, as if the gray eyes under his sandy hair had already set sail straight for the horizon and the rest of him had to catch up somehow.

"Are we going on the boat?"

"Not today," his father said. "This man says it's too—dangerous, right now. He thinks we should come back when the sea is . . ."

"Smaller," I said, trying to help him out.

"I'm not scared."

"Jacky Gilbert," his dad faltered—"you should be."

"No. I want to go on the boat. You said we would."

"Your dad's right, son," I told him, still trying to help. "You can't see them, but there's whales out there, and—sea monsters, and—"

Well, I sure didn't know how to dissuade a kid. Not this one, anyway: "You mean like *serpents*?" he said, like just getting to use the word as a practical term was making today Christmas for him. "Do you fight them?"

"Only when I have to."

"With swords?"

Confused, I looked around my boat's deck. There was a mop there. "Whatever comes to hand, I guess."

"I could help. I want to fight them. Mama could watch me fight them. Please, Poppy!" He tugged at Egan's belt.

Even beforehand, I wasn't sure if what I'd thought of doing was a good idea or not. But I figured it might be easier on Egan this way. "Lis-

ten, son. The truth is, your dad would let you go if he could," I told him.
"I'm the one says you can't."

"Why not?" the kid said, and I could tell that his father was tenser
than he was about hearing the answer.

I crouched down, putting my face close to his. "Because I'm a sea
monster," I said. "*YEEAARGH! BLAAGH!*," jumping up and waving
my arms.

Well, he sure scooted. He gave a yelp and backpedaled right out of my
new shadow, grabbing blindly for his father's hand. As soon as he found
it, he stood his ground, too, and bit back his scared look. But he was still
dumbfounded, and I could have picked up his old expression and tossed
it to the gulls for all the use his staring eyes and legs that quivered with
plans to run if necessary had for it now.

"Why, you son of a bitch," Egan said, herding the kid close. "And
here I thought you were all right, too. Guess I made a mistake."

I didn't know how to explain to him that I had only been trying to
make sure his boy wouldn't blame him, or guess at the real reason they
couldn't go on the boat. But I also saw it didn't matter, because the only
difference between what I'd done and what McHale, who I didn't even
know back then, would have in my place was that McHale wouldn't
have had good intentions. Or felt confused and crappy afterwards, as if I
had committed more of a sin by trying to do right than I would have if
I'd just been the hard-case S.O.B. that Egan thought I was.

"I guess you did, brother," I told him. "Now shove off. Can't you see
I got work to do?" Then I turned back to the bait buckets, because I
didn't want to watch him take his son back down the pier to his lousy
tow truck and his coughing, dying wife.

All that the years since then had done for me was get me fatter. But it
was strange to think that little Jacky Gilbert Egan was practically old
enough to be out here in the war with the rest of us now. Unless I had put
him off oceans for life, he might've already lied about his age to sign up
for the Navy. Or maybe the Marines, since the jarheads took them young.

I guessed I hadn't lied to him in the long run about the monsters, only
about being one myself. But my beer can was empty, and all of a sudden

I had no idea why all this had sprung to my mind. After a while, I called down, "Hey, Algligni! Hand me up another. The rest of you guys get one more, too. One," holding up my finger where everyone could see it.

I was just crumpling my second can when the motor conked. You think it gets quiet when guns leave off firing, try the first ten seconds after that grinding you're so used to just up and quits being there in your ears and under your feet. If there was a Richter scale for silence, we'd have been off it.

Well, those PT engines always were as nervous as a filly on her first day at the stud farm, and I was counting on my machinist's mate, a crazy Kraut from Pensacola whose handle was Harry Flugelhorn, to get us under way again. But after forty-five minutes, he put his greasy face, that all of a sudden there wasn't enough sun left to light, out of the hatch and said, "Nothing doing, Skipper. Motor's fine. I think something's fouling the propellers."

That's when, looking astern, we all saw the black dot in our wake. It kept dipping in and out of sight in the low swells, and I couldn't make out what it was even with binoculars. I wasn't even positive it was con-nected to the boat, and I didn't see how something that far off could be what was messing us up. But somehow, from your first sight of it, you knew that it had been there for a while.

"God damn it," I said. "One of you dumb assholes volunteer to go over the side and try to unsnaggle whatever is snaggling the propellers."

"Are you nuts, Skipper?" Ski said. "These are shark-infested waters." That was his fear, and he always expressed it exactly the same way: "shark-infested waters." He must have read it once in *Life* or some damn rag back in Chicago, and it had stuck with him. Damned if I know why he hadn't joined the Army instead. "Anyway," he said, "we don't even know what that *thing* is back there. Maybe it's a shark."

A drunk and nervous one, I thought. I was trying to make a joke in my head, but thinking it just got me jittery. "Shit," I said. "O.K. So we radio the Seabees for a tow. They'll laugh their asses off. God damn it. Get 'em on the blower, Algligni."

"Radio's busted, Skipper." Man, did he look scared.

I'll tell you, I sure blew my stack then. I pulled off my cap and slung it at the deck, which I had never done before. "*Algligni!*" I hollered. "What the fuck are you telling me, the radio's busted?"

"I mean it doesn't *work*," he said.

"Well, can't you fix it, for Christ's sake?"

"Tried to."

"And?"

"I failed?"

I picked my cap up, smacked it against my leg. "Oh, this is fucking *great*," I said, shaking my whole face at him and putting the cap back on with the brim pointing starboard before I got it squared away.

The boat was starting to roll in the current, had nothing to fight it with. "Doesn't matter anyways," my exec said, I wish I could remember his name. He'd started this war in Arlington, Virginia, and he was going to end it there, too. Kamikaze. "If they had boats on Fondawonda, they wouldn't need us to ferry all this crap around for them in the first place."

For the first time, staring blankly at him, I noticed how much my exec looked like an older, shrewder Algligni. Then again, they were both in the same boat, and so was I. "Shit," I said. "Well, shit."

I was trying to get an idea, but I didn't even know what I ought to be having an idea about. Water was lapping the hull with little slaps, sounding happy that now it could be heard. The black dot was still there behind us, getting harder to pick out of all the deeper blue. I took one look and gave up.

"Well," I said, "hand me another. You guys go ahead, too."

"Maybe once we drift in a little closer to shore," I hollered when my third can was empty, "I can talk one of you 'fraidy-cats into taking a swim and unsnafuing the goddam propellers." But I knew there wasn't much chance of that, and not only because the blur of Fondawonda was getting farther away, not closer, and fading back into being more of the horizon. From the looks in their eyes, I could tell that the boat was going to have to fetch up somewhere in Kansas before any of *them* went over the side.

Besides, I knew any skipper worth an unexpected belch wouldn't ask his boys to do anything he wouldn't do himself, and I wouldn't have gone in the same water as the black dot if they'd told me I could have

Betty Grable any damn way I pleased afterwards. For just a second, she winked at me over her shoulder even so, and believe you me she wasn't standing up in that cornball pose or wearing that holy bathing suit of hers either, but then it was night and I don't just mean not day. It was more like the sun had turned into a giant bowling ball, and was sending out rays of ink and black and dark the same way it did light when it was really there. We had stars by the bucketload but no moon, and the water lapping as we drifted had become the ordinary noise, the way our engines should've been.

After a while, the rest of them stopped waiting for me to give the O.K. before they got themselves another brew. We had cases of 3.2 ripped open all over the bow, and of C rations that we had opened by mistake, and we kept on bumping into them, and each other, and the nice torpedo tubes, the insect guns and who knows what-all in the dark, trying to find out from our fingers and each other's information where the boat ended, so we could be sure we were pissing out of it. Every time I told myself I'd better taper off, I'd think of the black dot in our wake. I started to almost mourn the time when we could see it, instead of just knowing it was there.

"Skipper?" somebody said, as I either belched or farted. I was too drunk to be sure which end of me was up.

"Lea' me 'lone. Fchrisesake all'you lea' me 'lone. Don' know anything either."

"I think we're on a sandbar." It was the exec.

I got on my hands and knees to see how the boat felt. He was right, we were still being tugged by the current but now something was stopping it from doing whatever the hell it wanted with us. The boat was keeling slightly but steadily to starboard, the bow pinned by the water onto whatever was holding it there, like a gray butterfly in a glass case of sea and night.

"Sonvabitch," I said. "Fits low tide now, we'll float off when it's high tide. Fits high tide now, we can build sand castles when it's low tide. Win-win."

"If this is a sandbar, then there must be an island," my exec reasoned. "Besides, I think I can hear surf."

I looked out over the gunwale, blinking and straining my ears. Part of the night dead ahead of me did look even more like night than the rest did, and along what I had decided was that part's lower edge there was an occasional faint scrawl of maybe-white chalk, in time to dim crashing. I stood up, grabbing at the gunwale.

"Well, God damn, let's go, then," I said, putting one leg over it. "Jesus, I can't tell you how glad I'm going to be to get off this bucket."

"Skipper!" He grabbed my arm. "It might be Jap-held."

"Aw, shit. We're at war with them, aren't we? That's fucking sad when you think about it. Isn't it just fucking sad?"

"If you don't get hold of yourself pretty soon, I'll do it for you," he said. "Besides, have you forgotten? *It's* still out there, Skipper."

Remembering the black dot in our wake sobered me up P.D.Q. "Can you see it?" I said.

"I don't need to. Do you— I mean, can you?"

"O.K.," I said. Trying to clear my head, I dragged my fingers down my cheeks. "No way we're going to know anything for sure before it's light. But I want guards. How tanked is Flugelhorn?"

"Three sheets. But awake."

"Stick him up in the bow with the Thompson—do we still have the Thompson? O.K. You stay put here with the leeward .50 cal. I'll be back in the stern with my .45. That sound about right to you?"

"Well, I don't have any better ideas." He let go of my arm, and I heard him stumbling forward to go figure out which the fuck one was Flugelhorn all over again and get him set up in the bow. I got down off the bridge, landed flat on my fat ass, pulled myself back up again and went toward the stern, tripping over a cigar of God's that I figured out a second later was the starboard torpedo tube. Making sure the flap on the holster of my .45 was undone, I settled down next to the sternmost starboard depth-charge canister. A couple of unopened cans of 3.2 had rolled back there, so I cracked one to keep myself company. No point in even trying to look at my watch.

I don't know if I dozed or not. But the soft bumping in the water against the stern brought me back from wherever I was. At first I didn't even name it bumping, I just knew that it was a new sound I was getting used to, and then my brain jumped with the thought that maybe I shouldn't, maybe I should find out what it was before I got more used to it and sleepy. I didn't want to look, but I worked up the nerve by reminding myself that I probably wouldn't be able to see much of anything. My mouth was all muzzy, and my brain not heart was in it, like a frog. If I opened my mouth, my brain would hop away, and land with a splash in the water. I had no idea if this would be a good thing or not. My brain wasn't working anyway. Maybe it deserved to be free.

Drawing my .45, I looked down past the stern. I might as well have stuck my head into the folds of a nun's habit, but it was still true something was down there. It was a shape of black on black that the swells kept nudging forward to tap against the hull, then pulling back again. No question it was driftwood, with one branch sticking up and a knobby part next to that. But it was still driftwood that looked kind of like a man, so I decided to kid myself along for a second by just pretending it was one and seeing how that went.

"Jack?" I said, keeping my voice low. "That you, Jack?"

It didn't answer. It just came forward, with its one branch waving hello, and then went back again. By now, I couldn't have told you what was funny, or scary, or stupid, or real, or anything. "Say, Jack," I told it. "You know I'm always glad to see you, buddy. But if you don't tell me what's going on, I'm going to have to plug you sooner or later."

The chunk of driftwood dipped and waved, but didn't talk. It wanted to let the water do the talking for it, but I didn't understand water. All these years, and now my brain had finally spilled the beans. It had never known what water was saying and always wanted it to talk slower, which the water never did. Even a five-year-old who'd never seen the ocean before had understood it better than I could.

Well, that pissed me off more ways than I could count. Putting my free hand over one eye to steady my aim, although I might as well have put it over both of them for all the good it did, I put a bullet right into the water that I didn't understand, the nun's habit of the night, and the driftwood that was Jack.

Christ. Of course, the next thing I knew, Flugelhorn was spraying everything in sightlessness with the Tommy gun, my exec was pounding a whole belt of .50 cal into that Cheshire-cat smile of maybe-white surf off to starboard, and Algligni, who I hadn't made part of my plans or even known was awake, had just lobbed a grenade over the *port* side of the damn boat, where there wasn't anything to blow up but the ocean. Meanwhile, all the guys who'd been passed out and hadn't even known about the sandbar, much less anything afterwards, were jumping up or taking cover or running around like headless chickens, all screaming "Jesus *fuck!*" and "God no please I'll be good" and "Skipper" and "I see it, Ski!" and finally, as the firing died away, "What the hell was *that* about?," which came from Flugelhorn in the bow.

"And on a related subject, where are we?" someone else called out.

"I don't know. But it's all right," I hollered back. "I think I killed it. It's all right, guys! I killed it."

Nobody had to ask what *it* was. Feeling my way along, I went forward to the bridge, where the exec was standing with his hands in his pockets, like he didn't want to admit he'd just tossed a stream of the U.S. government's best .50-caliber ammo at nothing. I didn't know why he felt that way, either all of us were embarrassed or none of us were, and it wasn't like anyone was watching.

"Well, at least now we know there aren't any Japs on that island, if there is an island there," one of us said. "Because if they had so much as a mortar on that island, if there is an island there, they'd have blown our heads and our ass in two different directions by now."

"Yeah," the other of us said. "So now we know one thing. But out of how many we ought to?"

Whichever of us was supposed to have the answer to that one didn't, so I told Laprezski to take over from Flugelhorn in the bow and everybody else to try to get some shut-eye, since I guessed we still had a few hours before daylight and there was nothing we could do till then. Even though I was pretty sure I hadn't been lying about killing the black dot, or driftwood, or whatever it was at least temporarily, I didn't much want to wander back to the stern. So I settled down across from the exec in a corner of the bridge, with our heads and feet going in opposite directions and only our beltlines matching up. He already had his hat down over his face, and I don't know if it was the 3.2, the black dot, the excitement or just bone-deep exhaustion, but I was in dreamland on the strangest goddam sail of my life. There was a black dot in our wake.

The Skipper's Dream

I was still a skipper, but my boat was white, and didn't have machine guns or torpedoes. My crew was in civvies, and when I looked close, some of them were dames. Two real lookers, one of whom was plainly much too nice a gal for someone like me to ever think of putting my meathooks on her. The other was a high-class tramp who'd be happy to lay me the day I struck oil, at least if my well was bigger than anybody else's in line. They were both making fun of a skinny guy who was Algligni until he turned into my exec, and then back into Algligni again whenever the two pretty dames laughed. There was a black dot in our wake.

Meanwhile, I was showing off my new steering wheel, which kept on spinning out of control like a lazy susan that had decided it would rather be a pinwheel and the hell with serving anybody, to an old gent dressed like a popinjay and his wife. There was a black dot in our wake. All the same, I kept on knowing at the back of my neck that there were someone else aboard, and so I looked astern when the two dames ran by me laughing.

But they had vanished, and there was only one girl back there. Even before she turned to look at me, naked to the waist and in McHale's arms in the sawmill at the back of the boat, I knew this must be Screw-Me Susie, the old gal I'd known back in the Zone before the war started and everything else got screwed along with her. Then the two dames from earlier trotted back up to the bow, still giggling, and the next time I looked behind me all the lumber was gone. A fellow of the type that even a couple of the nuns used to call an auntie in trousers stared back at me blandly. There was a black dot in our wake.

Everyone on our boat had started to whoop and wave by then, because the 109 had joined us. Jack had the con. He was wearing sunglasses. He looked great. There was a black dot in our wake. Both the dames took pictures. There was a black dot in our wake. He steered the 109 on out ahead of all of us, and I mean all of us, because the sea was packed with ships. The wind was playing music, and everyone was shouting greetings to each other as all our boats and ships and everything charged across the sea. There was a black dot in our wake.

I saw three ships come sailing on with Maltese crosses on their sails, crowded with civilians all watching the 109 out front, and another that seemed to be a prison ship for people with poor taste in headgear, waving turkey drumsticks and arguing about who was going to get to persecute who when they landed. Other ships packed with groaning and chains, some damn fool in a white peruke standing up in a longboat so he wouldn't have to help row, and a whaler whose captain kept yelling, "From hell's heart I stab at thee."

A kid on a raft with a nigger hollered over to our boat for a tow, and we gave him one on condition that the nigger didn't get any bright ideas about scrambling in here with the rest of us the next time a squall blew up. But the sea was as smooth as glass, and then I saw it *was* glass. Well, *clearly* that explains why it's as smooth as glass, I thought, feeling proud that I had finally understood something about water, or glass, or smoothness. Then again, there was a black dot in our wake.

And on top of that, just like a black dot in our wake wasn't plenty enough to cope with, I had lost to McHale at arm wrestling. I had to be the base Santa Claus. I was handing out cruficixes and candy bars as fast as my hands could grab them, and giving rosary beads to anybody that wanted rosary beads and leis to whoever asked for a lei. A teenage Screw-Me Susie, oh Christ she wasn't even out of high school, said she wanted both. Standing in the lumberyard at the back of the boat, with either McHale or the auntie in trousers winking at me over her shoulder, she still had nothing on above the waist, but had her arms folded crisscross so that I wouldn't see anything. There was a black dot in our wake. "You can't have both," I told her.

"But then how will I cover up my boobies?" she said, holding her arms wide. "It's only April Fool's Day. When they get cold, I get cold." Putting down the chalk that he'd been using to scribble numbers and gibberish all over the black dot in our wake, whoever was standing in the woodshed behind her grabbed her teenaged nips and squeezed, squeezed, squeezed.

I'll tell you, I slammed my eyes shut to that awful sight like I was throwing away the key to them, and wished I had eyelids on the insides of my eyes so I could close those too. But there was a black dot in our wake, and now I had to open them again, because everyone else on all the ships had started looking at the place that Jack was taking us, which they could see now standing up out of the horizon. Jack waved our boat ahead, giving us the honor of leading everybody in. It was an island— and somehow, still asleep, I knew it was *this* island, the one whose sand-bar we'd spent all night riding. Some gyrenes were planting a U.S. flag on top, I noticed. That seemed kind of pointless or redundant, since I knew we were at peace now and that this island was ours alone, and would be past the end of time. There was a black dot in our wake. Then, even though he was miles away and tiny, the second gyrene from the left turned to me.

"How," he said.

"What are you asking *me* for," I said, "how in the fuck would I know?" And he got hot, and huge, and white. After a few seconds, I understood he was the sky.

There was a black dot in our wake.

■

The island wasn't the way I'd pictured it, but it was something. Breakers ran up a white beach. Palm trees let the wind blow up the undersides of their skirts. Here's a word I found in a jailhouse dictionary once: verdant. Damn, it was verdant. I wondered if I'd ever see it again.

Then again, I was still looking at it now. I had a head my skull didn't like, they were going at it the way my parents used to, and the sun had already had an hour or so to stick in its two cents, so my eyes felt like two tired birds that just wanted to fly away from all the noise and mess behind them. Almost the only thing that made me feel easy in my mind, because it was familiar, was the noise of gentle bumping against the stern.

I knew I had to go back there, what with being the skipper and all. Everyone else, even the exec, was still toes up and drooling, making denim hieroglyphics here and there around the deck. The whole damn boat was strange under my feet, I felt I'd gotten to know it so much better in the dark but now it was different. All night, the boat had just been having fun with us poor bastards by pretending something here was something there and something somewhere else wasn't anywhere at all. I was surer than I wanted to be that I wasn't going to need it, but I drew my .45 anyway, just to have something in my hand.

Well, I damn near puked. He looked like one of those pictures from Hiroshima or Nagasaki, which I know is getting ahead of things warwise. But phosphorus grenades or plain old high explosive could do pretty much the same job on a human body, just not as many of them at once. My first guess was that he must have been blown off a Jap troopship or hit coming out of one of their landing barges, which were even more unwieldy and easily shot up than ours and that's saying something. Either way, it had happened a couple of days before, because after humanity had gotten done with him the sea had taken its turn. He was coming forward, bumping, and going back. I said a quick Our Father under my breath, and didn't finish it.

But then, as my brain went on pretending that it cared about the how of it, to keep itself distracted, I started to figure that whatever it was got him probably had to have happened on land, because that one claw reaching up to wave at the world had had time to stiffen with rigor mortis before he hit the water. The other hand was a fist of white bones curled up at the base of his neck against a uniform or flesh burned black, like he'd been trying to loosen his collar, and his face was way past any words in any dictionary except for the teeth that showed, some yellow, some brown, some gold and flashing in the sun. He looked on the outside like what cancer must do to people's insides, and if it hadn't been for the star that I could still pick out on his helmet, I might not have known if he was ours or theirs. Coiling up on itself in the clear water in lighter and darker shades of rubbery and mossy green, the long hank of seaweed that had found what was left of him first and our propellers second looked like the vegetative version of the sea serpents warning mariners off of the unknown in old navigational charts, before Columbus came along and made things safe for everybody.

Now, there's one basic trick to handling something like this, which is to *go on looking* at it. And wait until someone else has seen it at the same time as you before you back off, so that the reality of it keeps getting passed from eye to eye, like a baton in a relay. Then you have some control, and can think in a factual way about what steps you're going to take to deal with it.

But I hadn't done that, because they were all still asleep and I didn't know how long I'd have to wait. Instead, I had already skedaddled back past the depth-charge canisters and toward the bridge, to a place where first he couldn't peek at me, or then even wave, over the stern. Now it started to sink in on me just how bad a mistake that was. Even if other people saw it, I knew I wouldn't be able to go back and look at it again. I mean, now that I knew *exactly* how many steps I'd have to take toward the stern before the claw and then the helmet started showing, there was no way I'd be able to make myself take them.

Of course, I couldn't turn my back either. So I didn't have any way of finding a canteen for the water my mouth was telling me that it could use pretty badly, getting more and more puzzled that I didn't respond. My mouth was stupid, it didn't know anything. But I wasn't grateful to my eyes, either. That beautiful island and its white beach were all of fifty yards off to starboard, and my eyes weren't allowing me to spare so much as a glance in that direction.

Damn, I was an idiot. On top of everything else, I hadn't even looked to see if the bullet I'd fired at the black dot during the night had killed it. I could have found out if I was a liar before anybody else did. But thinking that made me realize that there was still something I could do. Pulling my .45 back out of the holster I'd stuffed it in as I backed away from the stern, I aimed it at the sky, no, the island?, the island, and squeezed off a shot.

By the third one, the whole boat was awake, and collected amidships around the bridge. They saw which way I was looking and knew it was bad, that it was worse than yesterday afternoon or even last night, and nobody had thought anything could be worse than last night.

"Well, Jesus!" I said, my voice not sounding too good, when they all went on waiting, even my exec. "Go on and see what's there. You're such a *rude* bunch of bastards, you know that? It wants to shake hands. It wants to say hello. You damn well do what it says. That's an order." I still had the .45 in my hand.

One after another, all twelve of them went down to the stern to meet their new shipmate. Everybody went in at least pairs, and some in bigger groups. Only Algligni went alone, because nobody else had remembered him. He also stayed there the longest, which got me plenty rattled even if I couldn't tell you why.

"Algligni, you moron!" I bawled, even though I couldn't make it anywhere near as strong as usual. "Are you gonna stare at it for the rest of your life? Get on back here!" When he came back, he had a look on his face I'd never seen before. Nor, probably, had anybody else alive, including Algligni's mother. It made you feel sorry for him and disgusted with him and scared for him and scared of him all at the same time.

He was the last one, too. After he got back, everybody stayed bunched up around the bridge, past even the two .50 cals. But nobody wanted to be the one who was the closest to the black dot, and so there was this constant, quiet, bunched-together wiggling going on, which normally would have had all of them punching each other's lights out in about five seconds but didn't, because nobody wanted to admit what was happening. Flugelhorn, of all people, was the first one to break for the bow, like it was his by right just because I'd posted him up there with the Thompson gun the night before. He sat down with his backbone scooted up against the tip of it, his hands sort of scrabbling around until he realized that the Thompson wasn't there anymore.

"Fuck this!" he yelled at the rest of us. "*Fuck all of this!*"

By then, the rest of them were making for the bow too, pushing at each other in the narrow space between the bridge and the torpedo tubes, and yelling in high voices because they had to turn their backs on the black dot to do it. To make room, the ones who got there first started heaving the cases of 3.2 and C rations over the side, some to starboard and some to the deep water to port, making two different kinds of splashing. Soon my exec and I were the only ones left amidships, and then he was gone too. Now, standing in the cockpit, I was the one nearest the black dot. I scrambled ass over teakettle past the front bridge casing and hunkered in the bow with the rest of them, all of us facing the stern.

Naturally, nobody had remembered to grab any water on the way up there, and the C rations and 3.2 had all been heaved over the side. We didn't even have any smokes. And the only thing moving was the sun, which kept on getting higher.

Nobody wanted to say a word. Or had to either, because the thing was that we all understood each other better than we ever had before, now that our world had been so drastically simplified. Since everything was so obvious, it was like all our thoughts were following pretty much the same routes to get to more or less the same places at roughly the same time. Each conclusion that we reached expressed itself in tiny collective nose-liftings and neck-turnings and eye-blinkings and butt-shiftings, which we knew were universal even though the first collective decision we had made was that none of us could or was going to look at anybody else directly. Sometimes, I thought Algligni of all people was maybe a beat ahead of the rest of us, but I wasn't even sure which one of the pairs of knees or shoulderblades around me he was, and of course I couldn't look at him to check.

As one, we remembered the island next to us, and silently contemplated it. As one, we calculated the distance between us and the breakers on the beach to be approximately fifty yards, and as one we owned up that it wouldn't be too hard a swim. As one, we recognized that the distance might as well be fifty miles, because we'd have to get into the water to do it and fifty yards would give the black dot all the time it needed to overtake us.

As one, we realized that we had been letting our eyes stray from the stern, and now because we had neglected it something horrible could be about to happen or already starting to happen there, something our eyes would be punished for their inattention by being unable to bear, and so they would bolt like screaming flying fish and horses from our skulls, leaving us blind and at the black dot's mercy. As one, we resumed our watch on the stern. We did all of these things over and over again, as the rising sun climbed and as one we noticed that the deck plates under our palms were getting too hot to touch. As one, we rested our elbows on our hitched-up knees.

But since I was still the skipper, I had to think separate thoughts too. One of these was that if so much as a Jap dinghy came along, its occupant or occupants could easily take all of us prisoner, because the .50 cals were out of reach and for the life of me I didn't see much of anything that we could do about that. A related thought was that to get captured might not be all bad, because as cruel as the Japanese were, and believe me we all knew about Bataan, whenever people got taken prisoner their captors still had to give them water. But then I had to admit to myself this wasn't foolproof-true, since the black dot hadn't given us any.

All the same, I knew I had to make some kind of command decision, since that was what my hat and bars meant. So I did. As skipper, I mutely gave the order that we were to do nothing until something else happened. As one, we all obeyed.

What finally happened, since something had to and did, wasn't a Jap dinghy taking us prisoner. Instead, we heard familiarly American-sounding, us-ish-sounding engines putt-putting along just out of sight behind part of the island, and a few seconds later another PT boat rounded the bend. It was McHale.

At first, we just sat there. But then it started to sink in that if they were in sight of us, then we were in sight of them, and we scrambled off the bow and back to our different stations around the boat, me and the exec in the cockpit, Laprezski near the torpedo tubes, Algligni at the portside .50 cal, and so on. Although no longer as one, we all knew the black dot was still in the water. But now McHale's boat was in it too, and McHale's boat was bigger and more normal.

Anyway, we hadn't moved in time. He'd seen us at it, all right. "What the fuck you doing, holding Sunday services?" he hollered, grinning and bringing the 73 up alongside us but well back off the sandbar, which he had spotted right away. Whatever else he was, McHale was a good sailor. "Don't you know it's Wednesday, for Christ sake? What the fuck happened, anyhow?"

"Radio conked," I hollered back. "The propellers are fouled. We're grounded on the sandbar."

"Well, why in the hell ain't you unfouled them?" he hollered, with his engines putt-putting away under his voice as he reversed throttle to hold the 73 at the same distance. He couldn't see the dead Jap from there. "You got the only fuckin' PT in the Navy without one man can swim?"

I knew I didn't want to answer that one. So I yelled, "How'd you find us, anyhow? Is this island even on the charts?"

McHale got about the biggest grin I'd ever seen on his face, and probably that anyone had ever seen on it. Except for Whatsername back in the Zone, and I knew I didn't want to think about her anymore.

"You're on the back side of Ireidahonda, you dumb son of a bitch," he yelled. "Nick's Fuckin' Snack Shack is about four miles due east-by-southwest of that pretty beach you all been lookin' at." His whole crew was laughing at us.

"Well, throw us a God damn line and give us a God damn tow back to it, then," I hollered.

"You heard 'im, boys." McHale put the 73 ahead to get us bow-to-stern, then throttled back and held her there. "Hey, you ain't run into nobody since yesterday, right?" he called back to me, as one of his boys heaved a coiled line that uncoiled in the air and hit our bow with a thud, where Laprezski and Flugelhorn grabbed it to make it fast. "That means you ain't heard the news."

"What?" I bawled.

"Jack Kennedy's not dead!" McHale shouted. "A Jap destroyer rammed the 109, which did sink God damn it, and he got almost his whole crew onto an island somewhere not too far from here. Got a message with the

location out to an Aussie coast watcher. Binghamton just sent out O'Reilly's boat to pick all of them up. Bobby should be bringing them in any time now."

"Well, I'll be a son of a bitch," I hollered. Couldn't think of much else to say. "Ski! We ready?" I called up to the bow.

"Aye aye, Skipper," Laprezski said. I gave McHale a big thumbs-up, he gave me back a circled thumb and forefinger and put the 73 ahead again. Coming back up out of the water, the line tightened and yanked us off the sandbar easy as a pat of butter, and the island—no, the back side of fucking Ireidahonda, and so what—started to show us more of its coast-line, which I realized I'd have recognized, dag nab it, if we'd been a little farther out to sea. But something else was coming along with us, and even though I don't think anybody on the 73 could see it, it turned out that now everybody on our boat wanted to take a look at what we were towing.

Just for a second, after the seaweed uncoiled and started to pull it, it got jerked across the bit of sandbar that showed above the waves, and we saw more of it than we ever had before. Then it got yanked back into the water, not making much of a splash, and disappeared again. Only now that we were moving one hell of a lot faster than we had been once it latched onto our propeller the afternoon before, the long hank of sea-weed got taut, and started to rise out of the sea, glistening. At the end of it, the dead Jap started rising too.

Soon he was out of the water up to his sternum, with one claw clutched against his collarbone and the other raised above his head, and his freshly wetted teeth glistening more than ever in the sun. In the skip-ping of the waves around it, you could see where the seaweed had him snagged around the waist.

"Oh, shit," my exec said. "Oh. Shit."

But you can never figure people. Now, the boys all thought it was funny. They were whooping and pointing as it came on behind us. Laprezski came back from the bow to see what the hell was up, and someone slapped him on the back and hollered, "Look at it, Ski!"

Well, it took them a second, but not much more. As far as they were concerned, this was the funniest damn thing anyone had said since the creation. "Look at it ski!" they kept bawling at each other. "Look at it *ski!*"

McHale and a couple of the boys on his boat had started looking back our way, wondering what was going on. I was thinking, as a skipper, that maybe this whole business wasn't so good for discipline. On top of that, I knew it wasn't going to be so funny if we were still dragging that corpse when we put in to the dock on the other side of Ireidahonda. If he was still half as savvy as he had been back when he was running his poker game in the Zone, McHale, for one, would probably guess what had happened, and that would be all she wrote as far as a tolerable life around the base was concerned.

"McHale!" I yelled. "*McHALE!*"

He looked back, and I saw him put a hand to his ear. His mouth moved, but I couldn't hear anything.

"More speed!" I hollered at the top of my lungs. "*GIVE US MORE SPEED!*" For what I had in mind, I needed that thing up out of the water as high as it could ride.

McHale looked baffled, and I saw him yelling "What." "*SPEED!*" I hollered, scooting one thumb upwards in front of my chest and rapidly stacking degrees in the air over my head with the other hand. He still looked confused, and no wonder. But we were too light for gunning the engine to put the 73 at any risk, and that was all he needed to worry about. It would just make our ride choppier, and why should he care if that's how we liked it? He shrugged and pushed the throttle forward.

I looked back. It was fully out of the water up to its waist now. Grabbing the Thompson gun out of the cockpit, I went back to where Flugelhorn was standing, next to the engine-room hatch, and practically tossed it at him. The Kraut was our best shot.

"Harry," I said. "I want you to blast that thing to kingdom come. I don't care about the seaweed. Just get rid of the Jap. Now. Everybody else get the hell out of his way."

"Me? Aye aye." Flugelhorn went down to the stern, past the depth-charge canisters, and crouched there, propping the gun against the gunwale to steady it. His first burst kicked up some flickers and spouts of water not too far from the corpse, and I saw his shoulders hunch as he braced to try again. He better do it damn quick, too, I thought, before McHale had time to wonder what in hell we could be shooting at. But the second burst just kicked up more water, and Flugelhorn yanked the Thompson's empty magazine out. "Skipper," he called back, "need more ammo."

Before I could start back to the bridge to see if we even *had* one more full magazine, a heavier gun started bucking right next to my God damned ear, and practically right over Flugelhorn's head. It was Algligni at the portside .50 cal, and I hope never to see anybody look like that again. It was worse now than when he'd first seen the corpse. Which, when I checked back, was disintegrating, the raised arm flying off and the rest getting torn apart like a paper bag filled with something black. A second later, with nothing left to tow, the seaweed smacked back into the surf behind us.

The rest of the trip in was quiet, since we didn't know anymore what we thought about anything, or maybe what anything thought about us. Mostly, we were sort of sheepish, I mean all of a sudden there wasn't anything particularly special about us anymore, now we were just a PT boat getting a tow with a big hunk of seaweed fouling its propellers.

Once he'd inched us back up the channel between Ireidahonda and Alwok, McHale did a hell of a job of putting us in at the dock, cutting the line and veering off with his own engines reversed right after he'd given us just enough momentum to drift in close enough for the swabbies along the dock to hook us with their grappling poles and make us fast. Then he brought the 73 around to tie up on the other side, and he and I met on the gangway going down to the beach.

"So what really happened, big buddy?" he asked with a big grin and a bigger har-har-har, clapping me on the back. "And why the hell were you towing a target? You telling me you can't find anything real to shoot at around here?"

"Aw, hell, big buddy, I don't know," I said, throwing an arm around his shoulders and figuring he'd never know how big a favor he'd just done me. I hadn't come up with any kind of story at all. "The boys were getting pretty rusty on their gunnery, so I had them rig it this morning to pass the time."

Before he could ask me why we hadn't unfouled the propellers first, which I would have if I was him, we saw Nick and his clipboard coming down the beach toward us, the sand flying off his shined black shoes. Oh, hell, oh, well. At least he didn't have that anxious smile on his pan anymore.

"I should have known the two of you got together to pull this one," he said, blinking at us. "The Seabees on Fondawonda want to know where the hell their God damn supplies are. And the Army on Liltiti wants to know what happened to their movie. And well, I guess I did make the wrong call on that one, because it turns out they'd all seen *Mrs. Miniver* before. But you know what? They'd still rather masturbate to Greer Garson than nothing. And you know something else? I didn't have an answer for either of them."

Still blinking, he looked from McHale to me and back with dark eyes that were hurt and angry, almost like some frustrated coyote's. And puzzled more than anything else.

"You really had it in for me, didn't you?" he said. "You really wanted to just stick it to me."

"Aw, fuck that, Nick," McHale said, "it wasn't like that. We—"

But now Nick was looking past us. Just as his darting eyes shifted, we heard another PT's engines out on the water, and heard something else too. The something else seemed so out of whack with this particular moment that for a second I honestly couldn't have placed it to save my life. But it was human voices, singing.

> *"Jesus loves me, this I know*
> *"For the Bible tells me so . . ."*

It was the crew of the 109. As O'Reilly's boat came up the channel, we could see them all sprawled around every which way in its bow, half naked, sunburned, and dead tired. But they had plenty of water, at least now, and they were singing and swigging from their canteens. Farther back, near the depth-charge canisters, an improvised canopy had been rigged up. That was where, I heard later, they were keeping McMahon, the crewman who'd been so badly burned that Jack had had to tow him as they swam by a life-belt strap held in his teeth.

The boat wasn't putting in at this dock, which was full anyway. It was going on up the channel, where there was a field hospital. But Bobby O'Reilly had brought it in close to shore so everyone there could see the men who had been saved, and wave if any of us felt like it.

I didn't spot Jack right away, because he wasn't in the bow with his crew. He was sitting in the cockpit, bare-chested, leaning back with one leg hooked over the casing and his face tilted up to the sky. He wasn't singing, but he was sort of idly tapping time with one hand on the outside of the bridge.

He was wearing sunglasses.

Next to me, McHale had started laughing. "Look at him! Six days on a rock out in the middle of the blue nothing, and he looks like a damn movie star! Where the *fuck* did he *get* those *shades*! Damn!"

He turned to me. "Big buddy, you know how come I'd like to be rich—really, really rich?"

"The money?" I said.

"Nah. You'd know *everything,*" McHale said. Then he started waving one hand over his head, and cupping his mouth with the other, and yelling. "Hey, *Jack! OVER HERE, JACK!*"

Jack heard McHale even over his own crew's singing, which wasn't all that powerful, and hiked his neck up to look our way. I'm not even sure he recognized us, but the arm that had been tapping time came up for a second or two. The hand at the end of it waved. Then the boat slid on out of sight up the channel, and when I turned, Nick was standing there in the sand with his black shoes and his clipboard, staring after it.

You probably know the look on Nick's face, because the whole God damn country saw it plenty enough times afterward. It was that expression he got that said that no matter how hard he tried, and how good he was at anything, and whichever way he applied himself, and how hard he tried, someone else was going to get all the candy.

And he didn't know why.

Noticing that I was watching, he smiled anxiously. Then, remembering that I had turned out to be one more of the people who spent their
whole lives trying to figure out how to stick it to him, he frowned.

A lot of people have asked me about it since, but I don't think they
ever met or spoke back then. If Nick had just felt some kind of inkling
even so, all I can say is I sure hadn't. You could have knocked me over
with a coconut when the two of them ran against each other for president. I'd have put my money on McHale.

Since he believed in nothing, he's the one who might've convinced
me there wasn't a black dot in our wake.

III

Alger and Dean and My Son and I and Whatnot

IT DID PAIN ME TO SEE MY FORMER PROTÉGÉ LED OFF LIKE A COM-
mon criminal, when at the least—between us, be it said!—Alger was an
uncommon one. Whatever confusions of Soviet personnel with Western
Union may have blotted his copybook in a youth whose icy fervor
nonetheless left me with fedora doffed, the man I still rejoice in calling
my former chum had far more merit than the shifty-eyed, unpleasant
junior Congressman from California who was to boast for decades, in an
idiom that struck me as curiously sexual, of having "nailed" Alger Hiss,
the spy. Perhaps it wasn't said until much later, but it was true from the
start: that other fellow was pure cancer.

In the usual way of such things, my family knew the Hisses without
quite knowing why, although my mother had been a Boo and I often
thought this might have some bearing on the matter. Once I inherited,
which couldn't have come at a worse time—my father had just died—I
removed my backgammon board and second-place trophy in the Groton
javelin toss from the Fifth Avenue pile of my now suspended childhood's
parodic treasure hunts and solo games of hide-and-seek. These memen-
tos of a youth as rich in confusion as everything else soon rested in my
dear pater's splendidly appointed suite at the center of our family's business headquarters, now eddying like newspapers over several floors of the
magnificent Woolworth Building down on good old lower Broadway.

Early on, it did sometimes trouble me that I had no conception, be it
worthy or woolly, of where our money came from. On my first visit to
our offices in the role of overlord, only a buoyant predisposition against
moodiness of any sort, the hale Howell strain having firmly gotten the
upper hand over the neurasthenic Boo blood in my genetic makeup, held
my ignorance back from making a terrorized leap, over an abatis of
accusing abacuses, into the chasm of self-doubt. However, the various
people I encountered telephoning and carrying papers to and fro on my
fascinated daily strolls through the premises all seemed to have a reasonably sure grip on what they were about. It would have seemed disloyal to
pater Walter's memory had I boldly climbed atop a nearby desk or
switchboard, firing a pistol ceilingward like Herr Hitler in his Bavarian

beer cellar (I had always wondered why he hadn't vanished in a shower of plaster), to announce that what had been good enough for him just wasn't good enough for me.

Alger was then a young associate in the progressive law firm of Crimson, Cerise, Ruby and Vermilion. Aside from a shared passion for ornithology, our paths had intersected very little. But then, one perfectly enchanting Manhattan afternoon (wild flocks of birds wafting through a windy Central Park down below, tumbling bursts of prothonotary warblers stunned to find themselves hurled up here from the Chesapeake marshes by an unexpected storm; home from the office at my usual one P.M., I delightedly placed an antique Royal Navy spyglass to watch the grand, mad scene through a plate-glass window), his secretary Rosa rang up with the message that her employer hoped I would consent to meet him in an hour at a restaurant on Carmine Street. This held a tang of adventure, as I was none too well posted on what lay between upper Fifth's bulky comforts and the Gothic origami of lower Broadway and Wall. However, my chauffeur had never let me down yet. Clapping on the figurative pith helmet of my second-best bowler as my fingers seized the nonce machete of my brolly, I gaily set off for Gothamite Bohemia.

Nonetheless, I must have been tardy. By the time my smoke-gray Rolls gave passersby a brief glimpse of its chamois innards outside a transposed Left Bank boîte by the quaint name of Le Perroquet de Moscou, impatience at my non-arrival had driven Alger, who normally retained a glacial reserve, to amuse himself by idly drawing a chalk mark on a trash receptacle. Tossing the chalk aside, he greeted me with an animation unique in my experience of him, and we exchanged hearty if, on his part, rather hectic witticisms about the unlikelihood of two experienced bird-watchers like ourselves taking an interest in the common pigeons and canaries waddling hereabouts. Despite an enjoyment of this sort of chaffing that has always been close to unslakable in my case, I had frankly begun to wonder why we weren't going inside when an explanation turned up in the form of a startling individual with whom, doubling my astonishment, Alger appeared to conclude he was acquainted almost on the spur of the moment.

Bearded like a lion's den and seemingly equipped with a dozen small facial variations on smiling and screwing up his eyes, the newcomer was rebuking our rather mild version of October with an overcoat of what I took to be poodle fur worn over square-toed but otherwise shapeless leather boots. Within, the poodle's owner puffed like a bellows on a black and silver paper tube that I only gradually came to realize the poor fellow had mistaken for a cigarette. Its exotic reek took my breath away, leaving my dungeoned lungs to imagine as best they could what the fumes must be doing for his. Apparently even less close than my own eager but clumsy mental hounds to treeing Greenwich Village's elusive sartorial *comme il faut*, he was also wearing a straw boater and nervously clutching a tennis racket by the neck and backwards.

"Why, that's no grip at all, old fellow!" I couldn't stop myself exclaiming. "It's not a *gun*, you know. Here, let me show you," as I helpfully reached for the racket.

Twin trails of that dreadful smoke marking his cranium's retrogressive jerk, he flinched back as if I'd lunged for his throat. What made him think I could have even estimated its probable location amid the mongrel merrymaking of poodle fur and human hirsutiae that hid his face from nostrils to tonsils and beyond, I can't say. With a look of hatred and terror that I knew jolly well no action of mine since the day of my birth could possibly warrant, he jerked the racket—still rather gauchely held, I noted with regret—aloft as if to strike, which was when Alger intervened.

"Thurston," he said, placing a restraining hand on the other fellow's forearm, "this is an old friend of my mother's family, Mr. Gulag Ivanovich Gliaglin. Of the, er, Baltimore Gliaglins. We were at Hopkins together. On behalf of the steering committee, he and I have been asked to invite you to consider a membership in the, ah, Explorers' Club."

"A perfect pleasure, Gliaglin," I cried. "And a fine institution. Do you know—"

"No, no," Gliaglin interrupted. "Explorers' Club very strict rules has," he explained to me. "Against many enemies we must protect—the Friars, Hasty Pudding. Password first," he hissed at Alger.

" 'I knew him, Horatio,' " Alger hissed back.

Visibly, or rather semi-visibly (his facial hair did take some getting used to, Wall Street and my other environs in 1933 being so universally clean-shaven that one often felt surrounded by thousands of mobile and talkative eggs), Gliaglin relaxed. "Good. We now go inside," he said, ushering me through the door. "My God, who does not exist, I could devour prostitutes."

While I bow to no man in admiring candor, that did startle me. But after some sort of rushed conference with a whispering Alger at my back, I heard Gliaglin clear his throat and say, "Horse. I could eat horse."

Unluckily, none was on offer, so poor Gliaglin had to content himself with tomato soup followed by a simple blood pudding. Prohibition having been repealed scant months before, Alger asked for a pink gin, a steak he wanted even pinker, and a side plate of beets. As for the third man at the table, having scanned the menu and always happy to try an unexpected dish, I ordered a soon delighted self a plate of moose-and-squirrel hash.

As we ate, we talked of trivial things—the Russian Revolution, the plight of the working classes in industrial societies, the historical imperative our era faced of bringing forth a whole new type of man from a corrupt world's charred guts (this last rather put me off requesting a wheel-by of the dessert cart, I must say!), and so on in the vein of amiable banter by which men of a certain standing like to demonstrate that they do scan the odd newspaper now and then. But I had a hunch we'd get down to brass tacks as soon as the plates were cleared, and right I was too.

"Thurston," said Alger abruptly, looking at the napkin wound up in his hands, "you told me once that your favorite birds were cardinals and robins, because of their beautiful coloring."

"So I did, by Jove," I agreed, delighted that he remembered. "Hues seldom otherwise found in the animal kingdom, and all the more glorious for the contrast."

"Well," Alger said, "I took that as a hint, to be candid."

"Only a hint? I'd have thought it was a fairly blunt statement, old fellow. Or did I err in thinking we two bird lovers spoke each other's language, my dear chap?" I said, mystified.

"Well, it *was* several years ago," Alger said casually, tossing aside the napkin and closing his eyes as if in thought. "Why, let me see—yes, it was just after Herbert Hoover became President."

He opened his eyes, which looked directly at me with an intensity I found disconcerting. Had I been a rare variety of thrush, or perhaps the last dodo, his gaze would have made more sense. "Hoover had no use for birds," Alger informed me. "But Roosevelt does—although he prefers a blue eagle to either cardinals or robins. And you? Do you still make the same choice?"

"Of course I do," I said. "When it comes to what matters most to him, a man doesn't change his opinions simply because of a headline or two," although I felt rather sorry to have missed the one about the new President's ornithological interests. I had never even heard of the blue eagle, but then my pater Walter's friend Franklin had always been whimsical. Not having seen him in many years, I wondered if he still leapt about while playing badminton as I remembered him doing in one flower-fleecy upstate summer of my boyhood, while fat bumblebees slowly ferried bits of sunlight to a meadow and L., my earliest and only love without feathers, began to wave her arms gravely as if to conduct their flight, in a broad-brimmed hat and a white dress with a sailor collar. Gradually, as an Abelard-ish young Thurston's springy steps across a variety of local flora—all made of air, all air!—brought me bounding nearer my hintless Heloise, I became aware that she was in a rowboat which had begun to sink, fortunately in a pond not more than two feet deep at its most menacing.

"I'm sorry?" I said, as the restaurant staff, whose waiters could have competed in the shot put at any track and field event on earth and indeed seemed disconsolate that attending to diners like ourselves had interrupted their practice, thoughtfully brought me back to Manhattan with a smashing of crockery.

"I was just saying," Alger informed me, "how glad Mr. Gliaglin and I both are to hear that you haven't changed your views."

"Well, I'm glad you're glad," I said, perhaps a bit tartly. "I hope the cardinals are glad, too."

Gliaglin had lit another of those foul tubes of his. "Indeed they are,

Gospodin Howell," he told me, with a luxurious exhalation of its noxious fumes. "I can say with authority the cardinals *are* glad."

"As are the robins, Gulag Ivanovich," Alger seconded him, his glacial reserve thawing noticeably.

In fact, Gliaglin was growing frankly if not rankly genial, so far as I could make out through the underbrush. "I think maybe you are understanding pretty quick how Explorers' Club can hang itself with rope I buy from it," he told me with what I could only assume, from a brief but newly friendly gleam of gray dentition amid the smoke and poodle fur, was a roguish grin. "I think maybe you are knowing before we meet that there is also politics here."

"Well, Mr. Gliaglin, it's not so easy as all that to pull the wool over my eyes," I said, I trust smoothly. "You're Democrats, aren't you?"

The look that flickered in Gliaglin's eye bore an uncanny resemblance to the expression that had passed across my old Latin tutor's face when I'd avowed my passionate desire to read Gibbon in the original. A moment later, however, he had emitted a laugh that crashed like surf, and was clapping me uproariously on the back with a hand whose hairy knuckles and slatelike nails the old Boo blood, making a rare cameo appearance in my jugular, would have voted to greet with a shudder had not that cowardly impulse been vetoed by the ruddier paternal corpuscles.

"*Da!*" Gliaglin cried. "As we all must be these days, if we wish to participate in the great events now ongoing in Washingtonograd. Nothing to fear we have but fear, plus FBI and Menshevik provocateurs—your worry, eh, *Tovarich*?" He turned and spoke rapidly to Alger in what I took to be some gurgling sort of Baltimorean patois, at whose audible note of reproof Alger bristled.

"Priscilla is *not* indiscreet," he said stiffly—instantly winning my own warm endorsement. Whatever the facts of the case, in my world no man lets his wife's character be impugned in public, even in an indecipherable Maryland dialect in a restaurant on Carmine Street. "I assure you, Gulag Ivanovich, none of the women at that flower show would have had the faintest idea *whose* nickname 'Koba' is. In any case, her rose won—and was the General Secretary so displeased about *that*? *Honestly?*"

"We never told him."

"You never *told* him?" Alger looked genuinely stunned; indeed, if only for Priscilla's sake, hurt.

"Be glad we never told him. You would have shared fate of rose. Head on display for few days until smell gets bad. Then ash-heap of history along with Kulaks and Zinoviev. Other roses," he said in a newly loud voice, addressing neither of us so far as I could see.

"Now, fellows," I made haste to interpose, not liking to see Alger less than spruce. "Keep in mind, I'm not even in the Explorers' Club yet! I'm sure your General Secretary wouldn't be happy to hear that you've been gossiping about club business in front of me." At this, Gliaglin looked at me with new respect, at least if I wasn't misconstruing the other facial elements in play as he blanched.

"Do tell me!" an eager self continued. "What do I need to do to join—is there some sort of hazing involved? Can't say I'd look forward to that much, but I've been upside down on the wrong end of a cricket bat before, and . . ."

"No, no, nothing like that," Alger said. "Just a trifle, really. Do you recall your old friend Henry Wallace?"

To be honest, when one boasts the scads and squads of acquaintances I was handed along with my name, address, future college, and stock portfolio—at birth, is what I mean—then combing through them on the sort of short notice Alger's eyes gave me can seem like the task of Rapunzel. But memory soon groped its way westward, found itself looking up at the gates of Colonel Wild Hiram Jones's New Mexico Ranch for Privileged Boys, slipped into the rustic dormitory on Mnemnesia's silent, limber feet, and stopped at an audibly buncombial bunk near my own. Thence—as the muscles of my now youthful frame began to ache from the unexpectedly spirited pony I'd been given that morning, temporarily dashing my plans to write an excited, pining letter to my beloved L. back East—a fatiguingly voluble voice was droning.

"*Hankie!*" I cried exultantly. "Three-Hankie Wallace. Of course I do."

"Are you aware that Roosevelt has named him Secretary of Agriculture?"

"Didn't altogether know the post existed, to be utterly candid with you. But I must write him my congratulations."

"Exactly," Alger said. "And when you do, Thurston, I'd like you to recommend me for a job."

"In the Department of Algerculture, Agri— Er, Agriculture, Alger? Whatever for? Isn't it a lot of . . . well, *crops*, and so on? Grim reapers, ordure, sleepily grappling with unknown udders at dawn and whatnot? I wouldn't have thought it was your sort of thing at all."

"I feel a vocation."

"Well! I can see you don't call it the Explorers' Club for nothing," I said.

"Neither does *Tovarich* Wallace," Gliaglin explained—that is, his tone was explanatory. "But a recommendation from you places the whole matter above suspicion."

"Well, that's flattering, Gliaglin. Many thanks," I beamed. "I do like the sound of that. That's me all over, I must say! 'Above suspicion'—and Forty-second Street, too!"

■

Despite my offer, heartily repeated amid our curbside adieux before Rolls and I became one once more, of assistance with his tennis game, I never saw Gliaglin again. Shortly after I had written my letter to Wallace, Alger informed me that our mutual friend had been called home to Baltimore after a bout of scarlet fever, and that our chapter of the Explorers' Club was being summarily disbanded. But I learned that only from a postcard, for Alger himself was already in Washington, making a brilliant career as one of the vibrant young minds whose suave zeal was to propel a confused nation—the self most patriotically included— through first the New Deal and then the war as dashingly as the wind making sense of the clatter of masts and rival rudders off Newport at the start of the America's Cup.

The higher his star climbed, the more I felt warmed by it, if you'll indulge what I don't doubt must be some fairly dubious physics. You see, I had often marked life's milestones by fretting, on one occasion aloud to L., that my own stint on the planet wasn't amounting to much, except in cash and securities. (Obeying her newly ringed hand's suggestion that boredom might reasonably flee a rampart only pity's sepoys could defend, my love's vague eyes drifted like paired starlings toward the passing night outside the clacking window, as pater Walter's private railway car hurled us toward a Palm Beach honeymoon.) But knowing that I was the man who'd gotten Alger Hiss his first job in Washington did brighten the otherwise muddled tableau with some sense of having contributed a small rocket to the universal fireworks display. Despite having long since exchanged a thrilled crouch on a parquet floor for somnolent recumbence in an armchair, in a progress whose one constant had been the voices of a succession of housekeepers politely requesting me to briefly agitate both feet in the air, I followed my protégé's ascent quite as avidly as I had the exploits of my favorite heroes of the Sunday funnies as a child, at that fist-to-nose age when one is still under a lovely impression, perhaps more easily retained in my case than most, that only one copy of the newspaper has been printed.

At the same time, may I say, I can put two and two together as expeditiously as any man. Once I have, two and two may well simply stare up like the urchins Ignorance and Want emerging from the Ghost of Christmas Present's cloak in Dickens, but there they are side by side just the same. In particular, a newsreel glimpse of a tobacco-less and thus twice tortured Gliaglin in the prisoners' dock at one of the Moscow show trials did make me sit bolt upright next to a snoozing L. in our private theater, not least with surprise that Stalin, notoriously mistrustful xenophobe that he was, had ever risked including a Baltimorean in his entourage to begin with. A later newsreel's glimpses of a Soviet flag fluttering madly alongside an equally energetic swastika at the signing of the Nazi-Soviet Pact also jolted recollection's ever idling engine into a belated recognition of the hammer-and-sickle symbol Alger had been tracing in chalk on the trash bin when I alighted outside Le Perroquet de Moscou that day in long-gone '33.

Wondering where my duty lay and whether I ought to get it to its feet, I asked myself if I should contact someone in authority. But a dread dating back to Groton days of simply advertising my status as the last to catch on, just as I had always been the first to stand a round of cocoa after intramurals, made the prospect too daunting for this old boy's hand to find either telephone receiver or quill.

In any case, Pearl Harbor soon made allies of the Soviet Union and ourselves and, in the *March of Time,* great pals out of Uncle Joe and my father's old chum Franklin (had he broken a leg? He was really much too old for skiing, particularly with the nation in crisis). With some relief, my memory revised the curious affair in which I'd played a none too nimble part into a privileged glimpse of my friend's political prescience— the very quality, so I assumed, that made him valuable in Washington.

Within three years, our country's great crusade was in sight of its dark, crook-mapped Jerusalem. I gathered victory was in the air on one of my periodic guided tours of the Stock Exchange, where that piratical parvenu Joseph P. Kennedy, glasses and choppers flashing in their perennial duel for his nose's rather modest favors, buttonholed me to crow about the return of his malarially frail second son from the rigors of the South Pacific. The bespoke, so to speak, issue of *Reader's Digest* detailing the lad's exploits that old Joe had thrust on me was still nestled between pin-striped arm and mildly bruised rib cage when I returned to the office via my private elevator. As I settled into an armchair for whose leather the bulls of half an Argentinian herd had been beheaded on the pampas, my secretary promptly buzzed me: "Mr. Acheson is on the line from Washington, sir."

The then Under Secretary of State and I had been at school together. "Dean!" I cried as *Reader's Digest* plopped softly carpetward, unread and unretrieved. "How goes the battle?"

"Well, I'm on my way out to Topeka and Santa Fe for some speeches, so I both would and will say 'Reasonably well'—not to put you on the same footing with hoi polloi," he answered in his usual tone, which was that of Mowgli's friend Bagheera in a good humor. "But something here can't wait till I get back. See here, Thurston: you've known Alger Hiss a long time, haven't you?"

"Indeed I have. Can't say I've seen much of him since Roosevelt came in, though—you fellows keep him too busy for more than the occasional Christmas card."

"He's still finding time to send those? We'll have to do something about that. In fact, we are, and that's the reason I'm calling. We're considering having him chair the organizing meeting of the United Nations next spring in San Francisco."

"Sounds impressive. What is it?"

"It's a mid-sized, rather lovely city on the West Coast of the United States," my caller retorted briskly. Dean, may I say, had been one of the least cruel of my Groton classmates, but the bent was pandemic. With a chipper apology for his lack of willpower, he gave me a quick rubdown—no, it's "rundown," isn't it?—on the nature and purpose of the world body at whose founding Alger was indeed to play concierge if not midwife come 1945.

"It's damned important, like every other job aside from the Vice Presidency these days," Dean said, "and once Alger's name came up, some of the lower orders here at State raised allegations that I must say I think are pure horse hockey. But I thought I'd better check in with you, since you were his first sponsor over at the Agriculture Department."

"And a proud one," I said.

"Well, just to reassure me, then. Look, as one haberdasher's favorite customer to another, or possibly the same haberdasher's favorite customer to another—hang it, Anglomane to Anglomane, old Grotonian to old Grotonian: is the fellow reliable?"

"Absolutely! He's a dedicated Communist. You know how disciplined they are."

Chuckling, Dean thanked me and rang off. Only some years later did it pop to my mind that he might well have thought I was joking.

Dean, of course, later famously said, "I will not turn my back on Alger Hiss." Fond as I was of Alger, I had to admit that I wouldn't have risked it either. Not that the self was required to do so microphonically before the committee of which surly, sweaty young Congressman Cancer was such an indefatigable member, busying himself in pursuit of Alger as urgently as if he feared that he too would turn into a pumpkin like the one in which had been hidden those ridiculous microfilms. Depriving me of the chance to hire a lawyer with whom I might later have played backgammon as we reminisced about the odd ordeal that had made us pals, they didn't call me as a witness, and indeed I can't fathom how my testimony would have done Alger any good.

Nor was I summoned at the perjury trial that eventually sent my old friend to the hoosegow, for which he departed from the steps of the Foley Square courthouse on a blustery March day whose hurrying clouds seemed to augur the future Senator Tumor and Vice President Malignancy. Having turned up with a few other well-wishers to provide what flimsy good cheer we could, I saw that Alger's handcuffs prevented a farewell handshake, and called his name instead. For the last time, my beclouded eyes met his glacial reserve. Then he was off to the pen, and I back to the penthouse.

As the postwar Cadillac that had replaced the Rolls purred us back to Central Park past streets shot from cannon, I saw that L.'s gaze was fogged too. But not, I'm afraid, noticeably more so than usual, although I took her gloved hand in my ungloved one nonetheless.

■

Yes—she was my earliest and only love. That's why I hope I'll be for-given for not having plucked up the courage from the proverbial rag-and-bone shop until now to admit that I wasn't hers, and never had been. Ever since our pre-*Titanic* to-and-fros in Mamzel Coudepiay's dancing class—the sacred, resin-squeaky spot where I first laid eyes on L., amid peers of both sexes for whom adolescence described a more or less lamentable condition, rather than the state of grace she made of it— I had been the besotted, madly volunteering partner, she the reluctant, easily distracted one. Although I don't mean to fault her dancing, for once in my devoted arms she'd swirl like caramel, her neck cast back in utter indifference to the goggling, boyish phiz ardent to nibble it—a heedlessness whose only interruptions were brief stares whenever one of my all but forgotten left feet would land with a thud in the wrong place, something *she* knew from the vibration alone.

From shared summer jaunts upstate to exclamatory *au hasard* encoun-ters on European tours, our moneyed families' long friendship kept put-ting me in her path throughout our teens, just as our shared social set would once we became adults. Yet candy-backed child or grown-up sylph, she'd drift toward me without the faintest worry that she'd bump into anything much. As I hardly cared to risk turning her obliviousness into active ill will by forcing her to think about my presence, all I could do was lift my cap and later skimmer with a smile as I stepped off into the poison ivy.

I also knew I had no hope of altering her nonexistent feelings, since I lacked the prerequisite that permits a wooer to sit down at the heart-shaped baccarat table in Cupid's Monte Carlo—whether he be flush or bankrupt when he stands and lights his final cigarette, tux wilted from the strain. Simply put, as we both knew, I utterly failed to interest her, and love without interest is as impossible as, in quite another realm, is interest without capital.

Since, with modest luck, L. and I will soon mark—although, to my undimmed regret, not celebrate; not with songs—an anniversary that Titania and Oberon might envy, I suppose the vulgar guess most likely to spring to mind, though I'd advise against lips if you value my indulgence, is that her people lost their loot in the Crash, making me the nearest sled in the blizzard if not the only boat in the storm. Port, whatever. In any case, chronology alone refutes that arid speculation, as we were married during the Boom.

Whatever prompted her to board the small craft of my love and push off from her mind's dark shore with a satin-slippered, trembling, but irreducibly graceful foot, material fears had nothing to do with it—as I can testify, since the fortune she came into upon her father's later death of apoplexy in California, in the midst of indelicate exertions, was to almost double my own. As to the actual reason that she wed the long rejected self, L. has never told me in the several decades since—and as it can plainly be no very happy story, I feel that only a bully, which I decline to be under any circumstances, would badger her to divulge it.

For some months, however, it had been apparent to me that what I saw as the *tour de force* social occasions of the merrymaking Manhattan we shared—banquets, avant-garde charity balls, and now more and more often weddings, as one after another couple first paired at Mamzel Coudepiay's went Charlestoning into madcap matrimony—were for L.

respites from other, visibly more exhausting amusements, at least when she even put in an appearance to raise dizzy dollars for lynched Negroes or watch the Carraways get hitched. As the twilight beneath her eyes turned to night, she developed modest eccentricities, as for instance her refusal to doff her fur coat amid her friends' evening gowns, brief and accidental views of one bare shoulder or the other now the closest one came to glimpsing her pale, delicately veined arms.

In a harsh voice, she'd speak of authors and vagabond artistic personalities unknown to the rest of us, not that their alien names would necessarily have been obscure outside a crowd whose members, the self fondly included, would as a rule experience an almost unbearable intellectual stimulus simply from being forced to read the coupons they clipped. At a farewell dinner for young Lindbergh, I watched in dismay as L. moodily set her place card on fire, dropping it into her finger bowl a moment before her own dear digits would have been burnt, then watched the charred remnants swirl until, to her surprise, her tiara suddenly fell forward over her eyes, like an encrusted blindfold.

Then she vanished to Provincetown for a week with one of her vivacious friends, a wealthy widow with a young child. On her return, L. found her invalid mother dead; it had long been expected, but the timing was obviously dreadful. That same day, she came to see me in my old Fifth Avenue pile. In terms that brooked no sentimental interpretation of her decision—although her swain's heart dove off a cliff for the pearl of its result as eagerly as any loinclothed Polynesian teen—she accepted my long-standing offer of marriage: a lamp long left in a window on no road she'd ever taken, and that no phaeton she'd ever thumbed a lift on had passed by.

Dazed to tears by the special sorrow of the happiness that was mine, I pressed her to announce our nuptials as speedily as possible. I was unsure if I played the role of question or answer to the urgency in her bruised eyes—which incidentally grew, to my bewilderment, downright haggard when, hoping to amuse an obviously disconsolate L., I sportively told her, "Well, my dear—if nothing else, I *can* afford a carriage! *And* the bicycle. And, by God, a zeppelin built for two, if you say the word." That sweetest of America's old songs had long held a special charm for me, but

as it seemed to disturb her I never once hummed it again, and had my
housekeeper remove its sheet music from the rack atop our Steinway.

Still, I won't have you think her behavior in all the years since has ever
given me cause for reproach. A search of my brain more thorough than
a burglar's, which is more or less how I feel when I set figurative and
stealthy foot inside those curtained, gray-and-pink precincts, yields only
one smudged memory. One desolate afternoon in the early Forties,
coming home to tell L. of some terrible news in the war, I found her in
a bower with our son's tutor, whose name eluded me even then. Her
makeup was disarranged, and the silver pot and china cups on the white-
linened table beneath the trellis had been untouched at my arrival,
despite the frantic tone in which she asked the fellow, "Won't you have
some more Maxwell House, Mr. X? There's always time for one more
cup." Yet the recollection itself is so flimsy and inconclusive—and the
dialogue so odd, not least since L. favored espresso; besides, our son
would have been a toddler—that I often lean toward calling this vivid
but elusive tidbit of reality a dream, or perhaps a story I heard about
another sad couple that lodged itself in an autobiographical cupboard by
mistake. I rather fear my inner life is something of a grand hotel in the
off season, with far too many vacancies despite its first-rate restaurant.

Whatever may be missing when I look into her eyes—a temporary
blurring of life's solitude in an exchange of glances, a tender ardor that,
in any case, I know only in imagination, though I am sure I'd recognize
it in an instant were L.'s face ever, miraculously or merely by accident, to
offer it to me—we have grown comfortable with each other. Given
longevity, almost any marriage, I suppose, eventually evolves into the
cozy story of Mr. and Mrs. Crusoe, who have always built the signal fire
in the same place, share pleasure in the promontories they have named
together and the birds that they call pets, and know the offshore shipwreck's skeleton in their sleep. Together, as we watch sunset coming on
from atop our hefty heap of the GNP, which gives us a view of the
emblazoned western sky far more magnificent than most, we are deco-
rous, mildly addled, considerate, even fond. I try not to think of what
might have been, and hope against hope that L. doesn't dwell on it
either—aware as I so painfully am that in her case no Thurston would

appear in the picture, unless it were as a gamboling clown juggling stocks and bonds to amuse children on the street below her clouds. Next to the heroes of star-crossed romances, for whom the sand in the awful hour-glass always sprints, I know I'm blessed. I've been allowed to spend a long, long life next to my love, for all that she feels none for me.

Her presence is my consolation for my inconsolability in her presence. If that's the best deal life could offer me, I'd still call it a bargain—a better one than any I ever encountered in the stock market, even during the Boom.

■

The son she bore me in September '39 may have bored, or rather disconcerted, her. But from where I sat—beside her bed, sporting a grin both grander and more grateful than any Roosevelt ever tossed the voters, and babbling more noticeably like an idiot than usual—he was the great proof that a marriage need not be a success to have one. On him I lavished the adoration that L.'s grimaces of distress forbade me to drown her in, giving him all that money could buy and love break its aortal bank to provide.

As he grew, I was delighted by his emerging bent for literature and sensitive but manly interest in the arts. And moved in other ways he didn't know, because of how those predilections mirrored his now indifferent mother's old pursuits. At his encouragement, I began to sample the dusty volumes he'd de-cobwebbed and the new ones he was adding to the shelves in the Fifth Avenue pile's long disused library, and found the experience unexpectedly congenial. The pinings I discovered could be soothed by poetry and fiction felt oddly familiar, and it did cross my mind that they might have been gratified with less anguish under a reading lamp all along.

Well, too late now, I told myself. But not for our son, who in any case had far less trouble than had Dad in getting the fairer sex to find him worth consideration. Suzanne, the French-Canadian girl he brought down from Andover for a few weekends one year, was a beauty from her parabolic hipbones to the light brown hair that flowed in two long waves from a central part on her high forehead. She was also as charming as Joan must have been to the dauphin, and utterly devoted to my boy.

The daughter, so he told me, of a fine old Montreal family called the Cohen-Chansons, she made a hobby of the second half of the name by singing artless but beguiling ditties of her own composition, accompanying herself on the guitar. As the fog of old age grounds more and more flights from this particular airport, I find that I can only remember part of one: *"Mes yeux sont verts, mes lèvres sont roses / En te donnant un baiser avec mes yeux, ne puis-je pas te regarder avec mes lèvres? / Non, je ne te trahiras jamais / Avec not' / professeur d'histoire / Pendant que ton père il meurt . . ."* In all honesty, it was breathtaking to see the loving intensity in the girl's green eyes as she crooned those lines—some puppy-love promise whose bone largely eluded me, since I can never venture onto the unfamiliar golf course of a foreign tongue without a hefty stock of mulligans—and gather that one's own flesh and blood had inspired it.

True, he did go through a mildly rebellious phase, during which he lurked about in blue jeans, white T-shirt and red windbreaker to an oddly John Philip Sousa–esque effect—while swigging milk directly from the bottle, an animalistic sight no doubt deliberately calculated to arouse more true horror in aging parental bosoms than would stealing strangers' cars or knifing unknown West Side Puerto Ricans. Later—at least on his summer vacation, since at Andover they probably wouldn't have permitted it—he grew a touchingly wispy goatee, went constantly about in a mangy sweatshirt, and began reading oddly titled books, often shaped like bathroom tiles, whose contents I was no longer invited to peruse in his wake. But I understood that he was simply asserting a separate identity for himself. In any case, throughout his adolescence, he and I had only one serious confrontation, the circumstances behind which will take some going into.

Sometime in the early Fifties, at no one's behest that I knew of, the paper boy had started chucking something new in the general direction of the Fifth Avenue pile's front door. To my quickly furtive bemusement, as I unwrapped the first bundle, I saw that it was, of all things, a comic book—one whose attention-compelling rubric had never so much as grazed my experience before. The next day, another turned up, featuring a different set of joyous thugs but under the same general banner. And so on, making about a dozen different titles in all until a second installment of the first one I'd seen was delivered, at which point the whole cycle began over again. As months and then years went by, if one adventure was retired, another would soon replace it.

Their provenance remained a mystery. But in what may have been an early sign of second childhood, I soon grew addicted to them—and stayed so for well over a decade, while they kept on plopping out of nowhere onto our massive stoop. Even after my son led me to take my first tottering steps into the realm of literature, the comic books retained a viselike grip on a Yukon-sized portion of my medulla oblongata.

For one thing, they were lavishly produced, with both a slickness and an aggregate thickness of pages that satisfied my once again boyish thumb and forefinger; for whatever reason, a great deal of money had plainly been sunk into contriving this new world of wonders and garden of delights. The drawing, in bold color, was splendidly vivid, the writing dynamic, and the storylines far-fetched, extravagant, and utterly irresistible—cunningly catering to callow fantasies of power and guile whose expression one might well have found repugnant if not actively dangerous in real life, but which could be gobbled up in perfect safety in a context of such blatant make-believe.

Unfortunately, I no longer own a single copy, having burnt the lot to please my son after our confrontation. But I did save one mid-Sixties editorial newsletter, which may give you some of the original flavor if I can find and you can see it in this fading light.

Two-Fisted U.S. Adventures:
What's Next, Straight from the Uncle's Mouth

*At ease, down boy, and hello sailor, which oughta cover pretty much every last mother-lovin' one of you **Two-Fisted** devotees and sons of guns out there from Bounding, Maine to Fifty, Cal.—at least the ones in uniform, or else who wish they were. And what it means is "Lissen up," because this is your Unka Sam behind the bullhorn, ready to give you the straight* *skivvy on what's gonna be hurtling into your long-suffering mailbox over the next couple 'a weeks. Buckle up, chow down, and joke if you got 'em, boys—the reading lamp is lit, the fan mail's in the fantail, and we all know it ain't over till the paper tiger roars. Here comes what you've been waiting for—Sam's inside scoop on what's next:*

*First off, shavetails, better hit the deck, because we've got a brand-new **Two-Fisted** series coming screaming out of the sky into your ever-lovin' lap. That's right, it's just what you've been begging for—**Alsop: Bird of Prey**. You all remember cigar-chompin' Joe was the newspaper columnist whose ability to turn himself into a hawk spitting bullets at will gave S/Sgt. Barry Sadler much-needed cover to get outta Laos in one piece awhile back (**Barry the Singing Killer**, ish #17). Now our gee-eyed Joe's getting his own comic, and all we can say is "Heads up!!!" In **Bird of Prey**'s action-packed debut ish, a finky squad of missile-toting Chicoms teaches Joe in a big hurry how to fly with just one wing—and if we need to tell you which one, then maybe it's time your Unka hired himself some new illustrators. Just kidding, Norm, LeRoy, Grandma! Meanwhile, as this guy named Joe revs his claws for takeoff, all we can tell him is that it's a jungle out there—and Brother!! he knows that already.*

*As for Joe's old foxhole buddy S/Sgt. Sadler himself, in the last **Barry the Singing Killer** (#19: "What Rhymes with Agent Orange, Sergeant?") we shipped him up-country on a pacification mission right after "The Ballad of the Green Berets" started duking it out with the peaceniks all over the Stateside music charts. Well, right now the Crewcut One's wondering if he'll ever get a chance to spend those ASCAP royalties on leave in Saigon's Hootchy-Kootchy Town, because a chopper's just dropped him on the spot in Hir Tu Long Hamlet, Nidipindamuc District, Gwaynow Province, Republic of South Vietnam, and the word for that spot is H-O-T. If you've ever wondered how you'd do holding off a horde of crazed Charlies with a blazing M-16 in one hand while roughing out the lyrics to your next hit single ("The A-Team") with the other, then bite down hard on that grenade ring, because this is Sadler like you've never seen him before. Two pages in, he's already been tied to a chair by his old Asiatic nemesis Domino—yup, the beautiful, unscrupulous, slant-eye Mata Hari who tried to talk the Sarge into putting his beret on backward in*

Singing Killer *#12 ("Mekong, You Kong"), and who first turned up battling Allen, Eleanor, and Foster way back in ish #6 of **The Fantastic Family** ("Why, Mr. Dulles—I Call This One Quemoy, and I Call That One Matsu"). And you know what, gang? Get ready to salute sitting down, because we haven't even given away any of the really good stuff— and that's a promise, Soldier!*

*And now just give your Unka Sam a second to get this telescope turned around and aimed out West and back about a hundred years, because I'm lookin' for somebody, and I bet you know who. Well, gitcher cotton-pickin' hands off and lemme look awready, pardner! Yep, I think I spot him. That ten-gallon white hat, those chaps, that glistening straight shooter in its holster, them black horn-rims—well, hang me from the Mojave's highest tree if it ain't **The Marshal of Tombstone,** coming over the rise just past that bleached cow skull and those cowering Washington redskins. Last month, we left the Sheriff riding hard out of O'Keeffe, N.M., where he'd found every last inhabitant dead ("The Village of Poisoned Water," ish #4). Now he's galloping South on Eternal Vigilance to get help rounding up a posse from Sheriff Bull Connor, who all you readers in our Dixie market met in ish #13 ("Selma Birthright? Nevuh!") of our **Two-Fisted Puts the White Back in the Old Red, White, and Blue** regional anthology. Unless you're a stranger to these parts, you know there's rough riding ahead—and if you can keep the sand out of your eyes as the bullets fly, look for the whole story in ish #5 ("Barry? Lyndon").*

Sounds good, right? Well, don't think old Unka is finished with you yet. Uh-uh. We've saved the best for last.

*That's right, gang. This is it. The Big One. The comic you'll be putting the squeeze on your pillow and your parents both until you get. You've been begging us for years, so now we've broken down and done our best by . . . the "Origins" issue of **JACK EGAN, CIA!!***

★ ★ ★

February 19, 1945. His boots still wet but his M-1 Garand already blazing, a 17-year-old Marine inches his determined way up a black, shell-

plowed, blood-soaked beach on Iwo Jima. As a Nip machine gun pounds and his best friends from boot camp drop around him, he's thinking desperately: "Maybe we can beat this enemy—but what about the next one? And the next? *And the NEXT?"*

You've seen CIA man Jack Egan in action in Guatemala (#3: "Well, When We Overthrow One, It Stays Overthrown, Paco—That's the Difference"). You've watched him banging his fist in frustration as his Brigade 2506 buddies get dragged down by a giant claw rising up out of the Caribbean (#11: "Dr. Castro and His Monstrous Mechanical Island"). You've seen him dodge French traffic and plastique bombs in a Paris where the O.A.S. wants de Gaulle dead, de Gaulle wants the O.A.S. kaput, and one tough, fast-thinking Yank has to figure out how to play both ends against the middle to keep an independent Algeria from going communist (#14 "Parlez-Vous Freedom, Mon General?"). And, yes, you've seen him in Nam (#7, "It's a Dirty Job, and These Frog Eaters Can't Do It"; #12, "Marvin the ARVN"; #15, "Flight of the Phoenix Program"). You've even seen him court his wife, the beautiful U.S. embassy consular officer Shirley Smith of Winston-Salem, N.C. (#8, "This World's No Place for a Woman, Baby—So Let Me Take You Home"). But until now, you've never seen . . .

The Way It All Began. And trust your Unka Sam—YOU AREN'T EVER GOING TO FORGET IT, SON.

■

In fact—this is rumpled, rheumy Thurston resuming the narrative, returning like MacArthur or a radish—the "Origins" issue of Jack Egan's exploits was the comic in residence on my lap the day my son confronted me. Next to the library in the Fifth Avenue pile was a den stacked high with turn-of-the-century board games for boys that, after rediscovering a key to the place, I was mildly surprised my own long-dead pater had found time for: *Philippine Insurrection, Leathernecks in Nicaragua, Canal.* Over the years, I had refashioned this room, which no one else ever entered, into nothing less than a private shrine devoted to

Two-Fisted U.S. Adventures. Every issue that I'd ever smuggled upstairs from the stoop was bagged in plastic and carefully filed on shelves, and a framed baker's half-dozen of the most corpuscle-rousing covers splashed the mahogany walls above the leather armchair I had moved in there.

It had become a sort of metastatic annex to the actual library, and I occasionally felt a twinge of guilt when a sudden flaring of nostrils and gulp in the chest would tell me that my path was taking me to the side door instead of proceeding straight on. Once I was ensconced within, however, I couldn't deny that the pleasures I found here were of a more robust type than the attenuated if genuine joys of the other universe to which my son had introduced me—but which had, after all, belonged to him first. In this room, by contrast, one felt rather like donning a smoking jacket, even though one had always been a nicotine teetotaler.

Although, to my knowledge, he had never before set foot in my cubby, I felt no surprise on looking up to see my boy in its doorway, holding a volume of Yeats whose pages played Leda to his index finger's swan. Nor did his face reveal any at the sight of my lurid treasure trove. Instead, after a moment, he merely asked: "You're reading about Jack Egan, aren't you, Papa?"

"Why, yes." My chest felt a sudden cresting of delight at the thought that mine need no longer be a solitary vice—for I did know it was a vice; still, the solitude was what had made it so. "Do you know who he is—have you read these?"

"Over and over." My son looked indecisive for a moment. "I hate him," he said unexpectedly.

"Hate him!" I chortled. "That's ridiculous. They're only comic books, and Jack Egan's a hero—my favorite, in fact. Why, just look, son, here he is, not much more than a boy—not much older than *you*, in fact—bayoneting a Jap machine gunner in the foothills of Mount Suribachi. Those others in the background are carrying a flag, you see?"

Wincing, my son turned away from the explosive panels I had held up for his benefit. "Maybe it's easier for me to hate him than to ask myself why a hero would do hateful things," he said, suddenly sounding like the lad he was.

"Easiest of all would be not to read his adventures, wouldn't you say? If he isn't to your taste, there's always *Pogo* . . . or television, I suppose."

My boy's gaze at his father combined affection, hesitation, stubbornness, and doubt in quantities that altered with each blink, as if he were seeking precisely the right formula for the unpleasant news he felt obliged to impart. Then his mouth came to a decision.

"Papa—the people in your comics aren't made up," he said.

Bucking merrily backward in my armchair, dexter hand to ascoted gorge and mate to knee for a brisk slap, I roared with laughter. "*What!?* You might as well tell me that I *am*. Or is your next announcement going to be that intrepid Jack Egan of the CIA is your real father, and I—your loving, doting Dad, who can flaunt bills from Andover, the dentist, the Gotham Book Mart, and F.A.O. Schwarz to prove it—am indeed fiction?"

He had no direct answer to that sally, which I had rather enjoyed. (I rather hoped Sally had, too.) Laying Yeats aside, he crouched in front of my armchair. His voice was even, but his face was odd: "It's not only him," he said, putting his own hand on the knee I'd just smacked. "*All* of them, Papa—they're all real. All those things in your comic books are really happening."

"If that's so—and I'm only going along because this seems to matter to you, absurd as the whole notion is—then why haven't I been reading about them in the newspaper?"

"When was the last time you saw one of *those* delivered here?" my son asked.

Well, that did give me pause. On reflection, it did seem to have been a while—since the very first day that *Two-Fisted U.S. Adventures* had shown up at my door, in what I now realized was their stead. I had simply assumed that the good old *Times* and *WSJ* were still arriving at the house and drifting about unread, as actually reading either had never had much to do with the quality of the reassurance they provided.

Still, the whole thing struck me as fantastic. "Frankly, all this strikes me as fantastic," I said. "Who'd go to all this trouble just for me?"

My son looked nonplussed—though not for the reason I was expecting, it turned out. "Oh, it's not just you," he finally explained. "Thousands and thousands of these go out to everyone like you. To your whole class, in fact."

"From *Groton?*" I gasped. "There were only a couple of hundred of us, my boy, and that was before the fellow with the scythe got to work."

"No, no. I mean, most of them probably do get the comics, but it's everybody with your kind of money. All the people so high on the ladder that they haven't had a clue for years who's actually running things or how, since they can take it for granted—accurately enough—that it's all for their benefit anyway."

"I suppose next you'll be telling me that all those nonsensical war films and assassinations on television are real, too," I said, perhaps somewhat huffily. "For all that a hambone like that Cronkite fellow would have been laughed off the stage in my youth—as would poor Vladimir Huntley and Estragon Brinkley, for that matter."

"I'm afraid so, Dad," my son said gently. "Whoever is doing this apparently didn't worry about TV. They knew that everyone your age wouldn't believe anything on the tube was real."

"But do you know *why* they're doing it?" I asked. "I mean, what are the comics *for*—to amuse us? Believe me, that was one thing we could always manage on our own, without too many casualties except among the servants."

"It's so you won't be completely uninformed about what's going on, but won't take any of it seriously. If you hear someone talking about any of it, and even if you join in, you'll think it's all just hobbies and conversation pieces."

Although I still couldn't credit what my son was telling me, its import had nonetheless begun to sink in. "But my God," I cried, looking up at my neatly bagged and filed shelves in a daze. "My God, if everything in there is *true*—*all* of it, from VJ Day on—then this is a *nightmare,* what we're living through."

" 'A nightmare from which I am trying to awake,' you could say," my boy cheerfully agreed, audibly quoting some author unknown to Dad.

A new thought now struck me smartly across the face, as if in challenge to a duel. Briefly, as I shook my head, I thought this slap was advising the old self never to speak of any but trivial matters again, which I found oddly soothing. Instead, it made me say this, although Alger's name had not passed my lips in many years:

"I used to know Alger Hiss, you know."

"Yes, I know."

"Well"—I was groping among unfamiliarities—"the truth is, my boy, in all this time I've never known if he actually did this country of ours real harm. Try as one might, it was hard to see much menace in that pumpkin. One's thoughts would drift to Halloween, Linus's vigil and so forth, and picture Alger as some sort of pin-striped trick-or-treater—for all that virtually unlimited treats apparently didn't dissuade him from secretly smashing eggs on one's car and writing rude words in soap on one's mirror."

"Perfect penmanship, though," my son proposed—mockingly? Defensively? I hardly knew.

"But all the same—and much as it pains me to say so—there isn't much question that he was indifferent to the *possibility* of placing this country at risk, at a time when one had put him in a position of trust. If he'd been a bank teller, all sorts of people who swear by Alger's innocence would have been calling for his head. And for *that,*" I said, surprised by my own conviction, "he jolly well *should* have been penalized—for all that even some of your mother's Newport friends developed a temporary but noticeable stammer when they electrocuted Julius and Ethel Rosenberg, presumably on the theory that two *more* Jews wouldn't matter much to anybody, while giving my fellow Anglo-Saxon a mild five-year prison term on a perjury rap."

"Well?" my son said.

"Well—but they were *traitors,* by Jove! Of *course* Alger and the Rosenbergs betrayed their country. That was their job—that's what traitors *do*! If I could see that, I assumed anyone could. But *these* people," I said, staring around my shelves, "call themselves the *patriots*—so what on earth is going on?"

"Nobody really knows," my son said. "I'm not sure even they do."

I sat back, feeling exhausted. "What would you like me to do with these?" I asked, waving my hand around the room.

"That's up to you," he said. "Some of the parents have gone on reading them, and thrown their kids out instead. But I'd like it if you burned them."

"Done, my boy!" I said, with what his eyes told me on the instant was a sad remnant of his father's hearty brio. A second earlier, lowering my hand, I had noticed it trembling. Now, although I'd planned to rise and hug my son before he took his leave, I found that my knees were advising—no, imploring—quite another plan, which was to stay put.

Though briefly mystified, I soon gathered what had happened: I was old. Well, here it was, with whatever experiences it would bring. I thought of Alger, still chipper and glacially reserved somewhere, and of virulent, raging Congressman Cancer. And even of Gliaglin, to whose fuzzy face, rescued from the brink of memory's oblivion, I saw my son's had a slight resemblance—at least in the boy's goateed phase, which I believe this was. They all swam about, like the framed but bursting covers of the comic books on my den's walls.

At the door, the only one of them who was present in the flesh had turned, and was hesitating: "Dad?"

"Yes, what is it?"

"Do you remember what you said earlier—about Jack Egan being my real father?"

"Who? Oh, Jack Egan . . . Did I say anything like that?" I asked, confused.

He paused.

"No," he said. "Neither of us did."

■

With some sheepishness, I will admit that I granted my comics collection several stays of execution from its fiery demise, and even considered an outright reprieve once the boy was back at Andover. But this was my son, so off to the incinerator the lot went one mild but windy day in April, in what year I don't recall. While I found I had no real regrets, I also had nothing to replace Jack Egan and his cohorts with, certainly not in the now dismal den. Neither could I stir much desire in myself to resume getting the good old *Times* and *WSJ*, which I couldn't help suspecting must have been somehow party to the whole enterprise.

In any case, the day's main drama soon became the moment of exchanging a view from one window for a view from another, with fine shadings of indecision and remorse provided by a comedy duo of kneecaps whose long-stanched flair for vaudeville had come at last into its own. All that tepidly went on until, as I was breakfasting with L. one morning, an invisible hyena leapt out of the floral arrangement to bury its teeth and all four paws in my chest. As the self keeled carpetward, L. dropped her napkin, knelt with a small cry, and wondered in a voice that waltzed and tangoed quite alarmingly about the room which telephone number was the one that summoned ambulances.

They must have given me a dose of painkillers, for I was woozy in the gurney that wheeled me into exploratory surgery at top speed—"a mile a minute," as we used to say in my youth, thinking that nothing could sound faster. Trotting alongside it, L. looked uncharacteristically distraught. But something else was pressing on her; apparently, she was worried—the things that women can dream up to divert their thoughts from the real danger!—that I might start babbling gibberish under the anesthetic.

"Just don't bring up our son, that's all," I thought I heard her say.

"Wha'?" I managed to mumble, above the noise of jiggling wheels and below the fluorescent flash of a thousand passing lights. "Is he in trouble? I'll—"

"Just don't bring up the kid, *all right*?" she said in harsh tones that were most unlike her, jabbing an equally atypical forefinger at my horizontal, already much beleaguered bosom. I had no idea what she was talking about, although my last, vague thought before a rubber mask pressed down to cup my face from nose to chin was that the boy had been at Andover for an awfully long time.

Afterward, when the doctors told me what they'd found, I asked that L. not be informed. Then I was sent home to resume my game of windowed hopscotch with the sunset. Having shared this bit of private terminology with him some years before, I took what amusement I could in writing my son that I'd been diagnosed with terminal nixon.

I still haven't told L. She is fragile, and—let me put this delicately—I fear that her fragility has made her all too resourceful in finding compensations for it. Having seen the results in our much younger years, I would rather be a memory than a temptation. However, I may have a few years left, and I've sometimes thought that she and I might yet sail away somewhere. Not that I'd really know the difference between here and elsewhere now!

Indeed, as I mentally palpate my nixon's daily encroachments on my innards, I'm often not even sure which of us is the malignancy, which the comfortable old self. But all that will get settled with no need for help from my cerebellum.

Our son, of course, is made of sterner stuff than his mother. On his most recent visit from Andover, I had just asked after Suzanne when he blurted out his wish that he and not I were the one afflicted with nixon-ous insides. Putting aside my reading (*The Man Who Was Thursday*), I said, Tut-tut, my boy: you've got a future.

We were in the now empty den off the once more disused library, him crouched as before in front of my armchair—the only survivor of my old burrow's trappings. He glanced around at the bare walls, where the patterns of lighter wallpaper left by the now absent frames still stood out, although faintly.

"Then fight, Daddy"—an unprecedented monicker in our relationship, may I say. He swallowed hard, looking most unlike himself; he'd shaved the goatee, I noticed. "Fight like you were still a Marine, and this was Iwo Jima."

"What an odd thing to say!" I guffawed. "Me a Marine! That's rich and so am I, as I always say. Unless Andover's wasting your time and my money, you know very well that the proper phrase is 'as if.' And this is Fifth Avenue, not some Godforsaken tiny island out in the Pacific, and you also know that there's no hope once you've got my kind of nixon. So what are you asking me to do—'Rage against the dying of the light'? Whatever for? To please Dylan Thomas, a Welsh sot who once vomited, *in my presence,* into Margie Dumont's best tureen, not long before making his own less than splendid goodnight? Did you know him—should I feel I owe him a personal favor of some sort? No, no, my darling child. There's no real point. When I die, I plan to slide into it like a bath at the end of a lovely long day of hunting."

IV

Sail Away

FOR THE LONGEST TIME, I DIDN'T KNOW DAISY BUCHANAN ALL THAT well. We knew *of* one another, of course; ours was a smaller world than you might guess from its equivalents in a later era's wan salad of saucy fun, where every suburban "gang" in possession of a hi-fi and a blender could fancy itself *le tout* Levittown. We Twenties free spirits were more exclusive but also more publicized, by a press whose goggling readers knew their place too well to mistake a vicarious participation in our frolics for equality. As our case might have been described by Sir Winston Churchill, whom my dear bear of a father, then floating a loan in London, bucked up over brandy in 1916 after the pudgy young First Lord of the Admiralty had been sacked in the wake of the Dardanelles disaster: Never have so many been so entranced by so few.

Father had most of the raising of me. In the years when I grew from a mere slip of a girl into a modest minx of a maiden, and needed her help and guidance most, Mother had become an addled recruit to the cause of women's suffrage instead. On the tiniest summons, she would duck down to Washington to parade unbecomingly before the White House with her fellow females, carrying wordy placards, while the poor, glowering man who put food on our table and paid for her train tickets took what comfort he could in laughing at my girlish pranks and teaching me my manners.

Even after Mother returned from one of her suffragette antics to breathlessly announce that she'd been knocked down by a pair of sailors while attempting to push a petition into President Wilson's carriage in a place called Lafayette Square, and Father had joshingly retorted, to my own barely muffled titters, that he might well have given her a good kick himself had he been a witness to the scene, she wouldn't abandon her mania. Increasingly, when Father brought his knife down with a crash at the dinner table to implore her once again to recognize how foolish and insulting to him her behavior was, she'd startle her daughter if not husband into silence by holding up her hand to stop his tongue, as if he were the butcher, and saying that she simply couldn't bear another tirade.

I found this most unjust, since she was causing all the trouble and wouldn't even hear him out. Instead, when Father then brought his fork down with another crash and continued straight on just like Admiral Farragut, as he invariably did, she'd flee to her upstairs drawing room in tears, babbling about headaches, exhaustion, and letters to write. Minutes later, nervously fingering her apron, Lil Gagni, the newest of our maids—a horrid young creature, from Denver by way of Sheboygan, on whom Mother had taken pity; her eyes poking out of her face like toes from a sprung shoe, she was as out of place under a white cap as was Mr. Twain's hero in that odd chapter where, to gather information, Huck dresses up in calico and sunbonnet—would come in to ask if it would be all right to take a tray up to the missus.

Eventually, the scandal that listening to Father had taught me to fear most occurred, and Mother was arrested with some other women after chaining herself to the White House gates one foggy dawn. Nor was this any mere formality, as Father learned to his considerable indignation when, already in a rage at having to set aside his business for the day, he bustled down to Washington himself. Mother had already been sent to the notorious Occoquan Workhouse in Virginia, where she and several dozen other suffragettes were incarcerated alongside women of the street and diseased Negresses. On his return, Father declared that, if nothing else, this ordeal was sure to make Mother finally see the light, and took me to Delmonico's for pastry.

Instead, within a few days, we heard with horror that she and the others had made things even worse by going on what they called a hunger strike for the right to be treated as "political prisoners," which made no sense to me whatsoever. As Father said, they could have called themselves *petunia* prisoners, and the noun rather than the adjective would still determine their situation. Mother spent *thirteen days* being led out of her cell and force-fed with some sort of horrible device pushed up her nose or down her throat by cursing prison guards, who after all were only concerned about her health.

When she was finally released and came back to New York, she took me to her drawing room, murmuring in a voice I'd come to dread that all she asked of me was to always remember this sight. I could have told her on the spot that doing so wouldn't be any problem, since I had nightmares for a week. It was the dingy prison shift she'd worn in Occoquan, which was of a dreadfully inelegant cut, had probably been touched by one or more of the diseased Negresses, and was also covered with perfectly repulsive bloodstains and food stains from when they had had to force-feed her. Father told Lil Gagni to burn it.

Particularly as she hadn't had a robust constitution to begin with, Mother's health never really recovered from her time in jail, and since the reason was so embarrassing, her friends and family seldom spoke of it. In fact, on Election Day in 1920, she was so ill that she couldn't even go out to the polling place and *vote,* which did strike both Father and me as some sort of poetic justice after all her carrying on.

Not long after that, Father made a killing on an investment in some oil wells in Oklahoma, and went out to Los Angeles to drill for more. It must have been a month or two before I understood he wasn't coming back, although Mother may have known this earlier than I. Once she had what she wanted outside the house and he had what he wanted in it, it was as if he had decided they no longer had a topic; without the distraction of disgust to beguile him, he simply lost interest in her. And in me too, now that I had stopped being the female in the family who wasn't Mother and was just someone else who wanted more of his time, as if I had been stupid Lil Gagni coming to bother him with stammered questions about the pantry keys.

In tearful letters, I begged to at least be allowed to visit him in California, if not come live in the marvelous Moorish-looking house that he'd had built for himself up in some hills there, of which he sent me a framed photograph for my birthday. But his replies to me were terse, and as I was no longer in reach of a tie whose knot I could playfully unravel with tongue pressed between my teeth, a gold watch chain that I could gigglingly tug out of its fob pocket, or a bald head I could kiss by surprising it in an armchair from behind, I had no means of changing his attitude. At twenty years old, I found myself trapped in a vast, gloomy brownstone from which the smell of cigar smoke had faded, with no company but a melancholy semi-invalid in an upstairs drawing room and some increasingly impertinent servants.

Luckily, besides paying for the help and all our other necessities, Father allowed us to charge whatever we liked to him, and also sent us a huge monthly allowance. If nothing else, that did give me a reason to be grateful that the Nineteenth Amendment had passed, since if it hadn't and her health had been better I was sure Mother would have promptly poured every extra cent we got from Father right down her favorite rat-hole. As it was, nowadays she hardly cared about the necessities, often sending trays of food back down the stairs untouched. So I had all the say in how we spent our loot, and the Hispano-Suiza barely made a dent in it. Although soon enough there was more than one dent in the Hispano-Suiza, after one of my new girl chums, shrilly exclaiming, "I don't care about the *vote,* what I want is the *wheel,*" had playfully wrestled the latter item out of our chauffeur's hands, Cheng not having access to the former in any case, on a wild ride back from West Egg one night.

It was sometime in that same spring of '21 that, tiptoeing at two A.M. past Mother's drawing room in my stocking feet, my shoes held in my hand, I heard her voice call faintly, "My dear, is that you?" My already practiced custom was to just keep going until either she stopped calling or I stopped hearing her, but as luck and a beaker of bathtub gin would have it, I lost my balance just then and slipped against the door, which had swung open before I could quite sort out which of my hands was free, though the answer proved to be neither, and stop it.

Under a brocaded lamp, Mother was at her escritoire in one of those starched white high-necked blouses that, along with her old-fashioned, high-piled chignon, made her look rather amusingly like a superannuated Gibson girl in a wheelchair. "It's so late, I was concerned for you," she started to say, to which I might have answered that it was much *too* late for that. But then she got a good look at me, and stopped saying anything.

Even I had to admit to a silent doubt that I was looking my best. Although my hair was bobbed too short by now to ever really look disarranged, except for Grace Scape's chewing-gum in my bangs, my white crepe gown with the scalloped hemline was practically off one shoulder, and one of my two Cuban-heeled pumps (I felt almost positive there had been two in all, back when I and they had first met) had just thudded to the floor from my hand. I also probably still had a big streak of soot on my face, left over from when drunken Dicky Foulard had started playing Jack the Ripper with the coal scuttle. One of our favorite games at parties was to pretend we were all murderers and then, surveying the room's available implements, announce what we would use to do each other in. The best weapon—which was always the unlikeliest, of course—won the match.

Not without a tingle of triumph, my other hand now informed me that it held Dicky's silver flask, from which, having dropped the other pump to the floor at some point in the recent present, I'd now concluded I could use a snort. As Mother went on staring, hands to her wheelchair's armrests, I felt the need for a ciggie to follow up the gin, and fished one from the beaded bag I'd found hanging from my not yet gown-free shoulder. "*What?*" I finally demanded, lighting it and blowing out smoke, some of which seemed to get stuck in the chewing-gum in my bangs.

That was when I heard a sound no one had in years, which was the tinkling little hiccup noises that Mother made when she laughed. It seemed to catch her by surprise as well, as if her throat was so long out of the habit that it had gotten giggling all mixed up with vomiting. Softly, she laughed in her wheelchair, and looked at me standing there, and blinked back lustrous tiny tears from her dark eyes.

"For this," she said. I wondered if her mind had finally gone off to join her health, wherever it was—still chained to the White House gates, I supposed. "For this," she said again. With an amused smile, she glanced down at the half-finished letter on the escritoire. "Dear Alice," she said, "wonderful news! It was for this."

That was when I finally understood what she was saying. "Oh, *go* on," I said scornfully, reaching down to collect my pumps and almost going head first into the escritoire. Once I straightened up, feeling that I had never understood the intricacy of that procedure in as much detail as I should and blowing disquietingly gum-weighted bangs out of my eyes, I thought that I had better start over. "*Go* on," I said, even more scornfully. "You and your silly suffragettes didn't have anything to do with it."

"Oh, but we did, my dear," Mother said. "We didn't know it, and

Alice Paul and Lucy Burns and I probably all hoped for better—or let's be kind, and just say different. But we did," and she laughed quietly again. "You—*you*—are our monument, not the one they still won't have put up at Occoquan eighty years from now, for all that my friends and I know it was our Valley Forge; where we suffered, where we won. The fact that you don't think we had anything to do with it is what proves that we did."

"Go—" But I'd already said "Go on" twice; I'd counted. "Go to *hell*," I told her, which was a first and so felt marvelously emancipating. Swinging the chewing-gum around in front of me like a carrot on a stick, I hauled flask, pumps, beaded bag, stockinged feet, and ciggie back into the hallway. But I hadn't been able to close the door with either hand or foot, which is why I heard Mother call gently after me, "I'm there, dear. But we did."

Ohh—let the old loony think anything she likes, I thought once I was back in my room, had found the electric light-switch, and could start strewing things about. She might depart the upstairs drawing room for the—attic, soon, at the fast clip she was fading. But she'd just better never *bother* me about it again, I thought, at the same time I discovered that I had made a sudden decision to fall into bed with one stocking on, while three or four of my Cuban-heeled pumps scuttled about the floor in the dark like friendly crabs.

She never did. Soon afterward, she began sending grotesque Lil Gagni, who had dusting and all sorts of better things to do, clumping off to the public library to obtain bound volumes of old newspapers from 1917 and 1918, which Mother kept as the fines mounted, writing gracious notes of apology instead of returning them. Her correspondence also grew more voluminous, and the letters that came in reply from Alice Paul and all those dreadful women she was so proud of having known in prison were sometimes so bulky that they would stay wedged in the mail slot of our front door, like the tongue of some atrocious dog, instead of dropping through to the carpet. Even if the light from her brocaded lamp still showed beneath the drawing room's door, I no longer had to worry about making noise when I went past it at ungodly hours, for I knew I wouldn't hear her voice; only, if I listened closely, the faint sound of Mother's pen going scratch-scratch, like a mouse's claws, across vellum.

Still, I felt it was my daughterly duty to look in on her once or twice a day. When I presented myself, she'd ask about my plans and friends, carefully keeping her voice and face clear of everything but a maddening gentleness so as to indicate in advance that no aspersions, or indeed opinion of any sort, would be forthcoming. Nonetheless, I was always relieved when my visit found her dozing in her wheelchair, her face cast up and blind in sleep and her mouth open like a sore. "It's nice to see you, Mother," I would murmur, "you're looking well. I'll just be going now."

Otherwise, I went on enjoying my new life. But not until Grace Scape, now Grace Foulard, made a slighting reference at a garden party to "your ratty old Hispano-Suiza" did I realize that it had become my old one. After finding a pretext to discharge Cheng, whose imperturbable face I now saw had always masked a critical attitude, I bought a Duesenberg, having startled Cheng into an actual widening of the eyes by telling him to take the Hispano-Suiza with him. Later, that led to his arrest, and all sorts of nonsense with beefy police detectives from Connecticut; I believe he was finally deported.

As his English was somewhat better and his racial stock less exotic, I was sure that Bruno, who had come with the Duesenberg, would be far more likely to talk himself out of that kind of trouble. All the same, as I came down for breakfast one afternoon, I did overhear him telling Lil Gagni in the kitchen dat onda day da Fraulein vired him he vud chust as sun valk.

Da Fraulein, as it happened, found it faintly disorienting to hear herself called that, as I had just turned twenty-six. Fortunately, we girls of the golden Twenties were under a good deal less pressure than the previous generation to get married immediately to whatever suitable man came knocking. I put this down to the fact that we were so much better at having fun than our dreary mothers had been, and also that now there was so much more fun to be had.

Not that there weren't risks involved, and penalties to pay. After one frankly rather sordid episode on a balcony of the Biltmore Hotel, of which I remembered very little except the spiky leaves of an inconveniently placed potted plant pricking the undersides of the bare thighs under my hoisted skirt, I had to ask Grace—who didn't know it had been Dicky—for help in finding a doctor, since I suspicioned I knew better than her hard-drinking husband why the Foulards had stayed childless. She took me to a dreadful man above a dreadful dive in dreadful Jersey City, and held my hand as he did horrid scraping and then plopping things to a distant continent of me and I thought Oh Mother Mother why didn't you chain yourself to a hospital instead. With Grace's help, I made my tottering way back to the Duesenberg, and from the flick of Bruno's eyes beneath his cap, I knew I'd have to count on his discretion. Had it still been Cheng under the visor, I could have just counted on his unintelligibility.

Aside from such escapades, which you'd be wrong to suppose were that numerous, I did have proper suitors. The blond scion of a meat fortune took me for a weekend to his parents' estate in Pennsylvania, where to my relief I saw that neither Ma nor Pa was wearing bloody aprons; nevertheless, on my return, I went on picturing them that way. The glib young heir to a drug-store chain soon began giving me headaches, and I broke off our brief engagement. And always, as a sort of human caesura between attachments, there was beaming, imbecilic, doggily doting Thurston, his face still crammed with earnest vouchers of a reverence I knew to be unalterable by any behavior of mine.

It had been so since our dancing-school days—when the blissful silliness of those keen eyes above that longing nose used to force me to tilt my head ceilingward on my neck, like a nodding rose at the end of its stem, for fear that gazing back would make me burst out laughing. Once or twice, in fact, it naughtily crossed my mind to drag *him* to some balcony, just to see if his adoration could survive hiked skirts, scraping brick, martini breath and a crushed corsage. But the burst-out-laughing problem swiftly reared its head again, and then I sobered up.

There were others, too. But promising, handsome, or simply well tailored, none of the boys I toyed with marrying could pass the test set by my memories of a bald head I could sneak up on to kiss, a lap large as a throne that I could sit on to tug a watch chain from its fob pocket, and a

lingering odor of cigar smoke. Of course, my chums knew exactly what
the problem was, the world being giddy with Freud in those days. Wafting onyx cigarette holders in patterns like a Cubist's paintbrushes, they'd
tease me about having predictably chosen the simplest complex I could
find, all of us delighted with our sophistication—which was never more
delightful than it was in the Twenties, when the very idea of sophistication was new and daring in itself, and hadn't yet been vulgarized by its
availability to any member of the boobish masses who could afford a
paperback or the down payment for a television on the installment plan.

As time went on, however, fewer and fewer of the people in my circle
went back far enough with me to have known Father, the friends I had
retained from childhood having largely drifted off to matrimony,
Boston, or both. Increasingly, I found myself instead playing the *doyenne*
of a set whose other members were my juniors by too wide a margin for
the thought that I'd ever *had* parents to spring very readily to their
minds. I missed the teasing then; in a way, it had kept Father close.

He wasn't dead, of course. But his letters, largely about household
matters, had dwindled to two or three per year, and as they often seemed
written by no one at all to no one at all, I felt that there was no one to
reply to them. He was more vivid to me incommunicado, as I forlornly
hoped I was to him; that would explain why the letters came so seldom.
By now, his Los Angeles oil wells having come in spectacularly, he was
establishing himself in the motion-picture business, and at the cinema I
would sometimes lose track of the story as a result of being distracted—
for this was still in silent days—by the sight of his name inscribed in dec-
orative curlicues along the lower border of the titles. He was prominent
enough in the movie industry for his doings to be reported with some
regularity in the newspapers; prominent enough, too, for a perfect
stranger's voice to crash in like a bowling ball from the next table as
Grace and I had tea at the Plaza one day in December of '26, repeating
the ribald gossip that Father was now living openly with an Irish woman
at his house in the Hollywood Hills, and had introduced her to the Governor of California as his daughter.

As Grace's hand pressed a handkerchief into my curled palm on the banquette in the powder room, I felt her other arm go around my shoulder. Managing to control my sobs, I choked out the whole story. "He wouldn't take me with him—wouldn't even let me visit," I wept. "It's such a lie—he'd never have let me live there, never."

When my tears had dwindled to sniffles and a final blink let me look at her directly, her expression was thoughtful. "But you've got plenty of money, you know," Grace said. "More than you know what to do with, and you're more than of age. In all these years, didn't it ever once occur to you that you could have gone out there anytime—without waiting for his permission? Your father might have felt differently when he saw you standing in front of him."

I stared at her. The thought had never crossed my mind.

I never spoke to her again.

■

The following spring was when Daisy B. and I became inseparable. As I've said, we had hardly been unaware of each other before that, in the way that a champion at tennis might keep track of a champion at golf. But the young-marrieds crowd where she set the pace only overlapped with the single-folk regatta to which I was a similar pennant at mobbed affairs where conversation that was either protracted or private was impossible, though we might smile a smile denied to lesser lights as we clutched each other's hands and talked about trifles. Even the whispers about the bootlegger who'd supposedly been having some sort of dalliance with her just before his murder had only reached my circle as the dimmest and sketchiest sort of gossip—the kind that starts everyone bringing up similar stories about other people they know better.

After Tom Buchanan's startling, ghastly death on the polo field, however—they said the crack of his neck as his shying horse trod on it was as loud as a pistol shot, just like the one that killed the dying rider's former mount two minutes later—his beautiful young widow began to frequent the same gaudy speaks and jammed house-parties where I was accustomed to ruling the roost. Instantly, it was clear to us both that if we didn't want to be enemies, we had better become intimates.

On the neutral ground of the wedding reception of some Midwestern second cousin of Daisy's—I knew the bride, an aviatrix, slightly—I sat down in a vacant chair next to hers. Not the least of my motives was to forestall Thurston, who was heeling toward me like a spaniel from the far side of the room, wearing that depressingly heartened expression he got whenever he spied me without a man incontrovertibly in evidence. Daisy greeted me with a splay of golden fingers on my forearm and an exclamation of genuine delight, and we started gabbing away like reunited sisters under a banner reading NICK AND AMELIA: MANY YEARS OF HAPPINESS.

After an hour of enchanted *bavardage,* she put her fingers on my neck to bring my ear close to her champagned mouth, although she'd had enough to drink that it took her a few giggly seconds to decide whether my right or left one was preferable. "I know where there's a better party than this one," she confided once that was settled, "only it hasn't started yet."

"Where?" I asked, a newly atomized earlobe still tingling.

"My house in East Egg. Do you have a car outside? I want to leave before the bore who brought me finishes his cigar, because that's when he'll remember that *I* was here, too."

Even so, as we sneaked doorward with the exaggerated footsteps of comedians in a Ziegfeld revue, Daisy whispered that we'd need supplies for the drive out to Long Island, and so we altered our escape route to go past the array of champagne bottles just behind Mr. Cigar's oblivious, smoke-wreathed head. Seizing two each, we spilled out onto the street with fur coats flying and elbows bump-a-bump and scrambled into the waiting Duesenberg together just as one of Daisy's champagnes slipped and went smash on the sidewalk.

That briefly stupefied us both, since we hadn't thought champagne bottles *could* break. Then Bruno clapped the door shut and got back in up front, I shrieked at him to drive, drive, the police were on our heels, and Daisy and I both fell back laughing as he gravely put the car in gear and she popped the cork on her remaining bottle.

Between the two of us, that one was empty by the time we started over the Williamsburg Bridge. Slipping as she did so, Daisy hiked herself over the sill that separated the front seat from ours.

"Bruno," she said idly. Then she crooned it: "*Broooo-no,*" and giggled. "What sort of name is that, Bruno?"

"Mine, Miss," Bruno said, driving. I could see his gloved hands, driving. "I have no other information."

"Broon-o. What's your last name, Bruno?"

He told her—something like Hockman or Hopman. How strange it is to hear him speaking German, I thought. But I was puzzled, too, and it took me a moment to understand why: "Isn't that funny," I remarked to a seagull over Brooklyn who seemed interested. "I've just realized that I always thought it was 'Duesenberg.' But that would certainly be a coincidence, wouldn't it?" As if to signal that it was one too, the seagull dipped its wings and dove away.

"And what sort of name is *that,* Broono?" Daisy was asking with mock sternness, meaning his real one.

"In my native language it means 'captain,' Miss," Bruno said.

"Oh, *no!*" Daisy cried, sitting back. "Bruno, you've been *demoted*! I think that's just *terrible*. We should treat you with more respect here in America. How do you say 'chauffeur' in German, Bruno?"

"*Fahrer,*" he said, which did sound so German I sat up, gathering my mink around me. "And I have so far found the respect I am given more than adequate. I can think of no reason why this should not continue, Miss."

"That's *nice,*" Daisy sighed, settling back. "Drive on, Brooono. Far'rer an' far'rer. Why have you kidnapped us, Broooono?" As I opened the first of my two bottles, I felt a new respect for her, since it had never crossed my mind to flirt with him. Then again, of course, he wasn't *her* chauffeur. And I too had flirted with other people's chauffeurs, when they weren't Asiatics. So she and I had something in common, I thought, a little driftily.

Compared to some of the inordinate heaps of ornamented and luminous slag already familiar to me in that part of Long Island, Daisy's place was architecturally rather sober. But its current character was quite at odds with its design. As we drove up to the main house, I was startled out of a demi-stupor by the sight of two or three fine horses loping or grazing contentedly on the lawn, now unmown to the point of having become a meadow, that spilled down to the Sound. From their opened gates to the tack left at the mercy of the elements, the stables we had just driven past were plainly long out of use.

"Oh, I gave them all their freedom, after—" Daisy's careless voice let a rag doll at the end of her wrist silently finish the sentence, and I knew that she meant her husband's death. "You see, I couldn't help but think it might have been *revenge,* and . . . well, why shouldn't it have been? I even let 'em come in the house if they like, although they don't, much. I think the smells there bother them. Every so often, one of them will clip-clop off to one of the other estates, and the neighbors complain to the police. I always say virtuously that I know *nothing* about it. Maybe someday they'll be completely wild again—the wild horses of East Egg!—and the Shinnecock Indians can ride them bareback over the Brooklyn Bridge to reconquer Manhattan at last." As my glance told Bruno to wait—and his nod said that no other scheme, however attractive or superficially plausible, could tempt him to do otherwise—she smilingly took me into the house.

There was no sunlight in it. The curtains of the living room's French windows were drawn, and the contents of Grant's Tomb had probably been aired more recently. As we entered, a white dog with enraged pink eyes was relieving itself on the carpet in the middle of the floor, quite visibly not for the first time.

"SooSoo!" Daisy exclaimed, going to pick it up. "Did oo make another mess? Will the Swede have to clean up? But you know the Swede doesn't *like* to clean up—*no,* SooSoo," looking it solemnly in the eye. "*Bad* SooSoo!" Yet she seemed delighted, not chagrined.

"I let all the servants go, too," she murmured as the dog hopped out of her arms, "except for my daughter's nanny. She's straight off the boat—speaks six words of English, all grumpy—and has absolutely no idea that *all* rich Americans don't live this way."

Now that my eyes were growing used to the gloom, I could see that a nearby coffee table and the sofa behind it were both piled high with books. Some were in French, and by authors with preposterous pseudonyms, like Tristan Tzara. Because of their peculiar design, the ones in English looked almost more foreign than the French ones, and came from publishers with names like the Three Mountains Press. Deciding that an attempt to palm off three stories and ten poems as a book was certainly the lazy man's way of joining the literary caravan, I tossed one near-pamphlet aside. In front of a large fireplace for which Daisy clearly had no other use was propped a large, framed black-and-white photograph of a seated woman in dorsal view, her lower back bizarrely transformed into the contours of a violin.

"It just came from P-P-Paris," Daisy said beside me, sounding as oddly out of breath as if she had somehow contrived to race through every room in the house in the last ten seconds. "Isn't it heavenly?" Taking the bottle of champagne from my hand, she tilted it and her throat back before wiping her mouth and turning away.

As I wandered, taking care where I stepped and also not entirely sure if Daisy was following or guiding me, I found myself in front of a table on which were laid out both a Ouija board and a Tarot deck, along with a few mah-jongg tiles that had evidently wandered into the party by accident. Under an almost spent candle was a copy of Madame Blavatsky or some other spiritualist manual, laid open to a chapter on séances.

This disconcerted me. "Were you trying to talk to your . . . Tom?" I asked, feeling dubious that such could be the case.

The scorn in Daisy's laugh was as dazzling as if I had *seen* it, like a sudden shower of gold coins tossed from somewhere high. "Whatever for?" she demanded, pushing her hair back off her pale brow. "So he could tell me about the cheap little doxy he's found in the afterlife, and the lovely, squalid orgies that the two of them are having in Hades?" She saw my lips trying to remember the name of the bootlegger people said had been her lover—unaided, for my brain had already given up the job— and shook her head. "No—not him, either. We had run out of things to say to each other *before* he died; just sat in a room, frozen like wax statues, while things went on somewhere else and we heard chairs and such being dragged back and forth in the wings."

"Then . . ." I didn't want to trespass. But I rather thought that she had wanted me to see this.

"I've been trying to contact my mother." Her voice had the matter-of-factness of true sorrow, an absence of vocal decoration that turned her words from the expression of a thing into the thing itself. "You see, she died when I was quite young."

Then I felt that we were truly sisters. "I might as well try using this to contact my father," I said, pushing the wheeled indicator over a few letters of the Ouija board.

Daisy, too, seemed to sense that this exchange sealed our intimacy; perhaps she had expected it would. "Come upstairs," she said gaily, in a superficial change of mood that I understood was actually the old one's apotheosis. "I want you to meet my secret lover."

The fantastic disorder of her lavishly appointed bedroom made the downstairs a view of a church. On her bed was a monogrammed shirt, the initials not her husband's, in which she'd apparently blown her nose more than a few times. Placing me on its unmade edge, she rummaged among vials and stone frogs on her vanity, knocking one or two over, and returned with an oblong velvet case. Sitting down next to me, she opened it; the two silver finger-holes on either side of the syringe stared up at me like a pair of steel-rimmed spectacles on a man with a large glass nose. "Hello, lover," Daisy's voice murmured, her cheek touching mine.

"Mommy? Are you home?"

For a lunatic moment, I thought the syringe had spoken. But the voice belonged to Daisy's daughter, whose small stocky body stood fidgeting in the doorway in an attitude whose combined confusion and determination reminded me of Lil Gagni. Beside me, Daisy had already clicked the case shut: "Ot-nay in ont-fray of the ild-chay," she said lightly.

Casually chucking the case onto the bed, she stood up, hands to knees: "Hello, precious!" she cooed. "Hello, my sweet baby. How are oo? What's the matter?"

"SooSoo crapped in my dollhouse."

"Oh, sweetie! We can get you another dollhouse. You didn't really like that crummy old one, anyhow."

"My dolls did," the child said. "And now there's crap on them too."

"Well, then they'll like the new one even better, darling," Daisy said. "We'll make it safe. Now run along and go find the Swede, and tell her to fix you some dinner—isn't it time for your dinner? Or have you had it already? Well, just tell her I said to give you whatever you like, even ice cream. Now go on, go on, quick! before the ice cream melts."

Reluctantly, the child backed out of the doorway. Then we heard her traipsing off, her small footsteps thumping on the way downstairs, one-two, one-two, until both thumps sounded at once on the final step. She'd been playing hopscotch on the stairs, I realized. By then, Daisy had gone to the door and closed and locked it. Pressing her back against it as she looked at me, she laughed with mingled excitement and relief, as if we'd both been out swimming and had been briefly caught in an undertow before batting our way back to shore.

Taking her old seat on the bed next to me again, she picked up the case—but didn't open it, which I found frustrating. "It was right after Tom's death," she explained. "I didn't love him, not anymore. But it was all just so *much* to have happen, in such a short time, that I think I was fairly hysterical. So a doctor gave me morphine—for the pain."

I understood what I had to say if I wanted to see the syringe again, which I did. Even so, I hesitated—but I wanted to say it, and it also sounded as if, as soon as I did say it, it would be the truth.

"I'm in a lot of pain too, Daisy," I finally blurted.

"I thought you might be," she said, in an oddly grateful tone.

Eyes closed, I lay back on the bed, listening to the tiny sounds of Daisy's preparations. For a bad moment, I imagined I was back in Jersey City, and pressed the palms of both my hands against the sheet to prove to myself it was silk. Then I felt her sit down, next to my hipbone. She'd already knotted something around my arm. Now she picked the arm up by the wrist, and startled me by giving it a couple of sharp, two-fingered taps at the crook of the elbow. As I instinctively started to pull free, I heard an amused, friendly "H'm," and then her voice telling me relax, it was all right. Something had just pricked my arm.

"Sail away," Daisy murmured. "This is how we sail away."

I did. First there was fog, which turned out to be ice. But it wasn't ice; it was the color of the world. Then Father was there. He was all around me, and soon I understood that I was finally inside him—in his stomach, behind his pocket watch, which I could hear ticking. This masculine womb, for so I sleepily identified it, was the one in whose walls I had always belonged: not Mother's, where I had only been a passenger. Here I could live.

The ticking of the watch had begun to go in turns, to the right at first, then to the left, then to the right again. I realized that Father was a bank, and I was his money. I was glad to be his and glad to be money, for I felt loved and knew it wouldn't be fleeting, as banks last forever. Hairily nude, an Irish woman squatted in a corner, like a dog doing its business. *Don't exist,* I ordered, and she vanished. But seeing her had made me naked too, although less hairy, and my being aware that this was the case, rather than the fact of it, was what had put me in the wrong. Now I'd be cast out of Father's womb, his bank. I would be marooned with Thurston, who did his best but had no stomach I could live in.

Since there was water all around us and no one else in sight, I tried to get in it anyway. But his was too small for me. It did have windows, though, through which morning sunlight poured. Daisy had opened the bedroom curtains before she went downstairs.

Gin having been my main guide to this sort of experience, I expected the hangover to be dreadful. But when I stood up, my brain stayed put where it belonged, and the rest of me felt as if it *was* where it belonged. That made me so happy that I didn't even bother to feel relieved first, and I started humming the first song that popped into my head. " '*Give me your answer, do,*' " I hummed. " '*I'm half crazy, all for . . .*' " Then I decided I couldn't really remember how the rest of it went.

Feeling ravenous, I found my way to the kitchen, which turned out to be sparkling clean. At the table, Daisy was already launched on her share of an enormous breakfast prepared by the Swedish nanny, who eyed me as if she had made up her mind not to comment on anything whatsoever until she found the right point of comparison to measure it by. Thus far, she had plainly found none such for a single incident since she came off the boat.

Waiting until her back was turned, Daisy put down her fork to squeeze my hand. "It's fun to share a lover, isn't it? If it were a man, we'd have to be jealous of each other," she whispered in a delicious rush.

Having finished the western one first, I was wolfing down my east egg when I suddenly sat bolt upright. "Oh my *God!*" I said, almost clapping a hand to my forehead before I remembered that there was a knife in it. My hand, I mean. "*Bruno!*"

"Has been fed," the Swede grunted. "Is on porch." But then, unexpectedly, she smiled, as if Bruno was someone she had known a very long time; though I was sure she'd never clapped eyes on him until now. I suppose he was something, or rather someone, that she did have a point of comparison for.

"Is looking at horses," she said.

■

Bruno gave notice two days later. "I haff been offered good job as auto mechanic," he told me in our brownstone's gloomy entrance hall, looking at his boots. "Here is the letter from Mr. Egan of Egan's Garage, Rochester, Minnesota. He is owner. I must of my future think, Miss."

"But Bruno," I gasped, "you'll get your *clothes* all dirty—and they won't be as nice, anyhow," I added, having just realized that of course he wouldn't be taking his chauffeur's uniform with him.

"Will still be working with autos," he said stolidly. "For me, Miss, it was always the cars: never the people, although I would appreciate if you remembered me to Frau Buchanan. Will two weeks be adequate?"

"Right *now* will be adequate," I told him, kicking the telephone table in frustration. He saluted and left, and neither Daisy nor I ever saw or heard of him again.

It was at her urging that, instead of hiring a new chauffeur or finding out if I could get Cheng back from China, I decided to learn to drive— although Daisy, who knew how to, always refused to take the wheel, and never did say why. Soon, feeling more thrilled about getting to scoot into the front seat than any other part of it, I was piloting the Duesenberg everywhere, out to Long Island and back and down to Greenwich Village, where we actually spent most of our time. Sometimes, as we drove around, Daisy would reach over, or forward from the back seat if she had decided to scramble in there, and clap Bruno's old chauffeur's cap on my head, tugging it this way and that as she giggled and I yelled at her to at least put it at an angle that would let me see out from under it. I think that there's a fading snapshot of her—or us, I suppose—doing that, in a trunk or a hatbox somewhere; but I don't know if she kept it or I did.

The reason that we went to the Village so often wasn't only that it was where Daisy got her—our, rather—morphine. Since her husband's death, she had also made herself familiar with and to a whole slew of bohemian writers, painters and simple eccentrics in that quarter, whose cramped gallery openings she went to, whose gouged-looking canvases she bought (we used to stack them in the Duesenberg's back seat, struggling like a couple of undersized stevedores), and whose fugitive little magazines she helped fund. The eccentrics, she just bought dinners for.

Her favorites in all those categories used to congregate in a restaurant on Carmine Street called Le Perroquet de Paris—in those days, at least; I believe it's changed its name since, perhaps more than once. There we'd hold court, with Daisy excitedly rattling on about Max Ernst and his imitators or James Joyce and his to our gang of artists in the vocabulary that she'd already acquired from them, while at my end of the table I prattled on as best I could in imitation Daisy, for she was trying to educate me in the avant-garde. But the bohemians who wound up down near me instead of up by her never seemed to mind much, if only because my monologues, however faltering, left their mouths free to wolf down food in as much quantity as they could. Our bill was always astronomical, but then we both had bank accounts the size of Jupiter, and it was nice to have so many interesting moons.

I always waited in the Duesenberg while she went to get our morphine stock. I never saw the man who sold it to us, if it was a man, or even knew the exact address she went to, since it was always dark. Then she'd come back, bright-eyed and smiling, and we'd set off.

Even though we'd feel impatient and Gramercy Park was a lot closer than Long Island, we never went to my brownstone to inject. I couldn't get past the thought that if I ever showed up there with Daisy, silver hypo, powder and Bunsen burner in tow, the smell of cigar smoke would be back at full force in the entrance hall, and it would be sulphuric. So I would drive us out to East Egg, while the wind washed our hair and Daisy sometimes sang her favorite song—the one whose chorus started with her name repeated, and in which I never quite dared join her even when she'd pretend to pout about that and stick out her tongue at me. So I'd just hum along, not forming the words.

Leaving the Duesenberg parked for the roaming horses to sniff at, we'd go upstairs, where Daisy would leave me alone in the bedroom while she looked in on her daughter to make sure she was asleep. When she came back and locked the door, we'd usually make a joke of having a little tiff about who got to go first. Of course, we knew it didn't really matter, since we would both sail away soon enough.

By now, I was adept enough to do for her with the syringe, just as she still did for me. But you must understand, there was nothing sordid about it. Daisy and I never stopped bathing, or dressing well, or having other interests and amusements. At the wheel of the Duesenberg, I never once nodded out. It wasn't like it is nowadays, God knows, when any Negro with the price of a fix can stagger about Harlem with a spike hanging out of his arm, recently widowed housewives in bathrobes stuff half a medicine cabinet up their rumps in broad daylight, heedless of being observed in the act by their sons, and any adolescent with a case of melancholia—some sixteen-year-old Jackie-boy or girlegan—can inhale every last vapor from a tube of airplane glue before collapsing to dream of who knows what, levitating out of Arlington, Virginia, to invented Minnesotas, South Pacifics, Manhattans or anywhere his television-addled brain may wander.

This world has long since grown so vile that as far as I'm concerned he can do anything he likes. But in the Twenties that my own age shared with the century's, civilization still persisted, the great unwashed hadn't yet gotten their grimy hands on our pleasures, and *everything* was more elegant: the cars, the clothes, the conversation, the music, the narcotics, the—well, everything, absolutely everything.

I'm not sure how long our lovely life went on that lovely, lovely way. Certainly for months, but which and how many elude me. It was long enough for me to grow more confident down at my end of the table in Le Perroquet de Paris, and once even take issue with a claim that Daisy had made about Picasso up at hers ("Now, dearest—we don't really *know* yet if his Blue Period is over, do we? It may just be in *abeyance,*" I called out, amid slurps of neighborly spaghetti). But on the night I'm about to describe, Daisy surprised me by waving a braceleted toodle-oo to the crowd at our usual table and leading me to a more secluded booth in back that was lit by a single candle.

Her smile as tender as the night, she produced a flat, elegantly wrapped package from her bag and pushed it across to me. "Well, it's a *present,* darling—not a bomb," she said brightly, to my mystified look. "Happy Whatever-Today-Is."

Even as I opened it, I knew what it must be. Inside an oblong velvet case was a syringe exactly like Daisy's, except that, while the metal parts of hers—or, as I thought of it, ours—were silver, mine was done in gold. As I mutely gazed down at it, she made a play of holding up her napkin like a curtain to hide the case's contents from anyone else's eyes, although no one was nearby.

"Mind taken a powder?" she asked finally, which was one of our favorite little jokes.

"No," I said. "It's just— I've just never seen such a *beautiful* hypo before," having indeed only seen one other in my life up to now and fancying gold rather better than silver. Then a new thought appeared in its glints, and I jerked my head up to stare at her. "Daisy!" I exclaimed, with what I'm sure was some alarm. "Is this *goodbye*?"

She laughed. "No, darling. It's 'hello.' From now on, you can do for me with mine—and I can do for you with yours. It's engraved, by the way; there, just past the last calibration mark." Her finger tapped it.

The engraving was tiny, and difficult to read by candlelight, especially as it went all the way around the hypo and I had to keep turning it to get to the next letters. *Give me your answer do,* it said. I felt somewhat at a loss. "Thank you," I finally said.

At the same time, however, I was as madly eager to try it out as she was, so we wasted no time paying the bill for the other table—we hadn't had a bite ourselves—and dashing for the Duesenberg as our bohemians shouted their gratitude with mouths full of food. As I got behind the wheel and Daisy slipped into the front seat from the other side, I felt that my previous response had been awfully inadequate.

"Daisy," I said, turning to her, "I really meant it. Thank—" Before I could finish, her mouth was on mine, as it had been once or twice before when our pecks on the cheek hadn't quite hit the bull's-eye. But then I felt her tongue start to delve between my lips.

I have no real idea how I got back to Gramercy Park. I may have found a taxi, although it seems to me I walked. Daisy didn't call after me or try to follow, either on foot or in the car.

The next morning, I was awakened by the sound of a horn in the street outside my window. When I looked down, there was the Duesenberg, and Daisy's Swede was climbing out of the driver's seat. Looking up, she saw that I had seen her; I heard a faint tinkle as she tossed the key onto the brownstone's stoop. Without a word, or any gesture except a heave of her broad shoulders implying that the trials of Job had been puny by comparison, she set off stoutly down the sidewalk, and was almost instantly out of sight beyond the nearest tree.

Although I did manage to creep out to retrieve the keys from the top step, that was the last I saw of the world beyond my room for four days. Of course, while I was walking home in the taxi, I had sworn to myself that I would never see Daisy again, and at first I told myself that the emotional strain and upset of this decision was the reason I could neither sleep nor picture myself going down the stairs for any reason until I died.

I told myself I'd surely start to mend soon. But aside from the relative reprieves of being able to pitch a shoe at the door and holler "Go *'way!*" every time Lil Gagni brought me a tray of food identical to the one she always brought for Mother—and even after, as a last resort, she tried one different from the tray she always brought for Mother—my condition grew worse rather than better. Once I started to hear mice scratching in the wall behind my bed's headboard—and soon, impossibly, in the headboard itself, leaving me in little doubt that my skull would be next—I finally had to face what the real problem was. Pulling on some clothes, and slinking out my bedroom door past the twelve shoes piled there, I stumbled down the stairs and got into the Duesenberg.

On the whole drive out to East Egg, I was heaving so much with nausea that I kept bumping my chin against the top of the steering wheel. The only news I had of how badly I must be handling the car was the endless roar of horns and squeal of brakes and thump of jerking tires around me. Luckily, no policeman who was happy in his job was likely to pull over a Duesenberg; while I *might* be a nobody, the odds weren't worth it. Somehow, in the midst of what I believe was the closest I've ever come to pure delirium, I found myself noticing that the billboard with the garish eyes on the way to Daisy's house had been replaced by a new one advertising Maxwell House coffee, although the image—a clock with far too many, peculiarly human-looking hands—was hardly much less of an inducement to stark madness than old Dr. T.J.'s stare had been. Then a gate was thankfully open without my needing to sound the horn, a horse was loping away from me down a long driveway, and I had shut off the Duesenberg's motor with a sob of exhaustion and relief.

The Swede opened the door to me with a dour and skeptical look, for which I repaid her by sticking my thumbs in my ears and wiggling my fingers while making a horrible gargoyle face the second her back was turned. Not bothering to take me to our mistress, she lumbered back toward the kitchen. I went on into the living room.

On a sofa from which the piles of books had now been dashed to the floor, as had the ones on the nearby table, Daisy was feeding bits of something to dreadful, pink-eyed SooSoo. Hearing my step, she glanced up, and we stared at each other in silence for some moments as SooSoo growled at me warningly.

"I need ore-may orphine-may," I said.

Lifting an eyebrow, she tilted her head toward SooSoo. "This is the dog, not the child," she said coolly. "Or had you already forgotten—" at which point her chin trembled. A moment later, she was sobbing in my arms.

"Oh, darling, it was terrifying!" her damp voice moaned in my hair. "I had to drive all the way back here—down *that road*—but you don't know—you must never know . . ." As, indeed, I do not; to this day.

Regaining some control of herself, she went back to the sofa, and fished out something that had been stuffed between its frame and cushions. Smiling and brushing the last tears from her eyes with one hand, she held out the velvet case with my gold hypo in it with the other.

After we had sailed away, we lay on her bed, our two heads touching but our feet angling off the coverlet in opposite directions. I felt as nervous as one could right after an injection of morphine—which, however hard I tried, wasn't very. But Daisy seemed to be in no great hurry to make the thing happen that I knew would have to happen, probably many times, unless and until I managed to locate a narcotics supplier of my own. Instead, I heard her voice asking dreamily, "Would you like to go to Provincetown with me tomorrow? A lot of our friends from the Village are up there just now, and I've rented a cottage for a week. We can hire a car if you don't feel like doing a drive that long."

Hard as I found it to explain, I was touched—and somehow humbled—by the "our" when Daisy said "our friends." I also didn't much want to drive back to New York, since it was so pleasant here just now, no matter the apprehensions knocking, so far vainly, at the back door of my head. But if we were going to be in Provincetown for a full week, I had an enormous amount of wardrobe to select and pack, even though Daisy assured me that neither its temporary nor its permanent residents were any great sticklers for formality.

At the door, she kissed me in full view of the Swede, and this time my lips obediently parted when her tongue's slither asked them to. But that was as far as it went.

In any case, the drive back to Gramercy Park was considerably easier than the drive out to East Egg had been. Early the next morning, I heard a car-horn outside the window, just as I had four days before. Oh, it's the Swede back with the Duesenberg again, I thought nonsensically. But this was a different horn, and when I looked, a long black Daimler was idling down below. From its back window, Daisy's face and arm protruded, waving and beaming enthusiastically.

Taking my four suitcases from Lil Gagni, who was rather overdoing the gasping and puffing, the Chinese chauffeur fit them into the Daimler's luggage compartment, next to Daisy's—three. Well, she'd certainly been fibbing about traveling light, I thought. Then the chauffeur opened the door, and I stepped in to find myself face-to-face with Daisy, her daughter, and SooSoo.

"The Swede quit last night." Daisy's smile was tight. "But it'll be all right, darling. It'll just have to, since it can't be helped!"

As the Daimler pulled away, I saw the chauffeur's eyes flick toward me in the mirror above his head. On the sidewalk, he had struck me as vaguely familiar. But now, seeing those eyes in the same elongated box where I had seen them so many times before, I realized instantly who this was.

"Cheng," I said.

"No," he said. "Wong." Hearing his voice, I *knew* it was Cheng. Had he snuck back in on another boat, or had he never been deported?

"I'm *not* wrong!" I said sharply. "You're Cheng."

"No," Cheng said. "My name Wong."

Daisy's daughter started to blubber.

Jumping into my lap, SooSoo bit me on the nose.

■

By the time the drive came to an end some eight or nine hours later, Provincetown would have had to be on fire to appear anything less than welcoming. And perhaps even that wouldn't have done it, for the afternoon sun that made the eaves and corners of everything glow orange simply gave a feeling that one was inside a gigantic paper lantern. The cottage Daisy had rented was called "The Waves," although marcels would have been more accurate, and on her instructions the Daimler trundled down a lane of flour to it, past a sign pointing people to the lighthouse. Which we could see, black against the sky beyond our roof. Behind the house were dunes declining to a somewhat marshy inlet into which the sea crept contentedly, like a blue kitten with white claws.

Once Cheng had unloaded the luggage, Daisy—who had been made rather peremptory by the fact that she, not I, had been in charge of the car—insisted that we all change into our bathing gear, except Cheng of course, and trot down to the beach. "Quick, quick! Before the sun goes down, and everything cools off. Wong, bring umbrella, um-*brel*-la." As he set it up, she went out into the water up to the first stripe above her knees, and bent down with a laugh to call some to her, reaching out for it as if it had been a child—a prettier one than her actual daughter, who was unfortunately turning out to be quite an ugly little fool.

After she and the sea had played awhile, she came back to drop onto the towel next to me, her blond head burnished by the sun and the tracery of punctures on her arms and legs looking like violet, delicate Rorschach blots. Naturally, I was used to those, having them myself. But as she turned to smile at me, a vein in her throat stood out more prominently than I had ever noticed it doing.

I started to watch Cheng, who, dutiless for the moment, had gone marching down the beach in his gray uniform and visored cap, his hands clasped behind his back and an interested expression on his neck. Seagulls flew around him, making noises. Behind him, the little waves scooted forward and washed away the indentations of the hobnailed footprints of his jackboots, a process I suddenly found fascinating.

"I always *knew* he was a spy—and look, the ocean's on his side," I said. "It's making sure no one will know he's been here."

"Tide's coming in." Daisy raised her voice. "Sweetheart, no! That's not your pail, nor SooSoo's either. No, I don't know whose it is, but I'm sure they'll come back for it soon, and then how will you look? Come back to Mummy now, we're going in the house."

Dinner, which involved a boisterous reunion with some of our bohemians at a sandy restaurant where crackling plates of strange, good things from the sea kept being passed behind and above all our heads, was more relaxing. One of the poets even made Daisy's daughter laugh, a phenomenon whose unfamiliarity the little girl signaled by catching up her small fat fists to her mouth as she did so. But as we strolled back to the cottage and Daisy slipped a shy, dry hand in mine as the dreadful dog yapped, my heart sank so fast that I could practically hear the cries of the drowning. Aside from the spot that we had fixed up for her daughter, or possibly SooSoo, on an ottoman in the front room, I had already observed that there was only one bed in the house.

I had rather hoped that we could sail away first, as I knew that afterward no great exertion would be possible, or seem all that inviting—to her, I mean. But Daisy gave a smile and said something about not wanting her recollections blurred, almost as if she already knew that the memory of it would be something she'd need to cling to.

As she attended to her child, I crept between rough cotton sheets, willing myself furiously to fall asleep on the instant. Of course, that was no great way to accomplish it, and soon I heard the door open and shut. But no one slipped into bed next to me, which was how I came to open my eyes at the moment Daisy's camisole fell to her feet. The moonlight made her skin blue, even as its softness effaced the needle marks. Then she had crouched beside me, and was tugging at my lacy nightgown. "Why do you have all this *on,* silly?" I heard her say, audibly trying to keep the fun in her voice and the urgency out of it.

That was how I finally learned what it was like to be a bad girl—to be a mad girl, between blue thighs. Then we lay with our two lanky, scrawny-breasted, period bodies fitted around each other, like two halves of the same Art Deco person. "Why, we're lovely," Daisy said, looking at us in the moonlight. Looking too, I had to admit that there was something aesthetically pleasing in our shared Juan Gris hips and two tufts. But it was like admiring a painting from a school with which one felt no real affinity. All the same, as Daisy's breathing grew even beside me, I had the strange thought, troubling because it was calming, that between two women this act was a transition from comforting, whereas when one was with a man it was a transition from suffering; that is, if one was lucky.

I also still wanted to sail away, and wondered if I could fix on my own and whether the bathroom light would wake up Daisy's little girl. But the door was a mile away, and then at the top of a tower inside which I was ever so slowly tumbling down.

By the next morning, it felt as if we had already developed a routine, which seldom varied over the next five days. We'd spend long, sun-dazed mornings on our little kitchen carpet of beach behind the cottage, in company with some of our bohemians—some of whom brought tense-faced, chunky girls with them, a rarity on Carmine Street. The conversations and flickering semi-arguments they all had with each other about painting and writing were nonetheless almost identical to the ones in Le Perroquet de Paris, as the new additions spoke little. Yet somehow it sounded different—at once less affected and more artificial, if that makes any sense—when we were all outside and in sunlight, tawny-headed and salty-lipped, as gulls cawed and one of the chunky girls, far out past the beach, determinedly inched her way along in the water below the gong-struck line that separated deeper from paler blue.

Then we'd stroll down Provincetown's main street, eating crunchy seafood wrapped in paper and peeking into moldy little shops with weathered fishing nets winding around whatever it was they sold. In the afternoons, we'd go back to our various little houses to nap, read, or play games, or else go on motor excursions—Cheng sweating in his gloves behind the wheel—to other parts of Cape Cod, which were pretty much like our bit except that the names were different and more people looked at us oddly the farther back toward the mainland we got. Once it was dark, everyone would gather for a riotous meal at the same restaurant we'd gone to the first night.

Then, night after night, I'd irritably drag my nightgown off over my head with one hand as I stomped across our tiny floor to throw myself with deliberate and punishing ungainliness on the bed. Even in the dark, I could see the hurt welling in Daisy's eyes. But she was never wounded enough to stop her caresses, her whispered requests for this and that here and there again and again, her maddening attempts to make all this a frolic by banging me on the head with a pillow or hiding my hairbrush.

On top of everything else, I had to sail away by myself a few times, clumsily fixing in the bathroom with the gold hypo whose engraved inscription I had tried several times by now to mar with my nails and teeth. Daisy sailed away often enough not to get sick, but she didn't seem that interested. "We don't really *need* it, do we?" she asked me on the beach one morning, before the first bohemians—later risers than we, to a man and chunky girl—had arrived. "With the sun on the water, and—well, each other? I mean, I know we *do*. But we can try *not* to need it, can't we?"

"Why should we?" I said. She didn't answer. After a moment, she picked up her book.

On the next-to-last night before we were supposed to go back, Daisy had arranged for something special—involving our whole crew and a movie theater, thank God, not me and some sort of there-she-blows apparatus acquired in a harpooning shop. She had rented Provincetown's tiny one and only motion-picture palace, which was another wood-frame house on Main Street like the rest except that it had a marquee instead of a fishnet or a shark's jaw over the door, and hired a projectionist to show some experimental movies from Europe that one of our bohemians was trying to convince the Metropolitan Museum in New York to run off for the public. I thought it strange that any movie should go to a museum without having, I don't know, rolled around in the world a bit first, but apparently with things experimental it was either that or permanent Coventry, since people wouldn't care unless they had been impressed *d'avance*. In Provincetown, at what I suppose would be called the premiere, we were most impressed by the fact that we could bring alcohol, since Daisy was paying for everything and there was no manager to object.

The first movie shown was so ghastly that I considered mailing the Metropolitan a private note hinting that the time had come to write off this medium as an art form. It was almost as if whoever had been entrusted with the camera had deliberately photographed the most revolting images he could imagine while rejecting all the beautiful ones, which I know sounds preposterous but does convey the general effect of watching ants crawl out of people's palms and dead mules lie atop pianos for twenty utterly repulsive minutes. Early on, when a woman's eye was slashed with a razor, Daisy's daughter screamed and buried her head in her mother's shoulder, and I felt caught between horror and envy myself. As the lights came up, I heard Daisy murmur a reproach to the bohemian who had arranged it all. "I didn't know," he muttered back.

"You hadn't *watched* it?" Daisy hissed.

"I didn't know your *daughter* was here. I didn't know she was in Provincetown. I didn't know you had a daughter. I thought she was your son. I've been drunk since Tuesday, for Christ's sake, and I'm not sure who you are either. Other than that, what did you think? I just hope the dame who shelled out for this wing-ding isn't going to be a ninny about it. But not much chance of that with these know-nothing, do-nothing rich twerps, I suppose."

I didn't catch her answer. But as for me, it had just crossed my mind that I had never really liked *any* of the art that knowing Daisy had subjected me to. Still, I couldn't have left without causing a stir. As we had a few minutes with the lights up while the projectionist got the next movie ready, I started to read the program notes for it to find out what I ought to be bracing myself for.

Das Herz von Avis

(The Heart of Avis)

ein Film von G. W. Langmur

Critical Remarks: This adaptation of Mack Schlechtkunst's famous fairy tale for adolescent lads employs very resource of the cinema. **Plot Synopsis:** Avis, the Boy-Prince of ancient Vommangia-zur-Alp, has been raised to reverence his prodigious father King Wuntag, whose throne he is intent to follow with his father's footsteps one day. One day, a passing crone indicates to Avis that his bride must be the Apline maiden Siegheidi, who is seen nearby milking and gives testimonials she is undefiled. Having been foretold long ago that he would be told this, Avis knows it to be truthful, and he and Siegheidi mount the Alp to sing of their engagement and impending demise. [**Note:** *Sheet music for organist attached.*]

Now we are returned to King Wuntag's court down below, where in his absence the vengeful sorcerer Mahlhaus has cast a spell on his clothing. Donning them on his return from war, Wuntag discovers he is evil. He struggles to doff the clothings but they are too strong even for Wuntag. Strangling his throat and running himself through with his sword Dolwahl, he is hurleed by his own feet into a nearby pit of fire.

When back to the top of the Alp we go, Avis and Siegheidi are ending their song of loving. As they return down, the warlock Frack-Frack espies them in the forest he is disguised as. Exposing himself, he casts a spell on Siegheidi that turns her into a statue. Continuing on, Avis reaches the castle, where he is told of Wuntag's turn to evil and subsequent death. He tries to lift Dolwahl but the great sword melts in front of the eyes of everybody. Going in search of the forest he remembers, he sees that Frack-Frack has defiled perhaps multiple times the statue of Siegheidi, which indicates by means of crumbling that it has been thinking of Avis the whole time. The ingenious warlock meanwhile turns into a noxious vapor and escapes while Avis is having illness.

Realizing that his weakness makes him unfit to rule, yet resolved to do his duty by his people, Avis re-mounts the Alp. There in one manly gesture he tears his heart from his chest and offers it to the sky. As birds begin to eat his heart, Avis expires. In an epilogue, we are shown that eating The Heart of Avis has given the birds strength, and they are reborn as a noble race of wingéd men.

■

To be honest, the epilogue *was* a bit funny, with nature photography of some distinctly noncommittal-looking seagulls on a rock dissolving into a view of a similar number of men striding around bare-chested in front of a black curtain in strapped-on papier-mâché wings, and trying hard to look like a noble race of wingéd men without getting unduly puffed up about it, as that wouldn't be noble. The lack of wingéd women also did leave one rather suspecting that, noble or not, this race was unwittingly doomed to the briefest of evolutionary trajectories. And the Heart of Avis itself, at which even Daisy coughed very suddenly, did look rather more like a bladder.

But even though some people snickered toward the end, overall *Das Herz von Avis* had been a smashing success in Provincetown, certainly compared to its awful predecessor. Whatever you thought of the story—which proved awfully hard to follow for those who hadn't troubled to read the program notes, especially after the organist, already somewhat off her feed after the razor sliced through the eyeball, accidentally played part of "My Country 'Tis of Thee" during Avis and Siegheidi's love song—the film was tremendously well done, with lots of gloom and mountains and warlocks leaping out from behind chunks of scenery. I had enjoyed it, but on our walk home, Daisy seemed preoccupied.

Her daughter was trotting along between us, gamely enough but looking as if it would be a very long time before she gambled on seeing a film again. The silence was making me uncomfortable, since around Daisy I wasn't used to it. "I thought the girl who played Siegheidi was awfully good," I volunteered.

Glancing up and smiling a tad too quickly, Daisy tapped me with her handbag. "Lech," she said. That made me sulky, because of course I hadn't meant anything of the kind. I just thought that the actress had done marvelously well at looking like a statue while Frack-Frack was defiling her; even her eyes hadn't moved. To see how long this could be done in reality, I began to stare at my nose as I walked. But soon I stumbled over Daisy's nightmarish little dog, who had just come running up from the surf, wondering as usual why the bone that it had found there had disappeared in its mouth. To get another, it ran back down to the waterline, barking squeaky little attacking barks.

When we got back to the cottage, I went into the bathroom. After only a few days, I noticed, I was getting much more nimble with the hypo when I had to inject myself. I forgot to shut off the electric light before I opened the door, and the silvered whites of Daisy's daughter's eyes looked back at me from her little bed in the darkened front room before I groped behind myself and found the switch.

In our room, Daisy was lying on our bed, looking at the ceiling. Even though the overhead light was on and she was fully dressed, I automatically started to pull my nightgown off over my head.

"You needn't bother." In those words, I heard how much my grudging ways at night had made her suffer, for all that she did what she wanted anyway, and I was glad that the nightgown covering my face had prevented me from seeing hers as she said it. By the time I poked my head back out of the collar, she had composed herself, if indeed she had been visibly discomposed at any point.

"I'm thinking of starting a little project, just for me," she said.

"If it's not for *me*, I don't care," I yawned. "What is it?"

"I'm thinking I might write a book."

"I've sailed away," I said. "I couldn't even read one."

"I don't mean tonight"—she smiled in bright desperation, realizing she couldn't afford to pass up a single chance to pretend we were amusing to each other—"silly. But I *should* write a book."

"What for?" I asked, sitting down on the bed and feeling the marvelous, euphoric morphine lassitude start to creep outward from my bones, which in defiance of physiology was where it always began.

"Because it's a book nobody's ever written," she said, sitting up as I lay down. In the bright light, which I wasn't accustomed to in this room at this hour, her eyes looked almost green. "About a *man*—a man that everybody thinks is wonderful, because his dreams soar so high and he's so full of ardor and he loves his idea of you so much more than the reality of you, which nobody else thinks deserves love anyway. And how nobody understands that this man is a tyrant and a dictator who carries your head around on a stick even though he calls it his banner, because he's in love with himself but he can never admit that, and so he makes you his idol and loves himself, adores himself, *worships* himself for having one."

One what? I wondered vaguely, as the lassitude reached my brain. But Daisy hadn't stopped talking:

"And all *you* ever wanted was a little bit of room where you could live as you pleased in your own mind, and you've gotten it by marrying someone who's too stupid and pigheaded to even know what you're talking about most of the time, but won't beat you or let you starve. But then the dreamer turns up one morning and knocks all that away—with never a by-your-leave, of course, because how could your opinion of the situation *possibly* compare to his, when he's been thinking of nothing else while you've been doing silly, shallow things like have children. He pushes you down and puts the pillow of his love over your face, right over your nose and mouth, telling you how pretty they are the whole time and how divine you look with a pillow on your face, and as you start to have a hard time breathing you hear him say, 'This is better than anything you could have possibly thought you wanted! This is *love,* my love! My *darling!*'"

I hated it when she called me that, I thought sleepily. But her voice hadn't stopped. In fact, it grew shriller:

"You try to push him away, but you're starting to suffocate and little lights are flashing in your head, and then you hear other voices, a crowd, you hear the whole *planet* all cooing at once, 'Isn't that beautiful! Isn't he wonderful! How shallow she is! How *self-centered* she is! Oh, look at how *he's* suffering! How little she deserves such great love! Oh, Daisy, it's so beautiful, what he's doing to you right now! Daisy, Daisy, look at the green light!' *I CAN'T LOOK AT THE GREEN LIGHT! I CAN'T SEE ANYTHING! I CAN'T BREATHE! CAN'T YOU SEE HE HAS A PILLOW OVER MY FACE! HE'S TRYING TO SMOTHER ME, FOR GOD'S SAKE!* And with your last . . . *ounce* . . . of strength, you push him off—and slowly you sit up, gasping for air—simple, precious air. And you think, my God—my *God*—*why*—did all those people— want me to—*die* . . ."

The sobs that were wracking Daisy's slender frame by then were the end of the only time she ever told me about what had happened between herself and Gatsby. And there I was so morphy-brained and noddy that I barely took in a word. If she tried to go on, and for all I know she may have, the only thing that answered her was a snore.

I awakened with a muddled recollection that she had told me something important the night before; something that should make me watch out. Mildly surprised that I had my nightgown on, I yawned my way into the front room. Daisy was sitting at the card table there, writing. Her pen stopped scratching as she heard me, and she looked up with a tranquil smile.

"Just making a few notes, dear," she said. "For my 'little project.' You know, I think I might really try it—why not? Did you sleep well?"

But something was missing, or possibly two things. As I tried to recall what they might be, through the back window I saw her daughter playing with SooSoo on the beach, apparently unattended. I looked back at Daisy, who read my mind:

"It's all right," she said. "Wong's watching them, but you can't see him. He's on the roof."

"Wong? Oh, Cheng," I said.

Daisy put down her pen. "You know, darling, I do think that joke has worn a bit thin. After all, it's not really true that 'they all look alike.'"

"Didn't say he all looks alike," I grumbled, scratching my derriere.

"Said he's Cheng. And what do you know: Cheng looks like Cheng. Ripso facto."

"Do you want a bath? I'll run the water."

"No. I want today to be tomorrow. I want to be back in New York."

"I don't want to go back to New York," Daisy said.

I shrugged. "Then so be it. You'll probably have to set the roof on fire to keep warm here in January. But I'm sure that Madame Bohemia's Provincetown Academy for Unmarried Chunkygirls will give your daughter an education that SooSoo will never forget, unless you've had to put SooSoo up on the flaming roof to roast her for food by then, of course."

Daisy's face was suspended between mild amusement at my absurdity and less mild alarm that I was talking about her living somewhere I wasn't. After a second, she gave a light-hearted laugh, and said, "No, silly. I don't want us to stay in Provincetown either. I want to go to Paris."

"What's in Paris? And don't say Parisians."

"No. Americans. Americans and other people who get to live in whatever way makes them happy, without worrying about what other people think. And they write and paint, instead of talking about writing and drinking about painting the way Carmine Street does. There's a woman named Djuna Barnes who lives on the Rue Jacob, and— and I want her life," Daisy said. "Or a little bit of one that's like it, anyway. Paris must be big enough for two of us to have it."

"Can you fix there?" I said.

Daisy's lip trembled for a second. "You could," she said quietly. "If you still wanted to."

"I can do that here."

"It doesn't have to be Paris, darling! I just want the two of us to be away somewhere, away from—things we've been. We'll even leave SooSoo behind," she smiled, making it clear to me that my powers of concealment had not been what I thought they were. "We could go to California."

"I despise California," I said sullenly.

"You've never been there, darling."

"I've seen pictures." One, anyway, I thought.

"It doesn't matter! Choose a place. Choose anywhere you like! Do anything you like, and I'll be happy, so long as you're with me. Why," Daisy giggled, her voice growing more and more desperate, "we could sneak down to Provincetown harbor tonight—and steal one of the fishing boats, what would you say to that? Yes, that's what we'll do! Freedom at last! We'll set out to sea, and—throw all the morphine and the hypos and even SooSoo overboard, if you like—and sail away . . . Sail away . . . Oh, don't you see, darling, we could just sail away—"

With unexpected strength, Daisy was clutching my wrist—and for all ten seconds of the most desperate moment of my life, I did not know which of my parents' faces I was looking into.

Behind her, the daughter stood in the door, SooSoo in her arms. I had no idea how long she—they—had been there.

"Let me O-GAY!" I screamed at Daisy, wrenching my arm free. Whirling on my heel, I marched into our room, slamming the door behind me. Pulling my nightgown off over my head with one hand, I chucked it into a corner. I got dressed with reckless haste, not even noticing until I was hooking the final button that my garters didn't match my hose. Well, no one was going to see that anyway. I put on the first dress I found—one of mine, one of Daisy's, nothing mattered now—flung my shoes here and there till I found two that matched, and checked my purse to make sure I had money.

When I stepped back out into the front room, Daisy was sitting on the ottoman, her daughter's head in her lap. As she stroked the little girl's hair, she was crying quietly. She didn't look up, and neither of us said a word.

Outside, I looked up at the roof, shielding my eyes from the white sun. "Cheng!" I called.

He scrambled to his feet—no small trick in jackboots, on shingles that steeply sloped. "Wong," he said.

"Come off the roof. You're taking me to New York. Now."

He jerked his head at the water. "Watch beach," he said. "Watch girl. No drown."

"Girl inside now. Also dog. Chop chop."

"Might come back," he said. "Early yet."

"You don't work for girl," I said. "Chop chop."

"Work for mother."

"Not anymore you don't, chum," I said, holding up a fat wad of green bills in the bright, hot morning.

After a moment, he skidded down to the roof's edge, and jumped off into the sand. Because of the dunes, it was only about five or six feet; he couldn't possibly have hurt himself, no matter how clumsy his jump was.

"Luggage?" he said.

I had forgotten. Some of my best dresses were back there. And my gold hypo in its case.

"Never mind," I said. "They'll probably need to burn it all to keep warm here, come January."

He looked at me uncomprehendingly. "No ruggage," I said. "We go."

He opened the back door for me. Then he got in behind the steering wheel, and started the Daimler's engine.

As we drove off, I thought I heard squeaky barking. But SooSoo must have stopped chasing us by the time we got to the main road, because then I didn't hear her anymore.

On an impulse, I reached forward and flicked my finger against the back of Cheng's cap. "Cheng," I said.

He didn't contradict me.

Then I giggled, and started singing as I settled back in the seat. "*Wong, Cheng, Wong,* Cheng," I sang—"*give me your answer, do . . .*"

I saw his eyes flick toward me in the mirror. Then they flicked away again, as precisely as a metronome; and suddenly, everything was back the way it always should have been.

■

Daisy died a few years later in Brussels, I don't really remember how. By then, she'd lost all the Buchanan money in the Crash, and had married a Belgian supplier of windsocks and other safety equipment to small airports in out-of-the-way places, of all the odd careers. She never wrote a book. Of course, her daughter, Pamela Buchanan, became a writer, and I suppose that's as good a way as any to fritter away your life when you're too homely to catch a man. But I don't even know where Daisy's buried—or if, somehow, she did contrive to have her ashes secretly scattered off the railing around the Statue of Liberty's torch, as she once whimsically told me she had decided would be best.

In our day—mine, rather—people used to be able to get up there, you know. Into the torch. However, if I had thought my troubles were over, I was wrong, for it turned out that I had a burial of my own to see to, once the Daimler glided to a halt in front of the Gramercy Park brownstone and Lil Gagni opened the door to me. Over the years, I had promoted her to housekeeper after the other servants drifted off, but she still had the same cretinous, blubbery look as ever. Then I saw she'd actually been crying.

"Oh, for God's sake, what is it?" I said. "Did you lose the pantry keys *again?*"

"Oh, Miss, Miss—your mother passed away this morning, Miss."

I stared at her.

"Where is she?" I demanded as I charged into the entrance hall, where for the first time in years I fancied I detected a faint smell of cigar smoke.

"Already at the mortician's, Miss."

Three steps up the stairs, hand on the banister, I turned to glare at her. "Without my *permission?*" I asked icily. Then a thought that for some reason I found truly horrific struck me: "*Did you call my father?*" I demanded.

"Today is Friday, Miss. Under the circumstances, I thought it would be better not to wait until the weekend—it's so much harder to arrange things then," she said, and started to blubber again. "We weren't sure when you'd return, Miss," she said, sniffling but now under control.

I hurried up the remaining steps and on into Mother's drawing room. Her empty wheelchair was parked behind the escritoire, from which I had so often seen her look up from her writing to greet me as I came in for my daily visit. On the escritoire was a thick stack of paper, neatly squared off and with no loose pages lying around, as there had always been before. She had waited to go until she was sure she was done, I thought; it irritated me, since I was never sure of such things. I looked down at the top page, and read this:

FOR OUR DAUGHTERS' FREEDOM
The Story of Occoquan

I started to push the stack apart, looking at a page here, a page there. But there were hundreds of them in the stack, and it wasn't getting any smaller, no matter how messy I was making it. Oh, it just went on and on—wads and wads of first-person reminiscences by Alice Paul, and Lucy Burns, and dozens and dozens of other suffragettes about all the good things that they'd done and all the bad things that had happened to them for it until they won the vote, all organized and collated into a single narrative in my mother's elegant, old-fashioned handwriting. She'd used violet ink to write it with, and—and no sane person would ever get to the end of all those pages, no matter how hard he tried.

Impulsively, I gathered the stack up, and practically danced to the window, whose sash I virtually hurled upward. "The *pigeons* want to vote!" I shouted into the street, as I threw wad after wad of the manuscript out the window, where it swirled and danced away, one page getting speared on the hood ornament of a passing Rolls-Royce. "The *cars* are political prisoners!" I shouted, giggling madly. "The *trees* are on a hunger strike!"

As I threw the last wad out, I heard a horrified gasp behind me. It was Lil Gagni. She was holding something clutched so tightly against her body that at first I thought it was a child. But then I recognized what it was—none too surprisingly, since it had once given me nightmares for a week. The cloth had faded to a pale blue-gray, but the stains, though faint, were still visible.

"I thought my father gave you orders to burn that years ago," I snapped.

"So he did, Miss." But then all the "Miss" went out of her voice and face. "I wouldn't have burned it for a million *dollars!*" she screamed at me, her eyes bulging and terrible. "*I wouldn't burn it in a million years!*"

"I believe that you've just given notice," I said, as crisply as I could. "And right now will be adequate."

"So I have. So it will." She backed out, still clutching the prison shift as if she feared I'd take it from her—as indeed I should have, as it was family property and burning it before her eyes would have taught her a good lesson about respecting Father's wishes. But I let her go, thinking that giving it to a maid was really the next thing to burning it, anyway.

Lil Gagni's footsteps went away, thump-thump. A breeze blew through the open window. It sank in that I was alone, which seemed preposterous. I never had been in my life, you see.

I went downstairs to the telephone table, and gave the switchboard operator the number I wanted. A couple of visiting cards lay on the salver next to the telephone, and I picked them up, startled to re-read two names that I'd glimpsed mere minutes earlier in the stack of paper on the escritoire. Louise Merskine and Christina Caldwell, two tiresome old biddies who'd been in jail with my mother, had already come to pay their condolences; one had written that she'd been here earlier, and the other that she'd be back soon.

Irritated both at the cards' existence and by how long it was taking for my call to go through, I tore them both up. Then I started to idly rearrange the fragments until one configuration stopped me, because it seemed to make a sort of nonsensical, mysterious sense, and for the life of me I couldn't understand why. Here's what I read:

TINA   ERSKINE

LOUISE   CALDWELL
            Will Be Here Soon

Annoyed, I dashed the salver to the floor, where it stopped clattering just as my connection went through. The conversation was a brief one. Of course Thurston would be delighted to see me, for any reason or none at all. Hadn't he always been?

I stepped outside, where I was nonplussed to see no Daimler. Then I remembered that I didn't own it, and Cheng—if it was Cheng—wasn't my chauffeur. Luckily, I soon found a taxi, which pulled up mere minutes later outside Thurston's dismal Fifth Avenue house. For a moment, I looked up at it, wondering what it was going to be like to spend the rest of my life there. But if I did this today, I knew he'd take care of all the funeral arrangements, so I rang the bell.

The butler showed me up to the library. Thurston was at the window, peering at birds, or something, through an ugly old telescope. (I would spend years trying to get him to discard it; it finally got "lost" one day.) Straightening up, he rushed forward to greet me with the same silly, euphoric look on his face that had been forcing me to fight back laughter since we were both in dancing school, both hands extended to take mine. But the first words out of his mouth were pure gibberish:

"It's because she was in a movie called *God's Little Acre,* you see," he said effusively. "Played some sort of white-trash temptress, I believe, although I've never actually seen it. Can't have, obviously, since the picture won't come out for another thirty years or so."

"Thurston, I can't make head or tail of what you're saying—particularly tail. What on earth are you talking about?"

He looked baffled. "I have no idea. My mind must have been elsewhere—and no surprise in that announcement, I must say! But it seems to be finding its way back to the old noggin. Yes—let's slay the fatted calf, by gosh. My dear, how can I oblige you?"

"Thurston, I'm going to marry you," I said, and mercifully—or otherwise—allowed him a few seconds of dazed bliss before proceeding to the second half of what I had to say. "But you had better know that I don't feel the least bit lovey-dovey about it."

"More of a business arrangement, then—emphasis on the 'contract' in the marriage contract," he said. Gallantly, he was trying to uncork champagne with his voice: "Well, my kind has always been on safer ground there, God knows. And now—now *you'll* be too, my dear."

That's why, whenever he calls me "Lovey" in that silly and adoring way, it makes me sad. But I don't know for who, or is it whom?

V

Hello Nurse

EVERY HE-MAN AND HIS YES-MAN IN HOLLYWOOD ALWAYS WANTED to get his hands on my upside-down heart. That's how I think of my sequined caboose, since the words convey its hymnable wobble to altogether wooziality-making perfection. When I twitched Old Smokey into Los Angeles, there was no visible wear on it, even though I'd hauled it all the way from Alabam'-don't-give-a-damn.

I came from a long line of slatternly women, but none of them had ever had anything to show for it. That's why Momma understood when I told her I was headed for California. She had tears in her eyes the day I left my childhood home of Jolene, AL (d-g-a-d). Twarn't just because this was the very first time she'd seen a daughter of hers wearing shoes, either, though that helped.

I was in the beautimous April of my years. Some blood relatives of ours were putting up a ruined shack in the distance. Only the lonely sun stood changeless and immortal in the placid sky above Jolene. Poppa, bless him whoever he was, was dead. My one souvenir of him was a rusty old church-key can-and-bottle opener that Momma claimed he'd left behind on his last visit, which she had just placed on a ribbon around my neck.

"Now, lissen, hun," she said. "Ah know you're a-gowe be in sum taht spots, an' hafta make some mahty hard cawls, along thet long an' wairy road to Awscar naht. But jiss whatevuh yew do, jiss don' sleep with no coon. *Chosen* peepul, Ah'll un'stann', Ah know how mewvies gits made, but yew promse me on the other'n. Lots folks out there thank an'thang kin happen, on account of they got enuff money to mayke iyt so. Well, yew better see iyt don't."

"Yes, Momma," I said, all a-tingle in my new high heels.

"Yew promse me, gal. Not wun. Not e'en thet Sayid-nee Pwa-chay ner 'at Harry Bilawfawnt, fer all I wun't blame yew fer wundrin' hew put the Mahntin Drew in yore undies if eiver of eym strawng brown gawds was ta ast yew in a p'laht way fer a paice of iyt at sum faincy porty in Malibew. But if'n yew's mah dawter, yew's steyl a-gonter draw yissef up t'cher full haaht n' say Much 'bliged but Naw Thanks Mist'

Pwa-chay raaht afore yew *flang* yore glass a' ixpensive waahn in hyez hansum black fayce, kaze we ain' neve' dun thet yit. Thass whah we Gumstump wimmen awways held our haids up haah, e'en when the nabors was runnin' us outta tahns they built jiss fo' thet purpose an' throwin' daid cats an' the cawnints a' whole truck gawdins at our hyp-nawtically resaydin' ruhmps. Even yore sister Sew-zannah wun't dew thet, an' yew gnaw whut *shey's* laahk. So yew promse. Iss mah daahn' request."

"Are you dyin', Momma?" I asked.

"Naw. But Ah will be sumtahm, prolly a' pure happiness when yew nab thet Awscar 'n show that kaahk Ellezbeth Taylor where she'n git off the bus. An' Ah ain' never ast yew fer an'thang before."

"You borried my one and only dress off'a me when I was in seventh grade," I said, wanting to keep the record straight.

"Din' fit. Don' count. Mah bewbs warn't big enuff. Yew got iyt back. Ain'chew wearin' iyt nah? Nah, skewt! 'Fore Ah hev ta fahr ol' Uncle Hewzit's shawtgun achore new shoes t'gitchew mewvin'.'"

"Yes, Momma," I said, and scooted. She was a crazy, bigoted old cretin who'd have sold me for a baloney sandwich, but I loved her. Leastways I missed her once the Greyhound had deposited my upside-down heart and right-side-up cardboard suitcase in Los Angeles, Califor-nia, where the road to Oscar night was to prove longer and wearier than Momma ever could have guessed as I waved my final farewell and our last surviving squirrel ran inside between her planted feet in Jolene, Alabam'-don't-give-a-damn.

But I didn't know that yet. Vowing to make Great-Grandma Jolene herself, after whom our town was named, proud of her progeny in this new land, I walked past the bus driver, a fat dyspeptic who had started gnawing his hat like a cheeseburger as I went by, and on out of the Grey-hound depot. "Hello there!" I hollered at the first Californian I saw. "Which way to Twentieth Century-Fox?"

"Oh, that's easy. Twuh, twuh, twuh," he started saying, staring at the home team coming off the bench for the victory celebration like he was the Apostle Paul struck blind on the road to Damascus. I think he had switched over to "Fuh, fuh, fuh," without a great deal more success, before I decided I'd do better trying to locate Mr. Darryl F. Zanuck's incomparable magic manufactory on my own.

As I strolled along, the string around my suitcase creaking bouncily in time to my steps—it had been Momma's very last piece, too—I got my first impression of Los Angeles, which was amazement at how few people here had learned to drive properly. Left and right and front and back of me, cars kept smashing into each other and fire hydrants and plowing into storefronts amid showers of glass, which sparkled like the very dreams I had heard the streets here were paved with. Off in the distance, even the owl eyes in the final syllable of the Hollywood sign seemed to be popping at all the June havoc here below. But then, catching sight of my reflection in a conveniently placed and as yet unbroken plate-glass window, I gathered that some clue to the commotion might lurk in my own not unstartlesome appearance, since at the moment I was verging on nine feet tall and, albeit only partially as a result, wearing a dress that a hamster couldn't have used for a hankie.

Not that I wasn't otherwise striking, even by Alabam'-don't-give-a-damn's high standards. If amber and rubies could burn, my hair would have been eternal fire. My bazooms were like a dual edition of the *Hindenburg*, with two cherry lollipops with red Jujubes stuck on them in charge of the navigating. My hips could have started the Timex folks weeping. In a bon-voyage view, my upside-down heart would have made King Kong jump off the Empire State Building, tossing poor Fay Wray like a candy wrapper, to follow me wherever I was headed, meanwhile obliging Lady Liberty to cast aside the torch that she secretly carries for him and dive into the bay in shame and self-abnegation. In fact, from my oncoming lollipops to my caboosial fare-thee-well on a good day, which they all were in my beautimous youth, I could have raised our sacred Confederate dead dicks first, turned that statue of the Thinker into something you'd use for doughnut-tossing practice, and given Our Lord Jesus Christ a king-of-kings-sized woody on the cross, its wrathful shadow forcing the centurions to back away in fear and awe and go nail up some other Canaanite instead.

As for whoever's making all this up about me, well—you go on and enjoy yourself, just like Jesus and our sacred Confederate dead. Have a good old time. Sure would appreciate if you restored me to my natural five eight, though, and not just because I don't want the model airplane I saw at rest on your closet shelf beside the jigsaw puzzle of the fifty states you hide me under, in forlorn memento mori Amsterdam of a previous kind of dreaming, to get itself tangled in the eternal fire of my hair. Before we're done, I've got to get through the door of none other than Mr. Frank Sinatra's home in Palm Springs, California Desert, U.S.A., and would prefer not to have to stoop upon entering his foyer like some hulking freak in a disingenuously compassionate Diane Arbus snapshot.

For *me*?

Thank you.

Believe me, Sprout, I'm used to this. The others aren't, which is why they never spotted you—although Lovey did come closer than she knew one time. Anyway, it don't bother me none, as we used to say in Jolene. For all I know, I'm dead by now, in which case I'm flattered by the spasmoosive immortality you bestow and ask you to imagine my two-dimensional ghost turning to make a small ectomorphic curtsy from the screen. Oh, no—I'm in a magazine this time, aren't I? Drat Gagilnil's old photographs! Not to be crass, Sprout, but I sure hope you've got some Kleenex handy. Don't make your momma wash those Elmer-ized sheets on top of everything else, she probably has to work real hard to keep things going and you know she's been feeling pretty low herself since your daddy passed away, which is why you should try to remember that she didn't know you were there. To tell the truth, he sounds to me like ninety-nine-point-eight percent pure son of a bitch in an cast-iron T-shirt, but never really having had one to call my own does put me at some disadvantage in determining where that puts him on the Dad-and-Husband-O-Meter.

But to resume. Charging out to find Darryl Zanuck, whose name I agree is intrinsically funny for reasons no one has ever been able to explain, I was beguiled by an index card tacked up in the lobby of the

Poil du Chien Arms, the hotel in which I had parked suitcase and caboose at the corner of Yucca Street and Cahuenga Boulevard. That was just two blocks from Hollywood and be-still-my-soul Vine, so I was sure I must be right near several major studios and producers' personal mansions. To my easily widened Alabam'-don't-give-a-damn eyes, the Poil was a pure humdinger of an establishment, featuring carpeting and doors that had real knobs instead of latches. The divine Carole Lombard had probably been here before me, though not for long. This index card looked classy, too: MODELS NEEDED $5 PER PRINTED POSE NO ANIMALS, it said, in what I soon learned was pen, not pencil.

Five dollars! Although Momma had disputed this so violently that bits of gummed corn flew from all three of her teeth as she did so, I had heard from a perambulatory sewing-machine agent name of Ratliff that the U.S. government actually did engrave and print a bill in that debominination. The prospect of laying eyes on one of these rarities, and thereby proving to myself that there was indeed a Santy Claus, sped my heels through a milk bath of Hollywood sunshine to the address on the card. This proved to be on a nearby street in a building whose rooftop sign declared that it was always time for some more Maxwell House, leading me to gather that they planned to erect an annex to it in the near future.

When my proud but breathless bazooms led their owner's way into the room marked *Gagilnil Art Photos and Fine Reproductions*, one of Momma's *Chosen* people, or so I strongly suspected, and from chin's droop to paunch's billow a mighty sorry physical specimen to boot, was maneuvering a box camera on a tripod in front of a painted ocean sky, before which stood a depressed-looking sofa and a plastic palm tree with one frond. "Well, here I am!" I told his plump, damp back. "And I didn't bring so much as a *parakeet* with me, fond as I am of the lil' devils."

With a groan of despair, Mr. Gagilnil—for I assumed that this could only be he—bashed at the snout of his camera, which folded back into the box part in hurt and surprise. Hands to hips that had loved potato chips not wisely but too well, knew Ruffles not only had ridges but gave them, and had long lost the bet about eating just one, he stared at the contraption, fuming. I had a distinct impression of having stepped off with the wrong bazoom, so to speak.

"Did I say the wrong thing a minute ago?" I asked.

"No, it's all right. When the sign's on the roof, I can't see it; that's why I moved in here. What do I call you, Miss?"

I told him, but when I got to "Gumst-," he stopped me. "Am I the telephone directory?" he said. "Just a first name'll do fine—or should I say a Christian one, as I eye you from beneath my beetling brows and my head swims at the doxy-from-Dixie boy-oh-goyishness of it all?"

"Golly," I said. "Are you really a Jew?"

"Golly, are you anti–Semitic?"

"Golly! So you *are* a Jew," I said, clapping my hands.

"Gumdrops! So you *are* anti-Semitic," he said, trying to clap his. He missed. I couldn't wait to see what kind of pictures he took.

"Not so far as I know," I explained, "although as it happens a lot of my mature attitude on the subject rests in your furry butterfingers, Mr. Gagilnil, since I've never actually *seen* one of you before—except for that fella who does all the double-talk on *Your Show of Shows,* and in Westerns playing unexpectedly large-nosed and thoughtful Apaches and such."

"A tribe's a tribe, lady. A genocide's a genocide. From Buchenwald to Plymouth Rock, it's all in a day's work hereabouts, and even though I'm not a busy man I do toss my whimpering vanity the occasional moldy dog biscuit by pretending otherwise here in my lonely six-pointed wig-wam, so let's see what you keep in the ruggage rack."

"Beg pardon?"

"The skimpy but nevertheless obstructing Daisy Mae blouse, discard," he explained, all with vigorous hand motions to match. "The oversized shiksa hello-nurses, make birthday-suit ta-dah with. The seedy Yid pho-tographer on Ivar Street whose grainy, sordid, yet mysteriously wistful black-and-white nudies' very existence you will deny if all goes better for you in Tinseltown than this seasoned observer honestly expects, impress. Or not, as the case may be."

"Jesus!" I said, undoing my polka-dotted top and reaching around to unhook Mount Rushmore. "Can't you at least buy me a Baby Ruth or maybe a box of Crackerjacks first, or anyway wait to play please-don't-squeeze-the-Charmin with my Goodyears till after the newsreel if not the Woody Woodpecker cartoon?"

"Don't flatter yourself, Miss. In more ways than you know, I see a lot of boobs in my line of work, and by now they might as well be—oy, the humanity," he said softly, as the gates to the Double-D Ranch for Way-ward Boys fell open before his eyes.

When I returned to the Maxwell House the next morning for my first glamor-photography session, Mr. Gagilnil had somebody for me to meet. One high heel a-dandle on the toes of an upraised and bestockinged foot, she was reading a movie magazine on a fake tiger rug on the floor, dressed in black undergarments that seemed to wrinkle and shift awry on her as if their material was perpetually astonished to find itself in actual contact with her skin, and feared hurting it. Looking up from under heavy auburn bangs that fell almost to her eyes, she gave me a lip-sticky and lopsided smile as she jumped to her feet in welcome. She struck me as an innocent, and as I had begun to suspect that by most standards I was one myself, that she had this effect on me filled me with a trepidative apprehensileness for her sake.

"This is Bettie," Mr. Gagilnil said. "And you may yet go as far in this business as she has if you just keep an eye peeled along with everything else, because she's the best that ever was."

"Honest, Mr. Gagilnil, am I?" Bettie said, goggling and pleased.

"Try to find a shutterbug between here and Wilshire who'll contra-dict me, doll."

"Okay! Oh, gosh, I'd better get dressed first." She took a few steps toward her clothes, then turned back with a worried frown. "If I can't find one, should I come back here anyway?" she asked. "Or am I done?"

Mr. Gagilnil sighed, but it was a fond type of noise. "Tell you what, Bettie, just take my word for it," he said.

"Where?"

"See?" Mr. Gagilnil said to me. "The best since Venus went on half pay, and she doesn't even know why. If she did, she'd have that mean, squinty look the rest of them get, and then it would all go down the toilet faster than you can lay Jackie Robinson. Okay! Now: which one of you wants to get spanked, and which one wants to do the spank-ing?"

Bettie's eyes clouded over. "Gee, Mr. Gagilnil," she said falteringly, "you know I'd always rather be spanked, if that's okay. The spank-*er* always has to look like they have some kind of clue why this is happen-ing, and no matter how hard I try you just go through roll after roll and start yelling at me. Besides, I think it's mean to act like you enjoy hitting somebody, even when it's only for glamor photography."

"But it doesn't bother you when whoever spanks *you* pretends to enjoy it," Mr. Gagilnil protested. "Or does enjoy it, for that matter."

"Oh, no!" Bettie said happily. "When I'm the one getting spanked, I always feel like I deserve it, because of something bad I probably did a long time ago."

"All right, then," Mr. Gagilnil said. "It's really only a courtesy ques-tion, Bettie, in case you ever change your mind."

"How do I do that?" she asked dubiously.

Mr. Gagilnil sighed again. "Will you please put her on your lap and lift your arm like you're paddling her with zest?" he asked me. "I'd like to be done sometime before you goyim celebrate the umpteenth birth-day of that simpering little bastard we bumped off back in the Old Country, with blood on our hands but a song in our hearts—*Hatikvah*, I think. Who knew the halo-happy *fegele* had hired a PR firm? Who knew?"

Soon afterward, Bettie got evicted from her apartment on Las Palmas for non-payment of rent. She had the money, but that wasn't what her landlord wanted, and sheer stupefactionalism at Bettie's willful refusal—or so he thought—to grasp his point, much less anything more engorged and tactile, led him to toss her and her belongings onto the street. You see, Bettie didn't even have any idea that men used the pictures that Gagilnil took of us for purposes of sexual self-stimulation. She thought we were underwear, rope, and gag-ball models, and when I idly grumped something about the chuckleheads at the newsstand all playing bell-pull with ol' Scrawny as Mr. Gagilnil and I were tying her up one day, I saw her eyes get as round as saucers and trembulamaticized as Bambi's while he made frantic throat-cutting and erasive motions at me from behind her shoulder. Anyhow, it was after she lost her old place that she moved into a vacant room a floor down from mine at the good old Poil du Chien Arms.

We had a pretty good group at the Poil, although the register could boast of only one big-time Hollywood moviemaker, a natty jokefest name of Wood who made a habit of borrowing Bettie's and my clothes. When we asked why he needed them so often, he explained that he made costume pictures—thus proving he was what he said he was, as this was a term I recognized from my earliest browsings of *Modern Screen* magazine, when I was still a splindly lass with a mere 36C bustline way back in Great-Grandmaville. My next-door neighbor was a polite fellow called Homer who used to be a hotel bookkeeper somewhere in the Midwest. He had moved to California in hopes of getting work as a cartoon character, for Warner Brothers if he could swing it but on the small screen if nothing better came along. And indeed, as far as all of us who were his friends were concerned, poor Homer was already well on his way to attaining that two-dimensional status in the book Mr. Nathanael West wrote about us, which was received with injured indignation in the improvised courtrooms of the Poil. Even Bettie, who heard parts of it read aloud, waxed wroth: "Why, that man's just *scared* of people!" she blurted out, blinking rapidly and jerking her lipsticky mouth in a rare effort to shape it into something other than a friendly smile. "And he makes them all awful to prove he's right."

Beside her, Homer nodded. "You know what hurt—he didn't even feel sorry for me," he said dolefully, wringing his large hands and then automatically groaning. "I thought at least he'd feel sorry for me. But he looked down on me more than anyone out here *ever* has."

"Or would," said Wood, putting a comforting hand on his shoulder. "Or would."

Meanwhile, Bettie's and my glamor-photography sessions at the Maxwell House continued apace. On days when we were both tied up and gagged—a situation whose true peril dawned on us only when a pair of Seventh-Day Adventists came to the unlocked door of *Gagilnil Art Photos and Fine Reproductions* and launched into their spiel, waving tracts before us as Bettie and I whimpered and rolled our eyes, until our employer re-emerged at last from the commode and drove the duo off with massive swattings of a rolled-up *Racing Form*—Mr. Gagilnil used to moan with impatience at we girls' dilatoriness in popping in the gag balls and helping each other secure them with tape or knotted cloth. "Come on, come on," he'd say—"I'm getting wise to that whole 'I got a code in the node' routine. The way the two of you sniffle and mope and carry on, you'd think this was *The Magic Mountain,* for shit's precious sake."

Yet my own magic mountains never did bring out the vestigial Mallory in him, except behind the camera. As for Bettie, Mr. Gagilnil once volunteered to me that he didn't care to test his disbelief in any God by inviting the wrath that he was sure would smite him if he ever put a paw on her perky yet vulnerable flesh; simultaneously granting the paradox that she was most sacred to atheists. That was one confession he made during what proved to be our final conversation, which took place after he had asked me, with an eye to playing the lead, to cast a glance over the scenario-treatment that, just like everyone else in Hollywood, he turned out to have been writing in his spare time.

The Puerile Maid

A Gagilnil Art Photos and Fine Reproductions Production

You are a scantily dressed, impudent maid in the otherwise untroubled household of a French Army officer, Captain Dreyfus. Though innocent of any crime, he is sent one day to Devil's Island. There he dies, unrehabilitated and unmourned.

At his funeral, which is nonetheless Catholic in the final insult, you are seen making goo-goo eyes at the priest. In an arbor in the Dreyfuses' backyard, you and he are making new wine from his hairy goyische grapes when the Captain's son, Alfred Dreyfus Jr., discovers you in the act. Enraged at the insult to his dead father's memory, and long in love with you himself as who could not be, he plans a terrible revenge.

Someone watches.

While dusting a telephone, you are seized from behind and blind-folded. Unknown hands drag you to a subterranean chamber. (I've got an old Signal Corps buddy in Tarzana whose basement we can probably use for this.) As your pouting lips quiver in sudden recognition of the crime you must now expiate, more unknown hands begin to tear at your saucy maid get-up.

Someone watches.

Your t*tties burst forth, in maddening cahoots with each other as usual. G-d himself has never seen such c*sabas. Realizing what must come next, you writhe in pr*test, but to no avail. As your frilly p*nties are pulled down, the glory of your t*shy is revealed in such gigantic closeup that the microscopic, indeed invis*ble blond ha*rs that inaugurate its nev*r p*netrated cl*ft are seen rippling like a field of wheat in the w*nd.

Someone watches.

You are made to lie f*cedown on a t*ble. Yet no one f*ndles your m*rvelo*s b**bs. Everyone ign*res your sweet c*nt. If th*s were the P*ris skyline, your Chr*stian b*tt would be Notre D*me. If the men in the r**m were a c*llege f**tball te*m, they would be N*tre D*me. A m*n approaches. He rams it *p your t*nder a-hole. A w*man approaches. Strapping on a pl*stic d*ngus the s*ze of the E*ffel T*w*r, she rams it *p your t*nder a-hole. Every*ne on the pl*net, d*gs included, rams it *p your t*nd*r a-hole.

Someone watches.

For the kicker, we cut to Alfred Junior as an awful suspicion dawns. Can it be—has his revenge failed, after he went to all this trouble? Striding to the table, he tears aside the blindfold. With bitterness, he sees that he was right, because—

You l*ked it.

Someone watches.

■

"Well, what do you think?" Gagilnil asked, lighting a cigarette as I handed the treatment back. "If you ask me, this could be the beginning of a whole new ball game. Not only does it have something to say—hell, *scream*—about the human condition, it's got *mood*."

"I'm sorry, but I don't think I can do this, Mr. Gagilnil," I broke it to him. "Much as I would truly adore having my very first movie part. I mean, what would my dear Rover say, back home? Either he'd be plumb mortified for my sake, or else he'd feel left out."

"But dogs don't even *go* to the movies," he protested.

"Y'ain't never been to Jolene, Alabam'," I said with some pridaciousness; mentally adding "don't-give-a-damn."

"There can't be any *art* cinemas in Jolene," he said, with hauteur.

"No, but there are a lot of *men* in Jolene," I explained, "and they usually go to watch the smokers straight from hunting. I used to play outside the door when I was a little girl, just listening to all that whooping and barking and the occasional gunshot and wondering which of those men was my poppa."

"But this part was *written* for you," Gagilnil complained. "How am I supposed to make *The Puerile Maid* now? It'd be like *Triumph of the Will* without Nazis, or *Birth of a Nation* without the Klan. Oh, sure, I could rewrite—but it won't be the same. And this was my big chance to break out." At which point, to my astonished consternation, he *did* break out, in sobs.

Although my mind was made up like Joan Crawford's face in her later years, when her maquillage approached the hull of the *Merrimac* in resiliency, I did feel pretty bad for him. But then inspiration struck. It would involve a sacrifice, but then Gagilnil had been mighty kind to me—what with giving me my first job in this town, and all.

"You know, Mr. Gagilnil, I can't do this. But my sister probably will," I said. "And she makes *me* look like a tongue depressor with pretensions. Can I have the use of your telephone?" Barely taking in what I was saying, he waved me to it, the cigarette on his lower lip still trembling.

At the telephone, I hesitated. Suzannah lived in the Shakespearean hamlet of Alcapp, Tennessee, raising soybeans by day and hell by night. But we had not spoken in some years. In our sisterly rivalry, she and I had long been like Joan Fontaine and Olivia de Havilland, except that no one knew of us and we were trash.

I looked back at Gagilnil on the sofa. He had buried his face in his hands. Between them, his cigarette stuck out like a little tombstone on fire. Sighing, I dialed Suzannah's number.

She picked up on the seventeenth ring. "Aw—heart attack, my abundant ass," I heard her hollering. "If you can't stand the heat, get to hell outta my Dixie cups. Now grab your pants and go, and don't forget to take your sample case with you."

When she heard who this was, she snickered cattily. "You got that Awscar yet?" she asked. "I must have fell asleep for that part of the broadcast, I guess. Or maybe my flushin' toilet just drowned out your acceptance speech, Sis."

"Now don't you cry for *me,* bitch," I said. "I'm here in California with a sad Jew on my hands. Listen—" and I told her of the situation. As I recounted the plot of *The Puerile Maid,* Suzannah kept making empathetical, nostalgicky "Mmm-hmmm" noises, as one or another element of its scenario reminded her of little memories of her own life. "Well, no wonder you can't handle it," she said when I was done. "Y'always were such a mousy lil' prude, even when we were puttin' on our shows for the boys down to the swimming hole and you never *would* somersault while you was doin' the cannonball. What's the money like?"

"Green and sort of rectangular. Got pictures of dead folks on it, mostly in wigs or whiskers."

"Well, it's gotta beat getting turnips back for soybeans, that's for sure. But why're you askin' *me* for? Why ain't you talkin' to Cousin Dewey Dell or Cousin Eula over t' Mississippi? Or Cousin Red in Arno, Texas? Or Cousin Maggie the Cat, way down Delta way? Maybe she's tired a' watchin' that nothin'-but-droop-in-these-drawers husband she's got drink himself into stark *in*-sensibility . . ."

She went on until she had named all of us—all nine of Great-Grandma Jolene's great-granddaughters. In the realm of male horniness, we were what the Muses were in the realm of artistic inspiration.

I hated to say it, but I had to. "Because you're the only one of us who'd do it, that's why," I said.

Suzannah crowed in malignant triumph. "That's right! That's *damn* right and mighty white of you, sister mine, and don't you ever forget it. Y'all are such 'fraidy-cat wusses I sometimes wonder if any a' you are real Gumstumps at all. Ony thing *I* won't do is sleep with a coon, and that's just 'cause Momma made me promise. It was her dyin' request."

"Is she dying?"

"No, but she will be sometime. Probably a' pure happiness when I wind up in the sack with the next Presi-dent of the United States, she told me."

After I had given her the practical instructions for getting to Los Angeles and finding the Maxwell House, I hung up. Having stopped crying, Gagilnil was staring bleakly at the plastic palm tree in front of the ocean-sky backdrop. Sitting down next to him and patting his hand, I told him of Suzannah, at which he brightened up considerably. Then, having come to another decision while I was on the phone, I took a deep breath. "And I guess I'll be moving on now, Mr. Gagilnil," I told him. "You've been good to me, but it's time for me to go in search of Darryl Zanuck once more and get on with my career."

Apparently having had some intimation of this, he nodded. "Bettie's going to miss you," he said.

"Miss who?" I said, and we both smiled. "Anyway, I'll still be seeing her at the Poil."

I stood to go, but then hesitated. I had to ask.

"Mr. Gagilnil?"

"Yes?"

"How come, in all this time, you never once tried to lay a finger on me? Not that I'm complaining, exactly—but I am curious."

"Why did I never touch the Happy Isles, you mean?" he said, with a wistful stare at my gazongas.

"Yes. Ivar Street is a sordid milieu, and on my arrival here, a girl like I would have struck most folks in your long unpolished shoes, one of which is presently unlaced as well—made you look!—as both an easy and a, not to flatter myself unduly, tempting, well let's split the difference and just say ripe, target for sexual victimization. Are you, by any chance, a decent man?"

"Jesus *Christ,* no!" Gagilnil almost shouted, reeling as if struck. "Bite your tongue. No, no, not with your lips parted, that just drives me insane. To tell you the truth, Miss, it would have violated my aesthetic sense—in which I do take some pride, however little our work together documents it. You see, *you*—from your creamy skin to your miraculous gazongas, from your hair of eternal ruby fire to your incredible caboose—are a wonder of nature and a human Baskin-Robbins. I, on the other hand, on my best day, which believe me is on a calendar that would leave you blind and choking if you tried to blow the dust off it, would have to strive to manage a fairly miserable approximation of an absconding CPA on his first and no doubt last weekend in Vegas, since the cops would have his tuchus to the fire as soon as he tried to seduce a chambermaid by proudly wiggling a single five-dollar poker chip before her disbelieving and contemptuous eyes. The *contrast* would have been unbearable, you see."

"I've slept with ugly folks before," I said—"sometimes even with the lights on and breakfast together afterwards, and no great harm has come of it. That can't be the only reason."

"It is."

"It is not," I said, noting with some unease that I was rapidly growing taller again. As my bazooms sprang forth like bouncy twin editions of the U.S.S. *Missouri* hastening to receive the surrender of the Japanese, my upside-down heart became two globes unholdable-up by any Atlas, or indeed any human agency save my own bodaciofied, endlessly ascending legs—aw, come on, Sprout! Let me *down.*

"All right!" Gagilnil said, as I resumed normal stature. "It's *because you make me feel so fucking Jewish,* all right? In just the *worst* goddam way. When I look at you, I feel so hairy and disgusting and Jewish and disgusting and potbellied and Jewish and impotent and Jewish and disgusting that it just makes me want to *plotz* to think that I'm inside this skin, for Chrissakes. Do you have *any fucking idea* how all you long-legged, big-boobed Southern broads make the rest of us feel, here in this meshuggenah promised land we all allegedly share? It's intolerable! You shouldn't tolerate us! You should stick us in ovens today! Go on!

Go on! I fucking dare you! Have the fucking courage of the fucking principles of your fucking tits! Act on what your ass is telling the world! Gas me with your farts! Burn me with your hair! Shovel me into the mass grave of your snatch! Mix my bones up with my grandfather's, as you grind them into pumice! What the fuck do you care! *You're all getting laid!*"

He took a breath.

"Don't you understand," he said, "that every time I stare at your jugs, I wonder if Hitler knew something I didn't? All in all, it's been enough to drive any reasonably intelligent man berserk."

■

I left him there—and maybe you should too, Sprout. You worry me. For one thing, far from being a middle-aged, broken-down nudie photographer, you aren't (*or weren't,* she breathes, in a sudden flash of intuition) hardly a day over sixteen, unless my formerly superb instincts have deserted me for good. And if you've ever so much as met anyone of the Hebraic persuasion, as Momma used to put it when minding her manners in front of them, I for one will be startled right out of my pink panties, not to give you more ideas than you know what to do with. I don't know why in soybeans or hell you're so down in the dumps, but you ought to try not to make the expression of it as unhealthy and woebegone-with-the-wind as the original feeling is.

There, that's better.

To resume. Exiting the Maxwell House, I stepped into the white skull and blue Jell-O of a Los Angeles high noon. It was a typical day on Ivar Street: the remaining letters on the marquee of the shuttered nightclub across the way, closed for many a moon since a freakish bolt of lighting crashed its skylight in, still advertised the triumphant re-urn of *USA AL XANDER K NE.* Plump Judy Maine, our local crazy lady—things hadn't gone that well for her, so my now former employer had told me, since the day her husband walked into the sea—came lurching along the sidewalk, still looking for her lost dog. Sauntering toward me from the bogus Riviera of his apartment building up the street was Gagilnil's debonair neighbor Joe Gillis, a scriptwriter whose smile's weak charm belied his experience as a veteran of both German and Japanese prison camps in the war. Thinking I might hitch a ride with him to Culver City or at least Schwab's, I hoisted my barely clad bazooms like the Jolly Roger; but the two-faced grin he gave them in reply froze unexpectedly into a look of panic, and he hurried past me to beat a couple of repo-company gumshoes to his car. Sliding into the driver's seat just as they reversed course to make for their own wheels, he floored the accelerator and sped off toward Sunset Boulevard.

As I peered after him, hand visored like Magellan's, I contemplated the unseemly haste with which our endlessly provisional Los Angeles lives could change. Just then, my own did, the unlikely announcement of the fact being a gigantic set of antlers that now glided to a halt before my nose. They turned out to be mounted on the hood of a long black limo, above an engraved silver plaque on the grille that asked: "Are These Yours, Buddy?"

A smoked window was rolled partly down, releasing the actual smoke behind it. From within a Havana cloud came a voice whose regional accent put me pleasantly in mind of my beginnings in Jolene.

"I was right—you look even better in color. Could you use a lift?"

"Well, I wasn't feeling especially depressed, to be honest," I cautiously replied. "But I'm always happy to hear a funny story."

Gurgling mirth from inside the limo. "Say, can you act?"

"Say, Mister—can you *pee*?" retorted I.

"Get in, then," said the voice, opening the door.

This was how I soon found myself a starlet under contract to Y. Avery Willingham Productions, makers of Westerns that featured up to four horses onscreen simultaneously and a variety of other B pictures in which you could often see the scenery wobbling when a character was slammed up against it and told to talk fast—but not too fast, as zippier dialogue tempos would have required lengthier and more elaborate scenarios to push the movie up to feature length. Budget-busting was ever the great fear at Y. Avery Willingham Productions, although its eponymous overseer was flush enough personally to own both a Tex-Mex restaurant, which was in Los Feliz, and a genuine Calder, which was in his foyer.

Over the next two years, I was to act in a variety of roles for this gentleman. In *The One-Armed Gun,* I played the town schoolteacher, whose big scene came when she jumped up and down in glee as the stagecoach arrived. In *The Crowded Balcony,* I played a French gangster's kidnapped moll, who spent virtually the movie's entire sixty-eight-minute running length tied to a chair, cords passed tautly over and under my bazooms to prevent either one's escape before the ransom money was delivered. Upstairs from the Calder, in a house in the Hollywood Hills, I played games that might well have given even my sister Suzannah pause.

Mr. Willingham himself was a plump fellow with somewhat bucked teeth and interested, friendly eyes—a clown with the bite of a ferret, as I believe he was once described by a rival and rather more pugnacious maker of thundering horse operas. I found him perfectly charming, not least because he hailed from the same part of the country as I, helping us to understand each other's not only moods but syntax. I also had a grown girl's healthy appreciation for his ornate house, a somewhat Moorish-looking edifice originally built for a onetime oil man and later silent-movie producer in a bygone day.

Be that as it may, it was still hard for me to leave the Poil, where my good friends from my early days in Hollywood all gathered in my dingy room to bid me adieu. "Homer," I said, knowing it would please him, "I think I'm going to miss you most of all." He stepped back, glowing and wringing his big hands. Turning to Wood, I handed him my, and also his, favorite angora sweater: "I know you'll give it a good home," I told him. He smiled under his little mustache and said, "Maybe more than one, if I'm lucky. You never know what might turn up." Smiling back, I then moved on to the goodbye I had deliberately saved for last.

"But what's going to happen to me now?" she asked.

"Everything under the sun, Bettie," I said, hugging her. "Everything under the sun. But with any luck, you'll be alive at the end of it, and that's something." Picking up my cardboard suitcase, I walked out onto Yucca Street, where the great antlered limo had begun diverting the neighborhood urchins—at least those not gainfully employed in selling oregano palmed off as marijuana to the tourists wandering up from Hollywood Boulevard by mistake.

Now, I had a pleasant time with Mr. Willingham. He was a delightful man who made me laugh more than any other I have known, and one of the few to understand how boasting a behind that Moses would have stayed in Egypt for did not preclude a girl from having a personality of depthishness and nuancification, or a mind whose insights could intrigue any writer of fiction less smug than, to pluck a name quite at random from the wet paper bag before me, Mr. John Updike. Yet while the stars never faded from my eyes, I soon discovered that the life of a movie actress was a fairly repetitive one—days of standing around waiting for the lighting to be adjusted and the camera put in position, nights of hanging off a chandelier dressed as a Dresden shepherdess as Mr. Willingham tore up and down the stairs in his boxer shorts, guffawing and trying to grab me, and Pilar the housekeeper tossed her apron up over her face and raced back to the kitchen to muffle a crisis of giggles. In any case, from *Cheyenne Summer* to *Navajo! Ho! Ho!* in the dust of the Old West, and from *Ginger Snaps Back* to *Shipwrecked* in the contemporary-comedy vein, nearly all the movies I made for Y. Avery Willingham Productions are available for rental—though not, unless the bucktoothed little bastard really pulled a fast one, the rather more special movies I starred in for plain Y. Avery Willingham. Therefore, in the interest of picking up the pace, I will simply skip forward to the ultimate climax in a relationship not short on them, during which I learned something that utterly astounded me.

Lustrously emerging from my marble bath one warm day, I wrapped my hourglass figure in a shortie robe whose silken skimpiness barely covered my beautimous hips, as I thoughtfully proved by bending and stretching in the miraculously unsteamed full-length mirror. Having misplaced my copy of the script for *Every Girl Is an Island,* my upcoming vehicle, somewhere in the Moorish house's vast confines, and believing Mr. Willingham to be sequestrating at the moment at the YAWP studios on Hyperion Avenue down in Silverlake, I ventured into his private office off the bedroom, into which I'd been requested not to go. Behind blue curtains, amid stacked scripts, I quickly found another copy of *Every Girl Is an Island*'s inane scenario, and had turned to depart when my gaze was snared by the sight of a rusty beer can standing alone on the highest shelf.

As there were empty beer cans all over the house, for which Pilar went daily scavenging with a large-capacity garbage bag and a net to snag the ones in the swimming pool, I shouldn't have found anything unusual in the sight. But the brand name on this one made my vision reel, for it was a can of Horspis Beer—which had never been sold anywhere but in the immediate environs of Jolene, Alabam'-don't-give-a-damn. On top of that, I knew full well that the old Horspis Brewery—which had soon relocated to St. Louis and changed its name to something both more unwieldy, what with the hyphen and all, and less accurate, as the recipe remained unchanged—had only sold this product under this label and in this container for a single year . . . the year preceding *my own birth.*

Climbing up on a convenient stepladder, and incidentally providing a dandy view to anyone lying beneath it had there been such a person present—hello, Sprout!—a slow-motion picture actress fetched the beer can down from the shelf. In a doozy of a daze, I reached into my capacious décolletage, now moving up and down like a matched pair of creamy concrete mixers as a result of my rapid gasps, to fish forth on its ribbon the rusty old church-key can-and-bottle opener that I had carried with me since I left Jolene. Hardly daring to believe that my fingers and hands were performing the task that my own stunned eyes were observing them to perform, I fitted the opener's triangular end to one of the triangular apertures cut into the top of the can.

They matched. They matched perfectly. There was no doubt in my mind that this can opener had opened this beer can.

Behind me, I heard Mr. Willingham's voice: "Oh, well, what the hell.

I guess that's it for that, huh?" When I turned, he stood before me in shirttails and boxers, evidently having come home early for what both ant and drumstick used to call an indoor picnic lunch in happier days. On his face, the remnants of a cheerful grin were fading; from his hand, my Dresden shepherdess's crook clattered to the floor.

I swallowed hard. "Mr. Willingham," I said, "are you my true Poppa?"

"Sort of. That is, I'm one of them," he said. "We never really did figure it out to anyone's satisfaction, least of all your Momma's. Horspis sold those things in six-packs, you know."

"She told me you were *dead*."

"That's because some of us are," he said. "I'm just one of the ones who's still around. And will be for a while, God willing, since my work here is far from done."

"And," my voice trembled, though whether with hurt or indignation I am not sure, "have you known this the whole time you've been repeatedly bestowing your not inconsiderable God-given endowment upon my grateful little college of one?"

He went from looking wolfish to looking sheepish. "Well, yeah," he said. "I do feel kind of crummy about it sometimes, usually while I'm shaving. That's why I've started this beard, but I'm only human. Jesus God, have you ever looked at yourself naked? Have you ever read the size tag on your bra and asked yourself just what those numbers *mean*?"

"Not to disregard what I believe is the intended compliment," I said, "but it has just become problematic for me to remain under your Moorish roof."

His face fell, and he punched a nearby armoire. "Aw, *damn*," he said. "I *knew* that's what would happen. This just *sucks*. Why didn't I toss that beer can out years ago?"

"Yes," I said, on the verge of tears, "why didn't you? Everything was going so well!"

"I'll tell you why. It's because I loved your Momma, that's why. I bet we all saved 'em—Bill Faulkner, Tex, everybody." He looked suddenly worried. "Hey, you're still gonna do *Every Girl Is an Island*, though, aren't you?"

"I am under contract to Y. Avery Willingham Productions, and I consider myself a professional," I said. "But things personal are over between us, Poppa mine."

"Not even one more swing on the chandelier for the road? Come on. It's Pilar's day off."

"Not one," I said.

Briefly, Mr. Willingham looked crestfallen. But then the old cheerful glint came into his eyes.

"Say," he said, "I've got an idea. You don't happen to know where your sister Suzannah is, do you? I bet she won't mind. Hell, you know what *she's* like—you've seen *The Puerile Maid,* although not nearly as many times as I have."

"Is she your daughter too?" I gasped. Though of course she would have been, as we were twins.

"You all are," he said. "All of you are all of ours. Bill, me, Tex, Frank Tashlin . . . all of us. Sometimes we hated ourselves for it, although maybe not quite as much as our wives did. Put it this way: we weren't throwing skillets at our *own* heads as soon as we got home. But we just couldn't find any women like you in real life."

■

Once the filming of *Every Girl Is an Island* was complete—in a rare stint at Zuma Beach, standing in for a mythicalacious Pacific archipelago, rather than the mock Old West of Griffith Park, where our shoestring productions had often bumped up against no fewer than three other Grade-Z Westerns in progress, amid any number of high-school field trips to the Planetarium and furtive homosexual getting-to-know-you sessions in nearby cars; we'd borrow each other's horses, and press the high-school students and the homosexuals into service as acned Indians or supercilious pairs of homesteaders—my duties to the Y. Avery Willingham organization were discharged in full. I had already moved from the Hollywood Hills to a small white house with blue trim in Echo Park. Now, having found myself an agent, I set about offering my services to Darryl Zanuck, along with any other studio not run by a chuckling, voluble, incest-crazed blood relative.

To my chagrin, however, the offers were few. I began to suspect that, unbeknownst to myself, I had either been a beneficiary of nepotism or was perceived as such, and in Hollywood the latter may well do more damage than the former. Having more or less run out of options, I had just signed to appear in a vapid situation comedy about some castaways when the telephone rang in my small Echo Park home. Assuming it was my agent calling back with more fine print for me to chew on, I picked it up; and here I reach the apotheosis of my tale.

As it turned out, it *was* my agent—a fellow who put me in mind slightly of a younger, more gullible, New Testament edition of Mr. Gagilnil, with whom I had long since lost touch. Giggling and nervous, for Swifty Lazar he wasn't, he announced that he had just secured me the opportunity of nine lifetimes, at least if I could be ready to depart for an unspecified location, dressed in my sultriooshiest gown and smelling like a spice shop, within the hour.

"Aw, Slowy, don't tell me Mr. Zanuck wants to see me *now*," I moaned. "I've already signed the contract to do *Gil*—"

"No, this isn't a movie part." He giggled again. "It's better, lots better. I can't explain, so just get ready. I'll pick you up at six."

Mystified, I disrobed and ran a bath, idly doing jumping jacks and deep-knee bends to pass the time as the tub filled. Coiffed, gowned in shimmering white, jeweled and perfumed, I was straightening one of the pictures of lilies with which my Echo Park house was decorated when the doorbell rang. Smirking like a guilty schoolboy as he ran a finger around his collar, my agent took me by the arm to escort me to a waiting limousine. This only deepened my confusion, as I knew perfectly well that Slowy couldn't afford a limo, certainly not one this big, long, and black. With momentary apprehensiatiousness, I checked to see if its hood perchance sported a massive set of antlers, and to my relief saw it did not.

Once the limo door opened and I scooted in, however, I discovered that I was not its only passenger—any more than I had been in my, our,

Momma's womb back in Jolene. Stacked like a fire sale at the International House of Pancakes and adjusting her skin-tight black gown to cross a pair of legs long enough to pass for the Chrysler Building in inverted alabaster duplicate, my sister looked as unaccustomed as ever to doing anything sitting up. At once beneath and amid the anarchic brunette coils and masses of her coiffure, her green eyes glittered with the same all too explicable hostility that I could feel my own gaze returning.

"Hello, Suzannah," I said coldly.

"Leavin' the little gold man at home tonight, Sis?" she sneered, with a drum roll of her lacquered fingernails upon her thigh. "Or has he run back on his little yaller legs through the streets to Bette Davis's house with panic in his little yaller eyes, havin' dee-duced he must of been the victim of a kid-*sis*-nappin'?"

"Being five minutes older ain't nothing to brag on," I said.

"Being about five yards smarter is, sister mine."

"You two know each other?" said Slowy as he got in with us, his surprised tone not entirely lacking in a certain idiot glee. He really wasn't much older than a sprout, I thought; no wonder I'd wound up with nothing but a sitcom.

"Somewhat," I said frostily.

"Somewhat," Suzannah said icily.

We had not seen each other since the world premiere of *The Puerile Maid* in a warehouse in San Pedro two years previous, which I had prevailed on Mr. Willingham to escort me to for old times' sake—not that he was disinclined, soon afterwards obtaining a private print of it to run off whenever I was busy with tight-costume fittings at the YAWP studios. As the movie uncesspooled, I had been unable to prevent myself from watching my sister's performance with a critical eye, considering the different ways in which I, Gagilnil's original choice, might have interpreted this or that aspect of the role. Evidently, the novice director had lost control of his star, for unless my recollections of the original scenario deceived me Suzannah had added a good deal of improvised business of her own, of a sordid lubricity that put my former employer's rather trite imaginings to shame: a classic case of the tail wagging the doghouse, you might say. Yet we had not exchanged a word either before the screening or after it, stalking out instead past the two flashlights that Gagilnil had hired Homer to keep waving in crisscross patterns outside the door to climb into our separate cars with no more than a single fiery glance of mutual hatred.

"So what you been up to?" I asked.

As if they were five tiny scarlet mirrors embedded in her fingertips, Suzannah was contemplating half her nails. "Puttin' on Chanel lipstick right after suckin' Woolworth's cock," she said, which even I had to admit did evoke Hollywood in a nutshell. "You?"

"I'm going to be starting a TV series soon," I said.

"Oh, yeah?" Suzannah snorted. "What's it called—*My Sister the Mattress*?"

"What makes you think it's about you?" I said.

"I wouldn't *fit* on TV," she said. "Takes a flat-chested lil' hunk a' itsy-bitsy nothin' like you to even get inside the box."

That seemed to have gotten us about as caught up as we cared to be. I turned to Slowy, who still wore the look of a candy lover who had woken up between two giant bonbons. "Where are we going, anyway?" I said.

"Palm Springs." He giggled again. "But I really can't tell you anything more than that."

Silence fell, and did not pick itself up by its own bootstraps afterwards. Lit within by beaded lights that put me in mind of an airplane somehow carrying its own portable runway, the limo sped on. Slowy fixed us all drinks, which added a gently syncopated clinking to the hummingbirdaciousness of whooshing tires and distant throb of engine. We had left the city behind and now glided across trackless wastes—well, trackless but for the highway we were on—whose burning sands were being cooled in a vast fridge of cobalt darkness.

After the perpetual phosphorescent glow that hangs above L.A. at night fell away in our rear window, more stars than there were at M-G-M appeared and glimmered white in the dark blue above. Through the front windshield, the tail-lights of the cars ahead of us and the headlights of oncoming ones drew alternating stripes of red and white across the desert. With nothing better to do, I began to count the stars, and had reached fifty when they all evaporated in another, smaller civic glow. We had just slid into Palm Springs.

I had never been there before. And deep down, I had always privately wondered if the people everybody else in America so desperately wanted to be actually existed, that is in the form we imagined them. Even in the joyous days when I felt thrilled to espy my own reflection in the mirror above the circular bedspread at the nerve center of Mr. Willingham's sumptuous Hollywood Hills abode, I had never been under any illusion of having attained or even being in sight of the ultimate height of heights, where the gods of celebrity played. In my fear that they would prove chimerical, and turn out to be more folks who wanted to be someone else too, I had sometimes supposed that their twinkling role in our lives was simply what Santy Claus did the other three-hundred-sixty-four days of the year. Now, as the limo prowled along quiet streets whose expensive-looking bungalows and ranch houses sprawled dimly well beyond an intervening no-fan's-land of lawns made complex and barbizoned by bladed splays of exotic desert plants, I suddenly guessed that I was closer than I had ever been, *physically* closer, to finding out if Santy Claus was real.

We pulled up in front of one of the estates. With a finger that quivered noticeably, Slowy mashed the button underneath the gate's speaker grille, with which he had an indistinct conversation. Then we were in the garden, a jumpy Slowy leading the way down a flagstoned path while I engaged in a small war of hips with Suzannah—the black-gowned Lilith to my white-gowned Eve—over which of us would take precedence in his wake.

At the house, light poured through a door left ajar. Pushing it gently, Slowy led us into a vast living room, the midpoint of whose vaulted ceiling was delineated by a balcony that ran around three of its four walls, with doors and hallways dimly discernible behind the rails. From an expensive-looking hi-fi by the bar, music played. The furnishings were elegant, although a few of the paintings struck even my indifferent eye as surprisingly undistinguished, albeit competent.

Unless the daubed clowns in those pictures counted, we were alone, and somewhat bemused. But then a voice I had been hearing my whole life, one so familiar that it seemed to be emanating from within my very brain, indeed the same voice that was on the hi-fi, spoke from above us. It called to Slowy by his proper name: "Adam, my man! Is that you down there? It just better be, buddy, that's all *I'm* going to say."

It was Sinatra. Behind him, as he slowly descended to received us, came a gentleman with face unknown to me, his grin strikingly if oddly reminiscent of autumn leaves with a pack of Chiclets at the center. "I was just showing Jack around the joint," said our host casually. "Hello, girls," more casually still.

"Well! Um, great seeing you, um, Frank," Slowy said unexpectedly. "I'm sorry I can't stay—something I can't get out of."

"Some*one* you'd like to get in*to*, more likely," Frank said, slapping him on the back; at which touch Slowy gulped as if swallowing the wafer at his first communion. "Come on, kid—I've got something I want to ask you on the way out." And off they strolled, leaving Suzannah and I to swap a glance of silent, instantaneous recognition that we had just been macked. This irked us both, as we had never needed any help before.

Frank came back from showing Slowy out. A man who needed no introduction himself, he introduced his beaming tagalong instead, who turned out to be a politician: Senator Jawn F. Knowbody, I didn't quite catch the name. Nor did I care, as I had small patience with either government or Yankees, and even less when they were conjoined—that particular combination, needless to say, having produced our sainted Dixie's Gotterdangeroong. And while his voice was pleasant, with nice wry bits around the edges, this crinkly son of a bitch's accent was Yankee enough to affect my ears as if my coiffure were Georgia and Sherman was coming through. He was genial as he greeted us, and just as genial when he turned to Frank and said, precisely as if my sister and I hadn't been standing thirty-six inches from his nose, "Angie couldn't make it, huh?" Not only was I miffed on my own behalf; I was miffed for my and Suzannah's whole, too, with a sisterly solidarity such as I hadn't felt since our shared girlhood in Jolene.

"No such luck, my friend. She's making a movie with Howard Hawks. Duke Wayne's in it too. So's Dean," Frank said, and was asking us what we'd care to drink when a sliding door's distinctive snicker-slither sounded behind us. Turning, I saw an apparently headless Negro, clad in swimming trunks and dark skin beaded with moisture, step into the room out of the night, one bright parallelogram of which behind him was dancing. Then the white towel in his hands came down off his face, and I found myself staring directly into the deep brown eyes—one real and the other, as I knew without being able to remember or guess which, glass—of Sammy Davis, Jr.

"Hello," he said, just as Frank turned to Senator Knowbody and muttered, "Sammy's been out looking for a land of the blind again. Wants to be its king, I think."

"As in Martin Luther, is the next knee-slapper," Sammy told me fairly dryly, the towel having done its job. "That's so you'll be prepared. What about Dean?" he asked.

"That Western for Hawks. They're on location now."

"I'm surprised they talked him into hauling his ass down there," Sammy said. "He's a religious man."

"I didn't think that was, ah, a drawback in *show business,* too," Senator Knowbody said drolly. "That's always been much more my own, ah, crucifix to bear. But what's being Catholic got to do with making a Western?"

"Who said anything about being Catholic? Not caring about anything, that's all Dean believes in. But he believes in it the way Gandhi believes in non-violence—or the way Sammy Cahn believes in Frank, here. But Catholicism? Forget it."

"So speaks the Jew of that which he ignores," Frank mock-rumbled, jabbing a blunt-nailed finger Sammy's way. "When you're raised in the Church, you never forget it, buddy of mine, and can you believe," he said to Senator Knowbody, "that this undersized black bastard I call my buddy decided to make life simpler for himself by converting to Judaism? That's like shooting craps with someone else's dice and complaining because *both* of them aren't loaded, sweet Jesus Mary mother of God. He's one-stop shopping for the Ku Klux Klan."

"Ah, Sammy," Senator Knowbody said, grinning broadly, "I want you know how important your people's support is to me. And I think my position on, ah, Israel will gratify you."

"Israel? Who's *she*?" Sammy said. "Try any position you like. I'm going to go get dressed."

This whole time, ignored by all three of them, Suzannah and I had been standing rooted to the spot, swiveling our coiffures from speaker to speaker like over-bebaubled spectators at a tennis match. As soon as Sammy trotted up the stairs, however, the other two men grew instantly aware of us, as if their intimacy was in fact a rivalry whose expression always had to be deflected to third parties if they didn't want to abruptly find themselves pinwheeling in the whirl and churn of an exaggerated cartoon fistfight. So Frank took my arm, and Senator Knowbody took Suzannah's—she looking distinctly nettled, at least to a sister's expert eyes, at getting second best—and with over-compensatory, genial solicitude they took us to the bar. There, Frank got busy mixing us a couple of highballs, and Senator Knowbody, seemingly to give himself some sort of presence and demonstrate that he too had the use of his hands, lit a cigar.

"Um, Mr. Sinatra?" Clearly, Suzannah was still hoping that she wasn't irretrievably destined for Senator Jawn Fucking Knowbody. But she also sounded something I had never heard her sound in all our lives together, namely nervous—and I could not avoid taking a certain malicious pleasure in this.

"Frank," he corrected her, pouring. "What is it, doll?"

Suzannah dipped her wild brunette mane at the hi-fi. "Well, I know that's *you*—but I've never heard these songs before, leastways not with you singing them. So I wondered . . ."

"It's the first acetate pressing of a new long–player we got done recording this week," he told her. "Normally, I don't listen to myself at home. I like to think that I'm a proud man but not a vain one, and it wouldn't be showing much class even if I did feel like it—you see that, don't you, doll. But right after we finish a record, I wear out the acetate making sure that everything's A-OK. Because it's got to be *perfect,* right down to the fourth son-of-a-bitching violin on track nine, or back to the studio we go."

"Well, how often do you have to go back?" I asked, largely because I had begun to miss the sound of my own voice. "Frank," I added, to irritate my sister.

"Not often." He handed me my drink, and then Suzannah hers. With a jerk of his head, he indicated that we were all going to move now to the facing couches out in the middle of the room. I ended up on the same one as him, at which Suzannah both indicated her displeasure and put in a bid for a shift in the arrangement by sticking out one hip more than she needed to as she turned to sit down, thereby letting any interested parties on *our* couch observe the mimetic fervor with which her black gown delineated the precise contours of her rump, and note in addition that she probably didn't have panties on underneath, not even of the sheerest, flimsiest sort—down, Sprout, hold on; we've got a ways to go here. Not that my sister's little let's-put-the-dumb-back-in-dumb-show mattered much, because as soon as we were all settled in, the men went right back to ignoring us.

Holding his highball in both hands, Frank counted the ice cubes. "*Should* I think anything special about Israel, Jack?" he asked unexpectedly, having kept that in his head the whole time.

"Oh, I don't think the, ah, Arabs are going to be taking another crack at them anytime soon, if that's what you mean," Senator Knowbody said affably, as interested in his cigar as Frank was in his drink. He grinned. "After all, they'll have to get their ordnance replaced first. But there's always plenty going on there. You know, the Israelis do us a lot of little favors in, ah, that part of the world, in exchange for our backup on the big thing of survival."

"Cloak-and-dagger stuff, you mean," Frank said. "CIA."

"Yes."

"So tell me: what should I think of *them*?" Frank asked. "Sometimes it sounds like a bunch of nonsense to me. Boys' games. Comic books."

"Don't you believe it," Senator Knowbody said. "They're good, Frank, really good. If I get in—*when* I get in—they are the bunch I'm going to go to whenever I need something in a hurry, because they're smart and fast and they don't dillydally about on-the-other-hand-what-

if-the-Queen-gets-her-tits-in-an-uproar the way State does. And they
don't miss a trick. I forget who said it first or what about, but it fits
them: the CIA is in the details."

"Give me a for instance," Frank said. Apparently, he was just interested; or considered it one of the duties of being Frank to collect
knowledge that would make him omniscient about anything of potential consequence. As for Suzannah and me, in another temporary sus-
pension of sibling hostilities, we kept on exchanging incredulous looks,
unable to believe that we were in Frank Sinatra's house—and bored. It
would have been so much more fun if this Baastin jackass wasn't here!
We even wished that Sammy would come back; Momma wouldn't have
approved, but at least he was entertaining.

Senator Knowbody had shut his eyes in thought for a second. "All
right," he said. "Right after they overthrew Arbenz in Guatemala, I
called over there and asked for a briefing—mostly because," he
laughed, "I was curious to hear how staging a coup *works,* if only so my
father will have some sort of backup plan ready if things don't work
out in '60. Well, they're good with the Hill, and even though I was still
in my first term and had no particular importance then, they sent over
a fellow who'd been there on the ground—Akin, Egan, something like
that. As I remember it, he made me feel old, because for all that it was
only a Central American one, he'd helped depose a government at the
age of all of twenty-six, and I—well, I *wasn't* twenty-six, all of a sudden. He was only supposed to brief me about Guatemala, but since I
wasn't bored and there's a very nice nameplate on my desk that says
'Senator,' he told me about some other little things he'd been involved
with."

"Iran?" Frank asked, with a shrewd expression. Some years later, I
found out this was a country.

"No—not that I'd have minded hearing about that one, believe me.
Even if the Shah was royalty the way I'm monogamous, putting in a
hereditary ruler is one trick that the Russians, for ideological reasons,
can't go tit for tat on us with, and I'll remember that if the opportunity
ever comes up. But there was one small operation this Egan fellow told

me about that stuck in my mind, just because it showed the infinite pains they can take."

"Well?"

"I'm trying to remember it exactly—oh yes. It seemed there was some company in Belgium whose business was supplying safety equipment to small regional airports—windsocks, backup generators for runway lights, things like that. Well, without even bothering to consult his superiors, it occurs to our man Egan that this could be a useful company for the Agency to have a hand in. So he checked out the owner, who turned out to be a fairly sad case; back before the war, he'd found his wife in the bathtub with her wrists slashed one day, and apparently he hadn't had much heart for anything from then on. In other words, it wouldn't take too big a nudge to move him out. So friend Egan arranges for the company to experience a few modest difficulties—nothing major, just enough to put the owner in a mood to sell. Well! Guess who bought it—and now it's one of their most reliable ways of moving some fairly nasty things around without much risk of customs people putting a finger in. What do you think of that?"

"Not too bad," said Frank, shaking his head. "That Egan sounds like a guy I wouldn't mind having around to listen to my acetate. What's happened to him since?"

"Oh, he's stationed in . . . Paris now, I think. We're not in touch, but I keep tabs."

"Sounds like he'll have an interesting future if you get in," Frank mused.

"*When* I get in—and yes, he may, along with everybody else in his shop. Sooner or later, we're obviously going to have to do something about Castro, unless he's gone away of his own volition by then—which I doubt, don't you? And that mess in Indochina could start heating up again anytime. So—"

But Frank—whose own enthusiasm appeared to be flagging, and not a moment too soon if you asked the Gumstump sisters—was glancing toward the stairs. "Hey, who put the lights out?" he called, in a considerably rougher tone than the one he'd used to quiz Senator Knowbody. "It just got *dark* in here. And what's with the shirt—you been trying to make wine from a watermelon again?"

"It's going to get a lot darker after I slug you," said Sammy, now nattily attired in slacks, pink silk shirt, and gold necklace from which dangled a six-pointed star. Dropping his Jack Johnson pose, he sat down in an armchair between the two couches. "What does a guy have to do to get a drink around here?" he asked, looking directly at me. I still couldn't figure out which eye was the glass one.

I glanced over at Frank for his dispensation to use his bar and got a flick of a nod in reply. "Scotch, baby, and right up to the top of the glass," Sammy called after me. "I'm not one of these bourbon drinkers—my throat and I have an understanding about that."

While I was fixing it for him, the last song ended, and the needle lifted off the hi-fi turntable. "Mr. . . . Frank?" I called, making the "Frank" louder so as to make the "Mister" retrospectively inaudible. "Should I turn it over?"

"If you wouldn't mind, doll," he called back. "But be careful, huh? You've probably never picked up an acetate before, but they're a little heavier than vinyl—and that's about three fucking grand worth of record player you're fooling with, baby-cakes."

As the beauty of his *other* voice filled the room again, and I came back to the couches and handed Sammy his drink, Senator Knowbody stood up, having stubbed out his cigar half-smoked. "You know," he remarked to no one in particular, "Frank's shown me the house. But I haven't really seen the grounds, and I'd like to while it's, ah, still dark yet. Not to insult your singing, Frank, but I've heard this about six times tonight—and anyway, I think my ear for music is the one van Gogh cut off. Runs in the family—we can't even remember what comes after 'Give me your answer do.'"

He looked down at Suzannah. "How'd you like to come with me?" he said. "I'll bet you haven't even seen the swimming pool."

Well, she had absolutely no choice in the matter. In a situation such as this one, girls like us don't choose; we get chosen, and Suzannah knew it. But that didn't prevent her from shooting me a dark look of pure maleviolence as she twitched her gown and self, looking rather like a black banana with each end partly peeled, up off the couch to accompany him.

Much later, of course, after Senator John F. Knowbody had become a distinct Somebody even to someone like me who only read *Variety,* I did have regrets—which I should probably mention. But no, too late: he went with Suzannah. He went with Lilith, my black-gowned sister.

In any case, she told me some time afterward that I hadn't missed a lot. The only fun part, she said, was right after they got their clothes off, when he towed her on a rubber raft around the pool for a while by a strap held in his teeth; but just as she was starting to seriously enjoy the whole Cleopatra's-barge aspect of this, he said something like, "Well, the choppers are still willing, but the back is now weak," and that was that for that. When they got down to business, she said that he was very indolent, leaning back on the steps at the pool's shallow end and getting her to straddle him, which gave her scrapes on both knees from bumping them repeatedly against the pool's concrete wall. But that, she said, was still an improvement on his first idea, which had been for her to give him head underwater—a task that even Suzannah, who had the lungs of a medieval glassblower and had acquired them in a similar way, found herself unable to perform for long without experiencing a serious diminution of the celebrated Gumstump brio.

However, at the time that my sister's rhythmically splashing keester was no doubt sending cascades of bright green water shivering all the way to the bougainvilleas, I hardly had space in my mind for curiosity about the state of things out in the swimming pool. I was too busy feeling stunned. You see, once Suzannah and Senator Knowbody split, I had simply assumed that Frank and I would soon depart upstairs to his vague but splendid bedroom, while Sammy wandered off to do whatever Negro sidekicks did in such circumstances—the dishes, I supposed, although we hadn't eaten. But after no more than a couple of minutes, whose conversational content I do not remember, Frank suddenly held up his hand, as if to either stop traffic or bestow a blessing. "What's today," he asked, "Saturday?"

"Yeah." Then Sammy glanced at his watch, which was flatter to his wrist than any I had ever seen. "Close to Sunday," he said, "if you want to get technical about it."

"I don't. Believe me, getting technical about anything is the last thing I want to do right now. I'm beat." He looked at his still upraised hand, as if only now recalling the chore it had been lifted to perform, and pressed thumb and forefinger to the bridge of his nose. "I've been in the studio for six days straight. I need to rest," he said, and stood up.

"See you in the morning, Nephew Remus. You know where everything is," he told Sammy. Then to me, "You've been a sweetie, dollcake. If you ever want to catch a show, there's two tickets waiting at the box office the minute you find the dime for a phone call." Then, as I was still blinking back my petrified astonishment, he was gone, back upstairs.

Since Sammy and I were both sitting down, and this now seemed a bit too much to have in common, I stood up. My plan was flawed, however, since he could stand up too; and promptly did so, to my resentment. With his one-glass-one-real-and-which-was-which eyes, he looked at me consideringly.

"You're right," he said abruptly, although I had said nothing. "I *could* have gotten that drink myself. But I decided that I wanted to accept it from your hand, because I wanted to see what your hand felt like."

"And?" I said.

He smiled. "Cold and wet. I hoped it was the highball glass talking."

The whole situation felt surreal to me, since this was Frank Sinatra's house in Palm Springs, and he was a Negro, and it was late, and he was a Negro, and we were alone, and he was a Negro. My gown felt too tight; also insufficient to its job. Also, to reiterate something I may not have stressed sufficiently, he was a Negro. And on top of that, as if we didn't have enough problems, he was a Negro. Plus which, I had just noticed something else: he was a Negro.

Abruptly, I felt dazed, as the realization came to me out of the black that he was a Negro. Why hadn't anyone informed me until this crucial moment, including myself, that Sammy Davis, Jr., was a Negro? And was he, himself, aware that he was a Negro? Clearly not, since we were alone and it was late and he was a Negro.

Briefly, I felt I had the upper hand, since evidently I knew something he didn't—namely, that he was a Negro. However, on reflection, this struck me as no advantage after all, since we were still alone and it was still late and he was still a Negro. I am giving you a much abbreviated version of my thoughts in these few seconds, during the entirety of which, the seconds and the thoughts alike, Sammy Davis, Jr., was and remained a Negro. Beyond that, murky but enormous, hovered the ultimate questions:

Why had Frank made Sammy a Negro? In what way was that part of his plan? And were we all equal in Frank's blue eyes?

"I have to know something," I said, and felt glad that I had stopped before saying "first."

"Sure."

"Did you and Frank *arrange* this?"

"Do you mean did I ask him to find me a girl tonight? Or do you mean did we flip a coin?"

"Both."

"Baby, it was neither," he said. "If I hadn't realized I was noticing things like the way you did your hair, I'd have gone to bed myself an hour ago."

"But I was *brought* here," I said. "My sister and I were brought some *two hundred miles* to this place. In a limousine," I added, in what I sincerely hoped was not a pathetic attempt to impress him with anything more than the seriousness of the case.

"Vampira's your *sister*? I'll be damned. Dean would love that," he said irrelevantly. "But now let me ask *you* something, all right?"

"Go ahead."

"Baby, did anybody ask for a cigarette tonight?"

I thought for a second. "No," I said.

Sammy flipped open a silver cigarette case on an end table. It was full. "They might have," he said, and strolled to the bar. "Did anybody ask for some Dom Perignon tonight?" he asked, and pulled two bottles that had been icing in twin buckets there. "They might have." Putting them down again, he walked to the record shelves next to the hi-fi. Yanking out a Johnny Mathis album, he displayed it for me without a word.

"That's how Frank *does* things," he said, tucking Johnny Mathis back in for the night.

Enraged by now, I stamped my foot. "Did anybody ask for a goddamn live performance of 'Ain't That a Kick in the Head' tonight, you black son of a bitch?" I shrieked. But he only smiled.

"Not yet," he said. "But nobody's asked you to go to bed with them yet, either."

At a loss, I walked to the hi-fi, and picked up the jacket to Frank's acetate so that I could pretend to be studying it. This was a dumb mistake, as the jacket was perfectly blank on both sides except for a scrawl reading "FAS Personal," and however desperate I might feel, I did not want to appear cretinous. Putting it down, I propped my hands to either side of the hi-fi's recessed turntable, peering down as the acetate went around and acting as if I were humming along with Frank's voice in a state of acute musical concentration that forbade anyone's breaking in on it, no matter how well intentioned, friendly, or burning with dark lust they might be. This too had its problems, chiefly that I had never heard this tune before and so had to guess at what I was humming as I hummed. Finally I gave that up and began pretending that I had been clearing my throat, albeit somewhat rhythmically and in the same state of acute musical concentration. In any case, the hi-fi's needle was now under an inch from the revolving blank white label at the acetate's center, and I had not bought myself any huge amount of time with this whole stratagem.

And now *the song is over. He's right behind me.* His arms encircle my waist. Now his hands come up and press my bazooms through my gown, his wiry fingers on the white silk and my pale-pink skin creating a color contrast that would have my Momma keeling over in a dead faint midway through fetching the shotgun. He's found my lollipops, which to my somewhat heavy-breathing consternation have begun to push out their red Jujubes. Yet his touch, while firm, is unexpectedly considerate. Plenty of men whose yearning looks have conveyed how very, very badly they want to fondle my bazooms have managed to do precisely that, either kneading them with the sort of brutality best reserved for pizza dough or squeezing them by their girth as if sufficient pressure will fire off lollipops and Jujubes like little red rocket ships from the launching pad. But this, I have begun to recognize, is different. Sammy's hands are gentle but authoritative, and the temperature of his breath on my neck feels just right, in the Goldilocksian sense of the term. My God, I have just noticed myself thinking, I can't wait another minute; let's get to hell out of here and find a bed, where I will give him the time of his life.

It had not yet occurred to me that he might give me the time of mine. However, I now grasped that I really *couldn't* wait another minute—and that we really did have to get to hell out of here, though to find what hardly mattered. I had remembered something Sammy didn't know, which was that my sister Suzannah, no less than I, could make men fire a gun faster than Wyatt Earp, and that she often did just this when she was bored with their exertions—or lack of same, though I could hardly know as yet how real the risk was in this case. Which meant that, at any moment, she and Senator Jawn F. Knowbody might come sauntering through the patio door all of six feet from my eyes, and slightly over five from where Sammy's hands were caressing me. So long as we were out of sight by the time the two of them returned, whatever he and I did or didn't wind up doing would matter a lot less, for I knew that Suzannah, upon finding the living room deserted, would simply take it for granted (no doubt with much bitterness, as I could not forbear interrupting these urgent specunabulations to note with some delight) that I was off somewhere making seismical, ring-a-ding-ding-dinging hunchy-punchy with Frank. But never Sammy, as the heritage that she and I shared—not to mention the promise that Momma had solemnly extracted from us both—would simply block the possibility from any access to her mind.

"Where are you taking me?" I murmured, to nudge Sammy's thoughts in the direction I now prayed they would go.

"Wherever you like, baby," he murmured back, his lips tender in my hair. "Wherever you want. Hey, I've got an idea: let's go all the way to the moon. How does that sound to you, baby?"

Clearly, this wasn't going to do at all. "*Sammy, for Christ's sake!*" I howled, whirling to face him. "*My sister Suzannah could walk in any second now, and she is hopelessly afflicted with every last one of the prejudices to which I am so evidently and blessedly immune! You can go on fiddling and farzeling around with my beautiful white bazooms till Doomsday if you like, but get me the fuck behind a door this instant!*"

From the look in Sammy's eyes, or eye—*which one was it?*—I saw that this outburst had changed the mood for him, and that he was trying to determine whether to swing with that or not. Having come to a decision, he quietly spoke two words whose meaning I found flabbergastingly cryptic—but only for a second.

"The left," he said. Taking my all but inert hand, he led me toward the stairs.

As we ascended, I thought of what I'd promised Momma. In a somewhat convoluted but nonetheless dandy piece of reasoning, I took what comfort I could from the thought that, after all, I wouldn't be sleeping with a coon in Los Angeles, the apocalyptic scenario of her worst nightmare. I'd be sleeping with a Jew in Palm Springs, and though not exactly recommended, wasn't that permissible in her book? God bless America when all is said and done, I thought, reaching around for my gown's zipper as we reached the top of the stairs.

Gallantly, he showed me through the door first, then stepped in and closed it behind me. Hearing another click afterward, I realized with a silent prayer of thanks that he both could lock and had locked it. There was nothing in the room but an enormous bed. Midway there, I turned to face him. Taking a deep breath, I let my gown fall to my waist, then pushed it down past hips and knees until I could kick it off and away from my still high-heeled feet.

Needless to say, like my sister, Suzannah, I wore no underwear. As he took in the sight before him—from hair of eternal fire to fire-engine-red high heels and back, pausing along the way at two gallumphing, peachy, red-tipped Dixie Flyers, a torso like a Stradivarius, and hips that flared out and soared up like cathedral arches to either side of the flaming mystery of all mysteries whose secrets he would soon penetrate even if of course he could not, as a man, ever entirely divine them—well, as he looked me over, I do not think I flatter myself beyond the pale by reporting that the expression in not only Sammy's right eye but his left one altered slightly.

It was Oscar night.

We hurled each other into our arms. We threw our mingled self upon the bed. We tested the springs until they snapped. I rolled over him. He rolled over me. We rolled over us. We came together until we came together. When we were finally done, I sat up in a daze, and felt the hot blood pound down like Niagara beneath my dazzled skin before, unlike Niagara, it pounded right back up again. Next to me, Sammy's breathing sounded slightly ragged; he glanced up with a smile. Tugging his wrist out from behind his head, I looked at his watch, and saw that I had just passed the most amazing ninety-two minutes in my far from inconsiderable experience as a mistress of the horizontal arts.

"Got another date?" he asked, with another smile.

"Not for the rest of my life," I said, and meant it.

"I'm sorry I couldn't stay with it any longer," he said. "But you really are something to look at, baby. And to touch. And to . . ."

"And to?"

"And to everything," he said.

Right then, I would have done whatever he asked. Not only would I have swung naked from a chandelier at the opera for him, I would have let my own dear Rover mount me in Macy's front window at high noon on a Sunday had such been his desire. Had he proposed it, which he did not, I might well have even let him diddle my caboose, which no man black white Martian or producer ever has, had or will.

Live with it, Sprout. Not gonna happen. Move on. You've got no one to resent but yourself. You could have tried to make all this stuff up about Suzannah instead of me, if you weren't so damn scared of her.

But to resume: at that moment, I was Sammy's slave.

It did not last.

And why, oh why, I wonder even now—why did I ever take it into my head to tell him about Momma?

■

". . . That's what she said," I giggled—"'whatever you do, just don't sleep with no coon!'" I may have been a little drunk, though whether with liquor or love I did not know, and now never will. In any case, ignoring the new tension in the body I was straddling, I then compounded my error by reaching forward to tug his ears, even as my newly competitional bazooms staged a shoving match over which one got to tickle his nose, and saying playfully: "What do you think, Samby— maybe that's just why I did it?"

In an instant, the room had become an empty glass, and Sammy was an ice cube that some giant hand—Frank's, I guess—had dropped in it. Wasn't melting none, either. For sure, no bourbon followed, nor libation of any sort.

"'*Samby*'?" he said.

"I didn't say 'Samby.' I said 'Sammy,'" I had a distinct feeling of dawning unhappiness. "I know I did."

He pushed me off him and stood up, reaching for a robe whose nearby presence on a hook I had not noticed in that breathless moment before the titanic collision of our black and white flesh in the now icy night—a moment now some ninety-seven minutes past. "You know you did not," he said. "And so do I. So do my ancestors, who went on singing like birds as they were hunted like dogs and packed in like sardines to be drowned like rats or else sold like cattle and worked to death like plain and simple," he paused, meaningfully I thought, "niggers."

"Well, I guess I sort of thought that we were friends now," I said.

"Skip it. Get dressed. You're lucky I'm not making you do that *after* I throw you out."

I slowly got up, allowing him and anyone else who might be interested a last, prolonged glimpse of my extraordinary, magnificently pale, Jujube-tipped and mystery-licked body—upon which even Sammy's anger did not prevent his right eye from lingering noticeably, even though his left eye didn't know what his right one was doing.

"But"—I had thought fast and hard during that interlude—"this isn't even your house. It's Frank's. Shouldn't we go wake him up first?" I asked, pulling up my gown.

"Why?"

"Well, don't you need his I don't know permission, before you throw me out?"

"For this? He'd need mine to keep you here."

"But earlier—"

He held up his hand. "I know—those dumb minstrel jokes. Baby, to say that St. Francis isn't from Assisi may be the definition of cutting a long story short. But can *you* sing like that album we were listening to downstairs, baby? I didn't think so. And you know why? I can't, either. But on a good night, when the drummer doesn't lag—I *hate* that!—then yes, I almost can, and I'm so much a better dancer it's not funny. No guinea from Hoboken is ever going to be able to do the splits worth a damn, and I'm the one with all the razzle-dazzle. Baby, he knows those things about me. I know them about him. That's a way we understand each other that nothing else can touch—not my skin, not bad jokes for the cheap seats, not Sam Giancana."

I had no idea who the last-named person was, but I forged ahead anyhow. "Too bad none of us in the cheap seats ever see what you're talking about," I said, trying to get his goat. But that wasn't even true, because I just *had*. You see, when he said "I *hate* that," his voice had more jump in it than at any other time in this conversation. Generally, he just sounded tired—bone-tired, skin-tired, skin-and-bone-tired. And I had thought about how the only department of the vast human endeavor in which my own voice spoke with a similar decisiveness and un-overrulable confidence of judgment was that which takes place in bed and occasionally taxicabs and such, and had reflected that here was where Sammy and I might have shared the same mutual respect, as one great athlete and Olympian to another, that he and Frank did in the realm of entertainment.

Then it occurred to me that had I only been half as up-front about the whole black-white thing as his hands had been on my gazongas when we were standing before the hi-fi, bringing the topic up before we hit the hay and alluding to myself rather than Momma, race might have been another such meeting ground. Put simply, whatever fearful and vicious notions might be clogging and clouding our brains in this regard, no white Southerner can be said to be *uninformed* on the subject, and black people know this even if our shared history has given them precious few reasons to throw roses at it ever since the first slaver dropped anchor and hoisted the "FOLKS FOR SALE" sign in lovely Charleston Bay. So do we know this about them; so had Sammy known this about me, and I him, from the moment our hands had fleetingly touched as I passed him his drink. He'd felt the Dixie in my fingers, I a trace of the old sun and the ships, the ships, the ships—the ships so gaily setting forth from West Africa, monstrous with creaking rigging and their white sails swollen like bazooms upon the sea, centuries ago—in his palm. We might have talked about it all. But I had waited to bring it up until the moment when he might have been enjoying a brief illusion that race was out of the picture, and it was too late now, for any of it. You can't *establish* things in retrospect, Sprout. Besides, he was about to throw me out, right on my upside-down heart.

"This isn't *fair,*" I faltered, as he marched me down the stairs; although how, and to whom, and if I was even referring to his actions, were all unplumbable to me.

"That's very interesting." He faced me at the door.

"You'd *never* do this to a girl," I said, and we both heard "dare" and "white" intrude although I hadn't spoken either word, "if you weren't rich and famous."

"Let's not get into sophistry, baby, I don't swing that way. If I weren't rich and famous, a chick like you would holler rape the second I smiled at you on the street. We both know I can only do that from a stage, or in a movie theater where I'm twenty feet high and you're eating popcorn, pretending that you don't ever wonder what it would be like if it was me feeling you up and not the cracker who brought you."

Opening the door, he nodded toward the street. It sank in that I was now going to be cast *outside* Frank Sinatra's house in Palm Springs, a town with which I was unfamiliar, and that I didn't have a dime anywhere on my begowned and flustered person. Somehow, when you're a Gumstump and you already know you ain't wearing underwear, you never think you'll need to bring a purse.

"Sam-*m*-my," I said, careful how I said it—"I bet you twenty dollars you can't mispronounce *my* name."

That did stop him, and he looked at me differently for a second. "You're right," he said. "I couldn't."

But then his mouth got tight again, and his right eye grew as hard and expressionless as his left one (and how could I have ever had the slightest doubt?) always was. "So go get famous," he said. "In this country, believe me, it's the only way."

"Believe me I am trying that," I said.

"Believe me, I wish I could wish you luck."

"Just maybe I won't need it," I said.

He looked briefly incredulous. "Are you kidding, baby? I don't know what you've got when you're standing up, but talent's the dice, not the throw. Why do you think Frank only feels at home in casinos?"

"So do I," I said.

"So do I," he said.

"Well, I guess I'll be heading on now," I said.

"I guess you will," he said.

"At least give me a hug goodbye first," I said, thinking that there might be money in the robe and maybe I could grab it and then run off real fast before he could catch me.

I do think Sammy hesitated. But then he said, "Forget it, baby. I'd sooner hug Richard Nixon. Hit the road. Scoot. Beat it. It's all been lovely, sweetest, but I'm tired now, and I've had enough."

"Sam-*m*-my," I said, "it's four A.M. I don't know anybody in Palm Springs. I don't even know if there's a bus from here back to L.A., or where I would present myself to get on it. Where am I going to go? What'll I *do*, for God's sake?"

"You know, frankly, I don't—"

And then he heard what he was about to say, and started laughing. It was a kind of laugh that we call laughing with your heart down South, and he never did finish the sentence; nor did he need to. "*Oh!*" he gasped, throwing back his head to drink of the entire indigo sky; and for a second, I had the feeling we'd been worth it to each other, after all.

You see, I had started laughing, too. It *was* as funny as the whole ding-dong country spread with mustard on a hot-dog bun, and we stood there, face to face outside of Frank's pad in Palm Springs, from which I had been banished, and laughed like it was killing us. Finally, in whatever laughter's equivalent of post-coitally is, we down-shifted to giggles.

"Yee-hah and adios, Samby," I said. "I bet you still don't know nothin' 'bout birthin' no babies."

"*Shalom,* my Dixie twat," he said. "Good luck getting a name." I was half a block away when I heard him call, "This country . . . *only way!*"

Trudging through alien Palm Springs streets, above whose still dark roofs some morning stars now glimmered, I soon spied a familiar shape that I recognized as the limo. Opening the door to my repeated and powerful kicks, a bleary Slowy blinked at me. At his feet was a nudie magazine he hadn't bothered to conceal, along with a five-sevenths empty tube of airplane glue. Beside him, one shoe clutched in her lap, snored Suzannah, smelling of lipstick, chlorine, and rank despair.

"So how'd it go?" asked Slowy, as I scrambled in there with them. He licked his lips, his eyes aglow like two little cameras packed with unexposed film. "Jesus! Tell me *everything*. Don't leave out a single detail."

"You're such a *schmuck*, Slowy," I said.

Next to him, Suzannah's head came up, and her eyes popped open. "Of *course* he is," she said in some surprise. "Hain't he got a *dick*, sister mine? Small, but nonetheless present." Then she conked out again.

Slowy tapped on the glass. "Driver!" he said, attempting to mimic a high-society penthouse hustler's playboy swank. "We're done here. Take us back to the real world."

"*L.A.?*" the driver said. "You're *shitting* me, right, sonny?" But he started the engine even so.

Some time later, I saw in the papers that Sammy had married Mai Britt. There was a picture that showed him looking natty and winking, and the bride just looking mighty blonde; and just my luck. I had slept with a coon, set Momma to whirling like a space-program simulator in the grave to which I no doubt instantly sent her via pure telepathic osmosis, and didn't even finish in the money. If he'd asked *me* to marry him I'd have done it, I mean to hell with my mother, with her three teeth and one vowel.

Sammy, you see, had acquired wealth and fame sufficient to not need to get his civil rights on the installment plan. All the same, I might have felt more wistful about our night of love together had I not heard that he was talking trash about me all over town. Getting called a stupid bitch by Sammy Davis, Jr.—even now, that gets me so all-fired-up indignant I could brain the little one-eyed jig with my bazooms. Of all the things he could have said, that was just a lie. He knew I was lots smarter than most actresses.

Or Southern gals.

Despite those assets, as you know, my career never did make good on what might have been. I never did nab that Oscar, for all that it was an honor just to be nominated—as I was, all too briefly, by a look on Sammy's face. I never returned to Palm Springs, in the capacity of either guest or property owner. After Suzannah and I had patched things up and become friends, and she moved into my little house in Echo Park with me, all we got was older.

But you know something, Sprout? These days, when I gaze down from the modestly glinting asteroid of minor fame that I now occupy, in orbit like a tiny but huge-breasted naked Sputnik high above the good old U.S.A.—and, gazing down, see you and the thousands of blue adolescents like you, all writhing on beds and hunched in basements, having quickly excused yourselves from the dinner table as my old TV show comes on—why, then, I sometimes think *I'm* what Santy Claus does the other three-hundred-sixty-four days of the year.

I'm sorry that you're taking everything about your dad so hard; not just his dying, which is understandable, but his life. On the other hand, I do think that you're being just a little rough on your ex-girlfriend—

what with turning her into an imbecilic Panama Canal Zone slut, a maddened little pink-eyed dog, my sister Suzannah, and so forth. I mean, I'm sure that seeing her with your teacher must have been *quite* the kick in the teeth at your age, but believe me: these things happen. Sometimes it just works out that way. Besides, she probably isn't any older than you are; plus which, she is female, and so is facing seas whose perils you will never know, in a craft so frail you'd be plumb petrified if you set foot in it. We often manage to make port, however. We women have learned to sail.

All right, Sprout. Close me now. Stick me back under the pillow. Toodle-oo, and au revoir, and yee-hah. Well, finally!—yes, indeed: those *are* my eyes.

That's really all. I'm not going to show you anything else.

Aaaaargh!

Enough already.

Now, scoot.

Amoose-vay. Scram.

Beat it, kid.

VI

Professor X

ROBERT OPPENHEIMER WAS THE MOST SELF-DRAMATIZING MAN I'VE ever met. That drives me batty in a scientist. For instance, in the desert at Los Alamos, just after we'd set off the first bomb, he quoted from the *Bhagavad Gita*. "'I am become death,'" he said in that sepulchral voice of his—so at odds with the sanguine American tone, genially ranging from gee-whiz to oh-well, whose breezy ability to redefine what one did as things that happened kept all but the refugees among us chipper throughout the Manhattan Project.

Well and good. But what the books don't tell you is that, after a brief but annoyed silence, one of the thick-goggled physicists clustered around Oppenheimer on the observation platform turned and said, "Oh, blow it out your ass, Bob. We've got it made now till the cows come home." While I don't use language of that type myself, I did enjoy the sentiment for its humor and its accuracy both, as did the rest of our little band. Soon all of us were chortling as if there were no tomorrow, except for our boss. He kept on moving around in the bomb's afterglow, as if seeking the best way for its light to sculpt the gauntness of his face.

Having removed my own goggles early in order to take a Laggilin pill for the heart condition with which I had been diagnosed even then, I watched him closely, as I did all my seniors in the Manhattan Project— obtaining not only pointers on my own future demeanor but, as in this case, useful musts to avoid. In fact, I believe that my final decision to conduct myself as a friendly, accommodating, rumpled sort of fellow, plainly brainy but too lacking in masculine vim and gumption to raise any sort of alarm, was taken at that moment.

Then and later, I often considered concealing my intellect as well, since in the United States a simulation of stupidity can be highly useful in generating camaraderie's bovinely democratic heat. But I soon realized that a bushel of the size required to hide this particular light simply hadn't been made yet, and the calculations that, first taking a few moments to collect my thoughts, I swiftly jotted down on a matchbook adorned with the name of the gay bar I was adorning at the moment informed me that it probably never would. So I settled for inflecting the intelligence that I knew might make me suspect in my cud-chewing compatriots' eyes with a soothingly ineffectual air of shambling and even somewhat hangdog affability.

Lest you think I'm some unappetizing sort of fossil, though, I should point out that *every* physicist at Los Alamos was my senior, in years and office if not merit. My youth made me quite conspicuous, not only for its own sake but because very few scientists of any age, from firefly-trapping tykehood all the way to bushy-browed, Nobel-crazed dotage, can be reasonably described as even physically presentable, let alone comely. Indeed, having racked my brains for your benefit—no trifling gesture, all in all—I find that, myself aside, I can't think of another. In that New Mexico summer of '45, as I strolled among the various Quonset huts and labs on my various labors, I would often feel my brisk solitude trespassed on by the besotted stares of, simply, every sentient creature on the site—male or female, young or old, unattached or spoken for, smart or stupid, citizen or refugee, superior or inferior, in civvies or in uniform, ugly or attractive, two-legged or four-legged, walking or crawling, plausible (many) or out of the question (few). In the thick salad of visual rapine to which my presence played the crouton, all eyes were straining to measure my broad shoulders, caress my tousled hair, and mentally palp the tautness of the glutes, throbbing in their imaginations and to my own pleasurably certain knowledge with the subcutaneous cinnamon of muscles healthily gorged on their own blood, beneath my deliberately baggy trousers and loose lab coat.

That was yet another reason for me to keep my distracted mask in place, for I had learned quite early on that beauty can place endless demands on one's time from those who come into this world less favored, and so never stop seeking favors. Their pleas for my kindness I might well be disposed to grant, but over the whole process I was determined to retain control.

My private education in these matters had been launched at fourteen, when in the space of twenty-four hours I found myself seduced by first the Homburged husband and then the witless wife of a family freshly moved in down the block from my parents' home in Schenectady. Intrigued, I then set about seducing the same household's adolescent son and barely nubile daughter, so as to experience this novel application for people from every conceivable vantage point. But the extra effort involved in playing the part of wooer chafed me from the start. From then on, whatever my partners' capacities, tastes, gender, and number, I preferred having others' obeisance to offering my own; in addition to maximizing my pleasure with a minimum of wasted activity, this assured me of staying the center of attention while allowing me to solve and then remuddle whatever abstruse riddles then occupied my mind.

Nor was this the only education I got from that first quartet of encounters. As I shifted both figuratively and literally from one room to another in our new neighbors' house, my reflexes envigorated by the mental knight's moves of recalling who was out on errands and which family member I hoped would answer my bold knock at one door or my surreptitious tap-tap at another, the ginger cat whose presence on the premises predated my own emerged as a rival—if not, in the arched back and furious hissing with which she greeted my advent, an antagonist. Naturally growing irritated, I mixed up some special pet food, and got obtrusive Puss out of the way with gratifying dispatch so as to have the household's caresses to myself. However, I was soon identified as the culprit (in hindsight, this was inevitable, as no other lad in the neighborhood even possessed a chemistry set), and all four corners of my self-designed sexual compass, however understandably enchanted with finding my lithe form next to their less prepossessing ones in bed, felt obliged to put themselves beyond the pull of my charisma. They moved away soon afterward, if only to be nearer the daughter's costly sanatorium and the son's harsh military academy while the parents got divorced without attracting much notice—and I too learned to be more circumspect.

I'd caught the inventing bug much earlier. At the age of seven, feeling that to stop at two seats had been nothing but a failure of engineering nerve, I first conceived and then successfully soldered together a bicycle built for three. Only after my prototype had been wheeled out to our driveway did I realize I was missing two key ingredients for a field test, whom I would have had to recruit from among quite nonexistent playmates. Aside from the considerable number of them in which susceptibility to my physical charms has been the sole determinant, personal relationships were never to hold a great appeal for me. In my rare forays in that line, the chore of shared inspections of those pale pellets of Freudian earwax that people offer up as revelations has invariably wound up striking me as an insult to a mind with better things to do, and I have never seen much point in discussing myself with people less insightful than I am. At any rate, although my three-seater prototype rusted against a wall in Schenectady until my undeserving parents—substantiation of chaos theory in the flesh!—took advantage of their son's absence at Stanford to donate it to a wartime scrap-metal drive, I soon turned to physics, the bulk of whose required apparatus, at least at that early stage of the game, already nestled comfortably between my faunlike ears.

At Stanford, I was soon renowned for my attempts to synthesize molecules and neurons into a new form of matter. Indeed, I was mulling possible names for this hybrid when a Western Union boy brought me my summons to Los Alamos, and got one to the nearest men's room in return. As he went on his nameless way some eight minutes later, and I quickly popped a Laggilin pill for my heart condition, I could only speculate on which of us had more real cause to call this day a highlight. After all, my intellectual progress had many grander milestones still in store, while his sexual experience had just peaked.

While I had a fine time at Los Alamos, I often felt under-used—though hardly under-using, so to speak, at least by the measure of a gallery of gaping mouths, thrust-apart thighs, and sleepily blinking, monocular buttocks that stretches, in my memory, as far into the distance as the Hall of Mirrors at Versailles. My mental palace drew fewer visitors, however. In our theoretical discussions, to my mute disgust, one or another of the refugees was always hauling out a letter from Niels Bohr or an overexposed in-both-senses prewar snapshot of himself sitting uncertainly with Heisenberg in some drab mittel-Europa chophouse as if that settled everything. Despite the scallop-edged Kodak of the three-seater I kept pinned inside my own trunk, which after all represented something I had done rather than merely vaunting my social connections, my relative lowliness on the scientific roster prevented me from taking either a hand or a stand as often as I might have liked. In fact, my single most memorable contribution to the Manhattan Project came after our strictly scientific work was done.

Once Hiroshima had crowned our endeavors with such an extraordinary first success, War Department and White House alike were frantic to drop our only other working bomb somewhere, anywhere—so long as it was in Japan, obviously. (Or perhaps not: there were scattered votes for Winnipeg, for the sheer deliciousness of the surprise of it, and one for San Diego, where the colonel in question had recently picked up a nasty case of the clap.) If it was to be done at all, it had to be done quickly, before the Japanese had time to pick themselves up, dust themselves off, and surrender.

Along with the other interested parties, we in Los Alamos had been asked for our recommendation on the most promising metropolis that a single B-29 could obliterate in less time than it took "to fill up that Jeep out there with gas," which was Edward Teller's favorite way of putting it. The list of guidelines sent from Washington included a reminder that the photographs and films of the great event would probably still be getting reproduced half a century hence, perhaps in media as yet uninvented; in other words, it would be nice if the pictures were good, those from the first explosion having been distinctly subpar.

At the final meeting in Quonset One, pacing back and forth before a wall map of Japan, Oppenheimer had predictably begun to dither, with maundering the inevitable next step. In his hand, as usual, he held a bit of chalk; at one point, he disconcerted everyone in the room by placing this object in his mouth while querulously asking for a light. All present were dreading the moment when he'd quote the *Bhagavad Gita* again.

"Maybe," he was saying, "we should recommend *against* dropping it—dropping it anywhere at all! Or find some uninhabited atoll—some uncharted desert isle, whatever." Removing the chalk from his lips, he cast his eyes up to the heavens, where only a ceiling fan revolved. "My God, I can't even *think* about this without wanting to throw up . . ."

A few people, colonels and physicists alike, exchanged alarmed looks. Was that last bit from the *Bhagavad Gita*? No one knew, but the throb in Oppenheimer's voice spelled danger. Leaning casually against a wall, still feeling a pleasurable tingle from the moderately unattractive WAC who had rejoiced to find herself up-ended and mined as briskly as Colorado atop a crate of uranium samples a quarter of an hour before—straightening the seams on her thick legs, she had just entered the conference room with another message from Washington pressing us for a decision, thus bringing the memory back to mind—I suddenly recalled the old children's game of Pin the Tail on the Donkey, which I had never played but often witnessed. Taking half a dozen decisive steps forward, I hurled my shapeless lab coat over the startled Oppenheimer's head, spun him around three times, and shoved him at the wall map chalk in hand. Having made contact, he removed the improvised blindfold, and bent in close to learn what city he'd marked.

" 'Na-ga-sa-ki,' " he read slowly, sounding somewhat shaken from the ordeal he'd been put through. "Oh, well— *Scheiss,* if I may quote my father briefly. At least we can all pronounce that one." Tossing the chalk over his shoulder, he started toward the door. "Honestly," he said, pausing and shaking a finger at us, "it was damned embarrassing, how long everyone around here went on saying '*Hee*-roe-*SHEE*-ma,' not 'Hi-*rosh*-ima.' And yes, I know some of us don't speak English all that well, and wouldn't need to speak it at all if it weren't for Adolf Hitler. But we're all starting from zero when it comes to Japanese, and there's no excuse for us to mispronounce the names of major cities. Absolutely no excuse—no excuse at all. Good day, gentlemen," he said, throwing the lab coat back at me.

The door closed on Oppenheimer, leaving behind a group of conferencing confreres in a state of high satisfaction, or at the very least relief. Every last one of them was grateful to, and quite probably almost unbearably aroused by, a slim young man now leaning casually against a wall again, who had recognized his true vocation at that moment. What the last two minutes had taught me was that I could think outside the confines of physics, or indeed any other scientific discipline to which I might yet apply myself—and I might yet apply myself to them all.

I had just learned that I was a genius at problem-solving.

■

Up to then, the prospect of peace had held few charms for this particular contributor to the war effort, not least because it would cut off the steady supply of thick-ankled or slope-shouldered WACs I had grown

used to in Los Alamos—as well as of excitingly sullen, grudgingly com-
pliant male draftees, some of whom had noticeable skin conditions.
Indeed, enjoying my New Mexico life as I did, I had hoped the Japanese
would be fanatical enough to keep fighting even after we had dropped
twenty, thirty, forty bombs, as fast as we could build them. Given their
militarism and generally perverted values, it hadn't seemed beyond the
realm of possibility.

Yet Washington now cried out for a mind like mine, perhaps more
loudly than it knew. Unpinning the Kodak of the three-seater from my
footlocker, I followed Oppenheimer to the new Atomic Energy Commission, whose head he had been appointed. "Bring that old lab coat of
yours, too. We may need it again," he told me upon inviting me to join
him, in the bleakly facetious manner he now adopted for any and all
conversations. With a hearty laugh—he was still my boss, after all—I did.

At a White House reception on Hiroshima's second anniversary for
those of us who'd played a role in the Manhattan Project, Eleanor Roosevelt's handshake was distinctly tepid. Perhaps the late President's
widow had been unfavorably comparing her own over-dentitioned
homeliness to the allure of the brainy young buck before her, reeking
with animal magnetism as the thought-storms crackling in his eyes
exposed his air of diffidence for the charade it was. Or perhaps, however
startlingly, not, for soon afterward, to my perfect horror, I overheard her
fluting voice say this to another guest—not one of us, but a female journalist and gadabout who went by the peculiar name of Clare Wilkes
Boothe Luce Quilty:

"Oh, don't misunderstand, Clare," said Mrs. Roosevelt; "I'm certain it
was necessary. I *pray* that it was, since it was so horrid. But at least now
it's *done,* and perhaps we can find our way back to the business of being
the good old America that we might have stayed all along, slowly learning how to be better to one another, if it hadn't been for Mr. Hitler and
Pearl Harbor."

Remote as they were from my own concerns, and rocking quietly as
they did in odd corners of her husband's splendid dynamo, Mrs. Roosevelt's well-known array of well-intentioned hobbyhorses had never
impressed me unduly. Until that moment, however, I had not known she

was mad. *Back* to business? We were *in* business. Glancing at the astonishing array of talent around me—the scientists, the generals, the bureaucrats, the contractors—I could feel my lustrous, tousled hair stand on end at the thought of such a team being disbanded. As indeed it might be, if the wrong advice reached the still shaky Harry Truman's all too susceptible ears.

Bantam-sized and crisply featured, as Missourian as a Milk Dud, he himself was across the room, listening in more or less the manner of that character in Steinbeck who wants to hear about the rabbits as a top-lofty Averell Harriman described some great event in which all had gone well once FDR had taken Averell's advice. Having been an awestruck, gliding eavesdropper to an earlier onslaught of auto-Harrimania, I knew I could count on this lasting a while.

Unobtrusively slipping out and padding swiftly down corridors whose layout I seemed to know in my blood—have I mentioned that my grandfather, a born tinkerer like myself, had had a hand in running the Bureau of Indian Affairs during the Grant Administration?—I soon found myself in Truman's deserted office. On his desk, confirming my worst fears of the new President's uncertain grip on the helm, lay a well-thumbed copy of Dale Carnegie's *How to Win Friends and Influence People.*

Uncapping my pen and sitting down, and taking a moment to collect my thoughts, I dashed off a plan for a vast national-security apparatus, rapidly filling the book's front and back flyleaves. For the dual purposes of self-concealment and heightened impact on Truman's mind, I disguised my handwriting as FDR's—itself easily mimicked from the jotted marginalia in the framed typescript of the Four Freedoms speech hung on the office wall.

As I completed my task, I heard a click. Saw a Filipino steward standing in the door. Above his uniform's white collar, his face was a coppery mask of inquisitiveness and confusion, soon complicated beyond its own powers by the dawning of a pathetic conviction that, whatever precisely was going on, he still belonged here more than I did. Closing Dale Carnegie, I rose from the desk. Chest thrown back and nostrils flaring, my lustrous hair grown thick, I advanced on the steward with the prancing steps of a centaur.

Five snorting, joyous minutes later—during which the only sounds were my grunts and his gurgling, for Truman's "The Buck Stops Here" sign, however vapid as a motto, had proved the perfect bit once I seized it from the desk between the Filipino's scrabbling hands, with which he was frantically but ineptly trying to brace himself at the angle that would give him the most pleasure—my latest admirer had backed out of the office to search for an unbloodied pair of duck trousers, his face flushed with a gratitude to King Priap so intense it left him mute. Patting my hair into place and downing a Laggilin for my heart condition, I suavely returned to the reception; Truman signed the CIA's founding charter the next month.

Hard as it is to remember now, that took some courage on our newly resolute leader's part. Up to then—and with the obvious exception of J. Edgar Hoover's FBI, from whose staggering success at hoodwinking the populace I drew much inspiration—no large new government bureaucracy had ever been created except in response to some pre-existing situation or condition that made the need for it unmistakable to the common citizenry. That was scarcely the case here, making my scheme far from risk-free. Paying off, in the event, more spectacularly still than I'd dared hope, the great gamble buried in my memo on the flyleaves of *How to Win Friends and Influence People* was that a public long accustomed to the old, common-sensical ways of organizing its affairs would be infinitely more likely to conclude that the government had to know what it was doing than leap to the wild, far-fetched, and perfectly accurate conclusion that the rulebook had been chucked.

This handily killed two birds with one stone, since anyone who accepted the need for a CIA and an NSA as the *first* postulate of an equation would be instantly catapulted into a state of highly useful panic by the belated recognition that they and the lesser agencies they spawned could be necessary only in a world gone mad. Even as I marveled at my own brilliance in convincing premise and conclusion to swap roles, I was aware that, at some future point or points down the road, the public might have second thoughts. But by then, with any luck, the whole, constantly expanding, endlessly recombinant national-security establishment I envisioned would have itself long since become a pre-existing condition—one grown too large to be excisable, or even to be contained except cosmetically.

And, of course, all this is precisely how it has worked out.

Naturally, my paternity in the whole affair remained a secret closely held between myself, Dale Carnegie's beaming dust-jacket photo, and a nameless Filipino White House steward who probably hadn't even understood any of what was happening except the part that had happened to him. Even so, I couldn't help but feel a proprietary pride as my institutional spawn began to put out its first baby tentacles, looping around a news-magazine publisher's neck here, an internationally oriented charity organization there. In fact, on the campus lecture tours I sometimes undertook at the behest of the AEC—still my formal employer—I would sometimes discreetly steer the most promising students I met toward a career in intelligence instead of talking up my own bailiwick.

As the AEC then had no speakers' bureau of its own, these tours were incidentally set up for us via a courtesy arrangement with General Electric's public relations office, then capably run by a mustachioed young veteran of the Battle of the Bulge whose Dutch or German name—Knut or Kurt Fungott or Vangut, something like that—I no longer recall precisely. On a personal level, I had little use for this fellow, whose omnipresent Pall Malls annoyed me no less than his refusal, despite the responsibility imposed by his current line of work, to speak with respect of anything or anyone save his own older brother Bernard, a scientist like myself. Or rather, as his dry tone somewhat insolently implied, distinctly unlike myself.

I believe he later quit GE. Still, for all his eccentricity, the middle-class sense of duty that my future masters and I were so often to rely on made Vangut or Fungott almost helplessly competent at his job, thereby incalculably assisting not only my official travels as an AEC speaker but, by extension, my sub-rosa recruitment efforts on the intelligence community's behalf. As it happens, my very first such nudge of a bright mind in the right direction is the one I remember best, largely because of the memorable way the sandy-haired young man in question introduced himself to me.

I'd just finished my standard talk on the potential uses of nuclear energy other than bomb-making. Partly because its risks had to be concealed, this was tiresome stuff, as I well knew even if the AEC didn't. Only the already practiced charm of my disarmingly self-surprised, fingers-raking-forelock delivery kept my audiences from suspecting as much. As I re-rubber-banded a slim stack of index cards at the podium, I was furtively ransacking the emptying hall for the special bulge of pink sweater that would satisfy my eyes, and soon afterward, I expected, their blind twins down below. As a result, I only noticed after several seconds that someone was standing directly in front of me, hand extended.

"Hello, sir," he said. "I don't know if this'll make sense to you, but I just wanted to say thanks for keeping me alive."

"Are you sure that you don't mean awake?" I said, mildly stupefied, as we shook hands.

"You mentioned in your lecture that you worked on the Manhattan Project, sir. My outfit was slated to land on Kyushu when we invaded Japan. I was on Iwo Jima, and we"—peculiarly, his attention seemed to wander for a moment; I wondered madly if he had spotted the pink sweater—"we were told that Japan would be worse, sir. Truth is, I probably wouldn't be here today, if it wasn't for Hiroshima."

"Don't forget Nagasaki," I said, perhaps a bit sharply.

"Yes, sir. I know a lot of people do. I wouldn't know why that is, sir. Anyhow, that's all I wanted to say. Appreciate your time." He nodded and turned to go.

I glanced around. No pink sweater. She was gone, and something about him—some quality of banked but stokable fire—had impressed me.

"Wait," I called. "Have a cup of coffee with me. My train doesn't leave for an hour yet—and I don't know a soul in Rochester, Minnesota."

■

As I recall, his name was some Scotch-Irish monosyllable or near-monosyllable, and it and he were a good match. Alert gray eyes, good jaw, a shrewd calm voice with attractively gruff lifeguard and police-radio undertones, the whole thing pinned together by the perennial cigarette that was his combat-tautened generation's universal badge of (ironic enough, this, when you recall the Surgeon General's conclusions some years later) survival. In fact, in former days, the sandy-haired fellow sitting across from me in the railroad station's coffee shop would almost surely have been the beneficiary of a surprise state visit from good King Priap—and the purring motor of my sexual charisma, once turned on, had outraced tighter train schedules than this one when it had to.

Somewhat to my own surprise, however, neither this kind of appeal nor its distaff equivalent aroused me that much anymore, and I hadn't even noticed him during my lecture. Instead, and virtually from opening joke to closing thought, my reason to value the podium's concealment had been the hunchbacked girl in the thick glasses midway back, the hump quite prominent beneath pink wool. The thought of her incredulous delight and abject gratitude when she was unexpectedly invited to pay fealty to my body with her imperfect one had been enfevering enough for the visiting speaker from the Atomic Energy Commission to start plucking at the loose rubber band around his wrist as he spoke— until the pings grew audible to the first row, which was how I found out I'd been doing it.

The urgings of the lower brain having been denied by her premature exit—with annoyance, I realized that I hadn't even gotten to see her spine's curve as she walked—I settled for keeping the upper one interested. Rochester was his hometown, he said, although he'd spent a short and apparently melancholy spell as a child in Florida. After his discharge from the Marines, he'd come back here to work in his father's garage. But Bruno, the immigrant mechanic his dad had saved from an almost certain doom back East by hiring him twenty-odd years ago, seemed to have things well in hand, so the son had started taking courses on the GI Bill instead.

What did he want to do next? A rare unfettered grin informed me that this was the most interesting question he'd ever heard, and that he'd heard it often from himself. He'd thought sometimes of becoming a journalist, and at other times of teaching; after being on the receiving end of it for a while, he guessed he'd gotten more interested in how history worked. Then again, about three days a week he thought of heading for the Gulf of Mexico, buying a fishing smack, and pointing it out to sea with no destination but the horizon, his dream since boyhood. So what did all of that add up to? Hands thrown apart above his elbows on the table, and joined only by the trailing rope of blue smoke from the cigarette in one of them, he amiably confessed he didn't know.

I did. For a man who had once cut a Gordian knot by whirling Robert Oppenheimer around three times before shoving him at a wall map, it was child's play to rearrange these only superficially random ingredients into a recipe. As I boarded my train and he called "Goodbye" and "Thanks, sir," I had no idea if he would take my advice—carefully hoarded until just before boarding time, to maximize its effect—that he should try for the CIA. Yet a year or so later came a postcard signed with a name I had long since forgotten, now briefly recalled, and soon forgot again, and showing the surprisingly small stream that is the Mississippi that far north. It let me know the sender had been accepted by "the shop," and thanked me warmly for my guidance.

Needless to say, I didn't answer. Unless you've got a pressing reason, you don't start a correspondence with a future spy. In any case, my only real concern had been to while away an hour, as un-idly as I could, before a train turned up to take me from somewhere to somewhere, and that hour was long since done.

As I recall, two or three other cards came over the next few years, until the sandy-haired, gray-eyed chap I'd steered to the Agency evidently concluded that I was indifferent—or else grew less grateful to me, I suppose, though I don't really. The last one came from Guatemala, I believe, and since it turned up in my AEC mailbox not many weeks before the coup down there, I imagine he was involved with that in some way. But I scarcely paid attention, for this was in 1954—the year of an encounter that was to have far greater consequences for me.

■

As at so many other crucial junctures of my life, it all began with a thump of Good King Priap's scepter.

I was leaning casually against a wall at Kay Josephs' piano bar on P Street in the lost blocks between Georgetown and Dupont Circle, right near the bridge above Rock Creek. If these two dimly lit rooms below street level in fact went by another name, the secret never passed the lips of Kay himself, an enticingly obese but disappointingly poised gent with a taste for hints, mints, and taunts. Denied the help of either a sign or telephone-directory listing in finding its way to his door, his all-male clientele had to rely instead on word of mouth, bathroom-stall graffitoes, and the guesswork invited by the chartreuse glow in the row of windows that hugged the sidewalk, too low for less gonadically goaded pedestrians to even notice they were there.

And to be candid, may I say that I find less enchantment in today's boisterous blatancies than I did in that urgent, quasi-conspiratorial furtiveness, so reminiscent of espionage in everything but its object. Among its other special joys, repression guaranteed that a high proportion of Kay Josephs' customers would lift their usual gin rickeys to mouths figuratively and sometimes literally twitching with an abject belief in their owners' ghastliness—and while neurosis hardly equaled physical deformity when it came to putting a crowbar in my pants, this self-loathing did add zeal to my generosity in letting such wretched creatures briefly share me with myself, like pigeons on a heroic statue.

Despite the rich field of masculine misery it offered to my good king's selflessness, their unhappiness otherwise left me mystified. But then I wasn't homosexual, and indeed rather looked down on the breed. Confirmed in Schenectady and never revised, my own attitude was simply that it made no sense to deprive half the planet's population of a chance to taste of life under good Priap's rule, on no better grounds than their particular spoonful of chromosomal alphabet soup.

Indeed, the only worry that I was obliged, willy-nilly, to share with these pansies was fear of the vice squad. The all too frequent surprise visits of D.C.'s finest explained the stacks of old *Washington Posts* left thoughtfully parked by Kay at all exits, enabling his clients to cover their faces should they chance to appear in the next day's edition. For the mute assertion of the bearer's normality they provided, sports sections were in particular demand, resulting in arrest photographs that often seemed to depict men dismayed by the Redskins' latest loss or setting grainily marched off to lockup for their faith in the Red Sox. I believe that such explanations were often fobbed off by parents on credulous children perusing the paper, thus not only preserving the tykes' naïveté but impressing them at an early age with the useful message that loyalty to a team is no laughing matter in America.

Needless to say, this apprehension was especially fraught for those of us who worked for the government. On an average night at Kay Josephs', that category probably included half if not two-thirds of the men eyeing one another along the bar or tentatively holding hands at one of the tables as Kay's piano player, known only as Clam even to regulars like myself, let two nimble pet white mice race back and forth along his keyboard. As a result, sheer probability may well have abetted my vague impression—acquired during our brief preliminary chat at the bar, so I believed, although more likely it came from newsreel images whose sullen mask I'd not yet matched to the pomaded head bobbing at my beltline—that the new subject kneeling to Priap at the moment in Kay Josephs' supply room, to which Kay supplied a select few of us with our own key, had some sort of official status equal to my own. Or possibly a more prominent one, I thought, having suddenly recalled that he and not I had unlocked the door.

Although distinctly unattractive, with eyes that slid around in their weak sockets like two smoldering oil drops in an enameled saucepan, pudgily smirking lips, and the pasty complexion that in Washington advertises one's importance by indicating business too pressing for one to ever see the sun—although in his case I certainly can't see why he and Schine, on their junketeering raids in search of disturbing library books and suspect embassy personnel at U.S. facilities overseas, couldn't have booked themselves into at least one country where they might get a tan—this chappie wasn't really my type. However, the primary problem wasn't physical. Despite the servility suggested by our respective attitudes, the mere lip service he was paying Priap told me he had mistaken the good king for a mendicant in *his* kingdom, instead of acknowledging that he was a supplicant in mine. A man in his position was supposed to be giving pleasure, not receiving it—and, despising that kind of selfishness as I do, I grew increasingly bored and annoyed. However, I could tell His Majesty was on the verge of delivering an edict even so, and cupped both the ears beneath me to yank forward the face they were attached to for the finale, as I always did.

At my touch, his neck jerked back like that of *Naja*—the taxonomic name, of course, for cobra, Mary-Ann. "Hands off the coif, pal," he snapped, giving the unpleasant sneer that, along with the smirk, comprised his sum total of facial reactions. "That's a twelve-dollar haircut you're messing up." In what little light came from the street through the smudged window above our heads, his teeth had gleamed like bullets from a . . .

Machine gun!

He set back to work, but my loins had become a republic. Now demoted to mere Citizen Priap, their former ruler went into exile, to Roy's evident disgust. After I'd gulped half a Laggilin for my heart condition as he watched, we departed the supply room in acrimonious silence, and chose stools far apart at the bar. A few minutes later, I saw him dangling his key before another prospect, whose repulsive physique—he looked like an Olympic swimmer—was soon following my recalcitrant former subject's hunched shoulders and, in rueful hindsight and palms-to-pants frottage, gratifyingly greasy hair down a corridor.

As this type of encounter, though not the wilted conclusion, was no rarity in my life, I had all but forgotten it when my office telephone gave a suspiciously strident ring some weeks later. Without preliminaries, in an arrogant whine, a voice I didn't yet recognize told me something interesting about my own life that I had never known. To wit, that—in the course of several long conversations we'd had at Los Alamos nine years earlier—Dr. Robert Oppenheimer had spoken sympathetically to me about Communism, and had even suggested I might read some Marx.

"He did no such thing," I protested. "We never had a single conversation like that. Who is this?"

"Jesus, don't answer right off the bat, Prof," the voice said. "This is important. Give yourself time to think. Maybe he even offered to loan you his own copy of *Das Kapital*—well, no, that won't fly. But still: are those little chats with the Doc while you and he were building the big one together starting to come back to you at all?"

"No, they are not," I said. "They never happened, and *this* conversation is preposterous. Who is this?"

"This is Washington, D.C., where preposterous is as preposterous does, pal—and it all depends on which story you'd rather see in the papers. The one about the pinko scientist up in Princeton who lost his security clearance, or the one about the faggot who got bounced out of the AEC for playing unlicensed hot-dog vendor at Kay Josephs'."

Suddenly, I knew who this was—or rather, realized who the stranger servicing me in Kay's supply room had been. The reason our preliminary chat before repairing there had been so brief, I now saw, was that his face was sufficiently familiar to me from newspapers and television that, without quite placing it, I had unconsciously behaved as if we already knew each other.

"Well, Roy," I said furiously, since under the circumstances I thought that he could hardly insist on being Mistered, "what if I were to mention to anyone who interviews me that—well—that *you* were the one on his knees?"

"That's sure not true now, is it? Anyway, I fished up some sad sack out of Kay's talent pool who now knows every detail of our little rendezvous, right down to the pattern of the ugly tie that kept on getting in my eyes, I mean his. And guess what, Prof? The poor bastard's broke, and we also look kind of alike. You so much as say that I was even in Washington that night—which it turns out I wasn't, you'll be happy to know—and I'll call it either a case of mistaken identity or a deliberate smear."

"What I'd call *this* is an awfully steep price to pay for one lost erection," I said angrily.

Roy sounded genuinely taken aback. "Christ, this isn't personal. Even if I'd wound up swallowing a whole milkshake, I'd be doing exactly the same thing. I guess you don't know me very well."

"How do you know *me*?" I asked. "I mean, how did you find me—how did you know who I was?"

"I know who everybody is," Roy said.

■

All the same, he plainly didn't know everything *about* everybody, providing a source of some merriment to us both over the next thirty years. Not the least reason his attempt at blackmail had left me spluttering was that it was so unnecessary, since if Oppenheimer needed smearing all Roy had to do was ask. I had lost all sympathy for my onetime chief some years earlier, when to my incredulity he and a majority of his fellow hand-wringers on the AEC's Advisory Committee had voted *against* developing a hydrogen bomb. I had even considered resigning my own post in protest, but soon realized I'd do better by both bomb and self by remaining in place, and quietly passed word to Teller—still out in Los Alamos—that he had a friend in court.

Subsequently, at least in Washington, D.C., Oppenheimer had become an increasingly vague presence in the corridors of nuclear power, devoting the bulk of his time to his other post as head of the Institute for Advanced Study in Princeton—a party to which, I noted with cold rage, I was distinctly *not* invited. Clearly, my ex-boss feared the competition of younger and more limber minds, since once in New Jersey he preferred to keep himself surrounded by a dismal clutch of has-beens and mediocrities—with Einstein, who hadn't had a new idea since 1905, as the most glaring example of the first category, and Oppenheimer himself leading the pack in the second.

The stunned look on my erstwhile superior's face as I gave my testimony, and the confusion of his faltering claims to have been barely aware of my existence at Los Alamos, are memories I shall always dote on. So is the recollection of how soon I found myself in a position to tease Roy about his miscalculation of the need for leverage in my case, for as I exited the hearing room, he hailed me from the window of a nearby taxicab.

Still inflamed to the point of being able to count the metal teeth on my zipper by thoughts of the dwarfishly stunted, almost hydrocephalic receptionist—her evident need for Priap's succor augmented almost to the point of madness by the milky cast in one eye—who had brought me coffee as I waited in an antechamber for my name to be called from the witness list, I made hasty use of a newspaper to hide my condition as I accepted Roy's invite to climb in alongside him. Nonetheless, when he saw Oppenheimer's always pained and now tentpoled face peering up at him from the front page of *The Washington Post*, he smirked knowingly.

"Lincoln Memorial," he told the driver. "Then just keep going around." Then he leaned back.

"I've had you checked out. Maybe I should be looking at you with new respect," he told me, instead looking at me with new chumminess.

"What do you mean?"

"I mean 1947. The Filipino talked," Roy explained. "As soon as you were done with him, he tottered off to find the Secret Service, clutching a copy of *How to Win Friends and Influence People* and babbling that he'd been raped."

"He was *raped*?" I gasped, horrified. "That same *day*? Was it before or after I had sex with him?"

Roy's expression grew slightly quizzical, but then he resumed his story. "Of course, the gook thought that what you'd written in the flyleaves must be some sort of threat. But the minute the Secret Service passed the book on to us, we realized it was an even smarter plan than the one we'd been working on. It just took us years to figure out you were responsible."

"And who is 'us'?" I asked.

"That," said Roy, "is the reason you're getting a ride in my taxi, pal. I think it's time you started working on purpose for the same people you've been working for by accident."

"And who are *they*?" I asked.

"The same people I work for."

"Joe McCarthy?" I was puzzled. "That's only one person. Unless he and his brother Charlie are in it together, of course."

Roy looked contemptuous. "*Joe?* That drunken nincompoop? Christ, no. He's on the skids anyhow, and what did he ever have to do with Oppenheimer? Tom Swift you're not, Prof, since the hearing you just testified at wasn't even on Capitol Hill. No, that's only my cover job—and not for a lot longer, either."

"What's your real one, then?" I asked.

"The same thing it's always been. The same thing it always will be, and don't let my boyish bad looks fool you—I turned fifty-four this year. I," said Roy somewhat floridly, "am the lawyer for the American Century. I represent the people this country is *for.*"

"And who are they?" I asked again, mystified again. At which my friend Roy grew less florid.

"How the hell would I know?" he said. "Most of them don't even know who each other are. I mean, they're all white, and they've all got money, and a lot of them live in Connecticut. But beyond that, pal," he shrugged helplessly, "we might as well be talking about the fucking man in the moon."

■

Having reached the Lincoln Memorial, the taxi began to circle it—something now no longer allowed, incidentally. Beyond Memorial Bridge, every time we came around, I could see the hill of Arlington on the far side of the Potomac, with its crowning mansion that had once fathered and now mothered graves. The view seemed oddly incomplete; some sort of small fire at midpoint would be the perfect finishing touch, I thought nonsensically. If my usually powerful mind struck even me as a tad disordered at the moment, that was because Roy had never stopped talking:

"Here's how it works," he was saying rapidly. "No one of them knows more than a dozen or so of the others—just enough so they can go on marrying each other and keep the loot in the family, or families. No one group ever communicates with any other group, since that would increase the risk of exposure."

"A cell system," I murmured. "It sounds as if they *did* learn something from the Communist Party, after all."

Briefly, Roy looked stumped—a rare condition that he deeply hated. "The which? Oh, the 'godless ratfink Commie bastards,'" he recited tonelessly. "Actually, I don't think they'll ever admit it, because they're such godless ratfink Commie bastards. But they got the idea from my clients."

"If the cells don't ever communicate with each other," I asked, having more than once felt the identical curiosity about the Comintern, "how do they figure out what they're all going to do next?"

"They don't," Roy said tersely.

"Then how do they even know what they want?"

"They don't. They never have. These people have the brains of pineapples, Prof, and the only thing they ever invented was croquet. But they don't need to know what they want. They just get it, because they're the people the country is for."

As a scientist, if nothing else, I was growing exasperated. "But how—"

"Do you remember the story of the centipede?" Roy interrupted, having anticipated me. "How it's walking along one day on its hundred legs—and then another insect, say a butterfly, floats up to it and says, 'Jesus, but that's impressive, Mr. Centipede. How do you ever manage to control all those legs?' Of course, nobody has ever asked the centipede that before. It's never even noticed that it's *got* a hundred legs—just figures something's keeping it moving down there, what the fuck, who cares, and now it's on to the next leaf, munch munch. But thanks to the butterfly, it starts to *think*, for the first time—and never takes another step until it dies. And ants start chowing down on it while it's still alive."

He exhaled noisily. "Well, nobody's ever asked my clients that question," he said. "And if I've got anything to do with it, which I do, no fucking butterfly ever will."

The cabdriver's neck, I now noticed, sported a huge goiter. From my lap, Oppenheimer's pained face began to rise again. "But Roy," I said, rapidly putting the business section atop it and dragging myself back to Topic B with some difficulty, "if we don't know who they are, and *they* don't know who they are—and don't even know what they *want*—why on earth do we work for them? It doesn't make any sense."

"It doesn't have to. Like I said, they're the people the country is for. And they're so stupid that they'd never get *anywhere* without us. Anyhow, the money and the perks are pretty good . . . Hey, *putzy*! You, with the goiter. Quit with the goddam circling already. Take us to the Smithsonian. You trying to make us sick?"

"I'm feeling a little dizzy myself," I confessed.

"Think so? Wait'll you see the nightclub underneath the Smithsonian," Roy said comfortably. "Prof, your whole family's life savings since 1776 wouldn't be enough to bribe the headwaiter. And you won't believe the main exhibit."

"Tell me," I said.

"Amelia Earhart!" He giggled happily. "We've had that bitch under lock and key for twenty years. Too many broads were starting to get funny looks in their eyes when they saw her up there, flying."

■

As usual, Roy was right. The money was staggering, and the perks—particularly for a man of my increasingly philanthropic brand of sexuality—nothing short of extraordinary. However, I won't have you think I simply spent my days egging on good Priap to do his kingly best for gasping old duffers in oxygen tents, three-hundred-pound women with skins all aglow from eczema, and grateful amputees of both sexes, forcing Laggilin pills for my heart condition down my throat by the fistful. Delighted that my genius at problem-solving had finally been recognized, had a sword clapped in its hand, and ordered to take that hill, I worked harder than I ever had in my life. My first major success was contriving the Suez crisis of 1956.

As Roy laid it out for me, the problem at hand was to find some means of preserving the anticolonialist reputation that the United States still enjoyed around the world at a time when we had, in fact, become its leading empire. Taking only a moment to collect my thoughts before grabbing a pencil and an envelope on which one of my predecessors appeared to have amused himself by working out a modest brain-teaser—the answer was "Eighty-seven," I noticed automatically—I quickly devised a beautiful little stratagem, whose first step was for Secretary of State John Foster Dulles to guarantee the World Bank loans required by Nasser's Egypt to build the Aswan Dam. A few months later, on a pretext, I had Dulles *rescind* the loan guarantees, leading Nasser to retaliate—as I had gambled he would, in my plan's single question mark—by nationalizing the Suez Canal.

Under a carefully nurtured illusion of being able to count on our tolerance if not consent, our *soi-disant* allies France and Great Britain, both of whom took a proprietary interest in the waterway that one nation had built and the other bought in happier times all around, mounted an invasion to re-open it, in covert collusion with the Israelis. Then came my great coup.

At the UN, I had Dulles denounce the Franco-British intervention as a flagrant act of old-fashioned imperialism—unlike, needless to say (and believe me, it wasn't), the newfangled kind on which we held the patent. Caught with their landing-craft ramps down, so to speak, and knowing full well that without our backing both their economies would be wrecked inside a week, London and Paris were obliged to give up the whole operation as a botch. As they sheepishly withdrew their baffled troops, we Americans basked in utterly undeserved adulation for the principled manner in which we had forced our very own "allies" to call off their bullying of a smaller nation. Partly to further muddy the waters, and partly because I enjoyed tickling Roy's funnybone, I had our own tame press demonize Nasser as a hysterical despot while permitting not a breath of criticism of the Israelis—who were as culpable as France and Britain, but had also been in on the whole scheme with us from the start.

It worked beautifully.

Although our own country's citizens were too docile and uninformed for us to worry overmuch about any rumblings from that corner, we did occasionally feel the need for some domestic prophylaxis. One of my best forays in that vein was the plan—scrawled, after I'd taken a few moments to collect my thoughts, with the end of a burnt match on the cuff of my shirt as I was watching *Gunsmoke* one day—to have President Eisenhower say goodbye to public life by denouncing what we decided to call "the military-industrial complex." That term occasioned no end of chortling in our vast sub-aquatic lair, located in the middle of the Potomac beneath the supposedly undeveloped woodlands of Theodore Roosevelt Island. Compared to what we knew to be the reality, for Ike to start babbling about a military-industrial complex was a bit like referring to the *Titanic* as the S.S. *Minnow,* or some other equally innocuous name.

In any case, the guile of it was my expectation—fully borne out by events—that by then everyone would be so sick of Eisenhower, whom we had carefully built up as a genial fool, and would find the sheer incongruity of a warning from this source so perplexing, that anyone who brought up the military-industrial complex from then on would simply sound as senile as he did. I'm told that Ike himself, in actuality about as doddering and kindly as a threshing machine, roared with laughter at my stratagem before agreeing to play the patsy, a decision he commemorated by sighing, "Thank Christ, thank Christ—no more golf. Jesus *God,* but I'm sick of that stupid game."

And lucky him, for at times our own work seemed endless. Coming over the speakerphone one day in 1961 in my lavish underwater office, past whose windows fish killed by the Potomac's increasing pollution had begun steadily drifting belly-up, Roy's voice sounded peevish even for him. "There's so much goddam money swimming around the country right now, sooner or later even the Gillies"—our organization's odd nickname for the imbecilic citizens not in the know, albeit one whose origin escapes me—"are going to start wondering how come there are still poor people and diseases, and all that other crap. Well, if there weren't, I'd have to start fucking rich ones—and you'd be stuck screwing healthy ones, Prof. Any ideas on how to distract them?"

Telling him to turn on a tape recorder, and taking a few moments to collect my thoughts, I removed one of my shoes and used my desk to bang out a plan in Morse code for a program dedicated to landing a man on the moon within the decade. Of course, there was nothing there, and even the slowest Gillie could have seen that; in this case, the naked eye was no liar. But the program would be fabulously expensive, and allow those of my fellow scientists who might otherwise have been tempted to try curing cancer or designing fuel-efficient cars to have a marvelous time instead building intricate $2 billion trinkets which they could then fire out past the slowly rotting ozone layer, placing these fascinating but perfectly useless objects well beyond the reach of suspicious minds.

Much as I'd like to, however, I can't claim credit for perhaps the single most celebrated idea ever hatched in our shop. Although modesty, among other things, forbade him from ever confessing his authorship, the war in Vietnam was the brainchild of my colleague Dr. Henry Kissinger, who had gone to work for Roy's clients well over a decade before that ultimate Gillie Richard Nixon innocently offered him a job "up top," as we called it in our underwater lair. Bored with watching dead fish float up past *his* window, as he didn't share my erotic fascination with them—or, at any rate, remained unwilling to admit it!—Hank took on the White House gig as a lark. Having hatched his plan to bump off nearly 60,000 Gillies and uncounted Vietnamese for the defense industry's sake back before the ink was even dry on the 1956 Geneva accords, it must have tickled him no end to reap all the glory of announcing "Peace is at hand" (well, on paper, anyway) some sixteen years of lucrative if otherwise pointless butchery later, even as his Gillie master fumed at his ostensible subordinate for hogging the kudos.

A sentimental fellow in his way, Hank used to phone down from up top to hear his old colleagues' amused reactions to his pranks: "Vot do you dink? Isn't my Cherman accent just a riot? Peter Sellers must be pissing his *pants,*" he used to crow over my speakerphone, switching to his natural Topanga Canyon tones midway through. When he was sure no TV cameras rolled or radio microphones recorded him, he sounded a bit like a member of the singing group the Mamas and the Papas.

Indeed, what I myself miss most about our sub-aquatic alma mater—for like dear Henry, one of the few human beings for whom I've ever felt genuine affection, I am now retired—are the laughs.

Although hardly on a par with Kissinger's, my own most whimsical project afforded Roy a good deal of amusement. In the mid-1960s, in order to conclusively prove the breed's stupidity—and, frankly, because I needed a vacation, not having been up top myself since 1954 except on brief sorties to visit good King Priap's subjects—I marooned six archetypal Gillies, chosen for us by a tame academic and canned-soup heir named Joseph Campbell, on what they were told was a desert island not found on any map. In fact, their floating environment was man-made, per my instructions down to the last palm and the white boat with a hole in it, and anchored just out of sight of California's coastline. If any of the fools had ever thought to climb up into the mountains on a clear day, they could have spotted Catalina.

Undetected, I moved among them in the guise of a fellow castaway, my old impersonation of the well-meaning but hapless egghead never more useful or successful. At night, in the secret complex I'd had built underneath the "island," I lived like a pasha, and Priap took his pick—although, at times, a shovel might have come in equally handy—from the flattered harem of the deformed, diseased, and freakish I'd had shipped here, at phenomenal expense, from all over the United States. Meanwhile, up top, as I still called it out of habit, none of my six specimens—male or female, sailor or landlubber, young or old, rich or poor—ever guessed that their thoughtful but somehow none too competent companion was not only the very man who had created their predicament, but the invariable saboteur of their pathetic schemes to escape.

I kept the game up some three years, until a call for help from Hank Kissinger—the semi-Gillie Lyndon Johnson's private qualms about Vietnam made extra work for us all down below until the day that broken man quit the White House—forced me to end the project and return to our sub-aquatic lair in the Potomac, whose last surviving fish turned out to have bit the ooze during my sabbatical. Still, by then I felt my point had been made, and my reaching Washington in one piece was the proof. In all our time together, just as I'd expected, not one of my artificial castaways off Catalina had even come close to unriddling the only true solution to their predicament, which my scientific integrity required me to include in the experiment's design. A mainstay of the concept from the moment that, having taken a few seconds to collect my thoughts, I'd roughed out the whole thing on a wall of my underwater office with a lump of coal left over from our annual Christmas party, the one way out I left in for the Gillies expressed my full contempt for them—a contempt that thirty-six months of familiarity had only bred like flies.

You see, as I had rigged the scheme, the only way they could have gotten off the island was to kill me.

■

Half a decade after my return to our underwater headquarters beneath Roosevelt Island, the clumsy conspiracies of Richard Nixon proved to be the near undoing of us. As a result, I went to live up top again for a while.

Nixon, you should know, was unusually smart for a Gillie. This caused him little else but torment, as his intelligence had led him to glean more than a few inklings of our existence over the years. His unctuous craving to prove his merit by serving our goals as best he could alternated with a mare's nest of resentments at never having been asked to join our golden combine himself, despite his undoubted industry and almost pathological eagerness to measure up by casting Gillie principle to the four winds.

As all this made him an imperfect stooge, placing him in the White House was something of a calculated risk on our part. At a secret meeting in Gettysburg, even our old standby Ike advised against it, shortly before his motor went on the fritz, the simpleton grin that we'd all taken such malicious pleasure in designing turned spasmodic, and we finally decided that we had repaired and rewired the whole apparatus one time too many. However, by the late 1960s our operations had grown so complex that we felt the need for a figurehead up top who had, so to speak, an ear for our special music—one good enough to let him limp along on the piano, apparently alone on the stage, as our unseen orchestra thrummed and sawed away in its masked pit. In that way, Nixon was a sort of distorted mirror image of his near-immediate predecessor, with the accidental Johnson playing the role of the equal sign in that particular let X=Y.

Far from being a Gillie of any sort, John Kennedy had been the rare member of Roy's clientele with enough perceptiveness to understand how the thing worked, and the wit to find it amusing. When he had a message smuggled to our underwater lair announcing he'd grown bored with a steady diet of amphetamines and starlets, and puckishly proposing that he be allowed to take the twenty-five-hundred-mile-long Caddy— our private nickname for the United States—out on a chicken run, we hesitated. But this was back in happier times, and we concluded that we could count on his sense of irony, which was marvelously tuned, to counteract his love of danger.

After his death, when the Gillies began to reverence him as their great idealist, we had some panicked moments down below. Of all things, picking out *earnestness* as Jack Kennedy's prime virtue struck us as so far-fetched that we feared they'd finally tumbled to the game, and were pulling our legs in turn. However, it turned out that they meant it, and after some mutually rolled eyes and bemused shrugs in our underwater corridors, we all contentedly went back to our jobs.

Incidentally, his murder was pure Gillie work, and nothing to do with us. But we certainly profited from the chance to divert all sorts of minds sharp enough to have detected our labors into wasting their careers instead on fruitless speculation and nonsensical conspiracy theories. Eventually, having decided that the Gillies' obsession with November 22, 1963, was adversely affecting their productivity, we gleefully put paid to the whole chapter by manipulating the biggest clod we could find in Hollywood—no easy search, given the competition—into making a movie about the assassination so ridiculous that no one in America ever took the topic seriously again. As I used to rather daringly tell my class during the interlude when I briefly turned high-school teacher up top in Arlington, knowing that my fuddy-duddy manner would prevent them from guessing that they were getting it straight from the horse's (no, Secretariat's!) mouth, the true story of history isn't what occurs, which is often perfectly haphazard, but how and by whom its events are turned to advantage.

But I'm getting ahead of myself, since I had yet to surface. Striding into my office one day in June 1972, a raging Roy threw down a copy of *The Washington Post* dated April 1973. Its headline screamed the news that Nixon had just fired the two animatronic devices we had code-named "Haldeman" and "Ehrlichman," and an inside page featured a rogues' gallery of conspirators, some robotic and some Gillie, all involved in something called Watergate. For some reason, one sandy-haired, gray-eyed face, far down in the postage-stamp-sized row of minor players, briefly caught my eye. In an instant, however, I had realized that the reason his hair looked sandy and his eyes seemed gray was that the photograph was black and white, and turned to the predictably indignant Herblock cartoon.

Although only an editorial cartoonist, Herblock was no dummy for a Gillie. In fact, I sometimes think he might have exposed the whole works if he hadn't been too nice a man to believe all this was really happening. However, Roy's rant was demanding my full attention:

"The son of a bitch has turned *freelancer*," he sputtered, meaning Nixon, "and *that*, or something very like it"—meaning the paper—"is going to come out inside a year. We can slow it down, but we can't stop it."

"Well, the Ford animatronic is coming along," I pointed out. "We can always send him up top ahead of schedule. It'll be a rush job, and he'll probably be pretty clumsy, but we can do it if we have to."

"That's a stopgap, and you know it," Roy fumed. "I want to make sure that nothing like this *ever* fucking happens again. I want a long-range plan. You've got five minutes." Seizing the newspaper, he stalked out.

I picked up a grease pencil and sat down in front of the nearest available writing surface, which happened to be the screen of the television set I always had on, with the sound off, in my office. Having taken a few moments to collect my thoughts, I began to jot random words and phrases on my screen—writing, as is my wont, in all directions, without particularly noticing where my nib has touched down from one idea to the next.

Imbecilic, I wrote in a long vertical, looping down one side of the screen.

Inspirational, I scrawled in another vertical, looping up opposite the first.

Docile, I inserted horizontally in between the two verticals, down near the bottom of the screen.

An uncanny ability to spout perfect nonsense with utter conviction. I scribbled, all in a bunch at the top.

Rugged, I wrote in a tiny circle, near the left-hand vertical.

(-looking), I qualified the previous thought, in another circle across from the first.

Patriotic, I wrote at the dead center of the screen, my grease pencil sliding unexpectedly in a vaguely Picasso-like hook.

Just as I got done outlining the qualities most needed in a perfect Gillie stooge, Roy charged back into my office. Seeing the screen, he stopped in his tracks. As agitated as he was, he burst out laughing.

"You're a sick bastard, you know that, Prof?" he said. "But it could work. Fuck everything! Desperate times call for desperate measures."

"Roy, I have no idea what you're talking about," I said.

"Come look."

Dropping the grease pencil and scrambling to my feet, I stepped back and saw the same thing he had. I was startled, but any half-bright Gillie could probably guess what it was. Showing through my outline, the screen flickered with random images, in bright and somehow soothing colors.

Unwittingly, I had drawn the face of Ronald Reagan.

Beside me, Roy shook his head admiringly. "I wish FDR could have seen this," he said. "It would give him the laugh of his life."

"FDR?" I said. "Why FDR?"

His eyes widened. "You don't know?"

"Don't know what?"

Wonderingly, he walked to my desk, and picked up Harry Truman's copy of Dale Carnegie's *How to Win Friends and Influence People.* Along with a plaque that read "The Buck Stops Here," its upper and lower rims incised with toothmarks, I kept the book in my office, as any man who has gone on to accomplish much might preserve a favorite memento of where it all began—say, a long-dried husk of coconut shell carved with the message NATIVE KNOWS POSIT HE CAN PILOT 11 ALIVE NEED SMALL BOAT KENNEDY, or some such thing.

"We always thought that's why you faked his handwriting," Roy said as he flipped the book open, to the front flyleaf first and then the back one. Putting it down, he shook his head: "Well, I'll be damned."

"He was in the know?" I asked.

"*In* the know? He *was* the know." Roy swept his hand around my office walls, and by implication our whole sub-aquatic lair. "Jesus Christ," he said, staring at me, "who do you think *built* this joint? It tickled the *ass* off him that the island was named for his cousin. Back in Teddy's day, we were working out of a broom closet in Union Station, and I should know: I was born in it. Anyway, my predecessor found me there in a brass spittoon, on January 1, 1900."

"But what about the Four Freedoms speech, and all the rest of that"— it had just sunk in—"hogwash?"

"Oh, come on—forget the crap he told the Gillies," Roy said. "The day he gave me my job, all he told *me* was two words."

"What were they?" I asked, and Roy smiled.

" 'Think big,' " he said, tilting his head back and clenching an imaginary cigarette holder in his teeth.

■

As the grooming of Ronald Reagan for the presidency got underway in earnest, our long-range future was assured. But we still had Watergate to get through, and that was no easy chore. As the months went by and the disaster spread like a living Rorschach blot across the calendar, Hank Kissinger grew increasingly rattled. These days, he wasn't even sure if Nixon's original decision to hire him had been all that unwitting, as his shaken voice reported over my speakerphone one day. In the Oval Office, he'd had a terrifying encounter with our drunken, baleful Gillie president, who had glared redly at him, eyes glowing like an animal's at bay, and midway through a lunatically erudite *tour d'horizon* of the foreign-policy situation frightened poor Hank out of his wits by suddenly snarling *Tell me about the fish, Henry. Tell me about the fucking fish. In the fucking Potomac, under Roosevelt Island. I know that you could get me down there. I know you bastards could have saved me if you'd wanted to*

"The hell with it," Roy said one afternoon late in the summer of 1973, as the Ervin Committee hearings silently flickered through Ronald Reagan's as yet unerased outline on my office television set. "Let's shut down for a while. Oh, we can keep a skeleton staff down here for the can't-wait stuff—holding Boeing's hand, keeping Chrysler in business, all that jazz. But I'm putting *Two-Fisted U.S. Adventures* on hold, and the rest of us might as well go on sabbatical until this whole ruckus fades. We're just lucky that you can always count on the Gillies to forget whatever horrible shit they've just found out about how this country really works one or two elections later. And call it—"

"Optimism," I said, having heard this lecture before. "But where will you go?" I asked. "What'll you do, Roy?"

"Frankly, Prof, I don't give a damn," he said. "But the prediction computer in Quonset Two has spat out something about a place called Studio 54 that's due to open any day now. It sounds like it might be worth my while to check out. And as for *you*, Prof," he winked, well aware of Priap's charitable endeavors, "there's a lot more cripples and burn victims up top than we could ever teach to swim their way down here."

The main portal to our sub-aquatic lair opened onto a grove of beech trees on the island above us, from which we could row to either the District or Virginia banks of the Potomac after dark. For my own sorties, however, I had come to prefer the emergency exit located at the river's bottom, from which, trailing air bubbles, one rose through murk and sludge whose slither on my own ripe skin I found peculiarly invigorating. As one simply bobbed up like a black dot in the current, without any indication of where one had come from, this could also be done in daylight without compromising the secret of Roosevelt Island. I chose to begin my sabbatical by this route.

I broke the surface, gasping and spouting water—and looking, I imagine, rather drolly reminiscent of one of those mythical creatures who decorate the unknown in maps made by medieval mariners. To my north, on the Washington side of the Potomac, loomed a spectacularly ugly building, its ameoba contours adorned with serrated balconies that resembled stacked dentures. As this was the Watergate itself, and the associations thereby conjured up struck me as on the painful side, I decided with a shudder to strike for Virginia, and turned to swim toward Arlington.

Just past the riverbank, intermittent automobile traffic slid by. Along the skyline in the background loomed Rosslyn's bulky apartment complexes, whose construction had actually been one of our own minor projects; Roy had wanted to find out if Gillies could get along without any prettiness in their lives whatsoever, and decided that the experiment might as well be a local one. In between the breezy traffic and the ugly buildings, a half-dozen uniformed men—looking gaunt, grim, and impossibly larger than life—were erecting a fluttering Stars and Stripes.

After a moment, I realized that I had reached shore directly in front of the Marine Corps Memorial, with its statue based on Joe Rosenthal's Pulitzer Prize–winning photograph of the flag raising on Iwo Jima.

Tousled hair dripping, I scrambled up the riverbank and set off. Two miles away was the secret cache where we sub-aquatics stored our spare clothes, credit cards and money, along with the keys to a dozen Ford Pintos parked in our secret garage nearby, all of which were rigged to explode the instant we were compromised. Soon enough, I had left the barracks of Fort Myer behind, and was moving through a series of quiet streets and red-brick residential warrens now sprinkled, as Arlington had been since at least 1941, with government families temporarily remanded back to the United States from the fathers' various outposts in our vast superpower diaspora: Foreign Service familes, Pentagon families, CIA families, and so on.

Eventually, I spotted the advertising billboard I was looking for. Our secret cache was directly beneath it. On my previous forays into Arlington, I had never particularly noticed the building that stood across the street; but I did now, and smiled. All in all, I found myself reflecting, this ad must be a fairly surreal thing for the relatives of grievously ill, perhaps dead or dying patients to see every time they came out of a hospital. It showed a clock with twelve hands, all human and clutching coffee cups.

"There's Always Time for Some More Maxwell House!" it said.

■

Within a day, I had rented an apartment and offered the Arlington County school board my services as a teacher. They accepted with as much abject gratitude as if I'd volunteered to throw Good King Priap's services into the bargain, for the expertly forged credentials and testimonials I had brought with me from Roosevelt Island, tugging them in a waterproof bag whose strap I held in my teeth, were as glowing as plausibility allowed.

What with one thing and another, though, I found myself teaching not science but modern American history—the same subject that my all but forgotten acquaintance back in Rochester, Minnesota, had talked about teaching before I steered him to intelligence work, although I'm frankly bewildered as to why that long-ago chat in a railroad-station coffee shop should suddenly pop into my mind in this context. Needless to say, it often felt distinctly peculiar to be guiding slack-faced, witless teenagers through a tale in so many of whose chapters I myself had played such a singular though *sotto voce* role. Yet for a man of my capacities, obviously, it would have been child's play to instruct adolescents in any topic under the sun; as I learned when one of them looked at me with green eyes.

By Priap's exacting standards, of course, Sue was no fit object of erotic interest. She had light brown hair that flowed in two waves from a central part on her high forehead, an amused and full-lipped mouth, a lanky midriff often left bare by the nubbly halter tops in favor with many girls her age that long-gone year of white-wine skies and Nixon's fall, and a rump that bobbed like an apple above her long legs inside the bell-bottomed hip-huggers in which I remember her most vividly. A hue of faintly roseate alabaster, her skin always had the faint, fresh, faintly moist smell of a just uncovered tuber; and her eyes' twin pools of dilute green light were bright, eager, tender, mocking, and observant all at once.

In short, I found her utterly grotesque, and indeed it was one of her classmates whom I'd initially marked down as the ideal recipient of Priap's generosity. This was one Sarah Wong, who belonged to a special subset of her generation whose arrival at sexual maturity I had awaited with half-mad impatience. At long last, though, the time had come, and I saw that Sarah and her kind were finally of an age to go half mad themselves—with gratitude, once Priap welcomed them into his kingdom.

What was she? Why, a thalidomide baby, of course.

Ironically enough, it was an unforeseen consequence of that very condition that cheated me of Sarah—or rather, cheated her of me. The curriculum I had been given by the Arlington County school board, which I was at no liberty to amend, devoted a week to studying the impact on America of twentieth-century immigration. To a son of the old Yankee stock—and I'm sure I speak for us all—this couldn't help but seem akin to telling the story of a champion greyhound via a minute examination of the fleas along for the ride. Yet there it was in the curriculum, and here was I in the school.

Having volunteered to give a presentation—in my brief and thus far much too remote experience of her, this was a first—Sarah read a paper about one of the earliest of her relatives to have migrated here from China, a chauffeur who had experienced a week of pure terror when a giddy heiress he was driving from hither to yon, and presumably back to hither afterward, mistook him for a second cousin who had been deported on a trumped-up (or so Sarah claimed) charge some months earlier. As her somewhat squeaky warble brought the tedious tale to an end, I made a mental note to reproach her for having depended on an unreliable family anecdote instead of hitting the books; in fact, I realized an instant later, this might be my excuse to tell her to speak to me after class, in a stern voice masking Priap's kingly glow. Did I have any Laggilin with me? I did. But then Sarah spoke this fateful sentence:

"You see—back then, white people thought that we all looked alike."

Dead silence fell. While I might have been some years out of high school myself, I hadn't forgotten my youth's classroom highjinks so far as to misread the thought in every suddenly bulging eye, the taboo but irresistible joke now alternately struggling for expression and suppression on twenty-odd clamped pairs of lips; in short, the twenty-odd mute variants on *Oh, well, Sarah—at least that's not true now* that had begun to writhe on all but one or two of the faces before me as the silence crashed and boomed like waves.

After five or ten seconds, the unspoken retort finally grew so loud that Sarah herself heard it, and fled the room with a sharp if squeaky cry—followed, in a sudden lithe detachment of hip-huggers from chair and alabaster arms from desk, by Sue. Who didn't return until the following day, glaring at her nonplussed fellow students with a hatred more properly reserved for someone like the apostate Robert Oppenheimer. As for Sarah, despite my several requests to the principal's office to remind her parents of their obligations, she never returned at all—and so never knew the unique joy that might have been hers, more than making up for the small prick of one of adolescence's inevitable petty embarrassments as she babbled and flippered her stunned gratitude.

"Why," Sue was to ask me a month later, green eyes blazing, "*why* didn't you *say* anything? My God, you just let her *sit* there—until the *dumbest* person in the *room,* which believe me in *that* room was saying *plenty,* would have known what everyone else was thinking. That poor girl!"

"My dear," I said, "I may teach history, but I try to build confidence. I don't interrupt my students when they've got the floor, and I wasn't sure if Sarah had finished her presentation. And now, dear Sue," I said, pushing her head down my chest, "I think it's time you started yours again."

Dear Sue. For a man such as myself, to whom being pursued is the natural order of things and wooing the partner's job, the odd intensity of her abrupt request for citizenship in Priap's kingdom made agreeing look like a chore less fatiguing than holding her off. At least by my good king's yardstick, so to speak, it was really all fairly innocuous, and she was a marvelous little baby tigress in bed. For the first and only time in my adult life, I found I didn't even need to take a Laggilin for my heart condition after a royal audience.

It might have gone on, pleasantly enough, for months more than it did if the predictable unwitting boyfriend, another student in my history class named Gil Somebody-or-Other, hadn't stumbled across us in mid-preliminary in some woods behind her house one day, thus learning of *his* Sue's (well, that's what he thought) cunning bid for extra credit. At our hasty final meeting, she reported that he had taken the whole business preposterously hard—a fairly pointless prelude to the more pressing information she had sought me out to impart, which was that "we" now had a little problem. No tyro in such matters, I made little Problem exclusively hers again by writing a medium-sized check to a local doctor, of whose services I had previously availed myself more than a few times. No doubt he was surprised to see a girl with the use of all four limbs and no visible disfigurements presenting herself for a change.

I might have brushed off Gil's resentment of me as even more of a trifle if one of the other teachers hadn't already mentioned, apropos of something else entirely, that the boy's father wasn't only a former Marine but an ex-Agency hand, and a hard man at parent-teacher conferences. Soon, though, my careful inquiries ferreted out the information that Somebody-or-Other Senior, far from being in any condition to bluster into my classroom and beat me up for causing his son's breakdown, was or had been in intensive care with a terminal case of lung cancer, no doubt a contributing factor to Gil's addled state. If not the primary one, and perhaps the father should have beaten *himself* up instead; ha, ha. The boy obviously got over it, though

No I did not you pigfuck bastard shitass fucker

since many years later, idly browsing through a newspaper, I saw my former student's face staring blurredly up, with a chain smoker's incomplete smile, from the author's photo next to a negative review of some inane 1960s television show's reunion movie—a show, incidentally, whose premise struck me as oddly familiar, although I could no longer place precisely why. In any case, that's how I learned that the wan high-schooler I'd cuckolded by letting Priap go a-cherry-picking where he was too unnerved to tread had gone on to become a pop-music and television critic, which I must say sounds to me like a remarkably silly profession, as most do compared to my own. But no doubt it's a lucrative one.

As for dear Sue, I have no idea what became of her, not to mention a most peculiar sensation of having company in my ignorance. But all in all, it had been an interesting detour on the royal road—to the point of inducing me to apply my old genius for problem-solving in a new arena by writing a brief treatise on love shortly before my return to Roosevelt Island, which took place far earlier than I had expected. As the treatise has been pressed inside my wallet ever since the day that, taking mere seconds to collect my thoughts, I tossed it off on a few blank sheets of two-ply toilet paper with a finger continually dipped and redipped in a freshly stirred mixture of cold tap water and my own dung, I'm not even sure it's all that legible. But let me fish it out now anyway.

On Love

By Professor X

Premise: Let us first postulate the existence of an ideal Object of Affection (or OAf for short). As he is a perfect OAf, all those drawn to him can reasonably be defined as Undeserving Ones (U1). Since this would logically include the entire Population of the Planet (PP), the number of U1, or simply U, to whom this OAf can grant his sexual favors is theoretically unlimited (U1/y). As he is a virile OAf, let us also assume that he would be happy to steep himself in PP every day.

Problem: In practice, what we shall call the Interference of Life (INT—L) has prevented the OAf from achieving his goal (G) of granting his favors to U1/y. He is surrounded by PP on all sides, yet as a result of other people's INT-L, if not his own, this particular G has so far eluded him.

Solution: Admittedly shifting our paradigm somewhat, let us further postulate that this particular OAf is also a Brilliant Scientist (BS). Therefore, it should be child's play for him to conceive a Means of Execution (ME) that keeps INT-L to an absolute minimum if not causing it to disappear entirely.

Conclusion: $OAf + BS + ME - INT\text{-}L = U1/\gamma\text{—}G$

Cautionary Note: *For brevity's sake, the step that has been omitted from the Solution is that of determining the nature of ME.*

■

What obliged me to break my contract with the Arlington County school board and return to Roosevelt Island in early 1974 was an urgent inquiry from Hank Kissinger about the status of the Ford animatronic, which might be needed sooner than we'd thought. In spite of knowing that frantic and yet numbingly repetitive weeks of pressing a "Walk" button, pressing a "Chew Gum" button, and hearing a disheartening crash lay ahead of me, I was glad to leave up-top behind.

Nonetheless, the rest of that decade spelled lean times under Roosevelt Island. Roy often stayed away at his lozenge-shaped bunker below Studio 54 for weeks or even months at a time. None of us truly felt that we were back in business at the old stand until our carefully nurtured project to place Ronald Reagan in the White House climaxed on January 20, 1981, with gala festivities whose lavish excess we deliberately made as insulting as we could in a first test of the Gillies' once again supine tolerance for crass displays of social hierarchy.

Ingeniously, Roy had whetted their appetite by allowing Jimmy Carter to do pretty much as he pleased, the sole restriction being that whatever he came up with had to stay charmless and uninteresting. Since even Carter admitted that this was approximately equivalent to forbidding him to play center for the Los Angeles Lakers—a team we sponsored, by the way, as I was curious to see how long the racial upheaval we all feared could be staved off simply by letting the inner city's deprived population share something meaningless but exciting with Jack Nicholson—all had gone swimmingly, so to speak, for us sub-aquatics. Just by having Carter advocate them with an air of nettled defensiveness and unpredictable nervous widenings of his eyes, we managed to discredit any number of more or less benign and reasonable notions that might well have tossed a spanner in the works.

Now we were back in the saddle, but in a changed world. Roy had planned all along to resume publication of *Two-Fisted U.S. Adventures* as soon as the new President was sworn in, and even we were dazed when we realized that it was now redundant. Compared to what Gillies across the economic and social spectrum were now prepared to believe—on their own hook and with no help from us—about what their country was up to in the world, our old comic-book versions of events looked like muckraking exposés. While the confession doesn't particularly flatter our shop's acumen, I might as well admit it: Reagan was better at the job we'd designed for him than even the designers had thought possible.

My own private celebration of his inaugural had been a romp with a young African-American cocaine addict afflicted with cystic fibrosis, an act of charity on Priap's part that left its beneficiary in such an advanced state of gratitude that afterward I had to take *two* Laggilins for my heart condition as I listened to his rasping final breaths. Almost as if—so I often thought, with a wry chuckle—our Air Force had been acting the pimp to Priap all along, more and more of the Asian children our planes had once sent screaming down Cambodian and Vietnamese roads with their flesh ablaze from napalm were also reaching what I called the age of gratitude, providing my philanthropic impulses with a whole new realm to succor. In one more of those ironic twists that used to send Hank Kissinger strolling down corridors, hands stuffed in pockets and whistling "Que Sera, Sera," large numbers of them had ended up as refugees right here in the United States, congregating in the Washington area in the amusing manner of youngsters squabbling over who gets to sit nearest the fireplace. For a while, I found myself breathlessly emerging onto one or the other bank of the Potomac from our lair's underwater exit, tousled hair drenched and my good king leading the way like Patton, almost every night.

As usual, though, the work came first. Finding yet another arena for my problem-solving genius, I spent a good part of the 1980s involved in urban planning—Roy having called my attention to the fact that the white exodus to the suburbs, while proceeding at a gratifying rate as a result of their natural instinct to pull up the ladder behind them, could use a jab from us. Taking only a moment to gather my thoughts, I strangled my receptionist's dog, sliced open its vitals, and used the cur's still warm blood to sketch out a plan on the office wall.

By finding some pretext to throw open the doors of the nation's psychiatric hospitals, I reasoned, we could effect the release of thousands of deeply disturbed mental patients onto the streets of all major U.S. cities. Their unpresentable appearance and unnerving behavior would instantly make urban environments even more unpleasant for well-off and therefore easily frightened white Americans. In addition, the mental patients' presence would considerably exacerbate the already existing "homeless" problem, tying up (in yet another silver lining) the time and resources of do-gooders whose endeavors would win them even more irritation from the general public, since those they were trying to help were so repellent and demented.

"Genius," Roy said, watching the blood dry on the wall.

"Roy," I said, only to find mind and tongue struggling to dredge up the unfamiliar word, "*why?* Why are we doing this? Isn't it just eroding the tax base, and making all these places unlivable?"

"*Tax base?*" he said incredulously. "You're kidding, right?"

"No. Well, I hadn't planned to be, anyway."

"I know he's a Gillie, but I think Ed Koch was the first big-city mayor to figure out something very simple. And that something very simple is this: when you've got enough rich people, you don't *need* a middle class," Roy explained.

"But the rich were the first to leave," I said.

"And they're going to be the first to come back. You ever see *Metropolis,* pal? By the year 2000, New York City's going to make it look like a documentary—and a pretty damned namby-pamby one, too."

"But what about the middle class?"

Hands braced on his knees, Roy bent toward the dead dog on the carpet. "Here, Rex!" he called. "Din-din!" Straightening up again, he shrugged.

"Guess he's not hungry, Prof."

■

My single greatest contribution to the 1980s, of course, was the Strategic Defense Initiative, more popularly known as Star Wars. Despite a slyly devised don't-tax-but-spend-anyway policy that was to send the national debt skyrocketing into the trillions, the Reagan Administration simply hadn't had enough imagination to create the firewall we needed against funding social programs of any sort well into the third millennium. "It's the same problem as always," Roy sighed. "This country's just so fuck-ing *rich*. We can spend ourselves blind on military Tupperware, we can gut the economy like a trout—and even so, it's never enough. By the late Nineties, there's probably going to be a goddamned budget surplus again, and just watch all the whimperers line up for gruel. So figure out what we can do about it now—and what we're going to do about it *then,* too. You've got three minutes."

Remembering my earlier success with the moon program, and recog-nizing that what had made Americans finally lose interest in that effort had been the lack of an enemy, I needed only a few moments to collect my thoughts before collecting a .357 Magnum from my desk. Striding out into the corridor, I blew away my receptionist, whose constant mop-ing about her dog had begun to irritate me in any case, and crouched on the floor to quickly sketch out the preliminary plan for SDI with her blood, in which my colleagues kept skidding on their way to their own current projects. Hank Kissinger took a real tumble, but picked himself up with a grin and a friendly wave of his red palm: "Used to it," he called cheerfully. "No problem. Carry on."

Needless to say, I knew perfectly well that any moderately bright tenth-grader would be able to guess immediately that Star Wars was impractical. But I also knew it would take twenty years or more and untold billions of dollars to *prove* it was impractical, meanwhile keep-ing occupied all sorts of able scientists who might otherwise have gotten busy fixing the hole in the ozone layer, to keep their minds from wandering, or saving the remnants of a tropical rain forest so dank and lush that when you were in it you could hardly see a single tree anyhow.

In other words, the unfeasibility of SDI was precisely what made it work—and, if this scientist may be allowed a personal note, it was also something of a sentimental journey, some forty years after the Manhattan Project, to be thinking about nuclear war again. Yet throughout my work on Star Wars, the reminiscent undercurrent generated by already having both Los Alamos and Apollo 11 on my résumé also troubled me. I worried that, like many men no longer all that young, I might be simply trying to repeat past glories.

In a brief chat as one of the charwomen scrubbed down the corridor outside my office, Hank Kissinger confessed to a similar concern. Emulating his own earlier triumph with the Vietnam War, he had recently contrived not one but two anti-Communist crusades in Central America. To ensure that no protest movement against either or both would be able to make itself intelligible to the public, he had decided—ah, the Henry touch—to have us fund the rebels in one country while supporting the government in the other. But he too found his whole enterprise's memory-lane aspect problematic.

"Oh, don't get me wrong," Hank said, quickly stuffing his hands in his pockets as usual. "I'm as nostalgic as the next man—maybe a little more so, since right now that seems to be you. Every time I see another hospital explode in Matagalpa or another ten-year-old kid step on a land mine in some Salvadoran village with a per-capita income of eighty-seven dollars a year, it's like old home week to me. And if we ever decide to legalize cocaine Stateside—say, what the hell, huh? Maybe we should talk to Roy—we'll have well-trained Green Berets who can take over the business in a fingersnap. Paratroopers with MBAs—believe me, that's the future of this country. But still, I dunno—I mean, it's *good*," he suddenly sighed. "But it's just not *as* good."

Although neither Hank nor I knew it that day, our future opportunities to talk to Roy about anything under the sun were dwindling fast. He died of AIDS in 1986—aged, of course, eighty-six, having come into the world, or at any rate into a spittoon in a Union Station broom closet, at dawn on the first day of the American Century, although the obituaries dutifully used the false and much later birthdate his vanity had invented.

As for AIDS itself, I can personally testify that it wasn't hatched under Roosevelt Island, despite the ravings of some of the more paranoid gay Gillies later on. But the endless struggle to prevent any meaningful amount of money from being spent on finding a cure occupied a good deal of my and my colleagues' time from the moment the disease was identified right up through my retirement. For all the public's natural hostility to homosexuals, stifling the average American's natural sympathy for any category of young men dying painful deaths in droves, no matter how perplexing their lifestyle or alien their sexual orientation, was one of the greatest challenges our shop ever faced. I'm pleased to say we all came through with flying colors.

In my final conversation with Roy, which took place at his deathbed in a New York City hospital, he implored me to hold fast. "Not a dime more, do you hear me?" he gasped on the pillow, his enfevered eyes glittering out of the new hollows of a face now positively nougated with lesions—distractingly so, given Priap's charitable propensities.

"Not a fucking dime," he repeated more harshly. Hoisting himself up on one elbow with difficulty, he grabbed my hand with an enfeebled lobster claw, pulling my face close. It was the first time he'd touched me, or I him, in thirty-two years.

"You know how it is, pal," he muttered—"you understand, Prof. When I think of everything we had to go through when we weren't even *queer,* not like those other nellies at Kay Josephs'—and then I look at all these arrogant bastards, with their bars that have the fucking signs right out in the fucking open, and their goddam public hand-holding and their fucking parades and their Stonewall and their Harvey Milks and their goddam ACT UP and their goddam Jim Fouratts and their *god damn gay pride*—all acting like it's *normal,* for Christ's sake, and some of them wanting to adopt *kids* and get *old* together! But we'll show them how normal they are. We'll teach them what love's got to do with it. *What kind of schmuck wants to get old?* Oh, don't you see they *deserve* it? They deserve everything they get," he whispered, and his head fell back onto the pillow.

He was still holding my hand when he died.

■

Afterward, I returned to Roosevelt Island, swimming down to the underwater exit in a state of some trepidation as to how I would proceed without Roy to guide me. Soon enough, however, I discovered that I needn't have worried, for it turned out I simply knew what ought to come next, without understanding how I knew it. One day, I asked my new receptionist to fetch me Hank Kissinger, and was informed that he'd retired a year previously. Gradually, it sank in that I was now in charge, and had been for some time; that must be why that fellow had summoned me to his deathbed.

Our labors continued apace, although few things fit my old friend Hank's catchphrase—"Good, but not *as* good"—like the ascent of Reagan's Vice President to the top job. Still, it would be uncharitable of me to say so. You see, in a roundabout fashion, I have George Bush, the elder I suppose I should say, to thank for helping me unriddle a desire I hadn't known had ruled me since the day at Los Alamos when I rolled my newly de-goggled eyes and swallowed a Laggilin for my heart condition as Robert Oppenheimer dolefully intoned, "I am become death."

Even granting that he too might be nearing the age of retirement, Priap could now be stirred to acts of generosity only by subjects so maimed and mutilated that it was often difficult to bestow my good king's favors on them in time for me to receive their silent thanks as they expired. Haunted by the thought that soon Priap would be unable to find anyone at all to be grateful to him, I tried to lose myself in work, to no avail. For the first time in my life, I had trouble sleeping at night.

Indeed, insomnia alone could explain how I came to be watching the 1992 Republican Convention on television. As a rule, we sub-aquatics troubled ourselves very little with the sideshows of Gillie politics; after all, the Gillies themselves could barely be bothered to lift a finger by then, and they were the ones who called it a democracy. Yet there I was, staring rather blearily at George Bush—who, to my momentary bewilderment, had abruptly grown almost a half century younger. No longer the nincompoop Chief Executive whose petulant voice over my speakerphone, near the window past which I had arranged for plastic fish to float belly-up at regular intervals, drove me almost daily to despair, he had just stepped out of the sea onto a corrugated metal deck, looking shaken and more exhausted at twenty than I, or possibly anyone, had ever seen him since.

Later on, I was often to marvel at the way that year's Gillie election seemed to come down to a contest between two bits of black-and-white film—the footage of Bush the youthful carrier pilot's rescue by one of our submarines after his plane was shot down in the Pacific late in World War Two, and the later but almost as archaic-looking clip that showed an even younger Bill Clinton shaking hands with Jack Kennedy in the Rose Garden. It was as if the Gillies had suddenly grasped that the twentieth century itself—that era that stayed unimaginable even as it happened, in which I counted my own glory days—was slipping irrefragably into history, and they wanted to gather up and clutch at the faded tickets and confetti still strewn on the dock now that the great ship was growing tiny as it sailed. For all the pro forma talk about the future in the candidates' speeches, it seemed to me that the real choice on offer, as our gallivanting epoch's waning grew real, was between those two dim rival echoes of two things alike only in that both were ghostly, somehow summoning, and gone.

Later still, I also marveled at the coincidence at both these relatively small events in the grand scheme of things having been caught by cameras—not that great a surprise in the case of the Rose Garden ceremony, but something to rock the laws of probability back hard on their heels as one watched a then anonymous pilot scramble aboard a sub's deck amid venerable light- and dark-gray waves. Having grown familiar with Franklin Roosevelt's puckish streak since the day I first learned of his paternity of our shop, I even wondered if *we* had had something to do with sticking that providential newsreel crew aboard the U.S.S. *Finback* on that cruise. But as we never kept records of anything, I had no way of determining if this had been so.

In any case, as I watched a twenty-year-old George Bush walk up to me out of a forty-seven-year-old sea, I suddenly understood the nature of my own final mission. An instant later, it already seemed extraordinary that Newton's apple should have taken so long to drop on my head, waiting until the latter began to nod beneath the spreading *Agaricus bisporus* of my now lengthily shadowed life. Yet only age's clouded thinking explained why it had taken me so long to see it—I, with my genius for problem-solving; I, Dr. Gordy N. Notcutter, to mention an alias I had used often with Gillie medicos over the years when negotiating Priap's more extreme missions of mercy. But now the old can-do spirit reasserted itself.

Shutting off the television, and taking several years to assemble my thoughts, I jotted down a plan on the nearest available writing surface. This turned out to be the back of a scallop-bordered old black-and-white Kodak I had never seen before, depicting an object whose nature and purpose baffled me. Finally, I concluded that it must be some monstrous sort of bicycle or icicle, and let it go at that.

At length, my other arrangements having been made, I booked a flight to Tokyo, and drippingly emerged from the Potomac to hail a cab to Dulles Airport. Then we spent forever in a glittering race with a huge sunset, I keeping mentally sharp the while by attempting to fathom what possible arrangement of recombinant light and particles could be creating the interesting illusion, visible each time we banked, of a black dot in our wake.

On the ground again in what my watch claimed was still yesterday and the calendar called tomorrow, having collected my ruggage amid bright flash floods of exotic noise and the next millennium's amoebal designs, I hailed another taxi. Rising skyward again from the bustling lobby of my elegant hotel, I showered, shaved, and donned fresh linen, wanting to put my best foot forward. Then, summoned at last by the telephone call I had been waiting for from first hasty toweling to last pat of my tousled hair, I sank once more, in a majestic silence, to the lobby, where I was expected at the bar.

Only the most compelling sense of duty had brought me to Tokyo, for the expense of setting all this up had been fantastic. Scarred by the blast and poisoned by radiation sickness, the last survivors were dying off like brown grass in a drought. Soon there would be none left, and I would have no one on whom to discharge my obligation. Still, one would be enough; would serve. Gordy N. Notcutter or no, I was only a single individual, and could not hope to sacrifice the remnants of my health on every last one of them.

Then or later, it never occurred to me to inquire this one's name. All I'd been told was her gender, which pleased me obscurely despite a lifetime of making no distinctions on that count, and that it was the Nagasaki bomb she had survived, which pleased me for reasons not obscure at all. Mind, if I'd been so obliged by either time or pocketbook, I'd have settled for Hiroshima. At times, beggars aren't the only ones who can't be choosers. But while Hiroshima would have been good, it wouldn't have been *as* good; so I had thought on the plane, paraphrasing a smiling man whose name I no longer recalled, although I was fairly sure that he'd been one of the only two friends I'd ever had. In any case, throughout the complicated business of arranging the affair, my one unalterable stipulation—which complicated matters a good deal, as so many of them had had their eyeballs melted at the instant that the century's new God had said "Let there be white light"—had been that she couldn't be blind. How could I look into her eyes for confirmation that my quest had succeeded, if there was nothing to look back?

As I crossed the lobby, I saw a cordon of Tokyo policemen in dress uniform beyond the hotel door, clearly on hand for the visit of some foreign potentate or other. An ambulance was pulling away. In the bar, a young doctor in a white coat waited, a bottle of Suntory whiskey before him. His face peculiarly strained, he cut short my attempts at quasi-collegial small talk.

"We have put her in a room upstairs," he told me. "We believe no one knows it was her in the ambulance, or why we brought her here. But if you are going to do this at all, you must do it quickly. She is sinking fast."

"How old is she?" I asked, somewhat idly. After all, it didn't make that much difference, and she would have to be fifty at least.

"Her age? Fourteen." Seeing my startled glance, he shook his head before my surprise could yield to the natural indignation of any man who has spent an exorbitant sum of money to do good and been cheated anyway. With crimped lips and averted eyes, he explained his mistake: "She *was* fourteen. She is sixty-four."

"Shall we go?" I said.

Now it was the turn of the doctor's eyes to widen somewhat. "If you feel ready. Forgive me—I thought perhaps you would want a restorative first."

"I think that showing up with alcohol on my breath would be disrespectful of the occasion, don't you?" I said brusquely, not troubling to explain that I never touched spirits and had always found others' need for artificial stimulation a mystery. "The sooner the better, and the best is right now."

Swooshing me back up to a floor higher than my own, the doctor led me to a door that he then opened, indicating that he would wait outside. With a nod, feeling every last one of my seventy-six years, I stepped over the transom.

It was August 9, 1995. It was the fiftieth anniversary of the forgotten second bomb, whose target had been chosen when I pushed a blindfolded man toward a wall map with a bit of chalk in his hand. From a bed across the room, two dark eyes stared at me like beads from a necklace long since scattered. Despite an opened window and the strong smell of saline and newly sprayed antiseptic that hung in the air like a cloud, the smell of suppuration was stronger.

Bringing my hands together, I inclined my tousled head slightly. "*Hajimemashita,*" I said, beaming. "*Dozo yoroshiku.*"

In attempted response, her lipless mouth may have trembled, though so slightly I had the illusion that its rims had merely been stirred by a faint breeze from the window. But her facial muscles were clearly too weak to form words—or, for that matter, close her mouth, which gaped like one more of her wounds. That suited my purposes, but I was saving her mouth for last.

Stripping off my recently donned clothes and joining her on the bed, I straight-fucked her first, her jellylike flesh ebbing and then liquefying under me until good Priap reported a strong chance that he was bestowing his favors on the rubber sheet below. Snorting and turning her over with a quick jerk of one hand, I parted the bronze, green, and blackened remnants of her buttocks, and Priapized her wasted anus—or so I can only hope. For all I know, my good king's first thrust might well have made literal a vulgarism I deplore, and simply torn her a new one; ha, ha.

Yet by now the thing below me might as well have been a puppet with sawdust and goo leaking out of it, and I knew time was running short. Scrambling from the bed and hauling her off it too, I dropped her on the floor on what were probably her knees. As I yanked her head back, we stared at each other, and I saw what I needed to see. To the screams of an exalted populace, my good Priap proclaimed himself the Emperor Priapus I; a moment later, a small bag of rot and broken chalk fell dead at my feet. Turning to my clothes, I reached for my vial of Laggilin.

It was empty.

Behind me, the door opened. Perhaps because my breathing had grown noisy at the sight of the Laggilin-less vial, the Japanese doctor's voice sounded inhumanly quiet.

"Are you finished with her, X-San?" he asked.

■

"Finished?" I said indignantly, turning six-foot-plus of leonine, still demi-royal Anglo-Saxon nudity to face his puny form. "Of *course* I'm finished, man! The woman's *dead*. What on earth would I do now? Why, she wouldn't even have been able to—"

"You are an American, X-San. Under the circumstances, given her native city and your track record, I thought it unwise to jump to conclusions."

"That's disgusting," I said, starting to get dressed. Clearly, this fellow didn't understand at all; East is East and so on, I suppose. Thrusting the empty Laggilin vial into my trousers pocket, I glanced around for my shoes. "I need to find a drugstore quickly, *quickly*," I told him. "Is there one in the hotel?"

Apparently he didn't hear me; he was looking down at the body. Now he said an odd thing: "She waited for you, you know. Or perhaps I should say watched for you."

"For me? That's preposterous," I told him, for I was not so vain as to believe that Good King Priap's fame had ever penetrated so far as Japan. "How would she even know of me?"

"She did not know it would be you. She didn't know that you had been at Los Alamos—that you had helped to build the bomb. Still less did she know that it was you who pinned Little Boy's tail on the city where she was a schoolgirl."

"Oppenheimer did that," I grunted, feeling the lack of Laggilin begin to tell. "All I did was blindfold him with a lab coat and spin him around three times first."

"I stand corrected, X-San. But be that as it may, she always believed that an American would come. She assumed that it would be a man. She hoped he would feel shame."

"Shame?" I was puzzled. "Do you mean before, or—after? Because I saw her eyes, and—"

"It made no difference," he interrupted me. "She knew that she'd be dead in moments. In any case, with her injuries, she should have died thirty years ago. And in fact, so far as we can tell"—he was looking at me steadily now—"she *did* die thirty years ago. All except her eyes."

"*What?*" I roared, as my spine rose beneath my shirt.

"By every medical indication," he said, "she was a corpse. We have not fed her since 1965. But something kept that corpse's eyes alive, in defiance of every law of nature. We believe that they were waiting to see you."

"And you call yourself a *doctor*?" I bellowed. "That's ridiculous nonsense! Either she was dead or she was alive. It's not possible to be both!"

"I didn't call myself a doctor, X-San. You did. But you are better proof than this woman that it is possible to be both. After all, *she,*" with a nod at the thing on the floor, "and thousands like her, kept death alive in *you* for half a century. And here you stand."

"Don't talk rot to me!" I roared. "I've got a heart condition. It's quite dangerous. The truth is, I should probably never have come here at all! Now call me a cab and get me to a drugstore where they speak English and stock Laggilin *right away,* do you hear me? Or do you want a dead American scientist on your conscience?"

He didn't answer immediately. In the course of my career, I've often found it interesting to watch Asians cry. One never knows what will provoke their tears, or precisely when they'll stop. He had been gazing down at the body as he wept, but now he looked up again.

"Are there really no lengths to which Americans will not go," he asked, "to prove that they cannot be damned—not by their own God, and not by anyone else's, either?"

I was stunned. "*Damned?* Have you gone *mad?*" I shouted. "You don't know what you're talking about. For *Christ's sake,*" letting a profanity escape my lips for the first time in my life, "you don't understand at all. Why do you think I came here? Look into her eyes! Thanks to me, she died *happy.*"

As the true extent of Priap's final act of generosity overcame his mind's lack of familiarity with our Western concept of benevolence, he was briefly speechless. Finally, he spoke:

"As she lived, X-San! As indeed she lived. Oh, it was a great privilege to be a bomb survivor, believe me! To us, they were like thousands of Beatles who did not need to make music—you had provided that. Their mere existence wiped out *any possibility* of war guilt on our part, for all that you will still find the thoughtful words 'Remember Pearl Harbor' inscribed by some of your compatriots in the visitors' book at the Hiroshima memorial itself. Then again, we should not complain: at least they care enough to visit! Indeed, *her* one regret, in the days before all of her died but her eyes, was that she had not been a Hiroshima victim. Oh, don't misunderstand—Nagasaki was *good,*" he assured me. "It just wasn't *as* good."

Laggilin deprivation had begun to make it difficult for me to speak. "If you aren't a doctor," I gasped, feeling something red scorch my nostrils, "who *do* you work for?"

He looked nonplussed. "The same people you do, X-San. You must know we've gone global."

"But if you—don't approve of American tourists," I said, still bewildered by his previous speech and sweeping my paw around the room in increasingly violent arcs, "then why did you arrange this?"

"X-San, you will forgive me—and many others—for hoping this is not permanent," he said. "But for fifty years and three days now, and into the foreseeable future, yours has been the country that the planet is for."

"Why, you ungrateful—"

At that point, though, the Laggilin wore off, as I had known it would. First, I belched fire.

Seizing him around the waist with a paw grown large enough to easily encircle it, I ate him in one gulp.

Then I belched fire again.

∎

The rest, as they say, was flattish and faded.

Having exited my hotel by destroying it, I stomped toward the waterfront through a Tokyo that my size had re-spelled Toy-ko, destroying buildings so shoddy that they seemed made of papier-mâché with mighty smacks of the tail I'd acquired and emptying entire busloads of terrified, tiny passengers into my vast maw. As fires began to spring up everywhere I'd breathed, I plunged into the Pacific in a huge hiss of steam, starting the long swim to California.

I still had hopes of making my fiftieth reunion at Stanford. While I'm no blubbering sentimentalist—except, perhaps, where Priap's good works are concerned—depriving my classmates of the presence of the single greatest success story *and* philanthropist among them would have been not only a slight but an actual throwing down of the gauntlet to the alumni association. Yet as I came ashore at Palo Alto, after a three-day swim whose one memorable meal was the white whale I briskly strangled off Hawaii, picking my teeth afterward with an old harpoon I had found embedded in his hump, I experienced the first of several shocks.

First, although my new size was unaltered, I found that the United States was built to scale for it—and possibly always had been. Secondly, it needed to be, for everyone else's appearance resembled my own—the only exceptions being recent immigrants unable or unwilling to adapt, who in the meantime did our scut-work and drove everyone around.

As we native-borns now conversed by means of belching fire, the new arrivals' frequent refusal to learn even the rudiments of our language was a handicap if we weren't hungry at the moment. Indeed, one of my fellow Stanford alums planned to remedy this by placing a proposition on that year's ballot known as the "Belching Fire Only Initiative," which would make anyone attempting to use any other tongue in our presence—and possibly even among themselves, a question that my old acquaintance Norman Lincoln Rockwell hadn't decided yet for sure—an instant candidate for assimilation via gobbling. Or so he told me as we strolled among striped tents, surrounded by our classmates' nostalgic flames and sulphur and idly tearing the arms off waiters when the urge for an hors d'oeuvre hit.

Gradually, the truth grew clear, which was that we had *all* been on Laggilin since 1945—and in some cases earlier than that. Now, too, the Gillies had finally caught up with us sub-aquatics, removing any need for concealment. Or else, unbeknownst to ourselves, perhaps we too had been Gillies all along. In any case, we'd all been re-created equal—belching fire, eating recent immigrants, and submitting camcorder tapes of our more amusing experiences while doing so to *America's Funniest Home Videos*.

After the reunion, I flew back into Dulles, diverting myself as did the others by obliging the immigrant stewards to hop over our flapping tails in the aisles as we belched fiery demands at them. On landing, I climbed into a cab, since that was what everyone else was doing. Feeling tired but elated after my long journey to wherever it was I'd gone, I gazed out the window, enjoying the view of the non-passing landscape.

While I had no complaints, some pleasant minutes later I noticed that the driver was still badgering me, in a recent immigrant's awkward charcoal and embers, for our destination. I took a few moments to collect my thoughts.

Or to attempt it. "I have no idea," I finally told him. "Isn't that *your* job now, my good man?"

After a indeterminate interlude of pure mutual confusion, I belched fire at him to just start driving, and perhaps something would come back to me. Yet the Virginia landscape remained obstinately unfamiliar. I found that I had no idea where I lived, if indeed I lived anywhere; and no idea where I worked, if I had a job.

I knew there was an island involved. It had some sort of underwater exit, and a white boat with a hole in the bow stranded on a beach.

Beyond that, no matter how long I took to collect my thoughts, I drew a blank.

As I had done this on the nearest available writing surface, which was a brochure handed out at the Dulles Airport taxi stand advising all passengers of the local cab regulations and giving typical fares to various buildings and statues in and around Washington, D.C., I showed the blank to the driver. He nodded in an interested way, but had no other reaction. After a while, he turned on the radio, which was playing a type of music I had never heard before.

"*Bhangra,*" he told me, turning around with a huge smile. I nodded in an interested way, not sure what type of information this was or whether a question of mine had elicited it.

Luckily, I still had plenty of money, so we were able to ride around for a while. Once I got him to understand the fire for "water," Bhangra took me to a river, and started driving alongside it. As it slid namelessly by, its surface of glassy tarmac providing my questing eyes with not a single clue to my origins or prospects, he told me something of himself—a conversation that left me at an unsettling disadvantage about responding in kind.

If Bhangra noticed this, however, he didn't appear perturbed. Perhaps he was used to alternations of random fire-belching and clumsy silence from his fares. In any case, he mostly spoke, with a paternal pride that managed to glow brightly despite his poor command of our flaming native tongue, of the eldest of his daughters, now in college. Despite having been confined since childhood to a wheelchair—a detail that caused my tail to thump feebly in the back seat, although I had no idea why—she hoped to enter politics. In his former country, Bhangra said, despite the example of Mrs. Gundy (a personage unknown to me; from Bhangra's tone, I took her for some sort of nanny gone bad), this would have been by and large impossible, for reasons of caste as much as gender.

Eventually, some ten miles downstream from what I was reasonably sure had been a city, we came to a decrepit plantation house. Pulling over, Bhangra glanced at me inquisitively; with his chin, he indicated a sign. As I had not the slightest clue what the words "Mount Vernon" ought to mean to me, and was indeed at a loss to know if they ever had meant anything to me, I shook my head. So he turned the cab around, and soon we were proceeding back the way we'd come. Some ten miles up the river, to my perfect astonishment, we came upon a city.

By the time we reached it, I had given him every penny I had, along with my Rolex and a matchbook bearing the cryptic legend "Hot Times at the Old Smithsonian Nightclub" that I had discovered on my person. Stopping the car near the riverbank, Bhangra indicated that our time together was rapidly reaching its end.

Alarmed at the prospect of continuing alone, I offered to teach him to belch fire more expressively, so as to win friends and influence people; but he declined. Although he'd taken pleasure in my company, he told me in embers and charcoal, he had a living to make; wanted all his daughters to get an education and better themselves. Belching fire to the effect that I too had enjoyed our ride along the river, I tore his arm off and got out.

That was six years ago. I have been wandering along this river ever since. I am homeless. I am eighty-two years old.

It seems to be Sunday. In my present condition, however, every day might as well be—ironically enough, as the last one to which I paid any attention fell on December 7, 1941. Since then, I'd never seen the need for days of rest.

Now that my teeth have fallen out, I live on the mud at the river's bottom. Whatever else happens, I am pleased to report that there is no immediate danger of starving. The only potential problem I can envision on that score is that I might forget how to eat. Given my circumstances, this is a distinct possibility.

Ten minutes ago, realizing that I ought to at least be able to describe my own current appearance, I emerged from the river and wandered up to a parked van, hoping to see my face in its rear window. I seemed to recall once taking pleasure in observing my reflection, and the river was much too muddy to serve. Across the top of the van's window, above the grime that spoiled my plan—I had a feeling I used to be better at concocting those, but wasn't entirely sure what I meant by this—was a bumper sticker that puzzled me.

GOD, GUTS, AND GUNS MADE AMERICA GREAT, it said. WE'RE DAMNED IF WE KNOW WHAT HAPPENED NEXT.

Under that, in the thick grime, someone had written this: "Do *you?*"

And under that, in another hand—or finger, I suppose—was written this: "Wash Me."

At that point, the van's lights came on, and it began to back over me. So I had to interrupt my reading, if there was any more to read. The next time I tried, approaching the van of my choice from an indirect angle, I found that I could no longer decipher the strange markings on its stickers.

Now I no longer recall why it was I wished to sneak up on vans. While clearly an element of surprise is involved, I am unable to determine on whose part with enough certainty to feel good about doing it, or indeed anything else. In any case, whether it was my hobby or my profession, this activity now strikes me as both dangerous and surprisingly pointless.

I can't remember my own name. Come to think of it, I'm not positive I ever had one—or if there was one or more of me, whoever I or we were. I have no information as to which town I'm in, or even if this is a town.

I believe that a van is about to back over me. As I don't have a clue what they are either, the whole situation has me at a loss. I'm trying to collect something, but I forget what. Garbage, perhaps.

In any case, I am almost certainly in this section of the country, in one town or another.

VII

Yesterday Never Knows

As I look back on my life, I see I never really knew just what the hell was going on—even though, to set the record straight about my being as corny as Kansas in August and so forth, I did study philosophy briefly at the Sorbonne in Paris, as taught by a man whose only book was called *Vie! Je te haïs!* I've forgotten his name, so he may have been right to feel that way. I also know Kansas in August, and believe me I don't compete. No human being ever could or has, which is why to stand up under its sky, as I used to, always awed me.

I grew up there. After not too long a walk in any direction, Russell just stops, like an island in a sea of growing gold. When I was a little girl, I had a tendency to disbelieve that people of any sort lived past our town's perfectly circular horizon. After the first sets appeared and we got one, television made this seem more possible, but not much more likely. My theory of it was that everybody on TV might be hidden in a basement somewhere right in Russell, pretending.

Dawson's Drug and both our movie theaters and both our right and left banks were all on Main Street, along with a couple of cafes and some feed and clothing stores. The county courthouse was set back from the street, our high school was a block behind it, and our American Legion post was a full half mile off, in a more open area where the houses had become sporadic. Our sixteen churches were distributed variously. Except for their steeples and the grain elevator, nothing was all that high; or could be, given the nature of the sky.

Aside from the obvious one, our town had only a single distinctive feature, or rather many repetitions of the same distinctive feature. These were the posts hewn from our amber-colored local variety of limestone, which was also the same stuff that the courthouse was built of. They were described as fence posts but often lacked railings, and also stood in places where there was no observable use for them, such as along Main Street or solitarily in front yards. It was never made clear to us when the people who put them there had started doing this, or why they had stopped. The lesser of Russell's two major secrets was that the posts were our form of paganism, argued with the churches, and had something stubborn and unspoken to do with the sky. But nobody ever admitted this, as it would have been difficult to bring up, particularly to a minister, while remaining laconic and easygoing, and all five thousand of us attended religious services regularly and with no sense of hypocrisy, primarily on foot except for the people from outlying farms.

My mother was the librarian of Russell. In a precocious moment, I once called her place of work our town's seventeenth church, at which point she looked at me. Her expression ended that conversation, which had not been atypically brief. Once I learned to read, it was easier for me to believe that people with whom I'd had no personal contact lived in other places, as it was evident the books weren't original to Russell. It was from several of these that I first learned of Paris and soon afterwards the Sorbonne, which my heart grew set on attending for reasons whose antagonism to easy articulability would have made local analysis of the fence posts seem voluble by comparison. But I knew the reasons to be of the ocean, rather than the sky, and this meant they were all hooked up, like wires strung from a telephone pole, to my daddy, Eddie Kilroy.

On weekend nights when I was small, I used to lie in bed and listen to all the daddies who had come back from the war going past my window, which was in one of the sporadic houses near the Legion post. They would be talking quietly when they went to it, and singing noisily when they came from it. I had very little notion of what went on in between, except that they drank beer and this was necessary. When it was late and their voices were moving from left to right outside my window, rather than from right to left, the song I heard most often, along with scuffling and laughter, was "Show Me the Way to Go Home." This always made me upset and confused, as to my understanding they were back there already.

My daddy wasn't. He was in a Marine cemetery on Iwo Jima, of which I had only seen a picture. The picture showed white crosses and a flag. Once I was old enough to grasp what this meant, it hurt me to discover that it had been the next-to-last battle, six months before Hiroshima. But I knew there was no common sense in singling this out as grief's focal point, as he would be just as dead if it had happened at Pearl Harbor. My mother, the librarian of Russell, would be just as melancholy, and the other daddies would still be singing "Show Me the

Way to Go Home" as their voices moved from left to right outside my window. When I was practicing common sense, the only significant difference I could see was that in that case I wouldn't exist.

Then again, I was also practicing speculation, since on February 29, 1945, which was the second date on the white cross closest to the camera in the picture, my daddy had been nineteen years old. My continuing awareness of this was to make my own twentieth birthday, when I reached it, seem unusually special and fraught, but I will get to that. The point I was making just now is that my daddy was only in tenth grade at Russell High on December 7, 1941, although as that was a Sunday I don't mean literally in a classroom. He and my mother, the future librarian of Russell, were listening to a ball game on the radio with her folks, she said. But the war had gone on; gone on just long enough, I guess you could say, and then six months more afterward. I'd have met my daddy if the scientists had hurried, I'd have run to the door and opened it for him. But they didn't know him and now neither did I.

One summer Sunday when I was small, my mother didn't lead me back to our house after services. Instead, she took me to the courthouse, where the rest of Russell also stood, having assembled from our sixteen churches. The only people from our town who weren't there were in Korea. The Russell High girls' choir sang "America the Beautiful," and then the sheet that had been put over the World War One memorial was pulled off again by my mother, the librarian of Russell. Pointing with her white-gloved finger, she showed me where my daddy's name was, along with the other new names from 1941–45 carved under the ones from 1918. The other mothers did the same with their children, and the parents of the men who hadn't been daddies went up and looked at the memorial, holding hands that they had to untangle if one or both of them wanted to touch the carving of that particular name. Then the girls' choir sang "Amazing Grace," after which we dispersed to our homes, primarily on foot except for the people from outlying farms, who were starting their pickup trucks to return to them as we left.

The photograph of my daddy that my mother kept on the mantel in our living room was his high-school graduation picture rather than their wedding photo, which was in her bedroom, or the one of him in his

Marine Corps uniform, which was in mine. Tucked into the back of the graduation picture was a V-mail letter that my mother had gotten in the summer of 1945 from someone who had been in the war with my daddy, and after I grew somewhat older I often plucked this letter out and read it. I always waited until my mother, the librarian of Russell, was away from the house before I did so, although she had never forbidden me to read it or given any indication that she would prefer not to see me in the act. As the letter was often tucked into the frame somewhat differently than it had been the last time I replaced it, I knew that she did exactly the same thing, but we never discussed it. Anyhow, this is what the letter said:

June 31, 1945

Dear Mrs. Kilroy,

    You don't know me, and I guess our CO has probably already written you about Eddie, since I know he always writes to all the families. I don't know if the regs say he needs to or he just does it, but I hope his letter helped. I know a couple of the other guys' wives wrote him back that it did, and maybe you did too or just felt that way. Anyway, I promised myself I would do this, and I'm sorry I didn't sooner. But they've put our outfit on a pretty heavy training schedule and so there isn't a whole lot of spare time, but I should have done it sooner anyway and I don't mean to make excuses.

    To tell you the truth, the training is irksome because all of us who were on Iwo sort of feel we have the gist, but we know the replacements don't. If I write where I think we're going next, the censor will just black it out. But I guess anybody can look at a map and see that there aren't many places left after Iwo and

The censor had blacked out the next word, probably because there was still fighting going on there. But it could only have been Okinawa, since that was the last battle.

    Anyway, I don't know if Eddie ever put my name in any of his letters to you. But he wrote you so many that I guess I probably must have cropped up in some of them, even if I was just the SOB yelling at him to hurry up and finish because I was collecting them from everybody. He and old Duke Stryker were pretty much my best friends in the whole outfit. I know Eddie said he was going to find out from our CO if Stryker had been lying about not having a family and write them, just to get Stryker's goat wherever he was now he said, but maybe Eddie didn't have time. So I should probably find out and then write them too, when I finish this one to you.

I don't know how much the censor will let me tell you about it or even if you want to hear the details, so you shouldn't keep reading if it would make things harder for you. I guess the important thing you need to know is that he didn't suffer at all.

After the first two days, Iwo was nothing but [there were a dozen or so words blacked out here by the censor]. We were going after one when a Jap came out of the ground with a [there was a word blacked out here], and Eddie had just stopped him from throwing it when it happened. I think he was gone right away, anyway he was gone by the time I got to him and that was about three seconds after, so I hope that's some kind of consolation to you. Anyway, I don't know if this will sound stupid to his wife and maybe I should cross it out or start over, but when I picked him up the only thing I could think of was how embarrassed he always was about still looking like such a kid, even though [there was a word scratched, not blacked, out here, although the apostrophe was still visible] he was two years older than me. The bar girls used to tease him about it when we were on pass, I don't mean that he was interested in the girls but they teased everybody, but anyway I thought that at least he wouldn't have to complain about the unfairness of me looking older than he did anymore. Otherwise, I guess we damned near looked like twins, excuse my French.

I guess that's about it. If I'm still around after the war and anywhere near [he had scratched out "Russell," and written] Kansas, I'll be sure to look you up. I'll call first to make sure you don't mind, I mean if I can. I don't know if you have a phone.

> Yours very truly,
> John G. Egan (Cpl., USMC)

■

For whatever reason—and I can think of one which would make me very unhappy—Corporal John G. Egan never did look us up, or try to; and it may seem a very long leap from here to Paris, France. But my ambition to attend the Sorbonne was conceived in honor of my daddy. I don't mean that I had any knowledge of a thwarted ambition on his part to attend it, which in fact strikes me as improbable, or even of a thwarted ambition on his part to see Paris, although since almost everyone does the odds on that one are much better. Because of the way his eyes looked in two of the three pictures on display in our house, I had simply developed a conviction that he was someone who would have liked to see all sorts of places, and it didn't matter much which ones.

The exceptional picture, of course, was the one of his wedding day. In it, he was looking at my mother, and the news that rocket ships were waiting outside to take anyone in Russell who was interested to see the Taj Mahal for free wouldn't have budged either one of them. As far as they were concerned, they were already there.

In any case, if I was going to travel in his stead, I figured I might as well start with a place whose name drew me compellingly. This the Sorbonne's name did from the moment I first read it on a page, although I concede the effect would have been less magnetic had the next words to greet me been "in Toledo, Ohio," rather than "in Paris." Above all, it was the first syllable that made my eyes dawdle before they resumed hightailing it after Sukey Santoit, Girl Detective, who actually was from Toledo, Ohio, or had been earlier in the series. But just now she had not let that deter her from chasing after some jewel thieves up a road called the Boulevard St. Michel, as soon as she had untied her fabulously wealthy father and pulled him up out of the Seine—which could have been anything, but was clearly wet. Once she had caught the brigands, I thought of being someplace I could soar, from which I could wave to my own daddy, and in vague imagination had Sukey Santoit untie him so he could wave back.

In any case, I now had my girlhood's magic thing, and no one ever knows what those will be. Becky Baum, who sat next to me in school, owned a dollhouse in which she kept discovering new rooms. Dorothy Haze, who joined us at lunch, had a turtle that talked to her, but only when they were alone. I had a mysterious place called the Sorbonne, which I soon learned was a university, not a restaurant, and which was magic because no one else but me had ever heard of it. In my mental picture, whose lack of confirmable particulars may well have been an advantage, even the wine-imbibing Kansans in slipshod berets and mustaches with whom I peopled the place had somehow never heard of it, because I wasn't there yet.

However, having made the point that magic things are unpredictable, I should rebut any implication that they are totally haphazard. Before she was born, Becky Baum's parents had lost their farm in the Depression. Dorothy Haze had an "uncle" whose visits to her house, whenever her father was away pursuing his profession of land surveyor, she continued to dislike even after mama's friend had bribed her with the turtle; any child, which we all were, could see that she was trying to turn the animal against him. My daddy was Eddie Kilroy, who had gone far away and not returned—and my mother was the librarian of Russell, Kansas, which was why I got to read every new Sukey Santoit book ahead of anybody else. If it wasn't for that, either Becky or Dorothy might well have had a pied-à-terre in the 6ième Arrondissement today, although you should not infer from this that I, Mary-Ann, do.

Then again, the turtle baked to death in Dorothy's back yard one day. The dollhouse fell prey to termites, who discovered more new rooms in it than Becky had thought possible. All three of us joined the Russell High girls' choir, and even after we had sung "My Country 'Tis of Thee" and "Rock of Ages" at the somewhat more sparsely attended ceremony unveiling the names of the Korean war dead on the memorial on the courthouse lawn, the Sorbonne remained intact. In fact, it grew more so, if that's possible—which it is with magic things, at least if they are purely mental and not made of either tasty wood or all too cookable turtle meat. At the same time, I having reached an age when college gradually quits shimmering to materialize as a tangible prospect, the Sorbonne also grew, at least in theory, attainable.

I had already learned that a government allotment for the children of daddies who hadn't come back from the war might well pay for part or all of my tuition. As I knew that no one else from Russell had even considered applying to the Sorbonne, I also can't say I was feeling much heat of competition. My mother's bemused but staunchly professional resourcefulness as a librarian having enabled me to lay my hands on the correct address, I wrote away for an application in the best French that two years of high-school language study unblemished by so much as a single B plus or lower could attain. At the post office, trying to enter into the spirit of the occasion—it was his way, the post office itself not having much spirit to enter into—Mr. Clark the clerk made a small production out of selling me an international "Par Avion" stamp. Yet while grateful for his support, I was also wildly impatient to see the letter pass from his hands into the bin behind him. Once out of my sight, it would be closer to Paris, if only by some eight feet.

Then came days of racing home from school to see if they had replied to me—as I commenced to do the very next afternoon, although I knew this was unrealistic. After a week, I started cutting girls' choir practices to get to the mailbox an hour earlier. On what turned out to be the day, I had just whizzed out the door of Russell High and was preparing to gather speed when I saw our County Attorney walking back to the courthouse from lunch. He had probably come from either Dawson Drug, where he had worked as a soda jerk back before I was born, or Maple Street, which was where his family's house was.

He was one of the men of Russell who had come back from the war my daddy hadn't. But as he had been badly hurt in Italy, and even closer to the end of the war in Europe than Iwo Jima had been to VJ Day, I felt closer to him than I did to the veterans who had come back more or less intact, although like everyone in Russell I felt that none of them could do wrong in my eyes. In fact, almost my earliest memory was of being held up by my mother so that I could empty my piggy bank, which probably only had about twelve or fifteen pennies in it, into a cigar box that our Legion post was using to collect money for an operation that he needed in Chicago, not long after he came back from the war.

In fact, I sometimes felt that if I got accepted to the Sorbonne and left Russell, I'd miss our County Attorney most of all.

He had an interesting face, and sometimes it looked as if it caused him more pain than his right shoulder, which the operation hadn't been able or intended to fix, just reorganize. I saw his mouth and eyes as betraying an acute curiosity about the expressions they might have if everyone in the world were merry and kind, and regretting their relatively scattered opportunities to explore this. But since I was only a senior in high school, and had been raised to be unfailingly pleasant, polite, and cheerful, I guess I was an opportunity.

"Hello, Mary-Ann!" he barked. "You in a hurry to get somewhere, like always?"

"Yes, *sir,* Mr. Dole," I said back, giving him my best smile. "Just like always!"

"Hope you get there soon, then!" he said, moving the pen that he kept gripped in his bad hand up and down like a baton. That was our standard conversation, which we both always enjoyed. But this time, as I waved and charged on, I felt as grateful as if our County Attorney had dropped twelve or fifteen pennies, of which he didn't have that many to spare, into a box marked "Mary-Ann"; and suddenly I knew today was the day.

Which it was—and as such, at least in the short run, a crushing disappointment. If the boggling sight and then the quaking touch of an envelope strange both in color (powder blue) and texture (crinklier than ours), and thrillingly addressed to "Mlle. Mary-Ann Kilroy, Russell, Kansas, Etats-Unis d'Amerique," almost burst my heart, the letter within, in what briefly struck me as amazingly good French until I remembered why, very nearly broke it. I read what the Sorbonne had to tell me several times, each time hoping against hope that my conceivably imperfect grasp of grammar and idiom had caused me to miss the tiny preposition, *accent grave* vs. *circonflexe,* or curlicue in the signature which would reveal that the letter said the exact opposite of what, each time, it did.

Unless my conceivably imperfect grasp of human nature was making me miss the sarcasm, however, they were very solemn and nice about it. While properly admiring of the academic record I had compiled at Russell High and in no doubt of the school's high standards, they regretted to inform me of their conclusion that four years there, even with the girls' choir as evidence that I was outgoing as well as competent, did not in their view constitute sufficient preparation for matriculating at the Sorbonne. While equally commendatory of my grasp of French, they also felt obliged to note their concern that my vocabulary might not yet be equal to the studies in philosophy, history and political science in which I had expressed a breathless interest. In what proved to be the letter's crucial passage, although at the time—desolate, in mental hock to youth's abbreviated calendar, and having already waited just about my whole sentient life—I barely took it in, they advised that I should plan to enroll in their summer program for foreign students after two years of further seasoning at an institution of higher learning in the United States, a program to whose waiting list they would be glad to add my name in the absence of instructions to the contrary.

In closing, they thanked me for my interest in their university, language, culture, city, country, and continent, and hoped it would continue. They also remembered the late Monsieur Kilroy, and begged his widow and daughter—which would be I, Mary-Ann—to please accept the expression of their most distinguished sentiments, whose warmth they were sure would not be diminished by the long trip from Paris to Russell, Kansas.

Having glumly prepared a fallback choice at the double-barreled behest of my mother's now bespectacled eyes, I soon found myself attending Ellfrank University in Topeka instead. There, amid the staircased new excitements of dorm life and more trees than I had ever seen, my youthful resiliency soon made me bounce back—and stay aloft, as I was naturally upbeat. Eagerly, I plunged into classes, cocoa, and pajama-clutching arguments about whether Dorothy Haze, who had joined me in the Ellfrank frosh, should join the cheerleading squad for the basketball team or play forward for the girls' one, a debate she finally made moot by calmly announcing that her pre–med studies would leave her time for neither. That unexpected career choice, by the way, won Dottie a stunned tribute from our mutual friend Becky Baum: "Wow," she said, wide-eyed and expertly licking a mini-marshmallow bit from the browned corona of her lips. "I guess your kids and husband'll *never* get sick for long."

As if the green campus had been tipping to spill them gently out, two

years slid by—and, to my instantly blinking shock and despite my continuing study of French, I had all but forgotten about the Sorbonne, having
let Topeka turn my head, when a familiarly blue and crinklier-than-ours
envelope was slipped under my dorm-room door, the forwarding address
from Russell scrawled in an all-caps hand to which my mother had been
unable to forbear adding a pair of exclamation points. After offering
good wishes for my health and politely inquiring about my current academic pursuits, the letter asked if I still cared to attend the Sorbonne's
summer program, for which a place had been held open for me should
my scholastic record prove adequate.

Once it had, the true magnitude of the journey I was to undertake
sank in. You have to understand that up to now I'd never seen an ocean,
much less crossed one. While it was possible to fly to Paris, and apparently done often, anyone who's ever spent a day in Russell—the most
that any of you can, of course—will doubtless understand my murky
sense that such swift, sleek transportation, crammed with people in posh
clothes, might well be barred to the likes of me. Not caring to suffer a
public rejection at TWA's hands, I took a train to New York City, whose
dizzying stone ladders and glass crossword puzzles my eyes had only a
single afternoon to scale and no time at all to read the clues to before,
third-class ticket firmly in hand, I trotted up a gangplank. Which was
hoisted soon afterward, amid tugboat toots and hurled paper ribbons.
Then, hands to the railing and hearing the goodbye cries of the seagulls
who were the last Americans we saw, on a sea that was a gifted child's
pretty watercolor of the sunset above it, I was on my way to Le Havre
aboard the S.S. *United States.*

Five days of shuffleboard, private conjugations of irregular verbs in
the past and future perfect, and meals full of fascination later—and
peeved only at the fat American kid who'd come across Richard New-
comb's *Iwo Jima* in the shipboard library and was reading it there, thick
glasses perched above two unknuckled hands, when I turned from the
gap in the shelf—I stood on French soil, or at least French concrete under
an audibly, from the flurry of fluid cursing overhead, French derrick.
Worn out with excitement, I napped on the boat train to Paris, and even
dozed, despite my neck's protesting jerks, in the undersized taxi that took

me to my small hotel in the narrow Rue de Lille on the Left Bank. But then, checked in and my stunned-looking suitcase hoisted in a tiny elevator to an only slightly larger room, I dashed back down the stairs, became an urgent compass for a second, rounded a corner and trotted a block. From across the Seine, which had always been and always would be a river, I was looking at the Louvre.

It was so enormous that at first my eyes had room for nothing else. But then, like a huge but toothless gray medieval dog, Notre Dame nudged them on my right. A barge was going under a bridge, and I, Mary-Ann, spoke words I did not flatter myself were original.

"My God," I gasped. "It's all *real.*"

"Every *day,*" I marveled. "Every last day of the year."

■

It's also fortunate that, as a result, life in Paris demands some attention to practicalities even for those not, such as I was, in town to attend the Sorbonne. Otherwise, the most famous local statuary would be the clumps of foreigners rooted to whatever spot they happened to be standing on when they first grasped this was Paris and they in it, and goggling with increasingly glazed eyes until starvation or Peugeots keeled them over. The best food in the world, and you can still forget you're hungry—for food, at any rate.

But I had the Sorbonne to locate, and classes to register for and then begin. Retracing Sukey Santoit's footsteps until I'd done the one, and letting a pencil tickle my lips and briefly go spelunking in my ear until I had a head start on the other, I realized that all this was the barest prologue to the dozens of other interesting decisions I now had to make and re-make, such as which kitten-and-wool route to take from the Rue de Lille to the Boulevard St. Michel each morning, which café to stop in for a chicoried and crumby breakfast en route to what in three days had become Boul' Mich', which museum or landmark to hasten off to after class with which guidebook under my arm, and which small piece of blue twilight to pick out for my special own before, clambering up the stairs or hoisted in the tiny elevator, I went back to do my nightly class reading and homework assignments in my not much larger room, whose single casement window's view of a sky stitched with entangled rooftops had shown me the origins of Cubism back on the very first day that I woke up in Paris, Paris, Paris, and went in my jammies to throw it open.

It was perfection cut in half by a river, and marred only by the intermittent sound of explosions whose reports were seemingly slowed but not stilled by the muggy summer sky. These, I soon discovered—having just stopped at a newspaper kiosk to buy a stack of undated newspapers, which for some reason almost all of them were, and now making my way through *Le Monde* with some difficulty—were the work of something called the Organisation Armée Secrète, or O.A.S., whose members were disaffected but still serving French Army officers and others who were bitterly opposed to granting independence or even limited autonomy to France's colony Algeria. These folks were currently attempting to win ordinary Parisians over to their point of view, the survivors anyway, by setting off bombs at random in public places.

They were also bitterly opposed to Charles de Gaulle, who they felt had betrayed their cause after a coup in Algiers had brought him back to power here—by this point, I was on my second *café crème*, and struggling through *Combat*—by occasionally letting drop gnomic but nonetheless lucid remarks to the effect that it might be best, or possibly just interesting, if the French war against the rebels in Algeria didn't drag on until the end of time. As the O.A.S. disagreed, they kept trying to assassinate him, meanwhile growing more and more enraged as he either foiled or flat-out ignored the coups they went on staging every few months in Algiers, apparently hoping that the seventeenth plan, or whichever, would be the charm.

But the O.A.S. wasn't the only outfit setting off explosions that summer. Adding to all the confusion in Paris, apparently from pure whimsy, were the mysterious operations of the Lili Gang, a pack of elusive safe-crackers whose mastery of disguise had so far stymied all attempts to apprehend them. The major difference between the O.A.S. and them—as I had just informed myself, humming my way through *Le Figaro*—was that the Lili Gang's bombs were much smaller and somewhat more artistically placed, and despite the minor damage that they might occasionally wreak on some ornate facade here or there, nobody had actually gotten killed or more than had their hair mussed as a result of them. If anything, going by the cryptic hints they dropped into their communications on unrelated matters, they also seemed to rather admire Charles de Gaulle, or at any rate to approve of his policies in Algeria.

In my whole time at the Sorbonne, I never saw de Gaulle in the flesh—not exactly. But once, on the Champs-Elysées, I did see a limousine that had him in it, or so I gathered from the excited or jittery mutterings of nearby bystanders, making its long-nosed way up the avenue from the Place de la Concorde to the Arc de Triomphe. Even the loud American girl hawking the *International Herald Tribune* in front of the Seberg Jeans boutique stopped to watch what happened next.

As the limousine passed the Avenue de Marigny, a man dashed out of a nearby park and began spraying it with a machine gun. His own bullets came ricocheting back at him off its door, and he had to dive inside a handily placed temporary *pissoir* to take cover.

At the Rond Point, two black sedans of different makes and years came tearing out from opposite directions, one from the Avenue Matignon and one from the Avenue Montaigne. As they reached the spot where the limousine should have been crushed between them, it vanished, and they collided instead as their target serenely reappeared some thirty feet away.

At the Rue Washington, which is where I was, a man hurled himself from a tall building and plunged toward the limousine's roof, brandishing a knife in one hand and a can opener in the other. As the limousine briefly picked up speed, he smacked into the street, picking himself up with an expression of disgusted resignation.

Resuming its stately pace, the limousine rolled past me, its horn gravely sounding a basso *"Mip-mip."* Then it was gone, heading toward the Étoile—if that's still its name today, anyhow. Not being in any position to go back, I wouldn't know.

"Wow," the *Herald Tribune* chick called to me, giggling and running a hand through her closely cropped blonde hair. "What do you suppose all *that* was about? Like I keep telling everybody back in Iowa, things can just get *kooky* here!"

I had no idea how she knew I was from the States too, but I wasn't surprised to be hailed in English. If my perfect Paris had a drawback other than the occasional explosions, it was a shortage of Parisians—ones I knew and could talk to about things more prolonged and vivid than our coinciding interests, respectively gustatory and financial, in *cafés crème*. The other students in my program at the Sorbonne were all either American or from foreign countries, and while it was interesting to meet my first Englishmen and stare at my first Germans, there were limits to both the appeal and use of practicing one's French on people who were practicing it too. At the hotel in the Rue de Lille, the whole roster of both short- and long-term guests was international, from the precious young *Vogue* model with the funny face who had the room down the hall from mine to superannuated old Lady Ashley up on the attic floor.

Along with this generalized shortage of actual French people to have prolonged and vivid dealings with, a more specific pinch of painful absence rode my other shoulder as I hurried to the Sorbonne each day. No lower than my shoulder did I ever let it travel, for in Russell I'd never gone past second, and even in college I only went to third once, briefly. In other words, I, Mary-Ann, was most definitely a good girl, and meant to remain one. But I also feared that I might never get back here, and I couldn't bear to miss out on being half of, rather than merely observing, a sight lovelier than the Louvre—and more famous, too. If the true test of a dream's beauty is its ability to withstand clichés, cartoons, and ten thousand bad songs all featuring accordions—although most people who have been on the spot would agree that car horns playing nothing but sharps would be a good deal more accurate, and not noticeably less musical or magical—then kissing someone with the Seine for a backdrop must be this planet's most beautiful dream, and so it certainly seemed to me. If I sailed for home without anything of the kind occurring—so I fretted in my tiny room in the hotel on the Rue de Lille, although more often and achingly at night than in the morning—I might well end up inside the withered flesh of an old age equipped with little more than a dim memory that I, Mary-Ann, had once attended the Sorbonne in Toledo, Ohio.

However, this was not to be the case. Killing two frogs with one stone, so to speak—if I may briefly resurrect the ugly tone of the all but forgotten professor who wrote *Vie! Je te haïs!*—someone soon came into my summer, if not precisely life. An utterly unheralded tribune, he promptly started judging my life if not summer. When he wasn't doing that, he wrote about movies, although he hoped to make them himself someday.

His name was Jean-Luc something. It's sad, but all these years later, I can't even remember the first initial of his surname.

■

"Gee," I realized I'd said aloud, attracting the attention of a previously unnoticed figure standing next to me as I stared at the movie poster outside a Left Bank revival house. Feeling a need to explain myself that somehow doubled as my first impression of Jean-Luc, I shrugged.

"I didn't know Joan Crawford was so big here," I said, in French more diffident than my norm. But this unshaven runt in the smoked glasses looked like he *really* talked it, all the time and quite a lot too.

"Crawford has her special hysteria that does not know how problematically it makes her actual hysterics difficult to distinguish from more routine behavior. But there are perceptions there. Still, her we can take or leave," he said, all with an impatience that seemed to be his version of friendliness—and was, as I soon learned, Jean-Luc's version of respect, although not to the exclusion of other, more predictable importunings. "The important name on that poster is much smaller." He pointed.

"*C'est qui, ça?*" I asked, peering. Guy could use a manicure, I thought.

"I wonder why I try to learn English," he grumbled in surprisingly good ditto, "when I reflect it will only bring me into closer contact with one hundred and seventy-five million people who have never heard of Nicholas Ray. In your country, I think he may feel fortunate to have heard of himself."

"*Explique-moi, alors,*" I said—and, in a very un-Mary-Ann-like gesture, which as a result left *both* of us disconcerted, seized the cigarette that he'd just started putting to his lips. "Uh-uh! Won't let you smoke it until you do," I said.

"I will need a whole package of them for that," he said in French, and led me into a *tabac* so he could buy one. Despite some four weeks in Paris, I found myself surprised that there were tables present, and told myself to snap out of it. It also seemed I would have time to, as he had asked for two *cafés crème* with his Gauloises. Later, I learned that his minuscule fee for a whole movie review had gone up in smoke—or steamed milk, anyhow—at that instant.

Jean-Luc gave me his view of who Nicholas Ray was. I explained that I could not go along with him there, having been raised a Lutheran (#9) and wishing to stay faithful to my creed. This made him temporarily abject and about five years younger, which was why I bought the next two *cafés crème*. By the time I returned with them, he had gotten older and perked up again, although I could see a certain chicken-and-egg aspect in wondering which one came first.

"Orson Welles," he announced, in a tone so knowledgeable and satisfied I actually glanced over my shoulder at the door his seat was facing toward. "Here I know I can convince you, if only because him I know you have at least heard of, Marianne."

"It's not Marianne," I told him, not for the first time. "It's Mary-Ann Kilroy. Mayr-ree-Ann."

He smiled—through smoked glasses, glassy smoke, hands, and bits of Paris. "Marianne is the personification of France," he said, which I knew. "Are you the personification of the United States, Mayr-ree-Ann?"

"Well, I'm not on a stamp, sir, if that's what you mean. And I'm not sure I'd much like being licked by strangers day in and day out while my back is turned," I said, thinking of poor Mr. Clark in the Russell post office. "So I guess that answers that."

We had been switching back and forth between languages, but I must have rattled this off in English, because I couldn't make jokes in French. In any case, as I spoke, his eyebrows had briefly appeared for the first time above the upper rims of his glasses, putting me disconcertingly in mind of Groundhog Day.

And I believe their retreat was the signal that I'd get six more weeks of Jean-Luc. For what he said next was "*Mon dieu.* And to think I was just bantering."

■

Along with many, many, many movies, my new boyfriend in Paris, Paris, Paris took me to see a play I kept calling *The Condemned of Altoona*, mostly to tease him. But as he had never heard of Altoona, P-A, and despite straining my ears and much increased command of French idiom alike I was none too clear on the location or actuality of Altona even afterward, it would be understatement to say this never became a running joke between us. It had barely staggered to its feet to try a shambling jog when it was shot down by both sides.

Jean-Luc and I both enjoyed ourselves more when he took me to see the play's author, Jean-Paul Sartre, of whose location and actuality neither I nor anyone in Paris, Paris, Paris was in any doubt. Not that such as we would ever dare to approach his table at Les Deux Magots to so much as genuflect, let alone remark that it sure looked like rain. Still, one could sit nearby, and listen to him and Simone de Beauvoir bicker about where they were going on vacation this year, whether they truly felt they had earned one, and if so whether it could be separate. Every once in a while as they did this, particularly if they were sitting outdoors, a tourist would step up and snap Sartre's picture, apparently feeling that he had come across the ideal combination of landmark and zoo animal. Although no teacher at the Sorbonne ever suggested as much, I have often wondered if the famous existentialist's views on human freedom, through the unlighted funhouse of which I was limping along in my schoolwork that summer, were colored in any way by this frequently repeated experience.

Then again, I couldn't help but ponder the obvious fact that Sartre could have drunk scads of coffee, smoked like a freighter, and rolled his walleye at de Beauvoir behind closed doors somewhere. This was his choice. He had been born free, but he was at Les Deux Magots.

There and elsewhere, Jean-Luc and I mostly kept to ourselves, holding hands except when he needed one to smoke with. A small tragedy of our six weeks together was that I didn't much care for his pals at *Cailloux du Cinéma* or whatever the magazine he reviewed for was called, and on their end they found me inexplicable at best. We more or less gave up group socializing after an evening in a transplanted Greenwich Village jazz club, somewhat ironically called Le Perroquet de New-York, at which I got into an argument with one particular *homme moyen avant-garde* who had decided to explain the true meaning of the Second World War to us all. But particularly to me, as I was evidently the least educated.

It had all been about America acquiring an empire, he said. From Lend-Lease to the Marshall Plan, the whole shebang had all been about us using our economic might to cut a pretty hefty piece of the pie for ourselves in the ingenious guise of saving the world. The Russians might have introduced tanks into Hungary, but we had introduced Coca-Cola into France, and *pas question* which one was turning a bigger profit— something I indeed wouldn't question, although I was unclear if this made the Russians more virtuous or just proved they weren't the folks you'd turn to for your estate planning.

In short, we had saved the world in order to make ourselves the masters of it, and he disapproved of this. He felt so, I gathered, partly on principle and partly because we were such bumblers at the job, though it seemed to me that even principled sorts might well find cretins with danceable music to be somewhat less of a stench in the nostrils than an ultra-efficient crew.

My eyes had begun to smart with a special form of astigmatism from which they occasionally suffered, and not from smoke either. But I allowed that I was not personally familiar with the thinking of my country's leaders during the period in question, or for that matter now. For all I knew, it might well have included or still include chicanery, gleeful or otherwise. I also agreed that imbibing a billion gallons of Coca-Cola *tout d'un coup* might well irritate any national palate raised on wine *half* as good as this third glass of burgundy I'd just downed. I even granted the point that, in the eyes of the world, the role of the United States might well seem at once naive and sinister, and that any apparent paradox in this characterization dissolved on the point that naïveté in today's world might well qualify as sinister by definition.

Having said all this, I nonetheless went on to express my distinct impression that, had it been the other way around—had, for instance, the Canadians revealed their true colors after centuries spent lulling us into a false sense of security by means of hockey, lumberjack shirts and beers with names like "Moosehead," and slammed their tanks south from Saskatchewan into our vitals like a shiv—that, *had the situation been reversed,* I for one could not help seriously doubting, despite my deep affection for many things and some people French and current wish to remain unfailingly pleasant, polite, and cheerful, that we in occupied America would have woken up one June morning to see a vast and mighty fleet off our coast, and watched with curiosity and interest the appearance therefrom of dozens of ungainly little boats packed with green-faced French boys from the farms and villages of Bordeaux, Alsace, Provence and, oh, just let me think a minute here, Normandy, all of them mighty confused about the whole thing and probably doing their business in their pants from dread but nonetheless prepared to soak the sands of Chincoteague with their blood and leave their brains smeared in the ruins of Norfolk if they had to before, having defeated the most fanatical units of fearsome Quebecois armor the butchers of Ottawa could throw at them in the Invasion of Chesapeake Bay, and now presumably singing the "Kissy-Missy from Trenton, N.J." song that their surviving daddies back in Bordeaux Alsace Provence and, oh, yes, Normandy had taught them after the *last* God Damned time they the French had had to do this for us spineless Americans, they drove up Constitution Avenue in triumph to throw off the yoke of Canadian tyranny, tear down the hated maple-leaf flag that had floated over the Washington Monument too long, and give us our God Damned freedom back on a God Damned olive-drab platter.

At this point, Jean-Luc, who had begun writing a monograph on Howard Hawks on his cocktail napkin so as to disoblige himself from taking an attitude, patted my arm and pointed out that the band had gone on break some minutes ago. I asked him what relevance this had to the intellectual discussion I was having, and he gently said none whatsoever except possibly as pertained to its volume.

So I stopped yelling. I did not mean to be rude, I said. I, Mary-Ann, merely wished to register my impression that all this would simply *not have occurred,* had our respective situations been reversed. Did he disagree?

What do you know, the son of a gun didn't. He just didn't think it mattered much. All hypothetical thinking aside, he said, we had never really had to come to grips with a bellicose Canada. Nor did he believe we had much reason to fear one's emergence, although he granted I might be better informed than he on that point.

Besides, he said, Washington, D.C., just wasn't as gosh-darn *pretty* as Paris. Not caring for travel, as few Parisians saw its point, he naturally hadn't been there, but he'd seen photographs and in any case I knew this to be irrefutable.

And finally, he said, had he and his compatriots been informed that afterward they'd need to prove day in day out and all the time that they'd been *deserving,* they might well have waved the fleet off.

At which point, he got a grin on his face so wide it almost made me like him.

"And *then* where would you *Amerloques* be? *Eh?*" he asked.

I thought about that. "Um, Jean-Luc?" I said.

"*Oui,* Mary-Ann?"

"How would you say 'without a paddle' in French?" I asked.

He told me there were many equivalents. They had found use for them over the years since Vercingetorix surrendered at Alesia. Often, as during the retreat from Moscow, for instance, or in 1940, the equivalents had served as large numbers of Frenchmen's final remarks on the situation before expiring, Jean-Luc said.

The going-away winner was "*Nous sommes foutus,*" he said. But since Vercingetorix's day, the tortoise to that particular hare had been "*Merde.*"

■

Otherwise, when no one but we two existed, which condition could last for periods ranging from two seconds up to several hours at a time, only one real bone of contention ever emerged between Jean-Luc and myself. I assume I am leaving you on fairly safe ground when I suggest that you guess whose.

I had gotten my wish, and been kissed with the Seine for a backdrop. I had been kissed somewhat gauchely on the Left Bank, which was where we tried it first, and rather more adroitly on the Right. I had been kissed in the Tuileries Gardens, at what I would calculate as the apex of a triangle whose other reference points were the statue of Joan of Arc in the Place des Pyramides and Gericault's painting of *The Raft of the Medusa* inside the Louvre. I hope you'll understand when I say that the succession of minute and cascading little awarenesses on my part that, working as secretly as silkworms, were to create my memory of these embraces—a pointillism of unshavenness, some seemingly random bumpings of smoked glasses in close-up, a complex reek of Gauloises new and old, and the downright eerie hush caused by the temporary cessation of Jean-Luc's voice—had, despite their prominent lack of resemblance to magazine advertisements, no downside, primarily because they made each kiss seem like the first, only improved.

Even those of you back home with four or more years of high-school French, however, may well depart the trolley when I say that the bone of contention between us came down to a grammatical struggle between the noun form of the French word for "kiss," which meant pretty much what ours did (with the addition of Gauloises, unshavenness, and a gold and mounted Joan of Arc raising her banner in the distance to a victory she understood; for all this was how I, Mary-Ann, saved France), and its verb form, which meant something else. As far as I was concerned, that something else, absent a wedding ring, kept the mere existence of the verb form of *baiser* akin to having a special word devised for no purpose other than describing a fast trip to Alpha Centauri; and I, Mary-Ann, far from caring to play a mutineer Buck Rogers and lay a course for there without permission from my galactic superiors, was, as I have said, a good girl.

That concept bedeviled my boyfriend not only for the mournful absence it prophesied of a shiny American coin tumbling into the little cigar box marked "Jean-Luc," but for the cultural differences it mapped between us even well this side of Alpha Centauri. For instance, as a good girl, the environment in which I was most used to being felt up was at the movies, and—well, enough said, at least if I have given an adequate picture of Jean-Luc's religious beliefs. Of course, he had so little respect for actual churches that, given the chance, he'd have been happy to despoil me successively in all sixteen of Russell's, tearing off my toreadors beneath #14's white steeple and bumping me quick-quick and gasping up against #6's red brick. However, even had it been physically possible for him to materialize there, which of course it wouldn't be until the next Unveiling, the image of Jean-Luc appearing in Russell, Kansas, in any capacity whatsoever—including that of projectionist at one or the other of our town's two movie houses, which had struck my imagination as the likeliest bet—was so surreal in itself that the image of him despoiling me there, which incidentally I quite often managed not to dwell upon unduly, seemed redundant.

As it goes without saying that Jean-Luc didn't own a car, my other customary domestic venue for getting felt up was equally inaccessible. That left opportunities for all but the most fleeting grope sessions, both aside from and during our public embraces, few and far between indeed, as I refused to let him come to my room in the Rue de Lille. Nor would I go to his apartment, protecting my past and future fondness for the noun form of *baiser* as well as my tense present feelings about the verb. While I had silently signed an armistice with Jean-Luc's personal hygiene some time previously, the prospect of seeing its trophies displayed museum-fashion was no great draw. In any case, the paucity and fleeting quality of any getting-felt-up sessions in our relationship probably left I, Mary-Ann, a good deal readier to sulk and kick furniture than my boyfriend was, as Jean-Luc found the whole practice of feeling girls up and leaving it at that too purely silly to be memorably frustrating.

In reaching this impasse that summer, Jean-Luc and I were not unique. Both Penny Wise and Cherry Maraschino, my two closest pals among the other American gals at the Sorbonne, reported similar wrangles with *their* French boyfriends, Claude being by far the more coldly contemptuous while François was often simply too curious to remember to be annoyed. Cherry, by the way, was the first American of Italian extraction that I'd ever swapped giggles, gum, and groans with, and by extrapolation the first Catholic. Yet her first name, if not her last, instantly gave us common ground—or a few cobblestones we shared that may have dated to the Middle Ages, that summer in Paris, Paris, Paris.

Since *my* boyfriend was not only the brainiest but the most polemical of the three, however, and hair-raisingly filthy-minded to boot, our debates about grammar were undoubtedly both more polytechnical and more licentious than either Penny and Claude's tart or Cherry and François's woebegone discussions of noun vs. verb. "*Mais, mais, mais, mais pourquoi enfin,* Mary-Ann"—so Jean-Luc used to get cranked up as we strolled, with blue Gauloise smoke hunting for Vercingetorix all around him—"*why* do you so cherish this absurd frontier between two utterly fictional countries named Today and Tomorrow, insisting that they not only engage in no commerce but do not even share a language? It's just more life, like birth and death."

"And the resurrection after death," I said automatically, in English. But that was a whole other argument, one that we had tacitly agreed to let Notre Dame cathedral and Père Lachaise cemetery fight out in our stead; knowing that the Seine prevented them from actually coming to blows.

"Has it ever occurred to you," he resumed, "that your most precious possession is something *all the world* starts out with—me, Hitler, Mickey Mouse? Good God, even Billy Wilder!" Suddenly, he had stopped dead on the sidewalk, Gauloise hand and non-Gauloise hand alike pressed to his temples. "You must forgive me," he said rapidly, "but I had never considered that before. Still, I must ask: how valuable can something once possessed by both de Gaulle and Laurel and Hardy truly be?"

"They don't have *mine*, though," I said, placing my hands on my hips. We were on the Boulevard St. Germain, where virtually every woman not sitting down in a café was doing this for one reason or another. De Beauvoir, although seated, just had too. But right now I, Mary-Ann, felt more like St. Joan Crawford of Arc than I did like Simone de Beauvoir; the idea that this distinction might well amount to hairsplitting not having yet occurred to me.

"Yes," Jean-Luc now said with great bitterness, "and it would take a second Hitler to change that little true fact. With an Annunciation in the form of Panzers, or is it Mickey that you save yourself for?"

"We'd still have to be married first, just like he was any other man or talking mouse in bright red shorts. One reason we like our Disney characters back in Russell is that they play by pretty much the same rules we do. Now Warner Brothers, I grant you, is a dicier matter altogether, which reminds me: when are you going to take me to Le Lapin Agile?"

"*L'Américaine, la petite pucelle—et voici la petite touriste! Coucou! Tu as vraiment du toupet! À ce moment, même découvrir un nouveau film de Jean Vigo tourné en Cinemascope et Technicolor ne me rendrait pas heureux! J'aimerais bien penser à autre chose qu'à ton cul pendant cinq minutes de ma vie! Ah, bon! Enfin, nouvelle bobine! Je pense à tes seins! Oh, les hurlements de joie que j'entends dans ma cervelle écrasée! Quel répit pour notre pauvre ami Jean-Luc! Et dire que tu vas partir pour ton fichu Kansas en moins d'une semaine! Si je n'ai pas l'air très gai, il faut peut-être se demander qui gagne, comme a dit Lenine! Merde! Je me fiche de toi*, Mary-Ann!"

By now, even Sartre had shut up. Had a tourist been handy, that would have been the moment for the snapshot of the century, believe me.

"Come on, Jean-Luc," I said, taking his trembling hand. "I bet Minnie will never divorce him, anyhow. Let me buy you a *café crème*."

Two sips, and lighting a Gauloise, calmed him considerably. "One day, perhaps," he said, smoking and patting my hand, "I will make a film in the manner of Mitch Leisen. And you will know who inspired it, because this will be its title: *Hail, Mary-Ann!*"

"Mitch Leisen?" I said.

"I know," he said, misunderstanding me slightly. "I too would prefer to say in the manner of Lubitsch. But Lubitsch would be hubris."

"Really? Lubis would be hubritch?" I said, to tease him.

"Yes, yes," he said irritably—"of course, Lubis would be hubritch." But then he heard himself, at the same moment he saw my face; and we smiled at each other across our table at Les Deux Magots, as women stood around us with fists to hips and Sartre smoked like a freighter, one day toward the all too rapid end of my summer in Paris, Paris, Paris.

■

Whether they were new or old, I always liked to go see American movies with my boyfriend. That was partly because it was fun to hear Humphrey Bogart say *"Les choses dont les rêves sont faits"* in a mellifluous couturier's voice at the end of *The Maltese Falcon*, and partly because what Jean-Luc thought was going on in most of our movies was so bughouse. In the second connection, I particularly remember the last one we saw, scant days before my departure. One reason for that is that we had to see it twice, owing to circumstances I will explain in their place.

Stubbing out his cigarette as my red Kansas-bought pumps clumped their last few clumps down to the hotel lobby, Jean-Luc gave me a new wave, choppier and more freewheeling than the old one. As we walked toward the theater, which was in the Quartier Latin, he gave me his usual densely choreographed earful about today's blue-smoke special. Although its producer-director, one Y. Avery Willingham, struck Jean-Luc as an auteur without hauteur, I can recall no further details, as I mostly just liked the sound of my boyfriend's voice when something interested and excited him. Nor, despite patting his pockets for ideas as if for Gauloises, was he ever short on commentary. We were not literally walking alongside the literal Seine at the moment, but I was strolling happily next to my private one; whose arm I got to hold, just listening to the river run.

Now, this movie, which was called *Every Girl Is an Island*, would have been chucked off the bottom half of a double bill at the Mecca Theater in Russell, Kansas, in well under a week. Considering that our town's Main Street arcade, not that far from the Mecca, has a sign ten feet high over its door bearing the legend "Something to Do," believe me this is no small claim. Set, or rather dumped, among the rickety shacks and amazingly interchangeable beaches of some mythical archipelago in the Pacific, the picture had the budget of a picnic, and its heroine was torn between an older man to whom she looked up, as he was taller, and a fellow her own age who did the same for Every Girl from his lower rung on the movie's structural ladder, which I personally wouldn't have used to change a light bulb.

While her predicament had clearly deranged Miss Island, that could and did not dissuade her from sporadically discovering her talent for the ukulele. In toto, said talent consisted of employing said ukulele as a sort of oddly shaped knick-knack shelf on which to prop her bosoms while some off-screen musician, discreetly ignoring our heroine's wildly flapping fingers, strummed away more or less proficiently on the soundtrack during the movie's song-and-dance numbers. These were as unpredictable as auto accidents, and left an observer similarly minded to summon doctors and police to the scene.

However, in defense of auto accidents, they are seldom if ever *dubbed*, which lent *Every Girl Is an Island* a whole extra dimension of lunacy. Meanwhile, in the background, a tourist contingent peculiarly long on acned adolescents and men with strikingly well-tended hair sometimes trooped through the shambles, all looking fairly glum about life except when four of them got to go on a horseback ride from which they never returned. But whether this was a subplot or sheer forgetfulness at work got lost in the murk between islands, or perhaps my attention had wandered.

When the lights came up, not a moment too soon but nonetheless slightly sooner than the plot seemed to warrant, Jean-Luc was too moved to speak. Since I learned this flabbergasting news from his own lips, the condition clearly wasn't absolute or medical, yet I could see he meant it. "*Formidable,*" he finally mumbled, patting his jacket as if to make sure he was still wearing one, as I pulled him out the theater exit.

Several minutes of mutually stunned, although from different causes, silence later, he stopped midway across Boul' Mich', to the fury of a number of drivers. "*Mais évidemment! Même quand Hitchcock s'en est servi dans* Saboteur, *la statue de la liberté était toujours une femme, après tout,*" he said, and walked on. Later still, at the junction of the Rue Dauphine and the Rue St. André des Arts, he paused again, running his fingers through his hair as if it was on fire. Inevitably, this prompted him to search for and light a Gauloise.

"Quiet, *please,* Mary-Ann!" he implored me, although I was neither a car horn nor a cursing cyclist. "I am trying to compose a review in my head that will do honor to Y. Avery Willingham. That movie was a masterpiece."

"Jean-Luc, compose *yourself*, for gosh sakes," I said. "The only thing that movie was was one of the dopiest things I've ever seen, says Mary-Ann Kilroy of the Kansas *Expatriate*. Why, a *cat* would be ashamed to be in it," I said, a white one with one pink and one green eye having just, in the wake of a nearby drunk's cry of "Shoo! Shoo!," bounded toward a nearby roof. "Jean-Luc, I swear: back in the States, B-movie studios churn these things out like pre-filled garbage bags for the lazy consumer. It's not worth thinking about!"

I might have gone on. I might very well have gotten as worked up about the imbecility of *Every Girl Is an Island* as I had about the true meaning of World War Two, that night in Le Perroquet de New-York, if Jean-Luc hadn't interrupted me. In an impatient voice whose cranky tone was somewhat offset by the fact that he'd just taken both my hands in his, he abruptly spoke the most touching words I was ever to hear from the strange boyfriend I had for some forty-two days, all those summers ago in Paris, Paris, Paris, just because they were the most like him.

"Prove it, Mary-Ann," he said. "I see what I see."

As did I, as Jean-Luc's eyes smiled he well knew. Or so I interpreted them through his smoked glasses, and we walked on, hand in hand and comfortable with each other. But now I too was pensive, somewhat against my better judgment. While I still had no more idea of what Jean-Luc could have found to admire in *Every Girl Is an Island* than I did of what the Lili Gang was up to, that hadn't stopped me from puzzling over the movie's abrupt and cryptic ending. With no explanation or excuse for her departure, Every Girl was briefly seen piloting a motorboat out to sea, alone and wearing a captain's cap.

Between my repeated attendance at our town's two theaters, at which being felt up had not always engaged my full attention—and also because I had the luck to have a mother who, while only a mild-mannered librarian of Russell by day, was transformed into a veritable Tiresias of the silver screen and she-wolf of the celluloid cave in the presence of *The Late, Late Show*—I knew that no American movie, or popular entertainment of whatever kind, had had an ending like that since the Civil War, that being approximately where my sense of how things functioned in America grew too dim for generalizations of this type. In fact, had Jean-Luc asked me, I would probably have teased him by maintaining that endings such as that of *Every Girl Is an Island* had long in fact been prohibited by the U.S. Constitution, either explicitly or by omission.

As a result, I had begun to rack my brains for some crucial plot point I had missed amid the song-and-dance numbers, the tourists, the four horsemen, and the general cavorting, because I knew in my bones, as a veteran moviegoer, that she *had* to have chosen either the Doctor or the water boy. After all, there wasn't any point to the story if she didn't. Why, they'd never have let her just sail away, I was thinking, as we passed the Rue Jacob.

Jean-Luc paused. "I don't know which hotel, but your American Djuna Barnes used to live on that street," he said. "You know, the woman who wrote *Nightwood.*"

"I've never heard of her," I said. As indeed I haven't to this day, so maybe Jean-Luc was pulling my leg. One of his favorite jokes was making up preposterous people with implausible-sounding names, and solemnly pretending they were real. So, with a shrug, I sent Djuna Barnes to the particular train compartment of oblivion already occupied by Man Ray and Rosa Luxembourg, and we walked on toward the Pont des Arts.

Past the Rue des Beaux-Arts, right before the Rue de Seine dog-legged to accommodate the side portico of the Institut de France's golden dome, a street musician with matted hair and a wild beard was playing the flute, a cap between his shoes. Drilled to seize any pretext to practice reading French, my eyes automatically went to the weathered words hewn in the wall behind him, which informed all those interested or not that here someone had been killed in August 1944. There were plaques of that type all over this stretch of the Left Bank, commemorating all the brave, newsreel-gray, quickly running people who had died during the Liberation.

Though one flute didn't stand much chance against the roar of traffic barreling along the Quai Malaquais close by, the wild-haired man was playing with determination, as if he didn't know what or who had put him here but he had work to do. After we'd gone a few steps more, I noticed I had developed a case of my special astigmatism, and that it was about to leak out of my eyes and down my cheeks. When I ran back to drop some francs in the musician's cap, he nodded and kept tootling away, not taking his eyes off the road Jean-Luc and I had traveled.

"What is it?" he asked when I rejoined him. "You're upset."

"Oh, it's nothing—just the song he was playing," I said, brushing astigmatism from my eyes. "I guess I was just surprised to hear it in Paris—I didn't think it had ever made it over here." Walking beside him, I started humming it under my breath, translating the lyrics to practice my language skills: "*Je suis presqu' fou / Tout par amour pour toi . . .*" Then I got stumped. "Jean-Luc," I asked, "how would you say 'a bicycle built for two' in French?"

"*Vélo à deux personnes.* But it would be dangerous here, don't you think?" he said, nodding at the view. We had reached the Quai Malaquais, and the rush-hour traffic was whizzing by.

"You're still talking to Mary-Ann Kilroy of the Kansas *Expatriate*," I said. "To me, all this would look plenty dangerous on a bicycle built for one."

Just as I said so, however, there was a break in the traffic, which meant that we could read the graffiti on the shuttered Seine bookstall across the street. In big, rust-colored, dripping letters, it said this: *O.A.S., AU POUVOIR.*

"*Salauds,*" Jean-Luc said. "*Toujours une nouvelle connerie.*"

"*T'inquiète pas, Jean-Luc,*" I said. "*Tout ça sera effacé par la nuit.*"

"No. If this continues, May-*ree* Ann, soon they'll be fighting in the street." He heaved a smile: "And the movies that I worship will be gone," he said.

As if its makers had been eavesdropping, a bomb went off somewhere nearby. "*Ah, non, c'est trop!*" Jean-Luc said, flipping his cigarette away. "*Et c'est trop dangereux pour toi,* Mary-Ann. Come on! I'm taking you back to your all-American hotel."

I started to follow him. But now, although the afternoon hadn't been a particularly unusual one up to this point, a series of rapid events occurred as if designed to prove that, as the Iowa girl selling the *Herald Tribune* outside Seberg Jeans on the Champs-Elysées had so cheerfully hallooed to me, things could get just *kooky* here in Paris, Paris, Paris.

First off, in the cries of the excited bystanders around us, two startling words began to spread like wildfire: "Lili Gang!" people were shouting, pointing down the Quai. "Lili Gang!" And the next thing Jean-Luc and

I knew, the people we'd been reading about all this time were running for their lives before our very eyes: Algligni, the young gunman who was rumored to have shot his own father; Gliaglin, the embittered ex-revolutionary; pert, sly Lil Gagni, who some whispered was really a man in disguise; and Laggilin, the apostate apothecary who'd turned to crime. At the same moment, throwing aside his flute and tearing off his wig and false beard as he came, the bug-eyed Mr. Gagilnil—who'd been their lookout, of course—dashed toward us down the Rue de Seine, brushing aside a middle-aged American tourist in a mackintosh and his lovely, startled wife. As he joined the others, he was yelling, "*Au Pont des Arts, les gars! À l'assaut du Louvre!*"

I felt a confused impulse to chase after them, but a calm hand on my shoulder detained me—and it wasn't Jean-Luc's, either. Instead, as I turned, my astonished eyes found themselves staring directly into the cool green ones of none other than Sukey Santoit, Girl Detective.

"Stay put, Mary-Ann," she said tightly. "I'll handle this." Quickly producing a gun from her compact, which sober reflection told me was no mean trick, she high-tailed it across the Pont des Arts in the Lili Gang's wake, firing into the air as if to alert them of her coming; leaving me unsure if she was in pursuit or had gone over to their side. Or they to hers, somewhere in the middle of it all. And in the general excitement, I had almost forgotten my boyfriend existed, until he made a remark.

"You know, that woman who's firing her pistol and running across the bridge just now—she seemed to know you," Jean-Luc remarked in a bemused way. "Do you know her?"

"I used to," I stammered, "or—will, or something. I'm not sure." Which was, I knew, a peculiar thing to say; also feel.

But what was even more peculiar, now that I had cause to mull the matter over, was that I had had precisely the same reaction to the actress playing the title role in Y. Avery Willingham's *Every Girl Is an Island*. Perhaps luckily, the feeling hadn't come near enough the surface in the dark for me to articulate it, Ginger and I still being on, so to speak, different islands then; besides which, of course, Jean-Luc hadn't asked me about my possible relationship to her, leaving the need for articulation moot.

In any case, you might as well read his review of the movie, which I perused with wonder and bewilderment in *Cailloux du Cinéma* the next morning. Having carried it in my purse ever since, I will now venture to put it into English—taking, you might say, my only remaining opportunity to reach out across a now invisible café table and hold hands with Jean-Luc, although he's unaware of it. Aside from a misspelling of the word "scarlet" that I really ought to correct, any gibberish in my version has what I would reckon as a fifty-fifty chance of being the fault of the translator's declining French skills, and is otherwise attributable to the translatee.

Unfortunately, parts of the heading and Jean-Luc's last name are now illegible, the contents of my purse having subsequently suffered some water damage. The rest is more or less complete. The nonsensical date, I believe, was intended to be facetious.

CA....DU CINÉMA

vol. 1, no. 7

19 Thermidor, Year 1

Quand les "elles" deviennent des Iles (Every Girl Is an Island)
a film by Y. Avery Willingham

TO FREEDOM BY MOTORBOAT

Before everything, he agitates himself [?] of this question: is the Self a proud lighthouse of solitude, or a little man in a boat in search of land, which never reveals itself to his anxious eyes? In Every Girl Is an Island, *Y. Avery Willingham shows himself to be an author of the cinema truly without fear, for he revises not only the Old Testament but Descartes. To the central problem of evading Pharoah's chariots pending [?] the flight from Egypt, he offers a new solution: rather than divide the Red Sea for a few moments, one must learn to navigate upon it in permanence.*

The Moses he proposes is no ferocious, barbed Charlton Heston—not, well heard [?], to imply that the magnificent Heston is an icon of the cinema one iota or roar less imposing than the Lion of M-G-M itself—but the charming young actress Gin . . . [more water damage, but of course you know her name anyway], *whose character "Louise" needs no more than a proud toss of her scarlett hair, below her saucy new captain's hat, to effectively replace the "Cogito, ergo sum" of graybeards become bluebeards with the female's own defiant correction: "Sum—ergo cogito!"*

Willingham's place-in-scene [??] *is a combination of artistic subtlety and elemental simplicity that has not been seen since the great films of silent days, such as G. W. Langmur's* Das Herz von Avis. *And yet, in the opinion of my clean heart, all the meanings are different now.*

The audacity of the scenario is to present Louise with a real problem posed in false terms—just as, for so many of her less fortunate sisters, life dwindles to a false problem posed in real terms. Of the two lovers between whom the plot—though not, in secret, the director!—urges her to choose, the Doctor seems to represent the best qualities of age: learning, authority, wisdom. His counterpart, Gilles the water boy, has all the ardor of youth, but also its confusions. Which represents her destiny? The viewer awaits at the end of his breath, but our Louise brooks no nonsense.

Ultimately, she recognizes that to choose either will deprive her of herself, for she will then only be a mirror of their *qualities. While they may also reflect some of hers, our heroine grasps the fallacy of mirrors—in short, that every mirror, however tempting, is restricted by its frame. Rejecting the spurious decision that life wishes to impose on her, she sets sail instead for an unknown harbor. Yet one might say Louise has reached her destination at the moment that her hand first grasps the wheel.*

At first, the fanciful environment put before us by Y. Avery Willingham seems to have few traits in common with our own. We, too, seek our separate and collective mirrors in the dark, and do not readily find them in this middle [?] *of resorts and tourists, through which our heroine moves as an itinerant ukulele player. (The actress's skills on this instrument are prominent.) Yet as we emerge from the theater into our own world of music and bombs, where we too look for freedom—and yes, perhaps, love too, although in Louise's case this is reserved for a sequel to be filmed only in our imaginations—among passing strangers unaware of the myriad small struggles and victories taking place in their very midst, we understand differently.*

Having begun with one question, I must end with another: is not Every
Girl Is an Island *the cinema of truth raised to poetry, and poetry become
the only cinema able to describe our age's strange new truths?*

                              —*Jean-Luc [quelque-chose]*

■

Unluckily for my boyfriend, although he stuck to his guns all the same,
the theater's management ran a public notice in the papers on the same
day his review appeared in *Cailloux* (or whatever) *du Cinéma*. It cleared
the mystery of the ending right up.

Apparently as a result of some unexplained private disorder at Y.
Avery Willingham Productions, this theater's print of *Every Girl Is an
Island* had inadvertently been shipped to Paris without the final reel,
which had now belatedly arrived. The management apologized, and
invited anyone who had seen the abridged version to come back and
view the complete one at no charge.

You can probably picture the fuming rapidity with which Jean-Luc
marched us back to the theater in the Quartier Latin—where this time,
of course, Louise ended up picking one of the men, just as I had known
in my bones she had to. I don't recall which one, as I could not have
cared less about either. Nor was I partial to the actors, for the Doctor
was a sort of grade-Z Robert Preston type whom I was more accustomed to seeing in cheap horror pictures. As for whoever played the kid,
he didn't seem able to decide whether he'd rather be James Dean or
Jerry Lewis—and talk about your false choices posed in real terms, at
least if you're asking Mary-Ann Kilroy of the Kansas *Expatriate*.

At any rate, when Louise set out on the motorboat with such an air of
jubilation, it turned out that she was only going around the corner, so to
speak, to tell her boss at the cardboard hotel where she worked that she
was giving up her career as an itinerant ukulele player. The last line in
the picture was this one, which my future fellow castaway delivered in
breathy close-up, batting eyelashes that bore an alarming resemblance to
pine needles under fresh snow, just after she'd chucked her ukulele in the

harbor: "Oh—what's making silly music matter, compared to finding the right man?"

And even the left man, whichever one he was, agreed with her.

Jean-Luc, you may not be surprised to hear, did not. Next to the bile he started venting the minute we hit the street, his previous outburst at me in front of Les Deux Magots was like something you'd find written in your yearbook by the shy classmate you had never guessed was such a sentimentalist.

"*Mon dieu,* Mary-Ann!" he raged. "The film we saw yesterday was as much an organic masterpiece, in its way, as *Way Down East.* The one we saw *today* is an abomination, a travesty—an insult, an atrocity, a joke!" he seethed. "Clearly, the new ending was forced by the gutless distributors onto the cowardly, despicable Y. Avery Willingham, who bent to their yoke with a smile and a wink at his accountant," he snarled.

"And I praised his artistic courage!" he spat. "*Il m'a trahi,* Mary-Ann! He has held up his tarnished mirror to my eyes, and shown me only a pathetic, useless dreamer gazing back," he moaned. "What's more important, he has betrayed both cinema and life, by making of his beautiful film an offering to the Golden Calf whose moo repeats the lie that cinema and life are divisible," he said quietly but menacingly. "Do *NOT* forgive him, André Bazin, do *NOT* forgive him, Otto Preminger, for he knows all too well what he does—*et tout ça me fait chier dans ta gueule, Monsieur* Y. Adolf Willingham!" he yelled.

"*Pah!*" he finished up.

Spent Gauloises lay all around us. I took Jean-Luc's trembling hands in mine.

"The *movie* is a travesty," I told him earnestly. "What you wrote is still true."

"But my review now hails a film that does not even exist," he lamented. "It *should* exist, as you and I exist—but it doesn't!"

Lifting my chin and shaking my head slightly to toss back my brown hair in a brief breeze that had sprung up—or had the Lili Gang set off another bomb?—I looked directly into his disconsolate smoked glasses.

"Prove it, Jean-Luc," I said. "I read what I read."

And while, to say the least, he never did need much encouragement to be headstrong, I like to think that I, Mary-Ann, played some small part in fixing his decision. Before noon of that same day, he had the entire staff of *Cailloux du Cinéma* out picketing the theater, distributing mimeographed leaflets headed *"Remettez Louise dans les chemins de la liberté!"* and chanting *"À bas* Willingham!" to alert the public and the theater management to their demand that the tacked-on, in Jean-Luc's view, final reel be destroyed and *Every Girl Is an Island* shown in its integral, in Jean-Luc's view, version. As the management had long depended on the *Cailloux du Cinéma* crowd to help drum up appreciative and respectful audiences for minor, mediocre American films, they really had no choice but to cave in. By nightfall, holding hands, Jean-Luc and I stood on the Rue St. Severin, watching a hundred eager, buzzing Parisians queue up to buy tickets to what was, in a sense, the first movie my boyfriend ever made.

As we strolled away, we heard an explosion; turning, we saw smoke. Quite fortunately, nobody got so much as a scratch. But the O.A.S. had just bombed the theater, apparently under a confused impression that Charles de Gaulle was inside attending a private screening of *Every Girl Is an Island*.

Which, events soon proved, he may well have been—and without the final reel, at that. The very next morning, every newspaper kiosk in Paris was a-blare with king-sized headlines screaming that he had granted every colony in France's empire the right to determine its own destiny. Whatever came next, they weren't going to be anyone's possessions ever again.

By afternoon, the O.A.S. had posters up all over the Right Bank denouncing the decision. They consisted of endless paragraphs of tiny type and strenuously convoluted argument, but everyone in Paris knew what they really said; and I've never heard more pedestrians whistling happy tunes as they walked along in my life.

"Nous sommes foutus," the O.A.S. posters never stopped repeating, between every line.

"Merde," the O.A.S. posters howled in invisible but deeply satisfying letters, which were rather larger than the graffiti on the bookstall on the

Quai Malaquais had been. The characteristic rust color had also deepened noticeably.

The retreat from Africa had begun. This time, at least from now on, almost nobody died on the way home.

Not long after, de Gaulle announced the end of the war in Algeria. Whatever became of it from now on, it too wasn't going to be anyone's possession ever again. But by that time, my summer program at the Sorbonne had ended, the regular students were coming back to reclaim their classrooms and, I guess, their streets—and I, Mary-Ann, had left Paris, Paris, Paris behind.

As I now know, it was forever.

■

My last full day in Paris was special for a number of reasons, that is besides the obvious one of being my last full day in Paris. For one thing, it was the first time all summer that I, Mary-Ann, went up to the top of the Eiffel Tower—whose scaffolding of aerial dentistry, you might have supposed, I had eagerly scrambled toward on my very first afternoon, but which something had told me to save for last. For another, it was also my last full day with Jean-Luc, which lasted longer than I had supposed.

For yet another, it was, by coincidence, my twentieth birthday—the first I had ever celebrated that my daddy hadn't had a chance to celebrate before me. Although he didn't know the last part, Jean-Luc had promised that we'd spend all day doing whatever I liked, and not even see a single movie if such was my choice. Knowing what that cost him, I was touched.

Yet while a promise was a promise, my boyfriend was so appalled by where I wanted to go first that his smoked glasses virtually blanched.

"*Ah, non! Surtout pas cette foutue Tour Eiffel,*" Jean-Luc protested Gauloise-ily, in the lobby of my soon-to-be-departed-from hotel in the Rue de Lille. "Really, Mary-Ann. It's one thing to personify America, and quite another to exaggerate it."

Fists to hips, I placed my red Kansas-bought pumps well apart. "You're sure wrong *there*, chum," I sassed him, "so just think again, Jean-

Luc. And we're going to the phoo-too Tour Eiffel, because I'm only going to turn twenty once in my whole life, and that's where I want it to happen."

From the grumbling that I had to listen to as we walked over there, you'd have thought my boyfriend had a peppermill for a brain. But his face grew somewhat queasy as we passed the Invalides, and by the time we two were soaring upward to the pinnacle of the Tour, he'd fallen completely and atypically silent in the elevator. And I'd been mighty slow in catching on that Jean-Luc had a fear of heights; making his many ascents, with or without me, fairly brave.

We stood there. I looked down. "It's beautiful," I said.

He lit a Gauloise, its blue smoke making a contrast with his green face that any Impressionist would have killed for. "Of *course* it's beautiful," he snapped, his Gauloise-bearing hand twitching. "It's *Paris,* name of God. It's its *job* to be beautiful—and it's beautiful *down there,* too. It's beautiful from an outside table at Les Deux Magots. It's beautiful at the cinema. And while, *à mon avis,* it would be especially beautiful in your soon-to-be-departed-from hotel room, which I have never seen, the truth is that it's beautiful almost *anywhere.* So how much longer do we need to stay *here,* name of God, Mary-Ann?"

"Just a little while longer," I said, patting his non-Gauloise-bearing hand. "I know it's corny, but so am I, and I like it."

At which point, with a grunt of surprise, Jean-Luc pulled his hand away, because he'd just found out he needed it. "Apparently," he said. "And why," he demanded, "why did you drag me up here, on our very last day before you go back to Kansas and I blow my brains out, when you've been up to the top of the Tour Eiffel before?"

On a nearby bit of railing, among the initials and messages scratched there over the years, he was pointing at an inscription. You may already have guessed what its three words were.

Kilroy Was Here, it said.

My eyes began to smart with their special astigmatism, and not from Jean-Luc's Gauloise smoke either. Yet you should not suppose from this that I, Mary-Ann, was living in some fantasy realm all my own. I was perfectly aware that thousands or possibly hundreds of thousands of men, few if any of them named Kilroy, had scratched those words wherever there was space and they had time, from Guadalcanal to El Guettar and from Iwo Jima to Remagen. And also, in letters too large and awful to be read by human eyes, on Hiroshima and Nagasaki, too; as I knew with, by now, some misgivings, for all I still wished the scientists had hurried. But all the same, I couldn't help myself, for I had always liked to imagine that whoever wrote those words, anywhere—or anywhere *else*, anyhow—had somehow been a little bit my daddy.

After a second, I got my nail file out of my purse, and scratched *Mary-Ann* in front of the other three words as Jean-Luc watched me, green-faced and impatient.

"Can we go now?" he asked.

"In a sec," I said, and it wasn't much. It was more of a jerk, really, and I brought my hand back down as if I were only smoothing my hair. But I had waved.

And down below, where a tiny but discernibly green-eyed Sukey Santoit had just pulled him up out of the Seine and untied him, my daddy, Eddie Kilroy—Corporal John G. Egan's missing twin, who was still only nineteen, and whom I was now older than, and would now be for however long I lived—had boyishly waved back.

■

Once we were back down on the ground, Jean-Luc grew less nauseated and more cheerful, as I knew as soon as he started describing the two or three things he might put into any movie *he* made about Paris, if he ever got to make movies. Perhaps predictably, the Tour Eiffel was not one of those two or three.

Somewhat less predictably, neither was Les Deux Magots. Yet there our footsteps took us next, so automatically that neither of us had to say a word. We found an outside table for two between the one occupied by Sartre and de Beauvoir and another at which sat a gray-eyed American with hair as sandy as Omaha Beach, alongside his pretty wife.

Although it was a clear day in August, we might as well have sat down in a fog. While Sartre was, as usual, smoking like a freighter, his sandy-haired opposite number smoked like a destroyer; it was almost as if they were conducting a silent duel between pipe and cigarette, in which the Marlboro man was pulling ahead. And if his conversation with his wife had left me in the smallest doubt we shared a country, which it did not, I would have needed no more confirmation of the fact than one look at their young son, a boy of three years old or so who was practicing his still fresh and therefore interesting skill at walking by coming up to his parents' table and then wandering away again. In one fist, he was clutching a tiny Stars and Stripes.

To my surprise, though, when he spoke in answer to a waiter's smiling request for some room to get past him and bring Sartre another *café crème,* it was in piping, fluent French. "*Mais c'est qui ce monsieur-là, après tout?*" he asked, pointing at Sartre, which turned the waiter's smile into a grin.

"Junior!" his father called sharply. "Quit getting tangled up in people's feet. They know where they're going and you don't. Come back here."

"*Oui, Papa,*" the boy said, trotting toward them with his flag.

"*Tu sais,*" Sartre was confiding to Beauvoir, giving the kid a walleyed glance as he did so, "*rien de ce qui se passe dans la rue ne m'importe.*" I didn't know what that was in reference to.

"Oh, Jack, please don't call him 'Junior,'" the American woman said. Her voice had a sunny lilt of the South in it; North Carolina, I would have guessed. "I don't know why, but I always thought that was sort of the worst of both worlds—to have no name of your own, but this strange *burden* to live up to," she laughed lightly, "all the same. We women may put up with a lot, but at least we're spared being Juniors."

Her husband's answering laugh was like hearing a police squawkbox enjoy itself. "Yeah? What is it you women have to put up with? Meet me at the office sometime, and you'll see what I put up with—that's all *I'm* going to say."

"Jack," his wife said gently, "I *did* meet you there. Maybe consular work didn't seem all that important, comp— seem very important, to you. But there was many a night in Bonn when I watched you lock up the office across the hall, and then went back to work in mine."

She glanced after their son—who, upon hearing himself talked about as if he weren't there, had evidently concluded that he wasn't. In search of wherever he should be instead, he'd gone toddling off again.

"Well, then, just be glad you're out of it," the man told her. "Honest to Christ, Shirl, sometimes I wish to hell *I* were. God damn, but I'd like to just get on a boat, and—"

" 'Set sail straight for the horizon,' " his wife quoted, fondly. Even if I couldn't see much cause for her fondness in her husband's alert gray eyes, it was plain she could; or else had seen it enough times, however long ago, that she didn't need to look for it now. "I know, honey—I wish you could, too."

"Sorry, Shirl. Pretty hectic times around the shop these days." While I couldn't be positive, I thought I detected faint quotation marks around the word "shop"—quotation marks no set of non-American ears would ever be able to pick up, however good their owner's English.

"*Et moi,*" Sartre had just told de Beauvoir, "*je fume ma pipe et j'espère,*" with a shrug that could have toppled governments, "*que nous ne nous rendrons pas ridicules encore une fois.*" I still had no idea what they were talking about.

"And any-*hoo*, Shirl," the American now said with a self-amused bearing-down on the word's folksiness, having resettled himself and lit a fresh Malboro as if he needed to do all these things to give himself permission to grin cheerfully at his wife, "I haven't heard *your* son complain about being called Junior. Not even once."

"He's three years old, Jack, and scared of—well, it's probably a pretty long list, come to think of it," his wife said, with a briefly troubled look. "But believe me, it's going to be a damn cold day in Rochester, Minnesota, before he complains about *anything* you do, and we've never even taken him back there."

"Why should we? The garage is sold. My dad's in Florida. Now it's just a name on a map. Why should he care?"

"Because you grew up there, honey. He doesn't think we're from anywhere."

"Well, what the hell. If 'Junior' 's out," her husband came back, with a slight but detectable lessening of good humor, "what am I supposed to call him? Unless I want to have to come running when *he's* who you want, or sound like I'm yelling at *myself* to put that damn thing down right *now,* 'Jack' is taken in this family. And everywhere else soon, at least if someone I used to know gets a job he wants to get," he laughed. "Bad luck all around. Anyway, *he* calls me '*Papa*,' for Christ's sake. Why can't he say 'Daddy,' like a normal kid?"

"Honey, I don't think it was *your* son's idea to live in Paris," his wife said. "Here, 'Papa' *is* what the normal kids say. That's what he's used to hearing, even if he hasn't let go of that flag since you gave it to him. But if we're only allowed one Jack in the family, we *could* try calling him by his middle name instead—which you ought to be able to remember and feel represented by, since it's yours too."

"Huh!" the man said in an intrigued way, putting out his cigarette. "Hey, *Junior!*" he called.

"*Oui, Papa, j'arrive,*" the little boy piped, trotting back to the table again with his tiny Stars and Stripes. Once there, he looked up at his father curiously.

Resting his large hands on the kid's shoulders, the American's hard and alert gray eyes peered intently into his son's three-year-old face. "Junior, I'm going to make you a deal, starting right now," he said. "If you'll call me 'Daddy' instead of '*Papa*,' I'll call you—"

But he never finished that sentence, at least not then and there. For at that exact moment, we all heard the last bomb ever set off in Paris by either the O.A.S. or the Lili Gang. It wasn't all that near, and a glance at the headlines in the newspaper kiosks that evening, after we'd made love for the first time, would tell Jean-Luc and me that no one had been injured. Even so, the noise sure upset Junior—and not only, I don't think, because it left him nameless for now. After a stunned and wide-eyed second, he started crying, with the kind of hysterical raucousness that sounds like a klaxon inside lungs you'd think were too small to produce that much noise, and lashing out blindly with his little American flag as he lurched around us all. I think he got Sartre right on the nose, which may have been the first time the great philosopher's eyes were ever in perfect alignment; not to mention blinking with a coordinated stunned expression, as the little boy turned and confusedly started toward the Boulevard St. Germain.

"Oh, for Christ's sake," the American father said, getting to his feet with jackknife speed. All in one swift, smooth, muscular movement, a Marlboro bobbing in his mouth, he took three steps out onto the sidewalk and scooped the sobbing kid up onto his shoulder before the last of the three was done.

"For Christ's sake, Gil! It's just a *bomb*," he said with startling rage. Then—in a pleasanter tone, as if he'd caught himself—he spoke to all of us at the outside tables. His own French, it turned out, wasn't that bad: "*Ce n'est qu'une bombe, après tout*," he repeated, smiling and flipping away his Marlboro. "*On en a entendu beaucoup, à l'époque.*"

"*Ah, oui! Nous autres, oui*," de Beauvoir said to Sartre. "*Et le père aussi—évidemment! Mais le gosse, non.*"

The American father hadn't heard her, but he looked at their table with a small lift and then incline of his chin. "Monsieur Sartre," he called. "*Je vous demande pardon—à cause de mon enfant, la.*"

"*À cause de* qui?" de Beauvoir gasped under her breath. But the American had already looked away in any case.

"Hey, Mrs. Egan!" he called to his wife. "Pay the nice man and let's get out of here. I don't like being embarrassed in public. Can't take you anywhere, can I?" he said, with what I presume he supposed was affection, to his son. "Except maybe back to the States, and you know something? *All* the kids say 'Daddy' there."

Indeed we did—and needless to say I, Mary-Ann, had caught the name he shouted. But that man now waiting for his wife to pay the bill could never have written the letter I still knew by heart. Or could he? Of course, I knew that whoever had written the letter had survived the battle for Iwo Jima, or it would never have been written. Yet Corporal John G. Egan, USMC, could still have died *of* it, I thought suddenly, watching the small American family start down the Boulevard St. Germain. Over the man's shoulder, the little boy was staring back at Les Deux Magots, and particularly at me for some reason. As they headed on toward God knows where, his father had already lit a fresh cigarette.

That man could have died of my own daddy's death, I thought; which was, incidentally or perhaps not, the moment when I realized that I hadn't.

I had been born of it instead, I saw.

But Sartre had been watching them go too, and now he nudged de Beauvoir. "*Eh bien!*" he snorted, with a quizzical look. "*Regarde-moi notre nouveau chef! Ma foi, Castor, il est pareil que l'ancien.*"

As I have noted, my translation skills are not what they were. But in English, what the great philosopher had just said would go something like, "Take a look at our new boss! I swear, Simone, he's the same as the old boss."

And Sartre—so I remembered with some wonder, as the American family vanished from sight—had lived through the Occupation, too.

■

After Jean-Luc and I had finished our *cafés crème* in turn, and started strolling toward the Seine, I was thoughtful. Once he finished telling me the true meaning of Howard Hawks's *Red River*, which took him several blocks although I had no idea how that particular movie had even come up, he noticed.

"What are you thinking about?" Jean-Luc asked.

"Being American," I said, moodily swinging my purse back and forth.

He laughed. "Should I go find a taxi? I thought you had to be riding in a car to do that—a Cadillac, at least. Or on horseback, driving cattle toward *Abilène*. 'Mathieu, there is a railroad in *Abilène*,'" he quoted happily.

"Maybe that's when we *stopped* thinking," I said, and stopped. To my mild non-surprise, I saw that I, and therefore we, had stopped right in front of my soon-to-be-departed-from hotel in the Rue de Lille. But even though I wasn't sure exactly how to do it, I knew I had something I wanted to say.

First.

"Jean-Luc," I said, "I know you've never been to the U.S.A., so maybe you'll just have to trust me on this one. But there's something so *sweet* about it, so nice you wouldn't believe it—no matter how many dumb mistakes we ever made, maybe because the sweetness always makes it so easy to forget them. And I guess we always thought the sweetness would make up for the mistakes as far as all the rest of you were concerned too. But what I'm thinking now is what if we stopped being sweet—and went right on being mistaken?"

"The mistake was what you started with," he said, shaking out a Gauloise. "Any country whose personification has the nerve to stand before me and call it *sweet*—and mean it, my God!—is *always* going to end up mistaken. And the world will suffer for it, as worlds tend to do."

"O.K., never mind about that," I said, snatching the cigarette from his lips and tossing it down the street. "The heck with it, this personification's getting on a boat back to what she personifies at four P.M. tomorrow anyway."

"Believe me, I know," he said, irritably reaching for another Gauloise. "And—"

"Upsy-daisy, Jean-Luc," I said, jerking my chin toward the hotel door. "The rules of the game have just changed, and whether this is the end or the beginning of a grand illusion is up to you. Here's the church, so where's the steeple? Let's go."

"*En français, s'il te plait*, Mary-Ann," he said.

"O.K.," I said, and took a breath. "*Baisez-moi.*"

"You might at least have *tutoie*'d me when you finally said it," he grumbled. Then, after we had gone upstairs—and after, glancing around my room as I demurely undressed behind him, Jean-Luc had marveled, "You never told me you were rich! Do *all* Americans have money?"—he showed me how everybody on the planet did it, which was lovely and interesting. As Ginger I'm not, you'll just have to live with it if I let things go at that.

After all, it would be very un-Kansas-ish and non-ladylike of me to go into any details whatsoever regarding how, in spite of never having been there in his life, Jean-Luc instinctively knew how to lay I, Mary-Ann, in every last church in Russell, tearing off my toreadors beneath #14's white steeple and bumping me quick-quick and gasping up against #6's red brick, or that one reason it was so lovely and interesting was that the whole time this was taking place he and I were in Paris, Paris, Paris, Paris, Paris, Paris, Paris, Paris PARIS parisparisparis PAAAAris Paris Paris ParrrrrrrIIIIIS parisparis Paris Paris

Parararararararararararararaririririririri̇RİRIS PARIS PARIS ParisParisParis andbrieflyalmostathens,untilisaid"ohcomeoffitjeanluc"andhedidPARIS PAAAAAAAAAAARIS pa pa pa pa pa pa pa pa PA-ris paRARARAris ris Paris Paris *paris Paris Paris PARIS!!!!*

Wouldn't it?

If I did tell you anything of the kind, I mean. As, of course, I haven't.

I'd never breathe it to a soul, because it's so inadequate a description.

■

Yet here's the thing, and a mystery to make my puzzlement over the ending of *Every Girl Is an Island* and the surprise appearance of Sukey Santoit near the Pont des Arts look like mazes on a diner place-mat by comparison. When I woke up the next morning, I was a virgin again. Virgo intacta, maidenhead of the class, hymen make yourself at home, the whole shebang. Or debang, now I think on it.

Even Jean-Luc agreed I was, and it drove him batty. "Personifying America is one thing," he was to fume before the morning was gone. "And since I know you do, believe me I try to be understanding. But *this,* Mary-Ann—*this* is just *too* foutu *much!*"

The night before, we had gone out after the first time we did it, and I had eaten the best meal of my life. (The service was slow, the food was awful, and the wine was pure Satan's grape juice; I'd recommend that restaurant to anyone who's just had lovely, interesting sex.) But then, when we had then gone back up to my hotel room to do it again, it had felt just like the first time. *Exactly* like it, is what I'm trying to convey, to the point that Jean-Luc had made a modestly quizzical noise and I had squinted briefly at the ceiling. But our minds, which in any case weren't being anything much more purposeful at the moment than barnacles on the S.S. *Jean-Luc Mary-Ann,* soon to be rechristened the X.X. *Jeanmary-lucann,* had soon been distracted by matters far more interesting and less puzzling. By the time, exhausted, I finally gasped, "My gosh! How do you say 'I'm out of breath' in French, Jean-Luc?" and he told me, and we went to sleep in each other's arms—actually, I think Jean-Luc stayed up awhile—I had just about forgotten that tiny, not entirely mental twinge of panic as I wondered if I was somehow, inexplicably, back at square one.

Just about.

But that morning, when we did it the third time, it was unmistakable and undeniable. After the fourth time, which was cutting it very close if I wanted to make the boat train, Jean-Luc *watched* it happen; it was genuinely amazing, he said, and seemed to take about five minutes. Being Jean-Luc, of course, he immediately wondered if he could *film* it happening—but there I put my foot down, even if I did have to take it off the wall first. Whatever the hell was going on, I told him, Christine Jorgensen I was not. Whatever the hell *had* gone on, I was still Mary-Ann Kilroy of Russell, Kansas.

And saying our town's name aloud put a horrible fear in my heart, for an all too obvious reason. It was well over a decade until the next Unveiling, by which time my mother, the librarian of Russell, might well have passed on. And even then, of course, I'd only get to go back for twenty-four hours, which might be more painful than blissful even if my mother was still with us—or with them, anyway, I forced myself to tell myself unhappily. But right now, and especially if I wanted to find out whether my private dread had any foundation, I had a train to catch from the Gare du Nord to Le Havre.

By the time we reached the Gare du Nord, Jean-Luc had grown bitter, the first blow to his previous attitude of pure fascination piled atop continuing lust—whatever the hell else was going on, he *had* been waiting six weeks—having been my refusal to let him film me becoming a virgin again. He just kept putting out half-smoked Gauloises in his *café crème* and calling for another, and muttering "*Merde*" even after, to tease him, I started asking sea of *what*, for gosh sakes; mother of *what*? Then it was all aboard.

When I reached for his hand for the last time, he didn't even look up as he said "*Adieu*, Mary-Ann." As I had just said "*Au revoir*, Jean-Luc," this caused me the worst case of special astigmatism I'd yet had as I stumbled out onto the platform, into the train—and away from Paris, Paris, Paris; for good, although I didn't know that yet.

Looking back, I can only hope that the experience didn't end up souring Jean-Luc on America and Americans permanently, especially since he loved our movies so. While it would perhaps be going too far to say that they had liberated him from whatever oppressed him, the messages he got from them had certainly helped him to begin his own resistance.

That's why I hope he still thinks well of us sometimes. But all I know is yesterday, and yesterday never knows.

■

As I was aware that Americans traveling overseas have the benefit of all sorts of protections and reprieves that they don't necessarily know about or understand, on the boat train I half worried—and half hoped—that becoming a virgin again and again was something that could happen to me only abroad. But assuming he is alive and track-downable, the assistant purser on the S.S. *America*, sister ship to the *United States*, can testify that I became a virgin again several times in international waters. Making the same proviso, although like the purser he'd be fairly old by now, a slick young advertising man bearing the odd name Holden Caulfield can vouch for it happening in New York, even if he was much too self-absorbed and complacently melancholy afterwards, in a *bonjour comme d'habitude tristesse* sort of way, and aren't those creeps who get the sad post-coital smiles just the *worst*, Ging, to pay a great deal of attention to the fact that he deflowered I, Mary-Ann, twice, at both the Plaza Hotel and in his locked office on Madison Avenue, before he put a once again *re*-flowered me in a cab to Idlewild.

You see, I had to find out; and was still Kansas-ish enough to realize that, as far as most of my fellow Americans were concerned, neither the shipboard project nor even the Manhattan one was conclusive proof that I could become a virgin again here in the good old U.S. of A. But once I'd hopped a plane to Topeka, a saintly motorcyclist who took me up a hill on his Harley and tumbled me on the grass—in full sight of my Ellfrank alma mater, although not, as the night was moonless, of any of its current students or faculty—removed the final shadow of a doubt. Before he'd so much as kick-started his chopper and jerked his head to indicate that I, Mary-Ann, should swing a leg over behind him, his temporary inamorata-rata-rata-*vroom* had felt herself become a virgin again—not just in these United States, not just in any state, but in *Kansas itself;* smelling its very wheat, along with motor oil, under the sky of my childhood, and of my daddy's childhood, and of all sorts of Kilroys before us.

Et in Arcadia virgo.

If that settled that, another question still pressed in on me; and was doing so like God's own fingers on my temples by the time, having patted a greasily stubbled cheek goodbye and rented a car in Topeka—Hertz or Avis, don't recall—I started the drive to Russell. Once I turned north toward our town off Route 40, not even a radio turned up to full volume and blasting out "Runaround Sue" could drown out the hoofbeats of my thumping anxiety. And soon and forever, I had my answer, for I had just pulled over and killed the engine in front of a sign that told all comers, just as it always had and always would, WELCOME TO RUSSELL, KANSAS, U.S.A.

Nothing besides remained. Boundless and rippling, the gold and level wheat stretched away to the horizon, under the same old sky.

Needless to say, I knew it was really all still right there in front of me: Main Street, Dawson's Drug, our two movie theaters, both our right bank and our left bank, our courthouse, my old high school. I knew that our townspeople still moved about mere yards from my nose, primarily on foot except the ones from outlying farms. I knew our sixteen churches stood, and that our limestone fence posts with no railings still poked upward to give their mute and stubborn testimony of having something to do with the sky. For all I knew, my mother, the librarian of Russell, was standing right in front of me, with her gun-barrel spectacles and an armful of Sukey Santoit books to pass on to the next generation of Russell girls, who might make better use of them than I had up to now.

If so, she could see me, of course. But unless I, Mary-Ann, stayed alive long enough—and remembered—to be here at the next Unveiling, or unless they broke the rules and stepped outside the town limits in my presence, causing their instant death, I'd never be able to see or make contact with her or any of them again; for the obvious reason.

Or maybe, now I ponder it, for the less than obvious reason. Looking back through these pages, I see I may have failed to clarify as comprehensively as I might the nature of Russell's other distinctive feature, and if so I'm sorry. But sometimes it's hard, or possibly just too likely to bring on my special astigmatism, for me to recall that I'm addressing people who don't already know the secret. Which is, of course, that our town only materializes, so far as what the rest of you call the real world is concerned, for one day every hundred years.

During that magic twenty-four hours, which we call the Unveiling, outsiders are at liberty to inspect Russell with both the naked eye and the shod foot, should they be in the vicinity and so desire. We will greet you, feed you, and even gladly give a hearing to your political opinions, however outlandish and poorly conceived they may be. But it all vanishes at midnight, and if you're still inside the town limits, you'll find yourself confronted with nothing but wheat fields and highway. Don't worry, though: your cars will still be present. But ours, along with the pickup trucks from the outlying farms, will have disappeared along with Main Street, Dawson's Drug, and so on.

Not having lived long enough, I, Mary-Ann, had never actually taken part in an Unveiling, the last occurrence having been in 1876. But when I was a little girl, a few people who had been children during that one were still around, and they described it for me. In any case, the lore would be hard to avoid, for when you are a town in this type of situation, it is something your family and neighbors tend to discuss, however laconic they may be by nature. Up to the moment of my return, however, there had been only two Unveilings in all, and the first was witnessed only by some Indians, since relocated elsewhere, and a handful of horsemen on the move west from a small fort called Detroit.

If there can possibly be so much as a single three-year-old child who feels incompetent to figure out the date of Russell's Unveilings with no help from I, Mary-Ann—and if so, then God protect you, and it will be a full-time job for Him—they happen, inevitably and gloriously, on the Fourth of July.

For the rest of each century, we natives of Russell can go in and out of our town at will, whether the summons in question is a college we'd like to attend, a war that we've heard on the radio we have to go fight in, or simply the lure of Topeka. We'd have to run out on errands in any case, such as fetching back newspapers, movies, TV sets and Sukey Santoit books. But if, on those visits to the outside world, we allow anything to *change* us—except for events in which we have no say whatsoever, such as our then future and now, I believe, former County Attorney's near death on a rocky hill in Italy, one day in April 1945—then we become outsiders, and cannot return except at the Unveiling. Those who recalled the Second Unveiling in my childhood said that none of those exiled up to then had come back, presumably finding it too painful.

Crouched on the hood of my rental car, looking out at the wheat fields past the WELCOME sign, I mulled the possible reasons for my banishment. And considering that, in the interim, I had allowed myself to be penetrated multiple and glorious times by an unshaven, chain-smoking movie critic and aspiring post-modern filmmaker in Paris, France, while attending a summer program at the Sorbonne, you may wonder why I even thought an ambiguity existed. But this is to underestimate Russell, Kansas.

We may have sixteen churches. We may live under a sky so unmoved that it could put the fear of God into God. But even our ministers agree that heck, these things happen. Heck, I knew a couple of girls from Russell High who'd come back from weekends in Topeka pregnant, and everybody dealt with it. Maybe they didn't get asked to help pass the collection plate during services or lead us all in "The Star-Spangled Banner" at pep rallies for a while, but beyond that they weren't ostracized, much less banished. Their children were raised with the whole town's help, just as barns were in the old days.

And by now, I had begun to suspect the true explanation for my own banishment, which was that I had come back not only un-pregnant but mysteriously undeflowered; this despite having allowed myself to be penetrated multiple and glorious times, &c., &c. Clearly, Russell found that too plain weird to fool with.

What had changed me beyond recourse, I now saw, was that I *should* have changed, and hadn't. Under the circumstances, my continued—or rather ever-renewable—virginity was abnormal, a mutation paradoxically defined by lack of mutability. Ours may be a town that only magically materializes one day every hundred years, and so forth, but for all that its people are not short on plain horse sense. They knew darned well that something should have happened to me when I went forth out of Russell into this century's bombs and music. Not unreasonably, they mistrusted the way my unaltered face, re-virginized body, pumping heart, and simple soul all kept insisting nothing had, for all that I myself might have wished otherwise. If I wasn't a lie of some unprecedented sort, then I was just too strange for them to keep in close proximity. That was that.

Being no fool, although fairly glum at the moment, I, Mary-Ann, did understand I had been given a kind of freedom; albeit one that I had no idea how to use responsibly, or even if it *could* be used responsibly. I could go away, or I could stay in Kansas—anywhere *else* in Kansas, that is, unless I wanted to live in my rental car. (The fees on which would soon be astronomical, were I to opt for this plan; I reconsidered.) I could go where I wanted, do as I pleased, and I would never stay deflowered for more than five minutes. Heck, I could take on a whole class of graduating midshipmen at Annapolis if I felt like it, the night before they all shipped out to fly fighter planes off aircraft carriers and fire sixteen-inch shells from battleships at some foreign coast somewhere—and I'd *still* be a virgin in the morning, by golly, and whether or not I cared to be one too.

While I wasn't sure if this was a curse or just some kind of super-power, one thing you couldn't call it was *restricting*. Except for one small limitation that a lot of people—maybe most—would likely find negligible, if they even noticed it existed in the first place.

That was the fact that I, Mary-Ann, the personification of America, wasn't ever going to see my hometown again.

At the time that I got back in my rental car and, blinking away my special astigmatism, started the engine up again, that limitation wasn't yet, strictly speaking, absolute. I was still only twenty, and the Third Unveiling wasn't that many years off. Indeed, in my childhood I had often been told that my generation was favored by fortune, as many people's life spans fell between two Unveilings and they never got to take part in one at all.

Of course, as a sign now reading EMOCLEW shrank into a greeting fit only for ants and then atoms before it disappeared entirely from my rear-view mirror, I had no way of knowing that I, Mary-Ann, would be in no position to turn up in Russell on that happy day. Since the years and for that matter the decades all tend to be pretty much alike on the island, I was only guessing that it was even 1976 on the bright, hot, enormous morning that, staring out to sea, I decided to pretend it was the Fourth—and then, an astigmatic moment or two later, to pretend instead it wasn't.

But before I'd turned the key in the ignition, I knew already, and I mean in my bones, why none of those banished had come back for the last Unveiling. Soon afterward, I reached Route 40; and not until then did it sink in that I could turn in either direction, east or west, and not have any more or any less of a destination. Pulling over and killing the engine while I thought, I now mulled two questions, viz.:

1. Where was I going to go?
2. What was I going to *do*?

No one was around to help me. Nor, with Jean-Luc several thousand sky- and Gauloise-blue miles away, was there even anyone to say he didn't give a damn—which might have been a goad, if not precisely a consolation. In any case, after new adventures too much like mimeographs of the old ones to be worth passing around, for all that the purple odor of that quaint reproductive process is memory's umbilicus to any graduate of Russell High, I ended up in New York.

There I found work as a translator at the United Nations, putting my French language skills and command of idiom, both still sharp as tacks then, to good use. While all the other girl translators were equally proficient if not more so, I had the distinction of being the only American citizen in the bunch, all of my co-workers having been recruited from abroad. Our own government was still reeling from the recent discovery that not one Anglo-Saxon in the United States—all except I, Mary-Ann—spoke a single foreign language anymore, as they found even capable handling of their first one a chore by then. Be that as it may, a second major difference between me and all the other girl translators, obviously, was that none of them had renewable virginities.

As a result, I soon had something of a reputation around the old UN. Still, I'm not sure it was all deserved; is any reputation, ever? The first time I strolled into the lobby of the Plaza, cloaked in a capote from Hats by Audrey and swinging my handbag as if I had a hammer, to see an evidently Latin gentleman in a befrogged and ornate uniform buying up weapons and torture implements at a trade show, I leaped to the same benign conclusion sure to have been lit upon by anybody similarly afflicted with a desire to think the best of people. This was that the hotel's doorman had just won the lottery, and was naturally of a mind to protect himself from possible desperadoes. Admittedly, as time went on, I did find it odd that the Latin and Asian doormen at both the Plaza and the Sherry-Netherland seemed to win lotteries with such frequency, and always bought weapons, torture implements, and cocktails for me with the proceeds. But then again, America—the land I, Mary-Ann, personify—is a land of opportunity if it's anything, as my best gal-pal would impishly remind me whenever Holly and I found ourselves bumping gloved elbows in the Four Seasons' powder room. Or seated together, behind an unforgettably sweet pair of goggling adolescents, at one of the pianist Henry Orient's madcap Carnegie Hall recitals, as a fractured fuss of whispers around us excitedly spread the gossip of the latest suicide in the Glass family.

At a loss to see a pleasant, polite, and cheerful way of doing so, I never once considered taking that way out myself. That much of Russell I still had in me, impulses to auto-destruction being ruled out not only by our sixteen churches but by our distrust of the hoity-toity and general desire to remain laconic. In Kansas, slashing your wrists is considered one more of the luxuries we'd only be tempted to if we had sophisticated folks' money and problems, and I was wary of being thought pretentious. Yet I was often bluer than Manhattan's stony sky.

Among other things, the time lags before my virginity renewed itself after a date had grown longer and more unpredictable. My single most protracted lapse began on a date in late November, 1963, after which I didn't become a virgin again for almost three whole months. As Thanksgiving's pilgrim migraine gave way to a coffin-shaped Christmas, a New Year's Eve without a hat or toot in sight, and then the prison of New York's bleak February, I wondered, with ambivalence, if this might be It. But one night not long before Valentine's Day, I was watching television in my apartment with the roommate I had just acquired, who was working on her Barnard master's thesis—or antithesis, as she oddly called it—and was intellectual but good company. To my surprise, I felt myself turn virginal again while watching *The Ed Sullivan Show;* but for no reason that I know.

Yesterday never knows.

Even after that reprieve—which was, all things said, a doozy—my mixed feelings persisted. In fact, they grew worse. If running around as a girl translator at the UN and waiting for my virginity to kick back in after every halfway memorable date was what personifying America called for, then I, Mary-Ann, was no longer sure that personifying America was my can of Coca-Cola, my jolt of Jim Beam, my mug of Maxwell House or my whiff of airplane glue. In moments of reflection, usually after seeing mine in some chance shiny duplication of a mobbed but briefly paralytic room, I often fell prey to a disturbing notion. In a mental state midway between rage and mirage, most likely induced by the way my New York life's peculiar flimsiness and generally makeshift air seemed to put out the welcome mat for delirium, I would catch myself more than half believing that everything I'd done since EMOCLEW receded in my rental car's rear-view mirror had been the actions of a painted puppet who bore my face and name, yet whose behavior and general situation were caprices over which I had no more control than did whatever stranger might be next to me. Increasingly convinced that none of this was my idea, I wanted to rebel against my own unasked-for nature, and probably would have if I'd known how to go about it.

As she had plainly never given an inch to anyone since whenever she'd lost *her* virginity, I sometimes thought of asking my new roommate for advice. But she seemed too engrossed in her burgeoning antithesis for me to feel comfortable barging in on her, and by the fall of the same year I was on the island with the others. Anyone can see that even if we had something to rebel against here, that is besides each other, there wouldn't be much point in trying. It would be like arguing with the sky.

Nor, for that matter, do I feel any desire to—and the distinct lack of get-up-and-go that my current life encourages isn't the only explanation. That summer of '64, not long before I left on the vacation that never quits, a chance encounter made me see my unexpectedly strange life in a new light.

In a furious and therefore most un- if not downright anti-Mary-Ann-ish mood, aching to kick off the traces and rid myself of this whole renewable-virgin, personifying-America load of you-know by hook or by crook, I suddenly found myself seated in a Greenwich Village saloon. To this day, I'm not sure what dragged me there, as I had grown leery of the artistic set after my fling with Jean-Luc ended in such acrimonious mutual perplexity; an aversion putting Carmine Street and environs well outside the ambit of a Mary-Ann-ized Manhattan that consisted in toto of the United Nations General Assembly, a nondescript apartment where I watched *Ed Sullivan* with my roommate, and a motley slew of midtown nightclubs, midnight powder rooms, and slaloming hotel beds. But I do recall the bar's name. Freshly painted and indeed being hoisted with some difficulty by a couple of burly workmen as I passed under it, next to a banner reading "Grand Re-Opening Under New Management," the sign above the door told me that this shadowy place, whatever its previous incarnations, was henceforward to be called The Bar of History.

One stool over, having slammed himself down on it mere moments after I came in, was a bright-eyed, slightly cracked-looking fellow in a mackintosh who looked to be in his early forties, drinking coffee and doodling on a napkin. Once he had drawn me into a conversation, it soon came out that he was even less a New Yorker than I, Mary-Ann, having just dashed up for the day from his home in Virginia.

His name, I think, was Gaingill.

Anywhere this side of a shipwreck, Gaingill and I would have had little in common, he being one of those irksome types whose private grins are more undercut by their public blinks than they know, as well as vice versa; not to mention a man whose jacket evidently hadn't had to match his pants a single workday of his life. Yet he must have struck me as a sympathetic auditor, for within a few minutes—and to my own astonishment, as I had never breathed a word of it to anyone—I found myself spilling the whole story: being Kilroy's daughter, sailing to Paris on the S.S. *United States,* my summer program at the Sorbonne, Jean-Luc, Sukey Santoit, sailing home on the S.S. *America,* my renewable virginity that I'd paid for with the loss of Russell, Kansas, and my current life as the UN's most notorious party girl. In short, the works, bedewed with more than one outbreak of my special astigmatism.

All in all and with no aim of self-flattery, I was reasonably sure that the story of my life up to then was a cut or two above the average anecdotes told in bars. Considering that, Gaingill took my narrative remarkably in stride. Then, with a grin whose clear preference for the far side of his face got me suspicious that he might be teasing me, much as Jean-Luc used to—the ashtray's little Père Lachaise of mashed stubs was familiar, though not the perky and brunette Notre Dame that my interlocutor's eyes were making of I, Mary-Ann, whose reflection in The Bar of History's mirror he almost seemed to prefer to looking at me directly, as if he feared that doing so too often would turn my features into Medusa's instead—he gave me his best guess as to the meaning of my uniqueness.

As far as he was concerned, Gaingill explained, my endlessly renewable virginity could only mean one thing. And that one thing was that, when and if I ever did get pregnant, it was going to be with Jesus.

■

Except on the jukebox, where the Everly Brothers were trying to wake someone up, things got awfully quiet then in The Bar of History, at least to my own hearing. Now that he'd said it, I was floored that I, Mary-Ann, despite having been raised amid sixteen church steeples, had never considered that possibility on my own. And so, Gaingill confessed, was he, since he had thought I'd be smart enough to guess without his help—a belief I promptly validated by figuring out the meaning of the meaning of my uniqueness.

"Wait a minute," I said, and we did.

"Do you mean God's my *pimp*?" I said, when it was up.

He nodded. It was the only explanation that made sense to him, he said, given my story. So far as he could tell, the Deity Himself had no idea what was really going on anymore, or any sure sense of how to accomplish whatever it was that He was trying to accomplish, and possibly why too; and so He just kept on sending me out into the world, hoping that I and so He would get lucky someday. He was, Gaingill imagined, sorry about Russell, Kansas. But even I, Mary-Ann, couldn't have everything, Gaingill supposed.

At this point, I gathered that I had some reason to be wary of my new friend; being, as he himself had pointed out, no fool. "Hold your horses, mister," I said. "I don't mean to be rude. But is all this just your way of hinting around that you wouldn't mind giving the job of fathering Our Savior the old college try yourself? Because—"

No, no, Gaingill interrupted me, with a scuttling sort of chortle and an upheld, smoke-wreathed hand. Unless my God's dark wit knew no bounds, he said, he was an unlikely choice to make a success out of the gig of Holy Ghost, as he was not only an agnostic but an atheist. Personally, he suspected that one reason I had yet to lose my virginity was that more people in this country believed in believing in God than actually believed in Him. But then again, being not only an a. but an a., he probably wasn't the best judge of that, he allowed. After all, he'd once considered buying a dog and naming it Robertson just so he could tell people to pat Robertson.

I didn't understand this, and Gaingill told me never mind. The fellow in question hosted a sort of cooking show minus utensils on TV, he said. Anyhow, he went on, even an atheist could have a sense of sacrilege, and the mere prospect of attempting sexual congress with the personification of America that I, Mary-Ann was left him feeling so pre-emptively overwhelmed and inadequate that he doubted he'd be able to rise to the occasion even if I were to suddenly up and say "O.K. let's go Gaingill," which he didn't consider likely. He'd had a previous experience in this vein in his youth, he said, and offered to tell me about it if I was interested.

"Sue me, mac, but I think I'll take a rain check on that one," I said—being preoccupied, understandably I would say, with my own new status as the future mother of a messiah. Shortly afterward, it appearing that we had run out of things to say to each other and I having a date to meet, I got up to leave. But at The Bar of History's door, I turned and looked back at Gaingill, still seated among the roseate shadows, the glints of silver and gold, the murmured conversations of strangers and the imaginary laughter of the dead.

"Tell me true," I said. "Have you just been having fun with me? If I'm going to spend the rest of my life waiting to give birth to Jesus just because some guy in a bar said I would, I kind of have to know."

He admitted that middle age had given him a weakness for trying to keep himself entertained. But I should never think that having fun was the same as making fun, something he'd never do with regard to I, Mary-Ann—or my hometown, either. Not when our existence filled him with such awe.

When he spoke next, though, it wasn't to me, but to his own now companionless reflection. "Nope—I wouldn't do that for a million dollars," he said as if reciting something *which, of course, I was.* "I wouldn't do that in a million years."

To my mind, it's poor manners when people go off somewhere by themselves without budging, even though they can see you standing there personifying America right in front of them and they will most likely never lay eyes on you again. But I was also raised in Russell, Kansas, which means that I was raised to be unfailingly pleasant, polite, and cheerful.

"Well, I'd better get going now. Goodbye-aye!" I called out pleasantly, politely, and cheerfully from the door.

Though he still wouldn't look at me—or maybe couldn't, for whatever reason—his hand shot up in salute: "So long, Mary-Ann!"

■

Just so as not to leave anyone in false suspense: whether or not Gaingill—
or was it Gillgain?—was pulling my leg, I'm still waiting. Not that
opportunities to get pregnant with Our Savior, or for that matter Little
Ricky, appear any too teeming at present, or indeed have for decades.
Even if any of the men looked the least bit plausible to my still virginal
but for all that somewhat jaded by now eyes, which they do not, none of
us can stand any of the others anyhow—with the sole exception, in my
case, of Ginger, who I'm proud to call my friend. But even if we were, as
Ging puts it, lesbiatically inclined, which we *shyly, tenderly, and ever so
gradually discovered we* are not, maternity obviously isn't in the cards on
that front.

Nonetheless, if Our Savior I must bear, then Our Savior I, Mary-Ann,
will bear. It's only a question of waiting.

Now, you may care to observe that, in light of the mission of which
I'd now been informed, a *smart* future Jesus' mom would have done better to stay in New York—since all sorts of people come through there,
and you never know. I won't dispute the point. But I had already booked
my vacation, not knowing yet that it would be the one that never quits.
Besides which, I had reason to feel some urgency as to getting out of
town. Ever since my pal Holly had split for parts unknown to avoid tes-
tifying before a grand jury about a man I too had had dates with, I had
nursed an obscure feeling that some sort of day of reckoning might be
looming ahead for I, Mary-Ann as well *et in Saigon virgo et in Hue virgo et
in Danang virgo et in Khe Sanh virgo et in My Lai virgo,* and I naturally
wished to avoid it by being somewhere else when it arrived.

At first, I wasn't sure which somewhere else to pick. I did consider
going back to Paris, but soon saw I could not. Not, that is, to I, Mary-
Ann's specific Paris, Paris, Paris, in what I now saw had been a time of
hope. Or rather—at least after my friend Karina, who was from there,
had goggled at my reflection in candid stupefaction when I idly mentioned the French preference for undated newspapers as we were lip-
sticking side by side in the girl translators' lounge, yé-yé-ing a Françoise

Hardy song, one afternoon at the UN—now saw as several times of hope, mysteriously jumbled together.

With Karina's help, she having been a *Cailloux* (or whatever) *du Cinéma* reader in her teens, I figured out that for Jean-Luc it could only have been the summer of either 1957 or 1958. But the Algerian war had ended in 1962, and de Gaulle had given France's colonies the right of self-determination at an altogether different time. And unaided by Karina, without knowing how I knew *hello Mary-Ann hello I'm with you on the Island*, I knew that for the three-year-old I had seen clutching a small Stars and Stripes one day on the Boulevard St. Germain, it had been the summer of 1960; even though the only thing that might have made that a time of hope for him was that he'd finally been given a name he could call his own, albeit in distressing circumstances.

Most bewildering of all, however, was the fact that in none of those years could I have celebrated my twentieth birthday in Paris or anywhere else, considering the date on which Eddie Kilroy's only child was born to my mother, the librarian of Russell. You see, I, Mary-Ann, came into this world on August 7, 1945. As my onetime boyfriend Jean-Luc might have phrased it, my birth was a bit of music between two bombs.

This whole tissue of colliding impossibilities seemed to prove that none of the things I thought had happened in my life could actually have happened, at least not to me *but they did*. And every time I tried to sort out how they could have happened to me anyway *because I wanted them to, that's why*, my mind kept returning to what hindsight now told me was an utterly inexplicable moment on the Quai Malaquais—a moment when people had been pointing and shouting, "Lili Gang! *Lili Gang!*," and I had turned to find myself staring into Sukey Santoit's green eyes.

Whatever the real explanation was, though, I could still practice Russell, Kansas, common sense when it was called for. Having had poor luck with said gambit before, no way was I about to fool with going back to anywhere I'd already been. I, Mary-Ann, did not want to step off an aircraft in front of a sign reading WELCOME TO PARIS, FRANCE, and see that nothing lay beyond it but absences: no Louvre, no Pont des Arts, no Rue de Lille, no Tour Eiffel, no Sorbonne. And no present, because those can't exist without pasts. Of course, the Seine would still have been there, for rivers are eternal, and this one had once divided perfection to my eyes. Yet they are less beautiful without bridges, and I feared those would be gone as well.

After some reflection, I booked a flight to the West Coast and points onward. Given my general direction, you may well ask if I had any notion of trying to visit an eight-square-mile island with beaches of black volcanic sand, on whose southern mountain peak the Stars and Stripes are being raised in a well-known photograph that shows absolutely none of the 6,822 Americans killed there, unless you count the three out of six flag raisers who were dead within days of Joe Rosenthal popping the shutter; and the answer is that, yes, it did cross my mind. But as it did, it trailed a small cloud of surprised recognition that I had hardly thought of *my father* in some time.

Since you know which island I washed up on instead, there is not that much more to tell. But there is some, for on the last night before my departure, once I'd finished packing the last of my bags, I realized that something was missing from my mental luggage, so to speak.

Despite the not inconsiderable interest level guaranteed by sheer chaos, my life had left me woefully ignorant of one of humanity's, and more specifically my own gender's, most elementary rites of passage. Yet I wasn't thinking of motherhood, most likely your first guess. As I'd been told that when and if I gave birth I would give birth to Jesus, I had a fair hunch that the average woman's report on the ups and downs of parturition would be no very useful guide as to what to expect in my case.

Instead, it had just struck me, with some pain, that after all I'd been through I, Mary-Ann, still had no conception of what it was like for a woman to lose her virginity. That is, for good, for real: forever. Even my recollections of the glorious first time with Jean-Luc had grown hazy, as I had been through the identical set of first-time sensations so often since. Nor had their aftermath ever lasted long enough for me to develop even a speculative sense of what losing one's virginity permanently would be like.

Given the nature of my peculiar predicament, it was obviously not the physiology of it I felt curious about. I'd had *cigars* up me, for gosh sakes.

What I suddenly ached to learn was whether the loss of virginity really did change a person, and if so, how essentially; or whether, on the other hand, it might be not that big a deal in the long run, as one nodded to oneself in that mirror and then turned to face a window or the sky. That would be every bit as useful to know, if it turned out that nodding and then getting on with whatever came next turned out to be more the general drift of things.

Put simply, either way, I, Mary-Ann, the personification of America, now found myself wondering for the first time what in hell it felt like to grow up.

After a frazzled day of shopping, packing, and fretting, I was tuckered out. In fact, thinking I could certainly use a good night's rest before I started my vacation, I had already gone to bed. But now, switching on my bedside lamp, I rose in my pink jammies and pushed open the door to my apartment's living room.

No doubt because I was so sleepy, making for perceptions as off-kilter as if the change in time zones was already in effect, I felt as if I'd never truly seen where I now lived. Smaller even than my hotel digs in the long-since-departed-from Rue de Lille, the living room held only a sofa, which I observed with irritation was so dilapidated that its proper home should have been in someone's basement, and a lawn chair with frayed webbings. Some important item appeared to be missing, but I couldn't put my finger on which.

More disconcerting than the lack of space as such, however, were the room's bizarrely foreshortened dimensions, at least to my befuddled eyes. Its two flanking walls were so narrow that you would need to maneuver like an Egyptian hieroglyph to cross it from left to right. Above the hoary old sofa, in the picture window that took up nearly all of the back wall, the whole city skyline—the UN, the Plaza, and the Sherry-Netherland—twinkled dingily, as if its mighty buildings were no more than an assortment of cheap Christmas-tree lights in the iron-cold Manhattan dark.

The fourth wall, which the sofa faced, was perfectly blank, and so thin as to seem almost translucent. In fact, with alarming clarity, I could hear some unknown neighbor knitting on its far side—all as if in an unnerving adumbration, so I, Mary-Ann, suddenly thought, of my New York life's peculiar flimsiness and generally makeshift air.

In a recumbent S shape on the ancient sofa, surrounded by books stacked on the cushions and spilled on the floor beside her, my room-mate was inspecting a sheaf of typed pages propped fanwise, in a parodic mimesis of childbirth, between her upthrust thighs. This must be the antithesis she was writing for her master's degree, I supposed, meanwhile noting with puzzlement that I had never once thought to ask her any-thing about it. In her far hand, she held another wad of paper, and her eyes shuttled between the two as if she were conducting a dialogue between them. On the floor was a radio playing music at such a low vol-ume that I couldn't make out the tune.

Then the song faded away, and a surprisingly strong-voiced announcer started spieling: "This is Double-You-Ache-Ay-Eee, your pop-classics station, where the Top Twenty's older than a lot of people who have died. Now—say, folks. When you're a nude descending a staircase under the brown fog of a winter noon, does the greed of this metropolis fill you with intolerance? Go to our sponsor: Refuge Paints. Art Refuge knows the secret of durable pigments, gang, and he's out to save you a stately, plump buck. Get on down there! Just catch the velvet underground to the corner of Twentieth and Century. Lots of curves, you bet! We're almost done. My engineer is leaving now. Goodbye, Joey—thanks for everything. Sitting in for Madeleine Proust on *The M.C. M Show* tonight, I'm . . ." *ZZT ZZT,* went an outbreak of static.

Another tune started in his wake. Or possibly another version of the same one, as I still couldn't catch the melody. Squeezing along the fourth wall to seat myself in the lawn chair, and realizing as I did so that I had no more idea how to launch this conversation than I did which impor-tant item was missing from the decor, I carefully cleared my throat.

As my roommate glanced up, the light brown hair that flowed in two waves from a central part on her high forehead fell away from her face, unveiling an amused and full-lipped mouth. Behind the glasses that she *almost certainly* wore these days, her eyes' twin pools of dilute green light looked at me inquisitively.

"Um," I said, "I was just wondering. How'd you lose it, Susan?"

■

After blinking at me for a nonplussed second, she gave a snort of merry and derisive laughter. "Oh, *God*! To my *history* teacher, believe it or not. He was a pompous ass—and a little pathetic, so hindsight informs me in its thoughtful way. Just another handsome guy in his thirties whose looks were starting to tiptoe the same direction his unfinished dissertation had, and wanted us to call him 'Professor.' Which I now know would probably have gotten him in lukewarm water with ye olde Arlington County school board, if they'd heard about *that* little vanity. Much less that he was boning me. 'No consequences,' we both said afterwards, over my first glass of Dart Drug's finest chardonnay—making me feel just splendidly sophisticated, because the candles I was used to had been the ones on birthday cakes, and a fine ho ho ho to that. But I knew he'd be too busy preening to even notice the door closing when I left—and I think that was how I wanted it, to be honest."

"It was in *high school*? How old were you?"

"Sixteen. First female captain of the debate team at George Pickett High, or anywhere in northern Virginia. Our football team was the Pickett Chargers—not the luckiest name, when you think about it. *Big* turmoil our junior year when the first black kid on the team got thrown right back out for putting tape over the Stars and Bars on his helmet. I had a quote in the *Post*. It was fervent. Anyway, we won more often than they did. Prof was our adviser. Now it can be told." With a deprecating facial shrug, letting her *honeyed* hair fall forward *in its swaying ballet move* on her cheek, my roommate went back to comparing her two typescripts.

"Um—*why* was that how you wanted it?" I asked.

With mild surprise, she laid aside her reading, gathering that—for reasons unknown to her, as a wry but tolerant dip of her mouth indicated—this conversation might go on for a while. "Well, to start with," she said, sitting up to hug her *bell-bottomed, blue-jeaned* knees, "I had a boyfriend."

Since this struck me as dis-explaining Prof rather than the reverse, I was confused. "What was the matter with him?"

"Oh, *no!*" As she let out a yowl, cascading hair romped at her throat; her hands scrubbed air. "You don't know what you're getting *into*, Mary-Ann, because that," she said, *in a glad voice that leaped through sentences like a just-born mountain creek, its eagerness to get on and find a river tumbling over its unpredictable infatuations with precision until even her sorrows sounded livelier than other people's joys*, "is a *very* long story, and it's also *been* quite a while. But let me see."

She'd misunderstood. Though to the best of my knowledge even living in New York had not turned me uncompassionate, at the moment I, Mary-Ann, wasn't especially interested in her boyfriend's problems, since I didn't know him *that's what you think*. I had only been asking how come she hadn't lost her virginity to him, if he was in the picture and she wanted to get it over with *believe me, you haven't wondered as long as I have*. "No," I said falteringly, "all I meant was—"

"*First* off, his father was CIA, and I never knew a CIA brat who wasn't either a basket case or a fink to beat the band. Or maybe a fink trapped in a basket case's body, because even the messed-up ones are sort of helplessly arrogant about it. If you don't mind me going all parenthetical and pop-sosh on you, it's different for the military brats: even when Sergeant Dad hauled them to Germany, they weren't really in foreign countries. They lived in little bits of America stuck here and there on the map, so it's not that hard for them to adapt when they get shipped back Stateside. In the pecking order of who's weirder, the State Department and Langley kids win going away. This guy Don Biehl that we were both friends with called them the government Martians—this whole subset of sore thumbs at Pickett who'd grown up everywhere but here, and hated being exotic."

I was having some trouble following this, particularly as the unaccountably prominent sound of knitting through the wall kept getting mixed up with the elusive tune on the radio and my nagging sense of an important item missing. But I was also getting interested despite myself. "Wait," I told her, "wait"—all but panting in my strangely narrow, all but oxygenless apartment, in the iron-cold Manhattan dark. "Do you mean foreigners?"

"*American* foreigners. You see, one peculiarity of the cold war was that the warriors took their children with them. They rode in triumph through Persepolis in baby carriages, wondering what baseball was. Naturally, this being the D.C. suburbs, a lot of *our* parents were government too. My father was Commerce, my mother was Justice. They're divorced. I think Don Biehl's dad was an FBI shrink. But we hadn't been stationed abroad. Big difference. *Their* dads were the glory guys. Sinbad with a diplomatic passport, and Mrs. Sinbad and Junior trotting off the plane in his wake. You should have seen their scrapbooks. Americans look very strange when nobody around them is."

Why, that's probably what *he'd* have done, I thought. But it took me me a second to sort out that I had meant my daddy, whom both I and the Marine Corps graves-registration office knew to have been a patriot and who I had always guessed would have liked to be a voyager. I would have given anything to have that childhood, and not only because then he would have been alive. With him holding my hand as I grew taller, and my mother now a librarian of photo albums, we Kilroys might have gone 'round and 'round the globe together for our country's sake, learning new languages, seeing fantastic sights and returning to Russell—arms laden with miniature Tour Eiffels and Taj Mahals—only for the Unveiling. "Oh, he was lucky," I said, meaning my roommate's boyfriend.

"That's sure as shit what *I* thought," she genially agreed—using the second-worst word in English with a casualness I, Mary-Ann, found flabbergasting. "But would you believe they all felt sorry for themselves? They envied *us*—because we got to stay in the U.S.A.! With sitcoms, and yard swings from Sears. They couldn't imagine it. Once they got posted back here, the kids would sort of try to go native phonetically, but they were like piñatas. Bop 'em at the right angle and 'When we were in Katmandu' comes out, just pissing everybody off. The only reason they weren't a clique was that they *shunned* each other—you know, like lepers tinkling 'Unclean, unclean.' They were all trying to pass for normal! But it was all mixed up with creepy vanity—'I am the only Martian. I am my favorite Martian.' One day, in a madcap mood, it occurred to me to point out to Boyfriend that maybe he'd have an easier time blending in beneath the blue suburban skies if he didn't natter on about how unique he was. Well, he couldn't decide which was more important to him. They're all like that—they don't make sense even to themselves."

"He thought you would," I said, not knowing how I had divined this.

"Exactly," my roommate said. "I was supposed to be *port*, you know—after all those three-year tours."

"Those what?" I said, for something in the sound of the words was inexplicably familiar.

"Three-year tours," she said. "I think he used to just feel *marooned* out there—in these places where just being American was the thing that made him different from anybody else, at the same time that he didn't know anything about being American except that he'd been told he was one. Or about America either, except from books and overheard adult conversation. The latter being both tantalizing and gnomic, of course, when your parents are having a cocktail party for Sam Screwsmith, the departing commercial attaché, and you can hear them chortling in their crewcut voices about Ohio and Ike and a new dance they've all read about in *Newsweek* called the Twist. But you're standing on tiptoe on the landing in your GI Joe pajamas, and you're trying so hard to understand that you've even forgotten to take off that idiotic fez your mom thinks is so darling and always *urges* you to wear for company. You can hear the call to prayer mixing with the roar of the brand-new jet fighters whose sale your daddy helped swing, nice item in his dossier, and they're up there ripping the evening sky a new one while your amah tries to get young sir to come to bed and the grownups fix another round of drinks. So then you're reading *Huckleberry Finn* by flashlight and feeling deeply puzzled by Huck's references to Cairo as they get out the old swing-band records downstairs and fix another round and talk about which foreign country you're all going to be posted to next. That was Boyfriend in his youth, which he spent nursing this sort of bonkers, unrequited love affair with the mysterious United States. You know? The way little boys who want to grow up to be astronauts are crazy about the moon. He'd learned to walk on the Champs-Elysées, but he'd have crawled to Virginia. He'd lived in Baghdad—but *we* were the Arabian Nights."

The truth is, it was worse than that: "By the rivers of Babylon . . ."

There in my apartment in the iron-cold Manhattan dark, where I, Mary-Ann, was still bedeviled by the sense that an important piece of furniture was missing, a feeling too indefinable for me to even call it intuition chose this moment to walk on spider legs across the back of my head. It was a spider that talked: "'*All* the kids say 'Daddy' there,'" it said. Worsening my confusion, I had just noticed that I hadn't changed into my jammies before going to bed after all. Instead, I was wearing a red-and-white checked top and blue denim short-shorts, as if I were already on my vacation. But my roommate was still talking:

"About the only thing he knew for sure about us was that we had won World War Two, which he had an inkling had something to do with his present situation. Including his father, of course, who had fought in it, of course. He told me he was nine before he fully grasped that it wasn't still going on somewhere. Bummed him out more than no Santa Claus. Even in Arlington, he still had a whole shelf in his bedroom closet filled with all the model warplanes and plastic PT boats he'd assembled on his personal desert island; as a result, I soon began expressing a preference for getting my firm young breasts mauled in the basement instead. There was something depressing about seeing those boats and planes over his shoulder and knowing you were getting a hickey from the guy who'd glued them together, especially since about every other time I could feel him coming *unglued* in my arms. He knew they were childish things, but he couldn't just toss them in the trash, you know, because they were sacramental. And so was I, putting me under a slightly unnerving obligation to behave symbolically."

Having spent some innings personifying America myself, I knew how burdensome this could be. "Boy! Isn't it just a pain in the *neck* sometimes?" I sympathetically exclaimed, meanwhile noticing—somehow without special surprise—that the skyline outside the window now showed sixteen church steeples in silhouette. From the casual way they had unveiled themselves, I gathered they would vanish just as casually. Since I was not one to waste time on phenomena over which I evidently had no control, my more immediate preoccupation at the moment was with the last mini-marshmallow in the cocoa I had made for myself at some point, which kept bobbing to the mug's far rim each time I ducked my mouth to retrieve it.

"Oh, no—you're not getting away that easy, Mister," I said. Setting down the mug on the lawn chair's armrest, I stood up and marched around it, fists to hips, until I had the mini-marshmallow where I wanted it. Then I swiftly crouched and my lips took it by surprise, filling me with satisfaction. "There," I said, resuming my seat. "It was driving me *crazy.*"

Clutching her own mug on the sofa, my roommate—who was now, I noted, wearing my pajamas—nodded approvingly. "It's really the only way," she said. "You can't think about anything else when you've got that white dot taunting you. But anyway: that was Boyfriend. Back in the promised land at last, and convinced in his own head that I was his manifest destiny. Sure we were, oh Christ, a love story for the ages, each other's one and only, and utterly oblivious to how all this is getting me *just* a little rattled, here and there around the teacups. Not only because you sort of have to measure up, but because everything was always all about how he felt about how he felt about me, and he didn't see how that made it all about *him*. But I didn't want to be the only person in the world who understood him—and he wanted to be the only person in the world who understood me, which it took me a while to realize was the proof he didn't."

I could see how surrendering your virginity to such a person might not be the wisest plan. "So that was why—" I started to say, and stopped. The halt was not volitional, since a blush can contract the throat as well as coloring one's face, and my eyes and skin alike had just given me the news that I didn't have a stitch on underneath the all but transparent shortie nightgown I was now wearing.

When I glanced at my roommate, her current apparel could have come straight from the finest lingerie shops in the Rue St. Honoré, although designer labels would have been a serious case of the tail wagging the dog so far as the amount of cloth involved went. But she seemed remarkably unfazed to find her alabaster torso bare between two upper and one lower shreds of irisdescent silk, above which her eyes added two additional green prizes to her body's startling invitation—though not to I, Mary-Ann, of course—to play Capture the Flag. As either water began to gurgle like faint music or music began to gurgle like faint water, a palm-frond fan above us gently dipped and rose.

"Yes and no," she said, "and ultimately yes. But it wasn't like we didn't try once. Or twice, depending on how you count."

"What happened?"

My father had built a doghouse for a dog who ran away, giving his son my first hint that moving back to the States wasn't going to be all idyll. Since it looked depressing out in the yard and we still talked sometimes about getting another dog, it had been moved down to the basement, but I didn't take having to step past it as an omen. When I did and saw her on the sofa, all she was wearing was a copy of The Great Gatsby—*face down over her pubic moss, and open to page One Thousand and One.*

With a sigh, my roommate stretched out on her back, hands clasped over her navel and gazing ceilingward. Only to erupt in giggles:

"Oh, *God*! The poor fucker came before he even got his shorts off. I was *six feet away*, Mary-Ann! Lying in more or less this position in his parents' basement, modestly nude but for my book and with my eyes closed since I'm waiting for my Christmas present, when instead of choirs I hear a strangled little voice say, 'Oh *merde*.' As this marks the first time I've gotten him to say *anything* in French to me, since as soon as he got back to the States he started refusing to speak it, I stubbornly tell myself that he's just being romantic. But then I open my eyes, and clearly it's just been whoops-a-daisy time. At which point I take a deep breath, lying modestly nude in his parents' basement, and gently suggest that we just hold each other for a while."

"I've been *there*," I, Mary-Ann, said with feeling, remembering the occasional misfires when I hadn't gotten to stop being a virgin for even a second before I became one again. You're each holding yourself, and you know it.

"I hadn't," she said. "But I didn't expect him to consider that this might be a little disconcerting for me too. At any rate, it's kind of an awkward transition. He's still got to walk those last six feet to get to me, and the look on his face is something only Chuck Jones could do justice to. Still, we manage. Doing my best to act playful about it, I indicate by means of gestures and tugging that maybe he should get rid of his Jockey shorts, since their sticky reminder of the recent unfortunate turn of events probably isn't going to help things a whole lot. So then we're lying there naked, both feeling somewhat at a loss for appropriate small talk—he knows that 'Gee, how's the debate team going?' won't do, and I know that neither will 'Say, talk French some more'—and pretending we aren't just counting the minutes and working up our nerve to try again. Even so, I'm doing what I hope is a reasonably good job of acting girlish and quite satisfied with things as they are, since I know it probably isn't a good idea for him to be thinking too much about how we're going to try again until we do."

"Let me guess," I said. "He thought about it."

"Oh, yes. So, of course, when we *did* work up our nerve to try again, he couldn't have gotten it up with a derrick. And, well—not much of a middle ground *here*, I can't help thinking to myself, as he keeps trying to screw his courage to the sticking place and rubbing against me like I'm Aladdin's lamp, and getting more and more frantic that no genie is in sight. Finally, we kind of collapsed like wet laundry, but it made for a mighty awkward sort of post-non-coital interlude. I mean, this was *not* someone you could rely on to laugh off the situation. Especially since, at the time, his dad—"

"Hang on a second." Getting out of my chair, I trotted over in my checked top and short-shorts to give the wall of my room in the hotel on the Rue de Lille a good smack. It quivered glassily. "Hey!" I called out. "*Madame Defarge!* Cut out the *gosh darn* knitting out there! I can't hear myself think, for gosh sakes." As I sat back down, my roommate—by then pulling a pair of jeans back on—had a droll expression on her face.

"Well, you know—'If at first you don't succeed,'" I quoted. And realized as I spoke that this saying had some claim to being my, Mary-Ann's, motto; though in a somewhat different context, which had had its origins in this very hotel room. Then my apartment reappeared, clamped on three sides by iron-cold Manhattan dark and on the fourth by that exasperating knitting. Something that should have been there still wasn't.

Now fully dressed again, my roommate shook her head. "You don't understand. After that, I realized I *couldn't*. Not with him. Even if we had been able to manage The Deed, which I assume we could have sooner or later. Shit, it's not *that* complicated," she giggled suddenly. "It really isn't, you dumb bastard. If it was, we'd all have died out a long time ago."

"Then why?" I said, blinking in the basement's yellow light as a nearby washer and dryer began to click and clack. In front of me was a record player, next to which was an LP jacket depicting a monolith standing in a slag heap. Four men with perplexingly long hair appeared to have just relieved themselves on the stone, which was distracting.

Sighing, my roommate drew a meditative finger along the ridge of the sofa *from which, since one of us was going to have to sooner or later, she finally swung herself onto her feet and started to collect her clothes. When I finally looked up, she was holding them bunched in front of her and looking back at me with a smile that—if I'd only known it then—was her real gift to me. "Since this is the kind of thing jerks always tell you you'll laugh about someday," she said cheerfully, "you want to try knocking 'em for loop and starting now?"*

"It meant too much to him," she said. "And I realized that I didn't want it to mean *that* much to *anybody*. And I *absolutely* didn't want it to mean more to *him* than it did to me, which it now dawned on me had been the problem all along. You know, sometimes it's the sensitive ones who are the real bullies, and they don't know it. He didn't, anyway. But even so, I realized that, basically, he was still a kid—and I wasn't, which I hadn't known before." She smiled. "So: 'Hello, Prof! In case you haven't noticed, I'm sixteen, and I'm not sure, but I think these are my boobies. Can you tell me if I'm right?'"

"My *God!*" I, Mary-Ann, squealed, having just sat bolt upright in what were, after all, my jammies. "Was that a *gunshot*? I swear, the big Apple wasn't anywhere *near* this dangerous when I moved in."

"Mackintosh," my roommate murmured, as if she knew something I didn't. "But I think it was just an exploding cigar," and she grinned. "Otherwise, Monsieur—I mean Madame—Defarge would have quit, and you could hear yourself think."

"Fat chance of *that!*" I said, jumping up in my corset and high-heeled black boots to give #6's brick wall another smack.

"It won't do any good," my roommate murmured. However, my banging must have changed the light, which incidentally had no evident source that I could see. As it quivered, it made her seem older, for she briefly appeared to be in her forties—or rather, like a luminous sketch of herself in her forties, drawn by a hand whose lack of firsthand information alternated with both a desire to believe and a flickering sense of utter impossibility. But then the tentative age lines vanished, though not the retrospective cast of her expression.

"So you never saw him again?" I asked.

"Boyfriend? I saw him all the time. In school, anyway; Prof's classroom, too, since we had history together. Even if I had wanted to stop having a relationship with him, which I didn't, I couldn't've. His idea of being gallant was to turn his suffering into a role—to amuse me, you know, so that my attention wouldn't have wandered by the time I came back to my senses. I mean, his family was as Catholic as you can get when Mom keeps making fish on Saturday from forgetfulness, but this was when Hollywood had just discovered Jewishness was funny, and since *everything* was mimicry for the government Martians, he decided that was his favorite fake him: 'I tried to assimilate, but you *schmatte* goyim would never tell me why you act the way you do. Then came the pogrom.' The pogrom was me. Not a lot of girls at Pickett were getting courted that way—which was what he was doing, of course. He didn't mind if everybody else thought he was goofy—or Jewish, for that matter—so long as he could still make me laugh."

"But it didn't work," I said.

"No. On top of everything else, his home life was turning into a horrible mess around then—and I did *not, not, not* want to be the *answer* to that horrible mess. I mean, *help*, yes—anything I could do, and he knew it. But answer? Call the fire department, because I'll just make it worse. Which I'm afraid I did anyway," she admitted—"but I didn't mean to."

"What happened?" I asked, glancing with fascination around the small patch of woods behind the tawny-bricked ranch house where my roommate had lived in high school. Off in the distance, in the skewed perspective of a primitive painting, I could see a fat-pillared mansion on a hill surrounded by Scrabble tiles. Unseen traffic honked. Closer by, a clickety-clacking weathervane was turning in an interesting manner, and I should probably explain that I was keeping my attention on the scenery because I was embarrassed to look at her. She had folded her arms to cover her bare bosom.

"It's another long story, so brace yourself." From the sofa, she looked at me quizzically; then glanced at Monsieur Defarge's wall, which now appeared to be growing somewhat more translucent. More unnervingly, it also seemed to have moved closer. With a good-natured roll of her eyes, my roommate brought them back to my face.

"No. I want to hear it," I forced my yawning mouth to say, *not having a whole lot of choice in the matter.* "Anything to distract me from that racket, my gosh! It sounds like fifty sweaters all getting made at once. Les Deux Magots was *never* this noisy before," I complained, sipping my *café crème*, as cups clicked and clacked into saucers all around us and Sartre and de Beauvoir began to bicker at the table next to ours.

"Well. He didn't know about Prof and me—*I* didn't know about Prof and me. Not yet. But the two of them went at it hammer and tongs in history class about two days a week. An inverted obsession is still an obsession, and America's sins were now a way of going on taking America personally. What it was really all about, needless to say, was that he couldn't get his head screwed on right about his own father—who was the bad-guy CIA, and had *been* one of those guys running around destabilizing governments and bribing officials and helping to keep dictators propped up, and all those other eagle-in-a-china-shop things we did and do. But Dad was also the brave Marine who'd fought on Iwo Jima, which complicated things a good deal."

That certainly gave I, Mary-Ann, a start—of not only recognition but an inexplicable suspicion *that I had invented her father to cope with mine, of course.* For the first time, I found myself mentally blinking at the date on my daddy's tombstone—and the one on Corporal John G. Egan's letter to my mother, too. "Well, that *does* complicate things," I told my roommate, in a slightly jumpy voice.

"It did for him. I think he was too awed by the Bronze Star in Dad's dresser drawer to ever figure out that his father had been, maybe, *seventeen* on Iwo Jima, or wonder what going through that must have done to a seventeen-year-old. But his dad was the kind of guy who'd made up his mind right afterward that *he* wasn't ever going to wonder about it, either. I mean, maybe what had frozen in his eyes were tears, but all there was there now was ice. It scared me to look at him, and I don't think it did a *whole* lot to relax his son, either."

"What about his mother?" I asked.

"Oh! Her I liked. She'd been in the Foreign Service before she got married, and I once made myself a mite unpopular with her husband by voicing my frisky curiosity as to why she hadn't gone on doing that afterward. By the time I knew her, she was one of those friendly blonde women in slightly accidental clothes, whose hands are on a first-name basis with everybody's arms and shoulders the minute she says hello, and who had concocted a sort of kidding fetish about the Rat Pack to give her personality a focal point. You know, like the birthstone necklace that someone tells you they *always* wear—meet me, meet my necklace. But she was nice."

"And beside the point," I guessed.

"For a lot of women her age, that's the only place they felt safe calling home," my roommate said. "She'd even had that little bit of a career, but when I met her, it was: 'Oh, I didn't know they had a girls' debate team at your school.' No, no, I said, it's just *the* debate team. 'Oh, my. Jack, did you hear that? It's *the* debate team.' But not to rebuke him: more as if she had been put in possession of a fact that she didn't want to be solely responsible for. She was passing it up the chain of command."

"And he—your boyfriend—was between a rock and a soft place," I guessed again. Though both the perception and the manner of articulating it made I, Mary-Ann, feel my old irksome sense of being no more than a convenient ventriloquist's dummy. "But if he wasn't your boyfriend anymore, how did you get to be part of the horrible mess? That's a really strange billboard behind you, by the way."

"Timing," my roommate said, as the hands on the Maxwell House clock began to tick and tock. "Just before he and I got together, the Phoenix program had started to stink so bad in the papers that *somebody* had to be the scapegoat—and his father was one of the gung-ho guys who'd helped set it up, which was another reason it was kind of scary to meet those eyes across a dinner table. Guess who carves the roast! But he fell on his electric knife, because he had just enough seniority to satisfy the Hill and not enough of it for Langley to protect him, and they gave him the boot from the Agency. That's Washington: the story runs below the fold, and mostly not even on Page One. There's somebody's picture, with that expressionless smile they all have in their work photograph— what are they *looking* at, to be that happy and that vague?—and you know you're reading an obituary. Between the lines is a small elegy for black passports and the day Suharto shook your hand, and that great time with old Joe Doakes in Rangoon, and a gray panic about making the car payment. Sometimes you went to school with their kid."

"But they didn't leave," I said.

"Oh, no. Nobody does. Nobody goes back to Kansas, unless it's to Leavenworth. Or back to Rochester, Minnesota, either. His dad was one of the lucky ones. He had friends in Nixon's re-election campaign. They found him a good job."

"Wait," I said, bewildered. "Re-elec-, what are you—"

My roommate's snicker was grim. "He ended up as one of the White House Plumbers, working for his fellow ex-gyrene Chuck Colson. That's some career progression, wouldn't you say—USMC, CIA, CREEP? I'm actually not sure if he would have gone to jail, but I guess he was still one of the lucky ones. He didn't end up in prison. Right in the middle of Watergate, he ended up in a hospital instead—with terminal cancer, at the age of all of forty-five."

Between the UN, the Plaza, and the Sherry-Netherland, I, Mary-Ann, did not consider myself uninformed. But to my ears, my roommate had started spouting gibberish, in the iron-cold Manhattan dark. I had no idea what she meant by "Watergate," and while I could see that working as a plumber, even in the Executive Mansion, might well qualify as a comedown for a white-collar type of fellow, my roommate's unexpected snobbery annoyed me to my Russell, Kansas, toes—now clad, I noticed, in the red pumps I'd worn to the top of the Tour Eiffel. Nor had I ever heard of any television show such as the "Phoenix" program, *which came under the heading of "pacification" in bureaucrat-speak and operated as a CIA-run assassination bureau in Vietnam.*

"O.K.," I said, "I'm getting lost here." Since we had just flown over what I knew perfectly well to be the Lincoln Memorial, which was now passing from sight beneath our helicopter as we dipped toward a large building whose scalloped balconies had an uncanny resemblance to stacked dentures before veering south over an island in what must be the Potomac River, this was not literally true. But I was beginning to feel frustrated.

"Well," my roommate shouted, as we crept out from underneath our chopper's clickety-clacking blades, "while his father was in intensive care, he came upon you and Prof—here in the woods behind your house. It was April Fool's Day, 1974."

And for me it was still winter, but for you it was already spring. So far as the weather went, you were right; it was so mild that I didn't even have a sweater on when I ran out of the hospital and past that damned billboard to find you, not so incidentally leaving my mother in the ICU alone. But if she and I tried to treat forgiveness for either my or her behavior at the time on a case-by-case basis, we'd still be at it today.

"He hadn't known?"

"No. And since you've got your top off"—with a yelp, I crossed my wrists over my collarbones—"you can't really tell him that Prof's just helping you work up your cards on that year's debate topic. Which was, by the by, and not without a certain irony, 'Was Alger Hiss Unjustly Accused?'"

"Was he?" I asked, shivering in her back yard.

"Well, this was debate. The trick was, if you built the case that the government fiddled the evidence to get him, you were going off on a tangent so far as the judges were concerned," my roommate explained briskly. "I had all that in my notes, but I surprised myself by deciding that anyone who thought the S.O.B. was *innocent* was definitely barking up the wrong crucifix. As I say, though, you can't really pretend that this is the point of your rendezvous—not when Boyfriend has just seen you with Prof's robust thumbs and index fingers twiddling your bare nipples like two pieces of pink classroom chalk, Mary-Ann."

"But hadn't you broken up with him by then?" I asked, relieved that we were back in my apartment, I had my checked top on again, and no strange hands were in sight.

"Try telling *him* that," my roommate said from the sofa. "One and only, love story for the ages, so on and so forth. It was a little scary, to be honest—he was more like his father than he thought."

"Well, I'd call that pretty good I'm-going-to-be-messed-up-there-for-a-while stuff," I said. "But is it really Grade-A I'll-hate-you-for-the-rest-of-my-life stuff?"

At which she looked blank; then realized what she'd left out. "The reason he'd come looking for me in the first place was to tell me that his father had just died."

"Oh," I said.

"April fool, Gil. Too bad, wouldn't you say? Too bad all around. Well, for everyone but Prof, I guess—he didn't give a damn."

Leaning forward, she turned up the volume on the radio. As the elusive tune gained on the knitting or else the knitting paused, I heard this:

"Monday, Monday . . . "

"What happened afterward?" I asked.

"Well—it wasn't *good.* I think he spent a solid *week* sniffing glue, which he used to do in between PT boats when he was younger, and listening over and over to that record whose cover you were glancing at in such perplexity a while back. It must have been something to be around the house, because Mom was losing herself to the delights of the medicine cabinet. And didn't much notice or care who saw—"

But then my roommate stopped, *because I told you that in confidence, and you aren't going to repeat it—not even to Mary-Ann. As I say, afterward we found it easier to forgive each other in bulk. I wish Lovey hadn't let it slip out, but too late now.*

"What about later?" I asked, as she apparently wasn't going to complete the sentence.

"Oh, later was all sorts of things. Later was June, when I found myself—courtesy of Prof—sitting in Doctor Rubicon's waiting room, a *very* scared almost-seventeen. When the nurse called my name, my knees were shaking so bad I wasn't sure I could even stand up." Lips compressed, she paused to inspect her clamped hands. "But I did, and slowly gathered that, even though it was what I had come there to prevent, somebody was going to get born anyway: me."

I had just realized what she meant; not, needless to say, that this had ever been a problem I, Mary-Ann, had had to contend with. "Lordy! Did you go to Tijuana, or—"

"Shit, no," she said. "I went to a clinic in the District. Why would— oh, right. You don't know yet. Never mind. Anyway: later was college. Gil and I ended up in facing dorms, but of course he was my bitter enemy by then. I'd walk past his window on my way to Commons, and hear him playing 'Aladdin Sane' at full blast as if he'd put it on when he saw me coming. It was all Bowie and Lou fucking Reed from freshman to junior year. But I don't think anything ever really made him happy until the Ramones came along."

"The who?" I stammered in confusion.

"No. I told you: that was earlier. But then he went away this way, and I went away that way, and we probably both tried real hard to grow up until one day we realized we'd succeeded beyond our wildest dreams at it. That's that."

"Do you know where he is now?"

"No." Her smile was rueful, but the way it pinched one side of her face made it look as if she'd winked. "I mean, I can *guess*—and so, I guess, can he. But we didn't exactly keep in touch."

"What did you say his name was?" I asked. "His whole name."

So she told me, which was how I learned that ex-Corporal John G. Egan—if that had indeed been him I'd seen briskly striding to hoist up a three-year-old, as a bomb went off and a Marlboro bobbed, on the Boulevard St. Germain one day—had kept his promise to stop calling his son "Junior" from then on. But then she re-pronounced the same three syllables she'd just spoken, whoopingly altering the stresses:

". . . I mean, the poor son of a bitch!" my roommate was saying, giggling and shaking her head. "You can imagine how long it took to spot *that* nickname in tenth grade—even though *I* never called him that," *for which I thank you.* "And he even *looked* a little like Bob Denver, so of course the nickname stuck. No wonder he could hardly stand the show."

"The show?" I said confusedly, *not yet remotely aware that she was* that *Mary-Ann.* Yet in my mind, I'd just re-seen the pointing bystanders near the Pont des Arts, and just re-heard what they were shouting; had re-felt a hand on my shoulder, and had re-looked into green eyes. I knew that this unveiling was connected to that one in some way I couldn't grasp, but all I wished for at the moment was an exit from this flimsy, endlessly mutable, peculiarly clickety-clacking maze. Sleepily, I longed to find a place whose reality—which I equated, simply and naively and despite everything that Jean-Luc ever tried to teach me, with its constancy—I could count on.

I'd like to be somewhere that never changes, I thought. Rather ironically, in hindsight.

"It's in my antithesis," my roommate said, apparently meaning the show, in a tone that suggested she was under an impression of explaining something. "The last chapter, in fact."

"What's your antithesis about?" I asked somewhat timidly, my summer program at the Sorbonne having stopped well short of connoisseurship of this type of project. I had heard of theses, but not antitheses.

"Sometimes I wish I had a good short answer to that one," my roommate said. "But Paul Burns—my adviser—thinks I ought to try to turn it into a book just the same. Want to take a look at the table of contents? It might give you an idea."

"Sure," I said, by now completely at sea and guessing that information of any sort would be helpful. Wrong again I was. Pulling a single sheet from her typescript, my roommate passed it over, and I stumbled my way through this:

A Cage Is a Cage Is a Cage
A Master's Antithesis
By Susan B. O'Hara

1. The Myth of Purity and the Cult of Hysteria:
   From Quentin Compson *to* The Catcher in the Rye

2. *Hung Up on GI Dad:*
   Find Your Own Big One or Shut Up

3. *Let's Call It "Macho-Chism":*
   Why Male Romantics Love to Rescue Women Who Might Have
   Learned to Swim Instead

4. *Dreams in a Funhouse Mirror:*
   Transcending the Self, Inventing the Other, and the Allure of the
   Lesbian Fantasy

5. *Goodbye, Doctor:*
   Cheesecake as Therapy

6. *We'll Be His Mirror:*
   The Narcissist (Male) as Superpower (Guess)

7. *Pre-Feminist Archetypes Marooned in a Midcentury Eden:*
   Was That "Uncharted Desert Isle" Paradise—or the Alamo?

"Well?" my roommate said, with a faint smile, as I handed it back. At which point I, Mary-Ann, exploded.

"What do you mean, 'Well?' " I hollered. "*None of this makes any sense to me! I am Mary-Ann Kilroy of Russell, Kansas, and briefly of the Sorbonne, and I have no idea what's going on!* You tell me an *interminable* story about you and your high-school *boyfriend,* when *all I wanted to hear about* was how you lost your virginity—and I don't even *know* why I felt curious about *that*! You keep mentioning all these crazy things I haven't heard of and don't want to hear of—*Phoenix* program! *Watergate!* Nixon's *re-election* campaign—for what, *dogcatcher*? For gosh sakes, *he couldn't even get elected governor of California!* Next, you'll be telling me that Ronald Reagan *did, AND GOD KNOWS WHAT-ALL ELSE!* I am Mary-Ann Kilroy of Russell, Kansas, and *I hardly even know what the CIA is, for gosh sakes*! And *that's* supposed to be an *oldies* station, *and I have never heard that song in my life until now! THE CLICKETY-CLACKING THROUGH THE DUMB WALL IS DRIVING ME PLUMB NUTS!* And you keep talking about a *TV show* that I never *saw* in my life—*and you get the most infuriating damn smirk on your face when you do*! And we're not *DONE, oh no*, because *THEN* you show me what you say is the *table of CON-TENTS* for something called a master's *antithesis*, of which I have never *heard*, and what do you know? *BIG surprise coming, folks! I CAN'T MAKE HEAD OR TAIL OF IT EITHER! It reads like one half of a tele-phone conversation on MARS*, and all I can tell you about *that* is that you start out *on Mars* sounding like you're *arguing* with somebody else *on Mars*, and *then* you decide you *agree* with them *on Mars*! Well, *JIM-DANDY! SO WHAT! WHAT IN HELL DOES ANY OF IT HAVE TO DO WITH ME? AND WHAT MAKES IT WORSE IS THAT THIS HAS BEEN HAPPENING TO ME MY WHOLE LIFE, AND I DON'T KNOW WHY!*"

Taking a breath, I looked around.

"Where's the TV set?" I said.

"Actually," Sukey Santoit, Girl Detective, told me comfortably, "I think it was the other way around. The argument, I mean—so far as which of us ended up agreeing with the other." Then, raising her voice and addressing Monsieur Defarge's increasingly translucent wall, she baf-flingly went on: "I didn't think you'd even *remember* the day I made you take me to Occoquan."

Come on. When you told me that you wanted to go, I'd only had my license for a week. It was the first time I'd driven anywhere outside of Arlington, and when we got there, we kept wandering around, because you were so stubbornly convinced that there must be a monument somewhere. But even at that little Tourist Information shack, they didn't know what you were talking about; all they could give us was directions to the prison. Then, among weeds and whizzing cars, we finally found that sad little plaque from the Fairfax County League of Women Voters, which was and is the only indication of what happened there in 1917, when a few women armed only with their own bodies fought a battle with the U.S. government and won. You sat down on the median strip in your white peasant blouse and jeans and started bawling, and even then I understood you well enough to know it wasn't grief. It was fury.

Before I could even get started trying to make sense of what my roommate had just said, which I suspected would be a fool's errand in any case, she had kindly resumed talking to me: "Anyway, you're right, Mary-Ann. I don't blame you for getting fed up. Even without the sudden dizzying changes of clothing and scenery, accompanied only by that persistent, annoying clacking sound, this whole conversation would be out of whack. In real life, I think I'm at least fifteen years younger than you are—or than Dawn Wells is, anyway. And if it's 1964, then feminism isn't much more than a gleam in Betty Friedan's eye—you know, sort of like a locomotive coming at you in the dark, but from *really* far away. And to be honest, while I've always been fond of you, I don't think that you and I would ever be roommates, much less the torrid lovers I suspect we briefly were in danger of becoming. But Gil never did get why I always rooted more for Ginger—and also objected to the choice."

Peculiarly, she raised her voice again. "I take it that's no longer the case," she called out. But there was no one there for her to be talking to—just the wall, which had now become so thin and translucent that endless parallel lines of regimented black markings showed through it from the far side.

"*Well Here we God Damn go again,*" I raged. "Will SOMEONE please tell me *what is going on?*"

As no doubt goes without saying, no one did. Instead, even as it visibly inched closer to us and the room began to grow more shallow and confining as a result, the wall became slightly concave—and I, Mary-Ann, would not be getting out of here a minute too soon, I told myself. When I got back from my vacation, I was definitely going to be in the market for another apartment; so I thought.

"I'm glad you tried to understand," Sukey Santoit told whoever she was talking to. "You know I didn't want you to find out the way you did, or God knows on the day you did. But Ginger's right: these things happen. Sometimes it just works out that way."

However, she no longer had to raise her voice to do this, as the room was now sufficiently narrow to make that unnecessary. At this rate, in only seconds more, whatever it was we were inside would be completely flat; and I had just seen the writing on the wall.

EMOCLEW, it said.

"For *God's sake, stop yakking and get me the hell out of here!*" I shrieked at Sukey Santoit. "Can't you see he's got us *trapped*?"

"Don't worry, Mary-Ann," she said. "We've both been gone a long time."

Apparently not the least perturbed that the room was now virtually two-dimensional—and we with it, I realized with a consternation I can only ask you to imagine, for now I could see through us both—she reached down with a shrug and picked up the typescript that she'd been comparing against her antithesis. To my utter stupefaction, and most un-Mary-Ann-ish rage.

"*What are you talking about?*" I screamed at her at the top of my lungs. "*Who are you? What are you? What are WE, for gosh sakes?*"

Tender, eager, mocking and amused, her eyes' twin vestiges of dilute green light—now all that was left of her—looked up from the last pages of her book.

"Memories," she said.

■

Dear Roadrunner,

Yes—and here I sit among my Acme traps and gizmos, watching you dash away. But you have somewhere to get to, and unlike my beloved master—the great Wile E. Coyote, whom we knew—I wasn't trying to catch you. You know I only wanted to see you one more time. And make you laugh, because you'd have to have changed a lot not to get a smile or two from this—especially since you know that the real story was so different.

Anyhow, this is all I really wanted to say: bless you. I started making up these jokes not long after they dropped the Times Square wrecking ball on the century you and I grew up in. Looking out of the small window that I had on it at sixteen—when you above all things were glad and young, as your favorite poem put it—I realized that the reason your eyes were green was that all of you was.

You see, in my memory, you were standing in New York Harbor.

Back then I didn't understand what freedom meant to you, and of course I couldn't see why anyone would want to be free of me—even though I sure did, which should probably have been some sort of tip-off. But everything I ever thought you did to me has turned out to be what you did for me, and I'm grateful. As is the woman I'm married to, who sends your youthful ghost bemused regards.

So it's thirty years later, and what do you know? I'm a middle-aged fat-head staring at a computer screen, still thinking about a girl I used to know in high school. Congratulate me, Susan—or S usa N, as I used to write it: that must prove I'm a real American at last.

Since I know you were fond of her, you'll probably be pleased to hear that my mom did rejoin the Consular Corps eventually. She served in many lands. I guess that's about it, except to say that I hope you like Daisy. I did, both times I was privileged to know her.

With old affection,

G.

■

Whatever.

The next morning, doing my best to shake off my complete bafflement as to why I'd ever dreamed I had a roommate, much less why she had been Sukey Santoit, Girl Detective—and unable to see a smidgen of rhyme or reason in the bizarre conversation we'd had—I, Mary-Ann, flew to Los Angeles. That was my first stop on what turned out to be the vacation that never quits, and there I changed planes.

On the next leg of the trip, my seatmate on the aisle was showing some. As the Pacific appeared under the slanting wing outside my window, I got to gabbing with her about how exciting it was for me to see my second ocean's blue for the first time; somewhat ironically, as it turned out, as she was a trashy-looking but entertaining redhead whose peculiar idea of appropriate traveling togs was a sequined white evening gown.

Guess who.

After we landed, both of us being at loose ends until nightfall and enjoying each other's company, we set out to look for, as the sign above the arcade on Main Street in my hometown of Russell, Kansas, used to and may still put it, Something to Do.

Guess what.

Soon after we put out to sea, just as the coastline dropped from sight, a gray and moving bulk showed up on the horizon. As it drew nearer and grew larger, Ging grabbed my as yet untanned forearm with one red-nailed, clattering-braceleted hand. "Hey, that's a *troopship!*" she exulted, and started to whoop and wave.

"How can you tell?" I asked, peering hard, for it was still quite far away and partly veiled in mist.

Ginger gave me a look. "Mary-Ann, how the hell you think my Momma taught me to swim, and why?" she drawled. We both laughed.

It kept swelling until it loomed over us. The railing was packed with what looked like a thousand young Marines in crewcuts and combat green. They whooped and waved. We whooped and waved, and Ginger gave them a few shimmies from the *Minnow*'s little deck, in her white evening gown. It was silly, since she could see perfectly well that they were just kids—probably all of nineteen. But that was what made it fun for them and us both, since we all knew how innocent it was.

Then we sailed away this way, and they sailed away that way. Soon they were gone, and we never did find out where they'd been going.

■

As for us, you know where we all washed up. And yes, the island is beautiful; especially at night, when the sky unveils its stars. But we have now been here, so far as we can compute, for going on forty years.

We try to make the best of things. But it's a downhill slide.

The reunion movies were a pack of lies. "A complete violation of the original's artistic integrity, as incredible as that sounds" according to the newspaper article about us, apparently written by one of my old boyfriend Jean-Luc's epigones, by which I learned of those movies' existence. Escorted there by her pet crabs, Ging found it lying on the beach at low tide a year or two or three ago, rolled inside an empty jar of Maxwell House instant coffee.

Oddly enough, one of the men said that the accompanying photograph of the reviewer reminded him of an old student of his. He couldn't place the name, though. Even so, when I'm done writing this, I'm going to put it all inside the jar and toss it back out to sea, and maybe it will find its way back to whoever sent it in the first place.

It did Mary-Ann Thank you

But anyway: we didn't escape from the gosh-darn island. We didn't return to the gosh-darn island. We never got off the gosh-darn island.

We never will get off the gosh-darn island.

We are the island. The island is us.

We have never gotten any older. Then again, we sure aren't getting any younger.

On top of which, as we have not been united in years, the prospect of being *re*-united holds few charms for us here.

■

Needless to say, it was Ginger who was the first to figure out that we must be fictional characters of some sort. Besides having the most prior experience of this kind of thing, she's also the smartest of us by miles. That's one reason why I, Mary-Ann, am proud to call her my friend.

But we don't know our purpose. We don't know when or how our unveilings take place, which may be why, for decades now, I've had recurring dreams. In these, a wry-faced, dry-voiced man with salt-and-pepper hair, dressed in a suit and tie and most often holding a cigarette, steps out from behind a palm tree at twilight and delivers a caustic yet somehow genial summary of our situation, which seems to be exemplary in some way. But I don't know who he is and can't make out what he's saying or reconstruct its import after I wake up, so I have no idea what the dreams signify.

Ging's theory is that we're some kind of refuge from the century that was just passing its two-thirds mark when we all washed up here. And yet, perhaps just because we're available to anyone who has a mind to, we all seem to have been equipped with histories that would make us instead, in however incomplete and veiled a way, that century's incarnation.

Her taste for philosophical conundrums having been whetted rather than sated by decades of nothing to do, Ging often likes to speculate at length on whether we're an incarnation that became a refuge, or a refuge that became an incarnation. But as I say, she's a lot brainier than the rest of us, and that includes me. So she usually loses me in her logic pretty fast, and I get up and wander off and go look at the mountains for a while as she continues talking to the crabs.

You should know it's understood between us that no offense will be taken—for all that, having been raised to be unfailingly pleasant, polite and cheerful and still remembering those lessons, I, Mary-Ann, nonetheless felt some discomfiture at wandering off to go look at the mountains during the first fifteen years or so. But we'll all be here forever, and my old friend will happily tell her theories to the crabs, who may be an audience more insightful than her human one, until night comes and the sky unveils its stars, and we build our separate fire here up at our end of the camp.

I need to hear Ging's voice behind me to keep looking at the mountains very long, because they frighten me; as they do all of us. Early on, the men got the bright idea of planting Old Glory on the island's southernmost peak—to signal passing ships, they said, although even back then Ginger and I already suspected that they simply needed to have projects and ambitions to keep themselves occupied. But we were all still one group then, and so we got the flag from the boat, put it on a pole that one of the men had made, and started climbing, Ginger leading the way in her white and starry evening gown. But we never got more than a couple of hundred yards up the slope, and when we turned to go back, we soon found ourselves running.

As we don't actually know the name of this island, assuming that it has one, we may have feared discovering that it had been done before. Or hadn't, but would seem completely pointless once we did. In any case, whatever the true reason for our fear of the mountains may be, now we all stay near the beach. We tell ourselves the ships will be more visible to us and we to them, and they more likely to come in and pick us up, if we're all closer to the water.

■

These days, however, Ging and I don't spend a lot of time with the others. Up at our end of the camp, we tend our own fire; we keep to our separate sisterhood. While I'm frankly not sure when we began to live apart from the other five, the day the Maxwell House coffee jar washed ashore was the first time we'd all clustered in one group in ages.

Even the non-egotists among us were eager to read about ourselves, in no matter how distorted and travestied a version. But that scrap of newspaper was also the first word we'd had of the outside world, or anyway America, since 1964, the year we all washed up here.

When one of the men finally turned the page over to see what was on the flip side of the review, he couldn't glean all that much from it, since it was mostly advertisements. There was a public notice announcing that Gang-A-Gley Pharmaceuticals was discontinuing the manufacture of its medication Laggilin, having determined that the condition it alleviated wasn't worth curing, and an ad for summer rentals in Provincetown. An antiques store specializing in things nautical announced a vintage Royal Navy spyglass for sale, and a recently unearthed bushel of genuine PT-109 tie clips from the 1960 Kennedy campaign. From an alarmingly blue-eyed commemorative plate offered by an apparent charitable organization for emotionally disturbed watercolorists calling itself the Franklin Mint, we gathered, with sorrow, that Frank Sinatra had passed. A local car show promoted itself as featuring an authentic Duesenberg, and so on.

In fact, the only actual news item on the page was part of a story about a young woman named Parvita Singh who, despite being confined to a wheelchair, had been elected to the county board in Arlington, Virginia. There was a picture of her flashing a victory sign on election night. Crouched next to her was her beaming father, identified as a Washington, D.C., cab driver.

He was flashing a victory sign, too.

"What the hell's going on back there, anyhow?" whichever one of the men had been reading complained. In fact, in his irritation and perplexity, he had almost started to crumple the paper up when I stopped him. He never knew that, behind his back, Ginger and I had looked at each other—with, as I believe the saying goes, a wild surmise.

Or that the unaccustomed tears in my friend's eyes were only prevented from dripping by the thickness of her false eyelashes, which caught them like bugs in amber.

■

Otherwise, you can probably see how it is from wherever you are. Too many for bridge, too few for football, and not much I care to say about any of them except Ging. Little boy and fat man; Mr. Magoo. The old dame with the empty spaces in her eyes that youth and then morphine once filled in, and a three-toed sloth in search of a mirror. It all got boring pretty fast.

If we were a medieval morality play, our names would be Youth, Clumsiness, Wealth, Cowardice, Hubba-Hubba, and Self-Love. Plus I, Mary-Ann, who am or may be all these things and more and yet am still and forever virgin; and still waiting, in my unfailingly pleasant, polite and cheerful way, to find myself pregnant with Jesus.

As I believe I have noted, current opportunities for this event to get rolling would appear to be nil. But to tell the truth, I'm not even sure we're alone now, not that the evidence is any great cause for huzzahs and champagne. One day not long ago, under ten years I would guess, I went out walking far from our camp, and saw something I thought was disgusting: a pig's head on a stick.

I don't believe that any of the men would have done that, although I can't be sure and don't really give a damn that I'm not. Nor do I see how any animals could, not even monkeys with their reversible thumbs and undoubted talent for mimicry. In any case, I didn't tell anyone what I'd seen, even Ginger. To be honest, things are plenty bad enough.

■

The men, of course, still have their plans and projects, and getting the next one settled can keep them contentedly arguing and bellowing for hours, down at their end of the camp. Then, with monotonous regular-ity, as I roll my eyes and she her eyelashes, Ging and I will have to over-hear the following conversation, reprised now for decades with only modest variations:

Hitching up his pants and brushing the sand off them, the fat one claps his hands together and says, "Okay, men! Let's *go!*"

"Oh, no—I just remembered," the sloth will moan. "We can't."

"Why on earth not?" says Magoo, in his unfailingly puzzled voice.

Pulling off his cap, the fat one dashes it to the ground, or beach. "Because God damn it, as usual, we're waiting for—"

That's when he shows up, shuffling hurriedly along the beach toward them in his sneakers and the red sweater that he always wears now, with that hurt and jumpy look in his eyes. Sometimes, as he shambles past our fire, he glances guiltily over at the two of us, as if hoping that he'll get invited to stop at our end of the camp for once, to settle down among the crabs and listen to my old friend spin her fabulous philosophy and her tales of brave Ulyssia, which is what Ging calls Amelia Earhart—our possible neighbor in this archipelago; or else to wander off hand in hand with I, Mary-Ann, to go look at the mountains for a while. But a yell comes from the men, and he trots on. Without knowing why, although God knows I am used to that by now, I sometimes blink to stop myself from picturing a tiny Stars and Stripes in his fist; and have to blink audi-torily as well, since I could swear that I've just heard him call, in piping French, "*Oui, Papa, j'arrive.*"

When night comes and the sky unveils its stars, and our two campfires wink in the dark like the widely spaced headlights of a gigantic, station-ary car, I don't know or care what the men talk about at their end. But every so often, Ging and I will reminisce about the old days, and try to unriddle the nature of what, taking my cue from her, I have begun to call *our* century—the one whose refuge, incarnation or both my friend believes we were. On occasion, tottering vaguely over to our campfire from the one she normally prefers, either although or because they pay her scant attention there, the old dame with the empty spaces in her eyes that youth and then morphine once filled in will let drop some cryptic, addled, sad remarks, apparently unsure of what if anything they mean, but always about something she lost; sometimes it's a manuscript, and sometimes a bouquet.

Once she's gone away again, and I, Mary-Ann, stare at the embers I'll have to kick out in a minute, I wonder if any of us—even Ginger— ever understood what it was all about before we washed up here. As I think back on it, what I come back to most is how often we were dimly surrounded by all sorts of people struggling for more of one or another kind of freedom, using strange or nonexistent weapons and sometimes not even able to name a goal that would have frightened them if they had. But even when they couldn't name it, they insisted on defining its meaning for themselves; and maybe they have named it now, too.

Even back before we washed up here, people always said our century had packed in more horrors than any other. That's probably true, even though I didn't live in any previous one and have no conception of the new one that we all, despite our lack of calendars, strongly suspect is underway. In *our* century, the country that all seven of us came from— and which I, Mary-Ann, still personify, even or especially here—fought some horrors and inflicted others, while being spared most of the worst. All that is beyond doubt, to my way of thinking. But I can't shake a hunch it wasn't the whole story, which means that there's another one we could tell; one you may know without our help, but then again may not.

That's when, leaving Ginger talking to the crabs, I walk alone to the far side of the island, where no one else has gone for decades. I head for a spot a few hundred yards below the tumbling, rocky jut that we once named the Mane, and easily twice that distance above the floury tongue of white sand to which Ging and I have often talked about moving our campfire once the day finally comes that we decide to retire from it all. Directly ahead of me is a sliver of sandbar that points straight out to sea, like a miniature long island.

Undoing my checked top and tossing it aside, I use a borrowed tube of my friend's undiminished supply of bright red lipstick to write the word *Rescue* above my right nipple, and the word *Us* above my left. And as I've been advised, via the private note Gil Egan stuck in the coffee jar and Ginger deftly slipped to me before the others came trotting up, that this moment imposes certain obligations—obligations that I, Mary-Ann, was raised to be much too unfailingly pleasant, polite and cheerful to even think of evading—they are brown and pointy, and somewhat small in relation to the overall size. Long ago, when they were finally unveiled to him—for what could have been much longer than twenty-four hours, and to my eternity-long regret was less—my old boyfriend in Paris couldn't get enough of them.

Even so, I always keep my short-shorts on, and my shoes in case I need to run. I've never dared to go all-the-way naked, much as I might like to. I wish I could climb up into the mountains, there I'd feel free.

Although I know it won't be seen from such a small island—not on such a hot, bright, enormous day—I light the bundled twigs I've brought with me. Blinking back my special astigmatism, and lifting breasts heavy as Lourdes with milk fit for a messiah and now bearing the message *Rescue Us,* I raise my torch to all comers.

■

There are no comers—only parrots, chimps, and unseen snakes behind me. I know there never will be.

I guess that's about it. Still, if you'll bear with me a moment longer, I'll make you my life's bequest; the only thing I've ever learned for sure, if you will only understand it.

At least for I, Mary-Ann, it was better to reign in Kansas than it has been to serve in Oz. Still, if Oz is all that's left you—that is, if our Oz has become your Kansas, as it must have by now—then get to it. Reign if you can. Even without calendars, we know our century has vanished. Yours has unveiled itself.

But wherever you go and whatever you do, just in case you need one—and you might, for whatever reason—carry along a map of where you started from. For better or worse, it was us.

Obviously, we'll never *know*, here on the island. As I can't seem to stop saying, yesterday never knows. But with any luck, before we washed up here—and along with everything else—we glimpsed the birth of your saviors.

which is
the end of
GILLIGAN'S WAKE

Afterword

A PASTICHE LIKE THIS OBVIOUSLY DRAWS ON MANY SOURCES, AND I want to identify at least some. For instance, Chapter One probably reads like a hodgepodge of everything but the kitchen sink, but in fact the kitchen sink is in there—in an echo of the mental-hospital scenes in Frederick Exley's *A Fan's Notes* that I can detect but not isolate. Here as elsewhere, my premise was that poor Gil had read it too, just as, like his fellow but less sympathetic embroiderer Mark David Chapman, he plainly had *The Catcher in the Rye*.

And yes, I know the "moose-and-squirrel hash" Chapter Three makes of the Alger Hiss case cheerfully garbles what it doesn't omit. A soberer account, sans Thurston, is Allen Weinstein's *Perjury*, which convinced me that, as I have "Sukey Santoit" say, anyone who thinks the son of a bitch was innocent is barking up the wrong crucifix.

While I deplore the future "Lovey"'s atrocious selfishness and cowardice, her slapstick in Chapter Four is by way of tribute to the most likable of all movie actresses—"the divine Carole Lombard," mentioned in Chapter Five as having recently passed through. The reason Calder Willingham is the patron saint of Chapter Five, the job of God being taken, is that only a nitwit would try one-upping America's greatest master of carnal comedy. Knowing my place, I aimed for the sincerest form of flattery instead. And so on.

Like Roy Cohn's, Henry Kissinger's role in Chapter Six is pure fantasy, as is the whole chapter. Even modern-day residents of Hiroshima and Nagasaki would no doubt agree that we are a benign and wonderful democracy, not Godzilla—unless, of course, it's possible to be both. Indeed, only one claim in the entire book states a fact: there is no monument to the heroic women of Occoquan. I think it's a shame.

I also hope the people of Russell, Kansas, will forgive me for turning their town into Brigadoon. I had no choice, since I was only there for twenty-four hours. My thanks to the *Village Voice*'s then editor, Karen Durbin, for sending me to write about their former County Attorney, to my eyes a more moving figure than he or most Americans will ever know. Like Amelia Earhart—but unlike Britney Spears, with whom he once shared a Pepsi commercial—he's one of *Gilligan's Wake*'s secret heroes.

Let me, too, express my gratitude to the cast members of *Gilligan's Island*, living and gone, for providing such vivid mannequins to populate Gil's hallucinations: Bob Denver, Alan Hale, Jr., Jim Backus, Natalie Schafer, Tina Louise, Russell Johnson, and especially Dawn Wells. And to series creator Sherwood Schwartz, whom I now find myself blessing, not without surprise, as *il miglior fabbro*.

Among my more witting helpmates, I want to thank my agent, Gary Morris of the David Black agency; my editor, Josh Kendall; and Glenn Kenny, Adrienne Miller, John Powers, Kit Rachlis, and Wendy Yoder. Along with the second of my dedicatees, without whom.

We numbered many in the ship.
—Alexander Pushkin, "Arion"